The Pull of the Earth

ALFRED ALCORN

Penguin Books

PENGUIN BOOKS
Viking Penguin Inc., 40 West 23rd Street,
New York, New York 10010, U.S.A.
Penguin Books Ltd, Harmondsworth,
Middlesex, England
Penguin Books Australia Ltd, Ringwood,
Victoria, Australia
Penguin Books Canada Limited, 2801 John Street,
Markham, Ontario, Canada L3R 1B4
Penguin Books (N.Z.) Ltd, 182–190 Wairau Road,
Auckland 10, New Zealand

First published in the United States of America
by Houghton Mifflin Company 1985
Published in Penguin Books 1986

LIBRARY OF CONGRESS CATALOGING IN PUBLICATION DATA
Alcorn, Alfred.
The pull of the earth.
(Contemporary American fiction)
I. Title. II. Series.
[PS3551.L29P8 1986] 813'.54 86-767
ISBN 0 14 00.8924 1

Printed in the United States of America by
R. R. Donnelley & Sons Company, Harrisonburg, Virginia
Set in Aster

CONTEMPORARY AMERICAN FICTION

THE PULL OF THE EARTH

Alfred Alcorn, who spent eleven years on a New England farm in his youth, now lives in Belmont, Massachusetts.

For Sally

❦ 1 ☙

TOGETHER, as if in prayer, the small hooves came first, glistening in the sunlight that stippled the floor of the pine grove. The cow arched her back and lowed. The caul-shrouded snout emerged, tucked along the forelegs like a cringing dog, then the rest of the head, slick as a seal's, the ears folded back. It stopped.

Bobby Dearborn slapped a mosquito, smudging blood. He saw crows flitting like shadows high in the pines above him. Silent now, they would come down afterward to pick at the afterbirth.

The dog whimpered and the boy shushed it.

Lowing again, the cow pivoted on her rear legs, which were sprung over her swollen udder. She had split red like a cleaved melon to let the shoulders through, and liquid dribbled down the dangling skein of shucked membrane. A gargoyle, the calf protruded from the body of the cow, stilled again for an agony of time on a late June afternoon in 1957.

The boy's awe at this spectacle of birth was muted by worry about the rest of the herd and by experience. He had watched cows calving before. He had watched his uncle reach a bare arm deep into a cow to loop a cord around the forelegs of a reluctant calf. He had watched Dillon's mare drop its foal and the back end of a hen blossom with an egg. He had watched the dog killing woodchucks and cats eating rats, and once, down near the creek, a snake, big-mouthed, swallowing whole a silent frog.

Slowly, almost imperceptibly, the calf began to angle downward. It seemed to take forever. It seemed to get stuck again. But it wasn't. The cow moved, coughed, and the calf, a fish out of water, fell through the gauzy light onto the pine needles. It lay inert, encased like a sausage. The cow turned through a smoke of flies and began to lick it dry.

The dog whined and started for the calf.

"No!"

The boy's voice snapped like a leash. The dog circled the wary cow and followed the boy to where the pines opened through a tumbled wall onto a boulder-strewn pasture. Standing on the rocks, the boy saw the herd of Holsteins strung out along the lane that led from the pasture through a patchwork of hayfields gray green with ripening grass. Some of the cows, their necks extended under the single strand of dead electric fence, swiped at the hay.

"Go get 'em!" the boy chanted at the dog. "Go get 'em!"

Digger, the black and white collie, jumped with excitement, barked, and ran out into the pasture, loping in a large circle before going back over the wall, heading for the calf.

The boy shouted again and threw a piece of dead pine end over end at the dog. The collie dodged the stick and retreated to crouch and pant in the shade.

Bobby Dearborn peered toward the herd again. A ridge of distant white caps etched the heat-bleached sky. A storm brewed. He squinted into the haze and tasted, in the clarity of his small panic, the salt on his lips. He had turned off the battery-driven fencer so as not to get a shock when he opened the wired gate. He wasn't supposed to do that. Left to themselves, the cows, hungry for good grass, would get into the hay. But he couldn't abandon the cow and the calf. She might take it deep into the woods and hide it. Back in there were swamps and dog packs. They'd really give him hell for that. He went back.

Free of its natal film, the calf lunged around, trying to rise. A bull calf, the boy thought, judging by size. In a few days Harry Manning would come by in his truck to take it to the butcher, because they already had a bull on the farm. The calf stood finally on wobbly legs and thrust its pink nose into the folds of its mother's dewlap, looking for the udder.

"Go on," the boy said and brandished a pine stick. The cow, trailing afterbirth, worried by the dog, turning and lowing to her stumbling calf, started for a gap in the wall.

A roar of sudden thunder sounded above them. Too early for the storm. The boy glanced up in time to catch the flash of swept-wing interceptors climbing in a practice scramble out of nearby Hanscom Air Force Base. The jets, Sabres, flashed above the trees, and he went with them, heroic and free behind his oxygen mask, the g's pressing his belted chest, the trigger stick in his hand as he spoke the terse language of a flight leader to his wingman over the static of shortwave. *Roger, Blue Hubbard, I read you. Bogeys closing at nine o'clock low* . . . And the jets would peel off into a screaming power dive, just the way they did in *The Bridges of Toko-Ri*. Up there, dueling with MIGs and blasting Russian bombers out of the sky, Captain Robert Dearborn, USAF, fighter pilot, bestrode an angel of death and power, and no one, absolutely no one, would be able to touch him.

He was too late to stop the herd. It had pushed through the fence into the canary grass that grew head high on bottomland where the creek ran. It moved in a wedge, leaving a broad swath of trampled hay.

Two figures appeared suddenly from the truck garden that spread from one side of the barn just beyond the hayfields. One was a tall thin man in overalls and the other a heavyset woman in a ragged cotton print dress. They moved with stumbling agitation down a slope of timothy grass toward the herd. The bass voice of the man cursing the cows came faintly through the heat-stilled air to the boy. Hedley Vaughn wasn't supposed to run. He had a bad heart. The cries of his wife, Janet Vaughn, mingled with his feckless shouting. Deep in the hay, leaving their own trails behind them, they approached the cattle, calling and waving their arms.

The cows wouldn't be herded. The hay made them frisky, and they fanned out, frolicking, leaving wakes like boats on a lake. One of the cows, brazen, challenged the approaching couple, dodged around them, and the rest of the herd followed it, stampeding up the slope. They tore into the garden, where, jumping and kicking, their udders swinging, they drove across the strawberries, the squash, the cucumbers, the potatoes, and the fragile fence of pole beans. They didn't stop until they reached the young corn, where, tails switching, they grazed contentedly.

The man, clutching at his chest, went up the slope after them. The woman had stopped and turned toward the lane, where the boy poked along with the cow and calf. Her hands were set on her hips. Above her to the west the vague clouds blurred the sun and showed an underbelly of dense, wet blue.

ક્ષ

Gaunt, serious Hedley Vaughn stood in the gloom of the dairy, facing the open door. His pipe fumed and the light glinted off his rimless glasses, hiding his eyes. He coughed and spat and dragged out his words in a flat, New England accent.

"You ought have brought the cows in from pasture."

The boy nodded as if agreeing. The concrete floor of the dairy felt cool under his bare feet.

"The cow was calving," he said, not looking at his uncle. "I thought she might take it into the swamps."

The man sucked on his pipe. It had gone bitter, with the rest of his life. He lived now in a pall of fatigue, and his world faded from around him. Through the doorway of the dairy, across Middlesex Road, and through the screen of dying elms that lined it, he looked to where the Marcello

Brothers were putting in a subdivision on what had been the Mayhew farm. All day now the hillside, a gentle slope, sounded to the whine of saws and the whack of hammers. Skeletons of houses, cages of two-by-fours, paltry things, the man thought, rose along bulldozed roads.

"They got into the hay and tore up the garden."

The boy nodded again, consenting to the seriousness of the thing. He watched as the plane of the man's face shifted from the light, and glanced away from the pained, passionless eyes. Uncle Hedley had a bad heart. The boy pictured it as an overripe tomato with black spots of rot on it. He felt sorry for his uncle.

The pipe rapped against the wall of the dairy, spilling ash and smoking shreds of tobacco on the damp floor. The man's feeble anger died to feeble remorse. His dead cousin's bastard.

"Your aunt's fit to be tied," he said.

"Yes," the boy answered, acknowledging the warning.

"Where did you put the cow?"

"In the stall next to the bull's."

The man approved. "A bull calf, you think?"

"It's big enough."

"Eyeah . . . Maybe we ought to keep it," he mused, then turned. "Start the milking," he said, and walked away, as though wounded, along the breezeway that connected the barn and dairy to the house.

Start the milking. That meant do the milking. Whatever else happened, the cows had to be milked. The boy sprinkled disinfectant into a pail and turned on the tap that came out of the wall. A ribbon of bright water flowed, and the boy cupped his hands under it, dashing it over his face and neck, soaking his T-shirt, suddenly cooled and exhilarated.

❧

Janet Vaughn stood over the black sink in the kitchen and scrubbed the skins off new potatoes. Her rage simmered along with the meat-poor stew cooking on the stove. She dipped a wet hand impulsively into the Ritz box, put the cracker in her mouth, chewed it to a mush, swallowing without tasting. Gladys Porley had just called about her husband's shirts. They had been due the day before. They rose in a white pile, the bleached ghosts of portly Charles Porley. Anger can be a mortal sin, Father Fahey said. And now Janet Vaughn was giving in to the temptation. But slowly, nursing it, starting with what was immediate and inanimate — her kitchen with its black sink stuck with rough plumbing, and the black Glenwood range that leaked smoke in winter, and the wide-board walls painted green forever, and the scuffed, heaved linoleum floor Hedley promised to fix, and Hedley's decrepit armchair, and the way Gladys Porley sniffed every time she came in, as if her husband's shirts might get tainted with the sour smell of cows, their milk and shit, which stank up every room in the house. Except the nursery. White and empty. Her rage tinged with a grief that always hovered, Janet Vaughn scrubbed the potatoes the cows had unearthed in their rampage through the garden. She crushed one in her hand and cursed. *The little bastard.*

That was better. She wiped the sweat from her face and rinsed the potatoes. They bobbed raw in the slick of the stew. She glanced in passing at her face in the dim mirror her husband used for shaving. The angry eyes startled her, made her relent and search the darkened glass for traces of that prettiness which had made her the belle of the Lowell High Officers' Ball. Twenty years ago. Janet Gilooly then. Michael Gavin from Shedd Park had taken a fancy to her. Loose that night with beer and reaching between her legs. She had let him. A quiver of panic for passing time, for age and old loves, touched her heart. She turned from herself and palmed another cracker.

The whir of the refrigerator faltered when she plugged in the iron. You know Charles wears two a day in hot weather. Gladys Porley was proud of that somehow. The collars have to be perfect. Now this one, the crease is wrong. He really won't wear it. He wants to use Tsongas, the dry cleaners in Lowell, but I know how you need . . . Gladys Porley's dentures gleamed white between the stretched lips of her false smile. Talking about her two boys. (David is going to Colgate in the fall.) Her white hands in white gloves driving her white Buick to Lowell for a permanent. Her going to Florida in January for a tan. Her seventeen-inch television. Her fitted kitchen with its immaculate floor (you could eat off it), and new Kelvinator and washer-dryer combination and the white tiling over the Formica, the chrome-edged Formica counter gleaming in the whiteness of fluorescence. The woman had everything, almost, that Janet Vaughn wanted from life.

Through the window frosted with steam from the ironing, she saw her husband and the boy talking in the doorway of the dairy. Hedley wouldn't tell him off the way he should. Leaving the fencer off like that. Letting them ruin the hay. And the garden. Her garden. No more spunk in the man. His heart attack.

She sprinkled water and the iron hissed. She pressed it along the spine of Charles Porley's seventeen-and-a-half-inch collar. She felt heavy. It was the heat. The work. The garden ruined. Her garden. She hissed with the iron, stoking her anger, working its pickled pleasure, calling him a little bastard, committing sins to take to Father Fahey for forgiveness. Bless me, Father. When you call the boy a bastard, my child, you are calling Jesus a bastard. Yes, Father, Janet Vaughn would whisper, grateful for the priest's seriousness, for the significance he gave her rage. Absolved again, she knelt before the Virgin and the bank of squat candles sleeved in ruby glass. Five Our Fathers and five Hail Marys and make a good Act of Contrition. It seemed a trifling penance for calling Christ a bastard.

The scrape of Hedley Vaughn's feet on the mat outside the door rasped on her nerves. Her blood quickened, and she waited expectantly, sorting through her accusations.

The screen door twanged, and he was scarcely in the house, shuffling across the nailed linoleum floor, her gray, failing husband, when she challenged him. "You told him."

"I did."

He settled into the disintegrating armchair next to the cold stove and opened the *Lowell Sun*. His energies, tentative at best, collapsed with the relief of sitting down.

She ironed furiously. "What did you tell him?"

"I told him to start the milking."

She knew it. Siding with the boy. "What about the cows?" she cried.

"What about them?" The paper rattled, a red rag to a bull.

"The hay. The garden." She choked, inarticulate in her rage.

"It wasn't his fault."

"It was his fault. He left the fencer off. He did it on purpose."

Hedley Vaughn did not have the heart to fight. A pressure, more debilitating than painful, but painful all the same, ballooned in his chest. He could sense his own weak and rapid pulse, and opened his mouth to ease the sensation of suffocating. Struggling, he kept the pain from showing. He thought he would die. "He did what I told him to do."

She stood over the gas burners that flanked one side of the Glenwood and stirred the stew. His impotence enraged her. His dead baby, too. Only he never mentioned it. Not once. Now he propped the paper between them.

"We have to do something about that boy, Hedley," she said, trying to sound ominous.

Hedley Vaughn grunted at her.

She spooned the greasy stew. Send him back to the orphanage in New Hampshire. That thought, though not in the catalogue of confessable sins, touched her with the guilt of dark hoping. They had promised to take him only for the summer. Two years ago. To give him fresh air. To have him help around the farm. Ernestine, Hedley's sister, had found him, had wanted him, but she wasn't married. So he came to the farm on a day in June with a suitcase full of clothes that didn't fit. And he had never liked her. She'd tried to love him, to show him some affection. But those silences. Those gray eyes, already old, looking right through her. And breaking things. The harrow. The milking machine pump. And letting all the pullets out. The time he tried to run away. And the time she turned and he had his finger up to her. She beat him bloody about the mouth that time; knocked out a tooth. You should not administer corporal punishment in anger, Father Fahey told her, giving her a whole rosary to say for penance.

"When are we going to send him back?" she said, her thoughts escaping, making her the supplicant.

Hedley Vaughn did not answer. They had come, as they usually did, to this argument so often voiced that now it scarcely needed stating. It hung between them, emblematic of deeper differences, a shame, another weight on his heart. He leaned forward and endured the malignant silence until the words in the paper he wasn't reading blurred into the grayness of his pain. He settled back, sighing, closed his eyes, and dozed.

The iron thumped and hissed. Outside the window the darkening sky lowered, compressing the heat. Sweat oiled the woman's face, her breasts and armpits, and the chafed smoothness between her thighs. She caught herself palming another cracker. She ate it anyway, glancing across the kitchen to where her husband of nine years sat sprawled, his breath rasping. Half dead, she thought, noticing the pallor beneath the scorch of sun. Like Dad when he began to go. Her pity, a shadow of the sorrow she felt for her father, soured quickly to contempt. If only he would sell the damn place. They could have everything. They could buy that house in Dracut near her brother's. Only twelve thousand five hundred. Small, but not too small. Cozy, really. She would have the kitchen redone. In white with a stainless steel double sink and washer-dryer combination. A good washer anyway. A washer and a picture window for the living room, with wall-to-wall beige carpeting and that matching chair and sofa in the Sears catalogue for only one seventy-five and a television and a nursery upstairs with a crib and tufted curtains just in case . . .

She gasped at the smell of singed cloth as if it were her own flesh burning. "Jesus!" she sinned, rubbing her fingers over the brown brand the iron had left on the snowy front of Charles Porley's shirt. A five-dollar shirt from Bon Marche. And Gladys Porley would make her pay for it. Two loads of ironing. Janet Vaughn's mouth went dry and the room went dark and red as her panic turned to fury. The little bastard!

The man woke to the slam of the screen door. "What?" he said to the empty kitchen, knowing what, and lapsed back to his fitful doze, rehearsing for a much longer sleep.

❧

The Holsteins ranged one next to the other down the north side of the barn, with their necks secured in long iron stanchions and their back ends poised over a gutter. Behind them the whitewashed wall had long since been splattered brown with manure. And although the windows had been removed from their casements for the summer, the air was an acrid mist wafting up from the piss and the gravy of green dung brought on by the corn that slicked the plank flooring. Milking in sync, going *shoo-choo, shoo-choo*, the machines sounded like a pair of mechanical lungs. The rhythm of Buddy Knox joined that of the machines — *Come along and be my party doll* — and the boy went down the line, working the plunger of a fly sprayer, pluming the air with clouds of DDT, a ritual that only temporarily relieved the place of flies. Captain Dearborn, USAF, was going to have a party doll to run her fingers through his hair, and *I'll make love to you, to you* . . . The music, coming from the plastic Zenith tuned to WCAP, Lowell, the voice of the Merrimack Valley, was supposed to help the cows give milk.

A gap midway down the row of cows led to a wide, high space that went down the center of the barn like the nave of a church. On the other side of this were bays, one used for hay, another for sawdust to bed the cows. There was also a feed room, where bags of grain were stored and, toward the back, several box stalls dimly lit by a single electric bulb and by light filtering through cobwebbed windows. One of the stalls contained the cow and the calf, and another, a corral of heavy timbers, held the bull. He was a white-faced beast with testicles the size of tennis balls slung elastically between thin hindquarters that widened out over a long back to a massive bulk of shoulder and neck. He had short, thick horns and a pink nose hung with a ring like the brass pull on a bureau drawer. His registered name was Lancaster's First Pride, and he was the one thing Hedley Vaughn still voiced any enthusiasm about. A real bull, he would say. A man from upstate New York had offered five thousand for him.

The boy quickly sprayed the cow and calf. Then he let himself down onto the bull's squishing bed of dung and straw. The bull pawed at it. Sometimes he could not be baited. Other times he slowly and methodically tracked the barefoot tormentor, who kept dodging just out of reach of the swinging horns. The boy moved close enough to tousle the curls of white hair between the lidded eyes. The bull had scared and fascinated him when he first arrived at the farm. He had played games with it, jumping in and out of the corral. He had grown bolder and now could take the ring in his hand and twist the animal into submission. He still felt fear, but it was fear he controlled, that he used to define his courage. An old bull was nothing next to what he would have to face as a fighter pilot. He backed away, spraying the DDT. The bull moved suddenly, lunging and snapping its horns at the boy, who, with the coolness of a toreador, stepped aside and gave it a punch in the ribs.

Pat Boone sang of love letters in the sand through the crackling static of approaching lightning. A breeze fretted the leaves of the maples that lined the far side of the barnyard. Maybe, he kept thinking, she won't come out. Maybe Uncle Hedley had quieted her down. He could do that sometimes. Sometimes he just made her worse. He lugged the half-filled machine pail out to the dairy and strained the milk into a twenty-gallon can. Large cats came stepping daintily through the muck and gathered near an old pie plate, snarling, their tails aloft as they waited for milk. Maybe she would leave him alone this time. It was Friday night. Sometimes they went out. He splashed milk into the pie plate. Ratters all, the cats prowled the beams of the loft and the hollow walls and the dark, dung-mounded cellar. With the rats and mice and bats and swallows and a pair of ghostly owls, they were part of the secret life of the barn.

The tumble of thunder came through the window. *A white sports coat and a pink carnation . . .*

The machines chugged on. The boy was kneeling between two cows, his cheek pressed against the taut swell of belly as he machine-stripped the last and richest milk, when he saw her legs and sneakered feet go by. The radio went dead. Above the pulse of the milkers he could hear the slap of her sneakers as she came back down behind the cows.

"Bobby!"

The boy rose up between the cows to the curse of his name. His ears had reddened. "Yes?" he answered, trying to sound innocent by sounding neutral.

"Yes what?"

"Yes, Auntie."

His flush deepened. She wasn't his aunt. She wasn't a real relative.

"Come out here."

He stepped across the gutter to where the woman stood next to an open window. The sky had darkened like a bruise, and the air had the dense stillness that precedes a storm. In that blighted, yellow light, her face gave off a sallow glow, and her hair, cropped short, lay flat against her skull so that to the boy her head appeared too small for the bulk of her body.

"Why did you leave the fencer off?"

He shook his head in a silent lie.

"Why did you let the cows get out?"

"I didn't . . ."

"Trying to kill your uncle, huh?"

"No . . ."

"You know his heart's no good."

"The cow was calving." He started through the motions of explanation, because silence would only make it worse. "Digger wouldn't herd them . . ."

"Blame the dog, huh? You knew they'd get out, didn't you? Get out into the hay. Into the garden. Everything ruined. My garden . . ."

She worked her clenched jaw, and the prow of flesh under her chin began to quiver. The thunder boomed closer. The milking machines skipped a beat.

His shoulders haunched defensively as he stood in the grip of her crippled voice and angry eyes, locked in the hollow heart of his fear.

"I . . ."

"You little bastard," she hissed and hit him, her right hand coming up off the side of his face with stunning power simultaneously with, as if part of, a flash and bang of blue light that filled the barn.

The woman turned to march away. She had gone only a few steps when she stopped and turned back to him. The thrill of her rage, gone suddenly bleak, made her reach for another cruelty. "And no swimming for you tonight."

Then she was gone. Outside, the rain came down across the rising wind in fat, splattering drops. A spike of blue-white fire stood over the orchard just beyond the barnyard and was followed by a splintering crack. The storm closed in, flashing and booming around the barn, and the boy, riding his rage now, was calling it down on the head of the woman.

෭ ·

Night, and the lights from cars and trucks passing on the road caught the windows of the boy's room and slid reticulated ghosts up the sloping ceiling, across the flat center to the corner where, trapped, they flickered for a moment and died. Sweaty and restless beneath a sheet, he watched the moving lights come and go with the sounds of traffic. In the silences he could hear the season's first crickets and the voices of the man and the woman in the kitchen below as they argued about the stranger.

The stranger had come at dusk when bats flew against the deepening indigo sky. The stranger had stood in front of the open barn and talked to Hedley Vaughn until all that could be seen of the two men was the point of red light from the stranger's cigarette. His rapid talk and frequent, nervous laugh carried to the house. He was looking for work.

I won't have Lucien Quirk in this house, the woman kept repeating. Hedley, he's a bum. He was up at Dillon's last year. They had to let him go. He's a wino. What will the neighbors say? I know, the man repeated back at her, as if agreeing, his voice trailing in the wake of hers, but resolute. He was the boss. We need him to bring the hay in. Wino, she said again, and the boy, catching the word, trying to decipher it, spelled it *w-h-i-n-o*, and thought it must mean someone who complained a lot, someone like the woman. Finally, silence, as if instilled by the heat, settled on them.

The swampy smell of pond water permeated the boy's room, mingling with the pungent odor of warmed, old wood. The woman had relented after supper and let him go swimming. She had given him a quarter to buy an ice cream at Earl's. She could be nice when she wanted to be. There were times when the boy could almost forgive her.

A convoy of trucks rumbled by on Middlesex Road, the two-lane highway that came out of Lowell and went southwest through Elmsbury toward Worcester. They rattled the house in passing. The dog barked and was answered by a melancholy howl from over near the lake. The faint wail carried like an echo, evoking for the boy the mystery of distance and the promise of escape. Downstairs the back door opened, and from underneath the open window near his head he heard the sound of his uncle pissing on the granite step. The splashing was followed by a cough, a spit, and the slam of the screen door. He heard them going up the stairs to their room on the other side of the house. Their door closed, and a silence of small sounds filled the night. Lights from a car went across the ceiling, soundless, fixed, part of the boy's dream.

❧ 2 ❧

JAP!

The rat sat on its haunches inches from the man's rolling eyes and delicately nibbled the crust of bread. An enfilade of machine gun fire issued from its mouth, sweeping the beach, kicking up water all around Lucien Quirk's struggling knees as the man rose vertiginously in his nightmare.

"Corpsman!"

The rat humped across the hay-smoothed floor of the mow. The man groped for the bottle. Empty. He thought he had. Didn't remember. Didn't remember, but he needed with an awful dry ache, worse than bad, worse than the burn of hunger.

From his bed of dry-rotted hay, Lucien Quirk peered up into the empty barn through a network of jointed ten-by-tens that framed the wide-board floors and raised a central loft of loose planking. Above that he could make out the steel railing that ran down the inner spine of the roof and, dangling from it in a web of ropes, the saber-shaped tongs used to lift loose hay from the barn floor. The tongs turned slightly in the breeze let in by high open windows and mutated to a giant spider, lowering for Lucien Quirk as he drifted back between the nightmares of his dreams and the nightmare of his life, seeking that ever-receding midpoint of oblivion.

The rat nibbled again. Lucien Quirk was off Tarawa, wading through bodies bobbing in the bullet-sprouted sea, then crouched on the beach, trying always to run as the mortars thumped, coming closer, finding the range, going thump, thump, THUMP, THUMP!

"Mister."

The boy bent over the restless body of the man. What he saw didn't quite fit the voice and laugh he had heard the night before. The slack elfin face showed missing teeth and a snub nose. The man was short and had freckles and red hair going gray, which made him appear boyish and old at the same time. The boy noticed the duffel bag, the holed shirt, and the vulnerable feet. He saw the bottle and smelled the cheap wine. Wino, he remembered, spelling it right — a bum. It made him prickle with an unpleasant flush of superiority. "Mister, you have to get up."

The eyes opened from a vanishing dream of death to the shock of life with death still pending. "What do you want?"

"You have to get up."

"Who the hell are you?"

"Bobby Dearborn."

The man rubbed his face. It took a few seconds for things to register. The Vaughn place. Haying. Five dollars a week and bed and board. Maybe. And this skinny hayseed, all ears and red face, standing over him and giving him orders like that lieutenant — what was his name? — who ate a Jap bullet with his breakfast one sunny morning on an island in the South Pacific.

"My uncle says you're to help with the mowing."

"Tell your uncle to kiss my ass."

He sat up on the mound of old hay and barked a mirthless laugh into the boy's confusion. Then he lit a cigarette and carelessly tossed the match. The smoke calmed his jitters. Hunger rumbled. His thirst pounded with his blood. Anything for a swig.

But the bottle was dry, dry as this empty mow and the boy's intent, appraising eyes.

"My uncle says you can have breakfast first."

"Your uncle's a real Christian."

Painfully he got to his feet. He was thinking about another bottle. Just one. A small one. A pint would do it. To get through the day. Woozing, he propped his head against a beam, unbuttoned his fly, and began to piss.

"Breakfast's ready now," said the boy.

The man's pissing in the mow offended his sense of things.

"Aye, aye, Lieutenant."

The boy blushed.

"I'm going to be a captain, an Air Force captain."

Lucien Quirk's mouth opened suddenly, compressing the rest of his face into gnomish lines. His laugh frightened the nesting swallows. "Okay, Captain, whatever you say."

"What's your name?"

The boy, stung by the man's mockery, was challenging him to have a name, as if, in his dereliction, he might have lost even that.

Still pissing, the soldier came to attention and snapped off a professional salute. "Lance Corporal Lucien Patrick Quirk, United States Marine Corps, reporting to duty, SIR!"

He laughed again and, shaking a last dribble, gestured an imaginary weapon in his free hand:

> "This is my rifle,
> This is my gun,
> This is for shooting,
> This is for fun."

The boy's heavy-lipped mouth hung open. Then: "You're a Marine?"

The bitter laugh sounded again. Yeah, I'm a Marine, Lucien Quirk said to himself. If I'm nothing else I'm a Marine, a leatherneck, a gyrene, a Marine. The names had consumed him with glory once. French-Irish from Lowell's Little Canada (his father is a Paddy, his mother is a Frog, which makes little Louie look just like a dog!), he had traded in what he was for a name and a uniform. It was all glory and swagger and neighborhood admiration until, squatting in a landing craft off Betio, sick with fear and courage, it had come down to a definition for which he had forfeited his life. But he had done it. He had fought. He had the medals to prove it. Now no one wanted to hear about it. No one believed, not even this gawky kid, telling him what to do.

Lucien Quirk sat on the hay to pull on his socks and tie his boots. He could read it in the boy's eyes. A bum. He had heard it two days before when they threw him out of the flophouse on Moody Street. No bums here, the Greek said, taking Lucien Quirk's disability check, which, in truth, he was owed, and more. But Lucien Quirk wasn't a bum. He had walked out of Lowell, toting his bag, walking his thirst through Westford and Acton, hitching from farm to farm, looking for work. The farmers were in their fields, busy with their machines. No, they said, they didn't need help. Even the farmers Lucien Quirk knew and who knew his story barely took time to be civil. Their sons smirked openly at him. Bum, their faces said. And standing then in those bright, safe New England fields, Lucien Quirk, still wounded, conjured up a banzai charge of Jap officers (at night, white-gloved in dress uniform, swords high, screaming), loosing his nightmare on their fat peace. Try Hedley Vaughn in Elmsbury, they told him. He doesn't bale; he needs help. Lucien Quirk, desperate, limped six miles to find Hedley Vaughn and a desperation to match his own. Five dollars a week. You can sleep in the mow tonight. Tomorrow we'll find you something better, maybe. A dollar till payday. Lucien Quirk followed the bowl-cut kid down the nailed ladder from the mow. No. He wasn't a bum. Not yet. He was a Marine. He had staked his life on it.

❧

"You cook an awful fine meal, Missus." Lucien Quirk guffawed, but obsequiously, humoring the woman, pinching

· 19 ·

her with his voice. She was a fine one, nice and plump, comfortable in a dark bed. Like Emma in San Diego. A bit on the cranky side. Maybe she just needs a good one.

"A man could work all day . . . and all night . . . on this cooking."

Janet Vaughn did not respond. She pretended busyness at the sink, an apron over her second-best dress, the blue rayon number with the white collar and belt, the one she could barely get into with a girdle that cruelly bound her waist and held up her best pair of nylons. She watched surreptitiously as the hired man ate more than his share of the bacon and eggs and the wedges of green tomato she had breaded and fried in the fat. She watched the way he sponged egg yolk with bits of bread and the way he spooned sugar into the three cups of coffee he poured from the percolator. It was mortifying. What would people say? What would Gladys Porley say, seeing an honest-to-God hobo sitting at the table with them? And she was likely to drop in any moment now to pick up her husband's shirts. And Priscilla Jewett, she'd tell Meg Greenwood. And Father Fahey. He'd ask about the man's moral character. Was it really wise to have that kind of man around the boy? He's at such an impressionable age. Of course, appearances were important too. And Ernestine, Hedley's sister, she would be so understanding, with her pity and her books and her education. And her own mom. Rose Gilooly would have a fit. I knew it would come to this, your marrying Hedley Vaughn. At least I've kept him out of the house, Janet Vaughn consoled herself. He wasn't actually going to live with them. The woman ran hot water for the dishes and could not quiet the hundred tongues wagging in her ear.

Still, she had made the coffee a little richer that morning; she had brought out the better cups from the living room closet; she had fried the bacon and eggs just right and placed them prettily on a platter with the green tomatoes the way she had seen it done in a magazine. She had put on her second-best dress, even though she knew she would have to change later to work in the garden. And when she had seen the man and the boy emerge from the barn and come toward the house, she had checked herself in the mirror over the sink and resisted an impulse to run upstairs to the bathroom and touch up her face. Now the man sat at the table behind her, another sorry-looking item in her poor kitchen, his eyes, she could tell, crawling all over her, his voice insinuating, flustering her with scandalous possibilities.

If only he would shave.

"Another hot one," Hedley Vaughn ventured.

His food, picked at, soured in his stomach. Since early morning he had sat in the armchair beside the stove, honing the mowing-machine blade with file and whetstone. The exertion had left him white and tremulous, but he had made the row of triangular teeth on the blade gleam with sharpness. He had decided it was time to start the haying.

"A scorcher," Lucien Quirk rejoined. "Just right for making hay."

The woman clucked but said nothing. Jesus, Hedley, she wanted to blurt, stop playing the fool. Can't you see you're being softened up for another touch for another bottle.

"If it lasts, we'll get the hay in all right."

"It'll last. No question about that. I've still got some Jap steel in me that lets me know when it's gonna rain, and I can tell you right now it ain't gonna rain."

Lucien Quirk was aggressive now in his agreement, animated, his eyes sweeping, his jaw working, talking and chewing. Then he laughed, slurped coffee, and winked at the boy, who listened and kept quiet. The stranger's presence, he could tell, had irked the woman while disarming her at the same time. More than that, the man's noisy, hollow optimism, his laugh and chat, had touched their lives with a kind of strange cheer.

Hedley Vaughn turned to the boy and repeated what he'd already said twice that morning. "I got the blade sharpened. You know where to start — the section between the brook and Jewett's woods." He blinked and coughed. Just thinking exhausted him. "Go in first along the bottomland where it's wet and go slow through the clover on the knoll. I want it cut close. And don't forget there's a rock 'bout dead center of the section. That damn thing gets bigger every year. If I didn't know better, I'd swear it was growing."

"Yes, sir."

Captain Robert Dearborn, USAF, sat in the briefing tent and listened closely. Target area vector four. Captain Dearborn will lead in the first group, establish air superiority, and suppress ground fire. Blue Ghost squadron will sortie from the northwest, drop their payloads, and return to base. Visibility is good. The target area is clear. Antiaircraft fire is expected to be heavy. Watch for the rock.

The crunch of tires on the gravel drive gave the woman a start. "Oh!" she gasped. "Oh," and toweled her hands. Her face was a panic of unhappy smiles as she went to answer the door.

Gladys Porley came through the side door into the short hallway that opened into both the kitchen and the dining room. "Good morning," the lady in the pink halter and white pedal pushers sang to the men, grimacing a smile that froze with curiosity at the sight of the stranger. Those poor Vaughns. He has a bad heart. And Janet does what she can for the boy. "Well . . . It smells so good!"

"Have a cup of coffee," Hedley Vaughn offered over his shoulder.

"Thank you, Hedley, but I can only stay a moment. Charles is waiting. We're off to the Cape for a couple of days if I can get the boys organized. I do hope this weather holds."

Then she went into the dining room to get the ironed shirts from poor Janet. But who is that wretched-looking fellow?

Janet Vaughn, for whom Gladys Porley's thoughts were

all too apparent, displayed the rack of ironed shirts, hoping the other woman, rummaging through her purse, would not notice the stain she had scraped and rebleached.

But she did notice as she checked the shirts, letting it go, getting compensated with what she wanted to know. "Who," she whispered, her shadowed eyes wide, "is that?" and fingered the bills.

"Lucien Quirk." Janet Vaughn mouthed the name in a swoon of embarrassment. "From Lowell. We've hired him to help with the haying. You know, Hedley's heart."

It was the truth, and the best face she could put on it.

Indeed. Mrs. Charles Porley, holding the shirts carefully, emerged into the sun and walked back to the car and her impatient husband, not knowing quite how to impart this tidbit of news, which both impressed and deflated her. Since when could people like the Vaughns afford to hire anyone, even a derelict?

❧

Built in the early nineteenth century, the Vaughn house was a white clapboard, two-story affair with black shutters that faced the road behind a short stretch of lawn. A kitchen and woodshed had been added later, changing the shape of the building into an L, the lower tip of which connected at a right angle to the breezeway, which in turn connected to the dairy and the barn. The barn, painted red, was topped by a shuttered cupola that bore a weathervane in the form of a bull. The barn also faced the road, but farther back than the house, allowing a driveway to sweep in from the road in a wide arc. This left a half-moon of lawn directly in front of the barn near the road, on which stood an ancient and ailing elm with a bole five feet in diameter. Connected to the back of the barn and forming another L where it extended into the barnyard was a dilapidated old house. The second floor of this structure contained about two hundred laying hens; the first floor, frame and front wall only, served as a shelter for young stock during the winter. Beyond the end of the barn and hen house and echoing the other arrangements was a free-standing, L-shaped equipment shed that stood with its back to the northeast and its open bays facing southwest. The house and barns proper were flanked, east and west, by two rows of old maples that in earlier times had been tapped for their sap to make sugar.

In the shade of one of these maples next to the equipment shed, a scuffed, weedy area of oil spills littered with bits of junk, the boy got the mowing machine ready to cut hay. The blade was warped and had to be tapped into place down the groove of the cutter bar. Sweat dripped from his face as he knelt behind the tractor, the steady *tap-tap* of the hammer sounding against the side of the shed.

Lucien Quirk sat with his back against the tree trunk, half-drowsing, watching the boy work. "How come the old man don't do the mowing?"

"My uncle?"

"Yeah."

The boy tapped for a moment, inching the blade down the bar. "He has a bad heart."

"What happened to it?"

"He had a heart attack."

The man laughed, and the boy tapped harder and faster with irritation. Marines didn't laugh at heart attacks, didn't laugh at nothing all the time.

"Why do you limp?" he challenged.

The man laughed again. In the shade, with his head down, it was difficult for the boy to see his eyes. "You really want to know, huh?" the man asked.

"I wouldn't ask if I didn't."

The boy flushed at his own words. It was heady stuff, giving lip to an adult, even if the adult was a wino.

"I got my ass blown off by a crazy Jap . . . half my ass, anyway."

The boy didn't believe him.

"Where?"

"Saipan."

"In the Pacific?"

"It wasn't Boston Harbor."

Bobby Dearborn felt dumb. Of course it had to be in the Pacific if the Japs did it. But that didn't prove the guy was a Marine. Anyone could know that stuff. He could have read it in books or watched "Victory at Sea." The boy went back to tapping the blade.

Lucien Quirk lit a Lucky Strike and closed his eyes. A bad heart and an easy touch, he thought, feeling already the pint bottle in his hand, the glowing burn in his gut. And the lady of the house, too. Touch her with what she needed. A push and a poke. Oh, let me help you, Mrs. Vaughn. Let me rub you where you need it. Let me, let me. With the same clarity with which he tasted his next mouthful of cheap sherry, Lucien Quirk tasted Janet Vaughn's ample charms in a scene of sharp words and aggressive surrender. Horny again. Amazing what a decent meal does for a man. He belched, opened his eyes, and gazed out, blinking, from the maple's shade to where the ascending sun sent down a stunning flood of heat and light. A pretty sight. Through heavy-lidded eyes he followed the curves of the land from where the truck garden, verdant and orderly despite the cows' rampage, ran along the road to a knoll of clover fringed by hardwoods, a tree line that fell back and rose with the land, turned to pine, and fenced an arc of more fields of ripening hay and the high ground of grazed pasture. The man took it in with the taste of wine in his throat and touched his thickening self, land and woman merging in a sleepy vision of empire, from which he awoke with a start. The possibility, flimsy and stark as a dream, ballooned and broke and he laughed it away.

"What's the joke?"

The man got up and watched the boy working.

"Life's a joke," he said. "You done this kind of thing before, Captain?"

Bobby Dearborn drove the blade home and snapped on

the spring-loaded clamp. He tried to sound offhand.

"Sure, I cut all of last year's second crop."

"All of last year's second crop. Is that right?"

The man didn't laugh, but his eyes were slit and his mouth set in a crooked smile, as if that too were to be the butt of a joke.

The boy didn't notice; he was up and down on the tractor, testing, oiling, adjusting, getting ready for his mission.

❧

They began on the knoll in the clover. The boy sat high on the tractor, perched between the two big wheels, and worked the lever that lowered the cutter bar hydraulically until it was buried in the green tangle of vegetation. He put the power takeoff in gear, and the blade, as he eased off the clutch, moved back and forth inside the cutter bar, scissoring. Then he clutched again, put the tractor in first, and began moving and mowing.

Because the bar extended out on the right side, they went clockwise, down from the clover to the thick grass along the creek and into the thin hay where the field wedged into the woods, then back to the clover at the bottom of the garden, covering a large rectangle of several acres. Submerged, the cutter bar swept under the grass, chattering, shearing the land as though it were a sheep. The grass shuddered and lay flat in windrows, covering its own stubble. A pheasant erupted from just in front of the blade. The year before he had cut one in half, leaving a mangle of feathers and blood on the field. Along the lowland where swamp grass had invaded in clumps, the blade jammed, the drive belt spun with a whine, and the boy, cursing manfully, stopped the tractor and backed off, raising the bar for Lucien Quirk, gimping up behind, to clean it off with his pitchfork. Then he drove forward again, perched sideways between the wheels, enclosed in a cone of noise and heat as he watched the back-slung mower doing its steady, precise work. As they went around once, twice, three times, the swatch of mown hay grew wider and started to bleach under the strong white sun.

For Lucien Quirk it was an agony. The fallen hay snared his feet. His butt hurt. His back ached. His head spun with the heat and visions of a cold beer. Just one. He could taste it. He thought: You keep hobbling after something that keeps moving farther and farther away from you until it stops and you can catch up to it to find it wasn't what you wanted, only a mess of swamp grass fouling up the works. But you kneel over it, risking your fingers (make sure that God damn thing ain't in gear!) to free it up, and then it moves off again and you start following, losing ground.

He dropped back until, at the corner of the cut near the brook, he sat down and lit a cigarette. The tractor went halfway up the cut and stopped. The boy got off and walked back to the man. "You're supposed to follow me."

"I'm taking a break."

Bobby Dearborn glanced toward the garden. The woman wasn't out yet. "We ain't got time for breaks."

"I got all the time in the world."

"My uncle won't like it."

The man shrugged.

"You'll get fired."

"No, I won't."

The man was smiling now and the boy didn't know what to say. He said what he was thinking. "Marines don't quit."

"This gyrene ain't quitting, Captain. He's just taking a fiver."

"It's your funeral," the boy said with dismissive anger and turned to go to the tractor.

"Listen."

"Yeah."

"Let's use our heads, huh? You're only getting stuck along this stretch, right? So why don't I just patrol along here while you're going around, okay? I'll just pull back the hay and tidy things up and that'll make it easier for you and easier for me."

The boy shrugged. Bum, he thought, getting back on the tractor, where he felt secure between the moving wheels; nothing but a lousy wino bum.

The rectangle shrank slowly. They cut the wetter section and most of the clover and were finally mowing a stretch of regular, gray-green hay. Around them swallows flew in great swooping arcs, snapping suddenly sideways after flying insects, and crows and grackles littered the mown swaths, stalking after frogs and bugs. A motion caught the boy's eye. He slowed and stopped and watched a kestrel hover, plunge, and rise with something wriggling in its talons. The hay had begun to dry in the heat, and the perfume of the wilting clover cloyed the already thin air.

❧

Around noontime Hedley Vaughn, followed by the dog, came down from the house with a lunch of cheese sandwiches and a jar of cherry-flavored Kool-Aid. The others stopped and drove over to the shade of Jewett's woods near the creek.

"I sharpened another blade," the farmer said. "I'll bring it down with some gas."

The boy nodded. "The one I've got's going dull."

Hedley Vaughn shaded his eyes and peered out over the area they had mowed.

"Doing a good job," he allowed. "If the weather holds we'll mow tomorrow morning and rake in the afternoon. Come Monday we can bring it in."

Then he set off across the hot field and returned shortly, lugging a five-gallon can of gasoline and a newly sharpened blade. While the hired man and the boy ate their lunch, the farmer worked. He hoisted the can to his shoulder and poured the gas into the tank, which was set back along the top of the tractor like the thorax of a large red insect. Sighing with the effort, he began to tap out the dulled blade. It was just about a year before, on a day like this one, when he was pitching hay up onto the wagon, that he had his heart attack. He remembered being grabbed and squeezed until lights flecked against a darkening sky, and he fell, drowning in air. The attack left him weak and half-alive in a thrall of dull pain. Everything seemed touched with the infinite grayness of death. And though Hedley Vaughn feared his own physical extinction, he feared more the cessation of work, the end of the farm. If I went now, he was always thinking, who would see that the cows got milked, the fences fixed, the winter rye planted, the manure shoveled, the haying done, the endless rounds of chores, the work of a lifetime, the work four generations of Vaughns had done on this piece of stony land since before the Civil War. Not to continue was far worse to the man than mere death.

He pulled the dull blade free and inserted the sharp one. He knew that things were desperate. Bringing in fifty acres of hay with a kid and a lame drunk. Jan balking at every turn. His heart. It tapped with the hammer. Dimly, through the heat, mocking, came the answering whack of hammers from the subdivision across the road. Mayhew had sold out. The Jewetts were old and childless. The Dillons only kept horses. He knew that when it happened, when his heart quit and died, the farm would die. He knew his wife would sell out for a few hundred an acre and that the land would be buried under roads and houses and a swarm of anonymous people. He, too, had wanted a child, a son to carry on.

With a leaky bucket he dipped water from the creek and carried it to the tractor for the radiator. Some of it spilled, and he went back for another bucketful. He sat for a moment on the bank of the stream where it flowed out of the woods. There the shadowed water gleamed and swirled over polished rocks, dimpling and eddying in a swift current between banks of peat. A form shot upstream underwater. A muskrat. The man had trapped them as a boy, walking his trap lines in the morning before school with the sky gray, the woods black, and the ground white. He remembered skinning them in the dairy, the pelts stretched inside out on wire frames as he scraped off the drying flecks of fat and got the pungent musk on his hands and clothes. In those days they sugared in March, and his father cut ice on the pond with a team of horses, and his grandfather, ancient and bearded as an Old Testament prophet, told stories about the Civil War and the time he saw Lincoln giving a speech.

Hedley Vaughn sighed and got up to finish filling the tractor radiator with water. The past was past, he mused ruefully. He was not, at heart, a sentimentalist, but there were times when, with his present a gray pall of pain and his future a dim and alien prospect, it seemed that all he had left was the past and its memories, which recurred now with strange, hallucinatory vividness. He resisted the tug. He wasn't quite ready yet. The tractor and the blade of the mowing machine, its teeth hung with snags of hay, were real, after all. They were getting the haying done. If the weather held, they would be finished in a few weeks. He would, for another season anyway, slow down time. It was another reprieve. He walked over to where the boy and the man were resting after their lunch.

"She's ready to go," he said to the boy. "Take her easy around the middle where that rock is. I figure it ought to be just about dead center."

The boy had gotten up and had sensed the unspoken order to get back to work. He watched as the man walked slowly across the mown hay toward the garden, where the woman worked on the row of damaged bean poles.

"Let's get started," he said.

Lucien Quirk, supine, head pillowed on drying hay, rustled to make himself more comfortable.

"Started? Christ, man, we just stopped. Gimme a break. Sit down, relax. You'll be old before your time."

"My aunt's in the garden. She can see us."

The man craned his neck to get a look. To an old tune he sang:

> "Nothing could be finer
> Than to be in her vagina
> In the morning.
> Nothing could be sweeter
> Than to have her eat my peter
> In the morning . . ."

The boy was not amused. He knew what the words meant and he couldn't imagine his aunt having anything to do with sex.

"You're afraid of her, ain't you?" the man taunted.

"No," the boy lied, stung by the truth. He pretended to work on the tractor.

"Sure you are. You're like a little rabbit around her."

"I ain't."

"Don't worry about it. That's what women do to men. I ought to know, I've had enough of them . . . all colors, sizes, shapes . . . Turn 'em upside down and they all look the same."

"Have you got a wife?"

The man had remained lying on the ferny ground, his head on the hay, his eyes closed. "Used to."

"What happened to her?"

"I don't know. I think she ran off with a vacuum-cleaner guy."

"Really?"

The boy glanced quickly at the man. He couldn't tell whether Lucien Quirk considered his wife's departure a singular tragedy or a stroke of luck.

"She never came back?"

"Never came back. I didn't exactly wait around for her." He opened his eyes and laughed. "Say, who was that babe that came in this morning?"

"Babe?"

"The lady in the white pants who came in for the shirts."

"Mrs. Porley?"

"Mrs. Porley, huh? Well, Mrs. Porley sure has a sweet-looking ass for an old dame. Wouldn't mind getting a hand or two on that."

A sweet-looking ass. Bobby Dearborn was twelve years old and sprouting intimations of manhood. Mostly, he noticed the breasts on women. But Mrs. Porley had a sweet-looking ass. It was like a revelation.

"Yeah," he said, trying to sound as if he knew, and got up on the tractor. And the man, rising, shaking himself, laughed as if he knew too, knew what the boy didn't know.

They mowed for an hour without stopping. The boy slowed to avoid snipping the head off a large and frantically racing black snake. Mrs. Porley's sweet-looking ass. She came down alone through Jewett's woods into the swamp to pick blueberries. She had got stuck and was sinking in one of the bottomless holes. He was hunting and heard her cries for help. Just in time he stretched out a pole that she clung to as he pulled her out. She was frightened and fainted. Because she was hurt he had to take her pedal pushers off. He saw it. (Coming to the edge of the cut, stopping, hydraulically lifting the cutter bar to clear the hay, reversing, lowering, starting again.) He saw her sweet-looking ass, clean and cleaved, as white as her white pedal pushers, and in front her secret, flossed furrow. The boy was roaring along in second gear, the gas up, his body prickling in its first sweet swoon of concupiscence, a throb in the groin amid the noise and vibration and shimmering heat, when the cutter bar slammed the rock with a nasty, crunching bang, bouncing up and came down, jammed and grinding.

Janet Vaughn had been watching them. The large field they had flattened around a diminishing rectangle of standing grass angered her. They were going to do it after all. Hedley would have another barnful of hay to keep them going through another bitter winter of work and frozen pipes and grain bills they couldn't pay. She had been straightening bean poles and refastening the twine hung with a web of vine and tendril when she heard the crack of steel on rock and knew instantly, with a surge of gleeful rage, what had happened. She resisted the first impulse to go down and cuff the boy around the ears. Father Fahey had said ... And the new man was down there. That stopped her and then, in no conscious way, impelled her to start across the garden to where the man sat chewing a blade of grass and watching the boy working on the machine.

Bobby Dearborn sweated in sheets as he loosened the nut securing the broken finger and tapped out the bolt with the hammer. He took a spare finger salvaged from an old cutter and positioned it, reinserting the bolt and twisting on the nut. Then the woman was there, standing off a little distance, bulky in the flatness of the field.

"What happened?"

"It hit a rock."

The boy turned to give her a look of shared disappointment, submission, guilt. Twice guilty. Mrs. Porley's sweet-looking ...

Lucien Quirk sat on a clump of hay, sucking on his stem of hay, observing and saying nothing.

"Can you fix it?"

The woman's voice was level, rational, and Bobby Dearborn went lightheaded with relief. The bent fingers straightened to his tap. The blade looked okay.

"It's almost fixed."

The man laughed for no reason at all.

Until then Janet Vaughn had ignored him and the way he was regarding her with an openly speculative gaze, as though he had taken off her clothes and left her standing naked in the field. But she hadn't been tempted so much as she had thought about temptation. The man's laugh insinuated more, touched her to an anger she turned on the boy.

"Didn't your uncle tell you to watch the rock?"

"I did."

"Those pieces cost money." She closed in on him.

"I got them off the old bar."

"Don't contradict me."

"I'm not . . ."

She hit him, cuffing him high on the head, delivering a humiliation worse than any hurt. What was worse for her was that the boy kept working as though it hadn't happened. Feeling awkward, confused, and finally defeated, she turned and stalked back toward the garden.

The man laughed again and got up. "She's a real firecracker, ain't she."

The boy was too enraged to speak. His jaw clenched, he started the tractor and resumed mowing. He could have murdered.

❧

That night, after dark, after he had milked the cows and had supper and gone for a swim, the boy helped Lucien Quirk settle into the brooder house that stood at the end of the maples on the north side of the house. A smoking kerosene lantern shed flickering yellow light and stark shadows around the low shack, a frame of two-by-fours covered by boards and tar-seamed tarpaper that perched precariously on cinderblocks. The two windows on the side were little more than openings tacked with wire screen and hung with burlap bags. Bobby Dearborn swept the floor, raising a fine white dust from the corners and from under the cowled brooder stove that two years before had warmed a mass of piping yellow chicks. His aunt had grumbled when they brought down the surplus Army cot from the attic. They had unfolded this next to a wooden cable reel laid on its side as a night table. The man had nailed a bushel box against the wall to put things in. When they finished sweeping and setting up, the man sat on the edge of the cot and smoked a cigarette.

"A regular fucking Taj Mahal," he said.

The boy nodded his head, missing the sarcasm. The shack appealed to him. If it had a real stove and some windows, he would have lived there himself, even in winter.

He envied Lucien Quirk his world. Sitting on a broken lawn chair, he watched the man pull things from his seemingly bottomless duffel bag.

"My dress blues."

The man carefully unrolled the crumpled uniform. He produced two hangers, one for the navy blue, almost black jacket, and the other for the light blue trousers, which had a red stripe down the side of each leg. On two nails at the back of the shack, where the ceiling came so low that even the man had to stoop, he hung the uniform on the two hangers, the jacket just above the trousers, and fixed the black-visored white hat so that in the eerie light of the lantern, seen sidelong, it appeared to the boy that a rumpled Marine was standing at attention.

Out of a cigar box Lucien Quirk produced a small framed picture of his mother, who looked dark and French and old-fashioned. Lucille Pelletier Quirk. She had spoken broken English and broken French. He placed it and a picture of the Virgin and Child on the cable reel.

"Are you a Catholic?" the boy asked.

The man blew smoke and shook his head ambiguously. "One of these days," he muttered, unrolling from a cardboard tube a pinup of a glossy-haired, red-lipped nude with pendulous, purple-nippled breasts. "My one and only true love," he exclaimed.

Bobby Dearborn glanced at it and away, a flush creeping over his skin right up to his scalp. Embarrassed and fascinated at the same time, he watched as the man pinned it with thumbtacks to the flaking boards over his cot.

"What's her name?"

"Mary Palm."

"She's pretty."

The boy, still abashed, was touched by the unearthly, evanescent lust he had experienced mowing hay. Her sweet ass.

"Is she going to visit you?"

"She comes to me all the time."

Then the man began to laugh and, showing the gaps in his teeth, sang:

> "Her lips are as pink
> As a rooster's dink,
> Her hair is a shitty brown.
> Her tits hang loose
> Like the balls on a goose,
> The girl from my home town."

He was chuckling, the joke private, as he unrolled another pinup, an Oriental woman seen from the back bending over a table arranging flowers.

"Who . . ." the boy started and checked himself, disappointed and relieved at the same time. They were just pictures of naked women like the ones on the calendar Smiley Grimes had on the wall inside his Shell station. They didn't even have names. He gazed at them boldly now, especially the Oriental, thinking he could see a wisp of her magic spot just beneath the cleft of delicate buttocks. His breathing came slower and his blood seemed to thicken and he sighed involuntarily, making the man, who was watching him, guffaw.

"You ain't pulled your peter yet, have you, Captain?"

Bobby Dearborn shook his head, ashamed, for some reason. Richie Fox, who was fifteen and still in the eighth grade and hung around the pond, jerked off all the time. He did it in the woods and let the kids watch him for a dime each. Sometimes he did it in math class in the back row, first asking Miss Joyce for a piece of math paper, which he tucked in his belt to catch the cum.

The man had produced another cigar box from within the magic duffel. Inside that was another box, this one of inlaid wood with delicate brass fittings. It contained three small cases of the kind jewelry comes in. He opened one of them like a jeweler displaying his wares and showed the boy his Good Conduct medal. It was a scarlet ribbon with a navy blue stripe down the middle and it was hung with a circular pendant.

"The Good Conduct medal," the man said, showing the boy. "I got it for not getting drunk too much."

Then he opened the next case, which held a purple and gold heart-shaped medallion hanging from a purple and white ribbon.

"The Purple Heart," the boy said, his eyes going big, his mouth dropping open. "What did you get that for?"

"For being dumb enough to get half my ass blown off."

He opened the last case. The medal hung from a red, white, and blue ribbon. "The Bronze Star."

The boy nodded, awestruck and cautious at the same time. The naked women had just been paper. He could have bought the medals in a pawn shop somewhere.

Lucien Quirk had risen and, with a ceremonial flourish that was half facetious and half serious, began pinning the medals on his hanging uniform.

"I got the Bronze on Tarawa," he said, keeping the talk of his exploits going. It wasn't often that he had such an appreciative audience.

"What did you do there?"

"I took out a Jap machine gun nest." He watched the boy's reaction. "We were pinned down. The lieutenant told me to do it. I did it. The son of a bitch should have just called in the artillery."

"Is that why you limp?"

"No, I got that on Saipan blowing up caves. You want to see something?"

And before the boy could answer, he unbuckled his belt and dropped his trousers. His right buttock, slug white on top, shelved in as if sliced by a rough knife that had left angry red tracks of stitching.

"Does it hurt?"

"Only when I'm screwing."

He laughed again, his crippled bark of mirth echoing through the cricket sounds of the night. He had pulled up his trousers and was sitting on the cot, bending forward, his face suddenly drained and serious, his eyes tracking and trapping the boy's, holding them. "Listen, I need a couple of bucks till pay day." He rubbed his chin. "For shaving gear. I need blades. I don't think the lady of the house likes the help to be unshaven."

"I've only got about a buck. It's in my drawer."

The man kept his face close so that the boy, even in the bad light, could see all the tiny blood vessels lacing the tip of his nose and the whites of his eyes.

"That'll do it."

"I was saving it to buy a new model jet, the Lockheed F-Ninety."

"Well, listen . . ." The man's voice took on a cooing sound. "If you lend me that dollar now, okay, I'll buy you that airplane come Friday."

"It costs one fifty-nine."

"We got a deal."

The boy wasn't sure. He heard the need in the man's voice and found himself able to look straight back into the fractured blue eyes. "I'll give you the buck if you'll give me one of your medals."

A silence of night sounds descended around them. The man had no laughter for this, the innocent mockery of a boy. "You can't buy those kinds of medals, sonny," he said in a voice low with menace.

"Just the one for good conduct."

"You'd better run along home."

"I was just . . ."

"Go home."

"I'll get you the dollar."

"Go home."

Confused, the boy stepped from the shack and closed the door. He wanted to say he was sorry, but he didn't know how. He lingered a moment, expecting the man to call him back. Then in the darkness he went up the old road under the maples to the house and was feeling rather than thinking that there was something to the man after all, that he was a real Marine.

3

THE SILKEN GREEN chasuble shimmered, a gaudy fish in a bowl of white light, and Father Francis J. Fahey, his hands parting, intoned: *"Gloria in excelsis Deo. Et in terra pax hominibus bonae voluntatis."*

He came up for air. *"Laudamus te. Benedicimus te. Adoramus te . . ."*

Then the effort of pronunciation failed him, and he lapsed into an unintelligible mutter. He finished the Gloria and bent before the tabernacle to kiss the saint's relic embedded in the altar slab. A drop of sweat rolled off his nose and spotted the linen. Damn heat. Again, as if in protest, his Latin rang with bass clarity through the small church: *"Dominus vobiscum."*

"Et cum spiritu tuo," responded the two altar boys, robed in black cassocks and white surplices and set like halfbacks at the bottom of the altar steps.

"Oremus," the priest urged and turned to the book.

Two standing fans swung back and forth, caged propellers stirring the heat in the church, which was filled with people who had hoped to escape the crowds and heat of later Masses. The faithful knelt dutifully, half slouched against pews in seersucker suits and light summer dresses. Above them saints and prophets in Life Saver colors etched with lead tilted at crazy angles where the double march of windows had been cranked open. From Blackman's farm across the parking lot, but seemingly closer, the mocking crow of a cock wafted in on the warm air.

(Through some extravagance of eccentricity and despite lawsuits and vandalism and selectmen's resolutions and offers of large sums of money, old man Parker Blackman and his ancient, dithered mother farmed seventy-some ramshackle acres smack in the middle of booming Elmsbury Centre. Their motley herd of milkers, their lame horse and querulous geese, their dusty chickens and stray dogs and army of cats, ruled a kingdom of dung defined by the parking lot of St. Cecilia's Catholic Church, the lawns of St. Paul's Episcopal Church, the back end of the town's first supermarket, the snapping pennants of Holtzman's Ford, and a weedy slice of railroad tracks.)

Janet Vaughn's nose wrinkled. Even here she could not escape the smell of cows. Her eyes wandered upward above the plastered walls and tilted saints to the high, pitched roof and the exposed beams that supported it. All nicely stained and polished, of course, but still it reminded her of the barn. She caught her thoughts and read silently in her missal: *Brethren, I speak in a human way because of the weakness of your flesh; for as you yielded your members as slaves of uncleanness and iniquity unto iniquity, so now yield your members as slaves of justice unto sanctification* . . .

The ornate language cloyed, then jolted her. *Flesh.*

She had waked that morning from a dream of love at once vaporous and explicit that returned now with pangs of guilt and pleasure. In the dream she had submitted with alacrity to a phantom lover who bestrode her, a rhythmic weight feeding her need and eluding her eyes as she squirmed to see his face. Who? The temptations of carnality and curiosity hovered like intimations. But it was a sin to probe such memories, to elicit the pleasure. Impure thoughts. Impure and irresistible. Her knees weakened on the uncushioned kneeler and she relaxed, letting her bottom touch the edge of the seat.

Like that!

The touch, the dazzle of altar lights, the humming fans, the polished railing fencing the sanctuary, the neck of the man in front of her — everything suddenly had a tumescent glow. She raised her eyes, imploring. Herod's purple robe . . . the bed of violets in the garden in the ell of the house. The scene flashed. Mary, she prayed, but it rose in her thick as suffocation, a yawn of need so distressingly physical, so immediate, she . . . Then it broke like a boil, lanced by the late entrance of the Langdons, all nine of them, from their shack by the cranberry bog, wandering as if lost down the center aisle in search of seats.

Father Fahey bowed at the center of the altar. *"Munda cor meum ac labia mea, omnipotens Deus . . ."*

Rebuked, Janet Vaughn stood for the Gospel. *At that time Jesus said to his disciples: Beware of false prophets, who come to you in sheep's clothing, but inwardly are ravenous wolves.*

She followed and faltered again. She wondered if the white sleeveless dress she wore, the one with the slimming pleats all the way down, made her arms seem too heavy. Fat and red. Really had to diet. Start today. No more starch. Yes, but it really did go nicely with the off-white pumps and the calfskin clasp with the mother-of-pearl bought on sale at Cherry & Webb. The whole ensemble was, she thought now, just a little too nursy, just a little too bleached-looking, especially with the boxy little hat of painted straw. Still, it was her best, and sometimes she wore it two weeks in a row, even though Connie Murphy down in front, wearing a dark blue short-sleeved number with tiny white polka dots and a white belt, never wore anything two weeks in a row. That somehow seemed more appropriate for Mass than all this whiteness. Of course, Connie Murphy could afford a new outfit every week. Married to Charles of the Murphy Brothers' Lumber — "Helping Elmsbury Grow" — and next to her Cindy and Sandy, her two darling little girls, in pigtails and summer frocks.

And the way they redid the house on the old Hutchins place, Gladys Porley never stopped raving about it, as if to say How could Catholics live in such splendor? Poisonous woman, with her Episcopalian airs when everyone knew she came from some kind of shouting Baptists. Just because . . .

More latecomers. A couple dressed for the beach. Beach Catholics, Father Fahey used to thunder before the fund drive got started to build a new church and rectory. Because now the beach Catholics from the new developments that had names like Grove Hill and Stage Pond and Post Road Estates packed the church. They came in new cars from raw split-level houses spaced with remnant oak and pine on raw plots carved from old pastures and woodlands. Janet Vaughn both envied them and felt a little superior. They were, after all, just newcomers.

They sat for the homily.

A sin is a sin is a sin, Father Francis J. Fahey was wont to say in the course of his ad-libbed sermons and in the admonitions he dealt out in the darkness of the confessional. A rules and regulations man, he liked to think of himself as a kind of master sergeant in the army of the Lord (having been passed up years before for the more or less officer rank of monsignor.) Thick-featured, with a red face and smooth baldness spreading back from his forehead, the pastor of St. Cecilia's appeared oddly trim and muscular for a man of nearly sixty. But, then, he ate in moderation and seldom had more than one drink before dinner. Celibacy had never been a problem and he had some difficulty comprehending the inordinate sexual preoccupations of his parishioners.

If Father Fahey had a weakness, it was his penchant for fires. The priest kept a short-wave radio in the rectory and served as unofficial chaplain to the Elmsbury Fire Department. Occasionally he was seen bent over the wheel of his sleek black Ford as it raced through town in the wake of fire engines. But it wasn't like the old days when he was a curate in Dorchester and the wooden three-deckers, sometimes whole blocks of them, went up like kindling. Sometimes there were victims and grieving families and, next morning in the Boston papers, pictures of the "fire priest," waterproof stole hung over his slicker as he administered the last rites to a blanketed form.

Then he found himself posted to a small town near the Cape, where there wasn't a decent fire from one end of the year to the next. Elmsbury didn't have many fires either, and Lowell was too far away. But the fires in his head did not go out, and the priest, whenever he could, fanned the flames of hell in his sermons.

"Every tree that does not bear good fruit is cut down and thrown in the fire." He paused meaningfully and pulled a handkerchief from the lace-fringed sleeve of his alb to wipe his hot face and the dome of his baldness. The silence filled with wheezing and barking coughs. "Fruit trees and fruit. Good trees and bad trees. What's our Lord trying to tell us here? Is God in the fruit business? Does he run a roadside stand? Does he truck produce into Boston at dawn?"

The priest paused again. It wasn't quite the direction he wanted to go. "In some ways, yes," he continued, modulating with a tone bordering on the hypothetical, begging their credence. "God the Father is also God the Farmer. As God the Farmer, the Almighty is the great reaper of souls in the universe." He stopped and let that sink in. Hot work, this musing on your feet. "For God the Farmer only the best is good enough. Only the best fruit is harvested in heaven and only the good trees are left to bear good fruit. The trees that bear blighted fruit, diseased fruit, deformed fruit, are cut down and thrown into the fire."

His words touched Janet Vaughn with terror. Deformed fruit. They had not let her see it. *It*. A girl, almost full term. She hadn't carried the others more than a month or two. Dr. Weller's voice had faltered and his eyes had looked away when he told her. And no baptism. The hospital chaplain had been adamant. No baptism. No funeral. No name. Janet Vaughn had named her anyway, and each year on April 17, with the world just turning green, she held a secret birthday party for her lost Jessica Lee.

She had wept for a week, lying on the bed in the hospital room with its desolate view of the Merrimack River lined with factories. She had stared at the river and the red brick factories and the few trees primping with green and had wanted to die. Because it went deeper than grief. She had felt emptied, useless. She had waited for the child to come and redeem her, to give her a second chance, a new start, a way vicariously to right the wrongs she had suffered and to avoid the mistakes she had made. Instead, she found herself deeper in the hell of a life gone wrong. Oh, yes, very bad, the old nurse with the starched face had told her, her mouth tutting life's brutal truths. The head was all wrong. You're better off, dear, she had cooed, sugaring it with thin kindness. You have time for lots more. But now Janet Vaughn felt time running out on her. Thirty-seven, closing in on forty. The last time she and Hedley even tried . . .

"The fires of hell," sweated Father Fahey, "are a thousand times hotter than the hottest day anyone here could ever imagine." He fake-coughed. "You've all burned yourself at one time or another. A mistake with a match. A hot pan on the stove. Now, imagine your whole body trapped in flames for all eternity. No escape. No hope. No tomorrow. I know because I've been there. That is to say, I've seen it. I've heard the screams. Only, the damned do not know the peace of death" — he caught himself again — "that is to say, the seeming peace of death, because none of us, saint or sinner, ever dies except for the death that is the loss of God's love. For better or worse, we are all immortal." He stopped, wiped his forehead, and squinted out over the rows of impassive faces staring up, hands in front of yawns, an orchard of blighted souls. "Yet," he whispered, inverting his thunder, "as tormenting, as painful, as awful, are the fires of hell, they are not the worst part of eternal damnation. No, my children. The worst pain of all is the loss for all eternity of God's love."

Janet Vaughn listened to the priest and assented. She wanted God's love. She believed in the storybook heaven of her girlhood as a place to go after this life. A shrine to the left of the altar with a pale blue and cream plaster Virgin lit softly by offertory candles cupped in ruby glass stood against a fresco of the Holy Land and was Janet Vaughn's secret doorway to paradise. In the foreground of this painting, cedar and cypress framed a green sward cut by a silver-blue stream along which shepherds with crooked staffs watched over gamboling lambs. In the background, on a distant hill, the golden domes of Jerusalem glowed under a radiant sky lit by the sun of a hundred-watt bulb fixed behind a cloud in the form of a cross. When the woman knelt there after confession to pray her penance, she walked toward a paradise of verdant lawns and white marble temples under an endlessly gorgeous sky where she was young and pretty again and could stroll hand in hand with her faultless Jessica Lee.

Yet her heaven was more than a kind of celestial suburb. Heaven held for her the promise of something whole and holy and perfect, something she'd never had in this life. In the life beyond the grave, in the time beyond the time to come (but real, something you could touch and hold), she didn't expect actually to meet God, who was too abstract, or Jesus, who was too important; but she did hope to be a good friend of the Virgin Mother and some of the nicer saints, like Francis of Assisi, who had been kind to birds. The very perfection of her dream, her walking with Jessica Lee, troubled her, however. She had doubts. In confession she had asked Father Fahey whether Jesus would bring her child from limbo if Mary asked him specially for her. Well, yes, the priest had answered. Anything was possible, given God's infinite power and infinite mercy. But he hadn't sounded very certain about it.

They stood for the Credo and sat again for the Offertory to a rustling for change and wallets.

As in holocausts of rams and bullocks, and as in thousands of fat rams, so let our sacrifice be made in thy sight this day that it may please thee, O Lord.

Two men came down the center aisle, each holding aloft

a varnished woven basket attached to the end of a pole. They genuflected and started back, gliding the baskets in and out of the rows with the bent, pumping motion of pool players.

Janet Vaughn put an extra fifty cents into the basket. It hadn't been a good Mass. That dream. She had watched Connie Murphy drop her envelope demurely into the basket. Big giver. She belonged to the Sodality and tried to be friendly. Do please come over for coffee. Her nice eyes harried with lines. She practically begged. But how could the invitation be returned with that kitchen even if the living room wasn't that bad although the couch did have that awful sag that no covering or cushions could hide though with another book of Green Stamps she could have the table lamp with the black and brass base and the washable fiber glass shade which was just the nicest blend of modern and old-fashioned and would go perfectly on the end of the table in the corner. One more book. Gladys Porley said she had some stamps she would give her. Would have to ask again. Begging, really. Although nothing would redeem that couch. The floral chintz cover only made it seem worse. And Hedley hadn't wanted to bid on the one at the auction the Lions Club held in the town hall. Thirty dollars, it went for. No money. No roadside stand after Hedley's attack. They sold to the competition what the cows didn't ruin. Frank Devito came by in his pickup for what they used to get good money for. God damn Dago, Hedley cursed. But Frank gave what he could for the strawberries and beans and squash, even when there was a glut. The way he went moony. The dark eyes hard, then soft, lingering, the voice solicitous. How is Hedley feeling? Can I get you anything in town? And he had clean hands for a farmer and fine, hairy wrists. Picking corn that time close in the row together. She went glum thinking about it. Like the dream . . . on the violets under the mulberry tree with the sun off the side of the house where the roses climbed, and she gasped then, remembering how in broad daylight she had opened, wanting it, twisting to see who was who, who, who . . .

Holy, holy, holy . . .

The bells of the Sanctus brought Janet Vaughn to her knees, thumbing for the place in her missal. *Lord God of Hosts. Heaven and earth are filled with Thy Glory. Hosanna in the highest.*

She followed closely again, making her concentration an act of contrition. She prayed for the living, for Hedley and Ernestine, for Bobby Dearborn and even the hired man. She prayed that God would help her family, sisters Mary and Ellen, brother Joe Jr., their children, and her mother, Rose Gilooly. She prayed that her family would help her. They never did. They came out to the farm for Sunday outings with their kids and sat around complaining and judging and waiting for their sliced ham and potato salad. But she resisted bitter thoughts. She commemorated the saints, Peter and Paul, Andrew, James, John, Thomas, James, Philip, Bartholomew, Matthew, Simon and Thaddeus, then Linus, Cletus, Clement, Sixtus, Cornelius, Cyprian, Lawrence, Chrysogonus, John and Paul, Cosmas and Damian.

On the altar, in the depths of the white light, his chasuble an oil of greens, Father Fahey muttered his way toward the consecration. The fans went off. The coughing ceased. Even the cock quieted. A car drifted by on ghostly wheels. The priest bent over, then straightened, then lifted the host between his fingertips and called down God.

"Hoc est enim Corpus meum."

This is my body. Janet Vaughn believed that the wafer of unleavened white bread in the priest's hands quite literally transubstantiated with those words into the living tissue of a Godman who had lived on earth two thousand years before. She closed her eyes and bowed her head and willed a mindless, deep piety, nodding again as the bells rang for the consecration of the wine into blood, remembering: . . . *offer unto thy supreme majesty, of the gifts bestowed upon us, the pure victim, the holy victim, the all perfect victim, the holy bread of life eternal and the chalice of unending salvation.*

She went by the book again, reading in English what the priest murmured in Latin. She prayed for her dead, her Jessica Lee and her father, Joseph Gilooly, whom she remembered as a retiring, decent man with thick, mortar-bitten hands and the smell of a pipe and a shag of black hair into his sixties until the sudden cancer whitened him to a ghost. He had disapproved of Hedley. Too old. Protestant. But he kept that to himself. Don't lose your faith, Jan, was all he said. In the end it's all you'll have. Yes. It's all you have now. It's all you'll ever have. And it's not enough. God keep Joseph Gilooly, she prayed, but where? His grave in the cemetery near East Chelmsford with the polished granite stone. A skeleton now; dust. O God, there was nothing but the grave. You ended in a box, buried. Nothing.

"Agnus Dei, qui tollis peccata mundi, dona nobis pacem."

Lamb of God, who takest away the sins of the world, grant us peace.

But Janet Vaughn had no peace. Her corset bit into the top of her thighs and into her belly, which was heavy and cramped just before her period. Around her the veneer of talcums and deodorants and aftershave lotions crumbled in the humid heat to a sickly sweetness mingling with ranker human smells so that even a whiff of Blackman's farm intruded now like freshness. The dream from the night before beckoned like a promise of deliverance and with an insistence she warded off by following her missal, but mechanically, keeping herself technically in a state of grace, waiting for communion, for a bite of the Godman to save her from herself. The bells sounded again. She repeated to herself: *Lord I am not worthy that thou shouldst come under my roof.*

Still, when the time came, she clasped her hands close to her breast like a medieval saint and got up from the pew and stood in line for communion. The line shuffled forward. She knelt at the railing, glad for the cushions, and waited for Father Fahey as he came along the kneeling row with the altar boy, who was gliding the plate under her chin. Then priest smell, wax and sherry, a murmured prayer, a touch of thumb, and the small wafer rested on her tongue.

With head bowed and eyes closed, Janet Vaughn knelt in the pew and shut out everything but the particle of God's perfection dissolving with wheaten taste in her mouth. She focused on it, praying for the strange and holy bliss that sometimes came to suffuse her being and lift her out of the mire of the world. She conjured up Christ's suffering face and the gates of heaven — massive iron things hung on towering stone piers — through which she had entered before to glimpse the distant glow and to hear the siren echoes of the ineffable reality she knew existed somehow, somewhere, in the universe. She swallowed her sliver of Christ. Her joy grew ascendant. The gates parted and she went through them, moving as if on angel's wings toward the light, leaving Christ's sad face behind. Serene, beyond the cares of the world, she let herself float with a tide that gripped and lulled her in a dreamy, then sensual rhythm, going and going and going until Blackman's cock crowed, waking her because she was in her dream, entwined with a lover in a scene so graphic she gasped and rubbed her eyes, blotting out the enthralling embrace, staunching the rising culmination, and scrabbling at the harsh side of holiness as she knelt, eyes covered until she came to a mastery of herself that left her empty in a church empty except for altar boys snuffing candles and old ladies kneeling before a statue of the Virgin, praying, as Janet Vaughn was praying — for deliverance.

❧ 4 ❧

HEDLEY VAUGHN fretted for nearly two days about whether to keep the bull calf or send it to the butcher. Several times, herdman's stick in hand, he went out to the barn to inspect the creature. Then he put a halter on the cow and led her out into the sunshine to get a better look at the calf, which had followed her, bleating. It was, he had to admit, of good size, with long legs, a straight back, and a fine head. He felt its neck and chest and the nubs of its testes. He could find nothing wrong with it. He called the vet, who examined the calf, declared the animal sound, and advised the farmer to use artificial insemination.

Hedley Vaughn paid the vet and thanked him, but he was having none of this artificial stuff which, as common sense told him, was contrary to nature and would ruin the herd. So he fretted, even mentioning it to his wife, whose response was scarcely civil. She would have sent the entire herd to the butcher if she had had her way. Finally, to resolve the matter, he brought the bull out and tied him to the tree. He also brought out the cow and the calf. He lined up the calf next to the bull and stood back. The comparison dismayed him, even allowing for the difficulty of comparing animals of such disparate ages. He remembered the beauty and size of the bull just after it was dropped and how he knew right away it was something special. His attention was drawn again and again to the excellence of the sire. It had been given, after all, the highest possible rating by the Holstein Association of America. It was one of a kind, even if it was getting on in years. It was irreplaceable. And that man from upstate New York . . . Hedley Vaughn, faint of heart, made up his mind. He led the animals back to their stalls and called Harry Manning to come get the calf in his truck.

❧ 5 ❧

THE HAY dried quickly and rustled underfoot on its stalks and gave off a clean, sweet smell. Bobby Dearborn perched sideways on the tractor, driving in second gear and watching the rake, which he tripped every few seconds as the hay gathered under it. The rake had been horse-drawn until just after the war, when Hedley Vaughn sold his last horse and bought a secondhand Farmall tractor. He had replaced the shafts and whiffletree of the rake with a drawbar and rigged the hand lever with a length of rope so that the tractor driver could trip the row of sprung steel prongs that curved like ribs between the slender, almost elegant iron wheels. The boy drove straight across the field, turned, and came back, overlapping where he had raked and tripping the loads so that the hay lay bunched in rows that patterned the starkly barbered land.

Lucien Quirk, naked to the waist, looking muscular under a sheen of sweat, forked the raked hay into cocks, building them to shed water in case it rained. He lifted and moved the hay with the slow, mechanical motions of an automaton. The man, when he stopped, did not bother to gaze around the baking field to see how much he had done or how much remained to be done. In the end he knew it was endless.

The monotony was broken when Janet Vaughn, who had

been working in the garden, went into the house to make the others a half-gallon jar of iced Kool-Aid. Her husband, sharpening a blade in the shade next to the barn, declined it, and she walked across the field toward Lucien Quirk, the jar jangling with ice by her side.

The hired man drove his pitchfork into the ground and wiped his face with a bandanna. "Obliged." He bowed, his courtliness not altogether theatrical. Then, tilting back the jug, he drank deeply, showing her his fine Adam's apple. "Thanks," he murmured, held the jar, and leveled his eyes into hers so that she had to pretend she hadn't been looking. His muscles and sweat repelled and fascinated her, and she was drawn to a tattoo, high on his right arm, of the American flag with an inscribed banner furling over it. Next to his nakedness she felt constricted and formless in the blue work shirt she wore with loose slacks of a thin denim.

"Well, it's coming along," she finally blurted into the squinting redness of his face when the silence lengthened into possibilities of unspoken understandings.

His irritating laugh kept her on the hook. He put the jug on the ground, tapped out a cigarette from a squashed pack, and offered her one.

She shook her head.

"Yeah, it's coming along." He lit the cigarette and plumed blue smoke at the hot sky. "But I sure as hell don't know where it's going."

She declined with a silence that seemed like an invitation to conspiracy. "Are you finished?" she finally asked.

"Don't I wish," he said, and his eyes scanned hers as though for a signal.

Picking up the jar and continuing across the field toward the boy, Janet Vaughn allowed herself a small flutter. The hired man wasn't much, she thought, but she couldn't help feeling richer for the temptation.

❧

The man and the boy finished cocking the hay before dark that evening. The next morning they began bringing it in. Hedley Vaughn drove the tractor, which now pulled the hay wagon — a great crate of two-by-fours bolted to a bed of planks suspended on four balding tires. Using long-handled forks, they pitched the hay into the wagon. When it filled up, the boy got in and tramped it down. Finally, he had to stay up on the wagon, building the load, taking the hay from Lucien Quirk's fork and placing it along the edges before binding it with large clumps in the center, always moving, tramping, knee-deep in the treacherous, dusty stuff. The load grew wide and high, so high that even the long forks couldn't reach, and Hedley Vaughn started for the barn in first, the wagon creaking and swaying behind the tractor like a thatched cottage on wheels.

He drove the tractor and the load of hay into the gloom of the barn through a wide opening where the center section of the front wall rolled to one side. When the engine died, the chittering of disturbed swallows could be heard. Bobby Dearborn stepped from the load onto the mow that roofed the feed room to the right. There, using a light guide rope, he pulled the hay tongs to the end of the railing that ran along the top of the barn. The tongs came complaining and then descended rapidly after disengaging from the wheel carriage that rolled them along the railing. The boy took the four curved tongs, spread them, and buried them deep into the hay on the wagon. A thick rope threaded wooden pulleys from the top of the tongs to the carriage on the railing, back to the back of the barn and back again to the front, down to the floor and the back end of an old Ford car stripped of its metal skirts and fitted with tractor wheels on the rear axle. Hedley Vaughn sat in the driver's seat of the tilted Ford and, at a signal from the boy, drove it slowly, kicking gravel, across the driveway toward the road. The rope tightened, the pulleys creaked, and a massive bite of hay rose from the wagon in the jaws of the tongs. It rose up and up until the tension suddenly released as the tongs snapped into the carriage and the load of hay went wheeling rapidly back into the loft. The boy, proud of his competence, played the burning guide rope through his hands and waited for the signal to yank it, dumping the load.

At first only Lucien Quirk had to climb into the loft to shout the signal to trip the tongs so that the hay spread evenly down the high central mow, forming a crown from which to tumble later loads. When they had accomplished that, it was necessary for Janet Vaughn to go up as well and stand beside the hired man with a pitchfork to stop the elephantine clumps of hay as they charged along the apex of the barn toward them, perched high now over the side mows. After stopping a load, they would brace their forks into its side, pushing and releasing, pushing and releasing, until it swung out wide over the empty mow. At the right moment, the man yelled, "Trip it!" The boy yanked the rope, and the hay dropped from the tongs into the mow with a satisfying thump. But sometimes the guide rope snagged when the boy pulled it, then caught just as the load swung back, half burying the pair in the loft.

"God damn it, kid!" Lucien Quirk would shout.

"Bobby, what are you doing?" Janet Vaughn would cry.

"It snagged."

"We'll snag you!"

The man and the woman were united momentarily in anger and in labor as they pushed and pulled the misplaced pile into a mow. But Janet Vaughn kept her distance. No small talk for the hired man as they sweated and struggled with the dry, neutral hay that had begun to fill with surprising rapidity the cavernous emptiness of the loft. She kept her distance, but once, coming up late, she saw him silhouetted against the light from the windows ranged across the rear wall of the barn. He sat on a beam, head back against another beam, one knee up, pensive and handsome in profile. Another time he had the end of the handle of his fork coming out between his legs at a provocative angle, and for a blood-racing moment she thought . . . The strangely pleasant shock turned to disappointment she disguised to herself as disgust. Disgust came easily anyway. It hung in the air with the dust that clogged her sweating pores so that she came down from the loft and fled to the house to wash her face and fix herself up just in case Gladys Porley showed up for her load of ironing. And there were times, working with the man, sweating and pulling at the hay, and shouting at the boy, when she felt all but naked.

It was true that Lucien Quirk watched her move and had seen the shape of her body changing through the thinness of her clothes that clung at times with the perspiration she could not stop. Nice big bum. He lusted for her half the time and half the time dreamed of cold beer or red wine and the fires it kindled in his blood. And sometimes both. Wine and a woman, and hell, he'd make his own song. Then the boy was yelling "Ready!" and the old Ford coughed across the sun-struck gravel. The rope sighed and threatened to break and whip them all to death as from the wagon another shag of hay rose to the roof, snapped, and charged. Then Lucien Quirk's idle lustings died in the blank brunt of work, the heaving of hay in the close air of the loft or under the drenching sun, another cock in the endless field they slowly cleared and fed to the big-mouthed barn.

The man wooed the woman in his own way. A loser with nothing to lose, he could more than match her distance, even if sometimes his eyes, boyish and hungry in their net of premature lines, betrayed him. He could tease her with vague insinuations and he could be friendly and casual and always, maddeningly, tongue in cheek. One day he could not resist being more direct when she bent over her fork and flowered for his spading hand. The boy, manning the ropes, heard the angry bark of her voice from the back end of the barn. For the rest of the day Lucien Quirk kept touching his left cheek, as though treasuring the place where her slap showed pink through the brown of his tan.

They brought in the last of the first hay late one night and waited until the morning to unload it. Then they bolted the mowing machine onto the tractor again and tapped home a fresh blade and again the boy perched in the heat and noise, concentrating, as the hay quivered and fell in long straight swaths. His time moved in a haze of work. Hardly had his eyes closed at night when his uncle's hand tugged at his toes. Time to get the cows. But he could be idle for a while in the early morning freshness, dawdling down the rough road to the pasture and watching a bobolink rise from the side of the creek and bubble into hovering song. He could throw stones at rabbits and dream of hunting them with Hedley Vaughn's double-barreled twelve gauge that stood in the kitchen closet. Sometimes he watched a scramble out of Hanscom, the swept wings of the jets slicing the rising sun of another hot day. Someday. Soon the rhythm of work took over as the machines pumped milk from the stanchioned cows and Dale Hawkins sang "Susie Q, my Susie Q" on the radio, chattering with sounds of the great world beyond the farm. It was still early when he sat at the table with the two men while the woman dished up a solid country breakfast of bacon and eggs and coffee and toast. They hayed together. The days blurred as he toiled in the sun with the sweat and prickly hay and dust forever embedded in the memory of his skin. Sometimes there was time for a dip in the tepid water of the pond after it became too dark to work. Then an ice cream at Earl's in a wet bathing suit, the bugs buzzing the fluorescence. Then the sheet chafing his irritated skin as he drifted through exhaustion to the oblivion of dreams too deep to remember.

Hedley Vaughn's sick heart grew stronger at the sight of the filling barn — or seemed to, anyway. Something of his old form returned as he directed the others with energy and assurance, picking up a pitchfork now and then in a gesture to what had been. He had an inkling that this was a reprieve of sorts, a time beyond his time, a gift. And Hedley Vaughn was not a man to pass up such a bargain. Besides, it would not occur to him that he had a choice. In the end Hadley Vaughn could no more not do the haying than he could will himself to stop breathing. It was habit and ritual and necessity — the momentum of generations. You slept better with a full barn in winter. You might even die in peace. Good crop for a dry year, he begrudged to Lucien Quirk, and checked the sky to see whether the clouds boiling up in the west would come to anything.

The hired man had nodded and peered up at the sky almost as if he cared as well. The haying had had its effect on him. His sarcasms and griping had dwindled to the mere formality of a soldier who does his share of the work and bitches about it. And while he ached for the taste and burn of wine, he found himself too ready for his cot at night to hoof it all the way into Elmsbury Centre to Durkin's Package Store, even with a crisp new fiver tucked in his gear. Now he rose before the boy finished milking and went up to the kitchen for a pan of hot water to use with a bristle brush and razor blade on his face scattered in a piece of cracked mirror tacked to the dairy wall.

"You are my sunshine, my only sunshine," he would sing with mock bravura. And then he would whistle it so that it followed him like a theme song after he splashed water on his hair and brushed it and arrived for breakfast looking for a smile from the lady of the house.

She tried not to smile. Not that she didn't notice the improvement in the appearance of the man as he gimped in for breakfast, humming his tune, to eat more than his share of what she cooked. Not that she didn't remember the hand caressing her fanny as she had pulled at the hay. And she knew where it would have gone from there if she hadn't slapped him — to something wordless and quick and sweaty in the hay. And that look he'd given her, then, as though she had kissed him instead. It was out of the question. Things were bad enough. Already she imagined people imagining. The sly look Gladys Porley gave her when she asked how the "hired man" was working out. And sister

Ellen's oblique questions. Let's not tell Mom about it; it'll only make her worry. So Janet Vaughn kept her distance, holding him beyond contempt or anger or pity or anything that might knit a bond between them. But she wasn't entirely successful. Through some insidious, corrosive process, the calculated coolness of her responses was twisted into a code he elaborated in gentle mockery and half smiles, catching her looking even when she wasn't so that she had to watch every glance and tone and gesture. And there was no one, absolutely no one, she could explain it to.

They hayed for nearly three weeks, every day, all day, including the Fourth of July, and sometimes into the dark, coming up from the fields following the lights of the tractor through a world gone soft and shapeless. Their luck broke when, on a Friday, the knuckled gear that transmits power from the tractor to the mower snapped and spun loose. Hedley Vaughn and the boy drove in the old Chevy to the International Harvester dealer in Acton to get a replacement. The man behind the counter said he didn't have the part and couldn't get it till Monday. He called the dealer in Andover for them, but they didn't have the part there either. Hedley Vaughn sucked on his pipe; the boy wandered around the showroom, inspecting the gleaming new equipment painted in primary colors. He couldn't imagine it being used in the muck of a real farm. And what a nice job it must be, he thought, to stand behind a counter in a clean shirt and look up things in a book and talk to customers. There's a junk dealer in Littleton who has a few old mowers, said the man. Hedley Vaughn blew pipe smoke and shook his head. No, he didn't want junk. He'd be in first thing Monday for the part. Had most of the hay in, anyway. Not a bad crop, either, for a bad year. Think the weather'll hold? Weatherman said something about a hurricane starting up down south. That'd mean rain. Could use some, actually. Time to think about the second crop. Hedley Vaughn remained at the counter, strangely garrulous, talking hay and weather, seeking something like assurance from the man, who only politely listened and who was not, the boy could tell, a farmer.

Before dark that night, Bobby Dearborn walked the mile and a half to the pond for a swim. Going south, Middlesex Road climbed a long hill, from the top of which, glancing back, the boy could see the farm lying like a swept rug where they had done the haying. Across the road in Mayhew's old place, matchstick houses grew along new roads, and farther to the north, in what seemed like dense woods, rose the white steeples of Elmsbury Centre. From the top of the hill the road descended abruptly to an elm-shaded intersection, where the village of South Elmsbury — a store, Earl's Ice Cream Palace, and a few clapboard Colonials — gathered around the Congregational church and a cemetery dating back to the seventeenth century. The village trailed off to the left down Travis Road with a few nondescript houses and ended, more or less, in the cars junked around Archambault's Sunoco station. Not far beyond that a gravel road led off to the right through a swampy woodland that breathed mosquitoes; it was where people went to change their clothes and relieve themselves. Where it swung close to the pond, the road widened into a gravel parking lot on one side and a beach of trucked-in sand on the other. Among the cars parked there was a clutch of hot-rodders, doors open, radios playing rock and roll, engines running. One of them always seemed to be coming or going, roaring out of the place trailing a storm of dust, squealing onto the asphalt of Travis Road, irking the older folks, who sat on folding chairs on the narrow beach and watched their children playing in the water.

The boy hid his clothes and towel under a bush in the woods and stepped gingerly across the gravel to the beach. He entered the water slowly, wading through a rank of noisy children before stopping to cup the smooth water over his arms and chest and to see if there was anyone he wanted to see. A new girl from school named Cynthia Kirkpatrick had been on the raft a few weeks before. He had said hello and turned from her vague acknowledgment, feeling absurdly inadequate in the presence of such freckled, chestnut beauty. He couldn't find her and dived in and swam underwater toward the sound of jostled barrels and thumping boards where the Langdon brothers and some other kids he knew were playing king of the raft.

≥∂

Later, in the moth-flecked light outside Earl's, the boy ordered a black raspberry cone. The screened takeout window opened into fluorescent depths where chromed fixtures gleamed and where framed pictures of a Jersey cow and bull hung on the tiled wall like family portraits. Stepping back from the window, he was able to glance through the screen of the door into a room lined with booths. The Everly Brothers crooned from the jukebox with *dree ee ee eem, dream, dream, dream* . . . Cynthia Kirkpatrick wasn't there either, but two other girls, both pretty, sat in a booth with boys from the high school. One of the girls, a blonde, wore a thin, powder-blue sweater showing uplifted breasts. Bobby Dearborn paid for his cone and hung around the door, trying to seem casual. He could hear the girl's laughing voice, and with furtive glances saw the nape of her neck through parted hair. He licked at the purple taste as though it might fill the exquisite void welling within him and stood transfixed outside the screen until one of the high school boys noticed him and began to glance back. And it was getting late. His aunt would give him hell. So he started up the road to the farm, tonguing the ice cream and dreaming.

Someday when he was a man, he would drive up to Earl's in a white convertible. He'd be in uniform. No, actually he'd be in his flight suit with all its zippers because he'd be on his way to Hanscom to test one of the new deltawing F-105s they were having trouble with. And Cynthia Kirkpatrick would be at Earl's, sitting in a booth alone. They'd get to talking about things. She'd notice what a nice car he had, and he'd ask her if she wanted to take a ride. Then they'd ride out to Bedford together, and he'd be able to wheel right out onto the runway apron, even with her in the car, where the ground crew had the jet waiting. It's all ready to go, sir, the ground crew chief would say. Captain Dearborn would put on his helmet with the oxygen mask and its attached air hose dangling casually to one side, and with the cockpit cover still open above him like a knight's raised visor, he would wave to his girl in the convertible and taxi away to take off. Then he'd come roaring down the runway, pivot upward right next to the apron, kick in the afterburner, and with a tremendous bang rocket into the sky. He would climb up and up to become a dot of pure freedom, rolling and looping and diving and climbing and finally coming down for a few low-altitude, wing-snapping fly-bys before dropping his gear and bringing her in, gently, like a bird coming to perch. Top up again, he'd roll his F-105 back to the apron and climb down and go over a few details on a clipboard with a likable crew chief named Al. Then, tapping out a Camel, he'd saunter casually back to the convertible and say something like I hope you didn't get too bored. And she'd say of course she didn't and have on a sexy sweater and take one of his cigarettes, which he'd light with a car lighter that worked, and together they'd drive off into a white convertible future so fabulous it could not be imagined.

It was nearly ten when he got home, but the old Chevy wasn't in the yard. Good, he thought; the woman is at her sister's watching television. He went quietly through the darkened house, shushing the dog when it began to growl. In the bathroom upstairs he heard his uncle in the next room mumbling in his thin sleep. And through the window of the bathroom, which opened onto the barnyard and the pastures beyond, he could see the yellow light in the shack where the hired man kept. It was a weak, uncertain light, but the boy found some strange comfort in it. He put his sneakers back on and went silently down the stairs and let himself out without twanging the screen door.

"Who's that?"

"Bobby."

Lucien Quirk sat propped against the wall on his cot. A bottle of Pastene sherry stood on the bedside cable reel next to the pictures of his mother and the Virgin and Child and an empty bottle with the same label. The man's eyes seemed buried in a brittle face that broke from a scowl in sudden laughter. "What the hell do *you* want?"

"Nothing," the boy said. Uncertain of what to do, he stood on the cinderblock step outside the door, fascinated by the effigy of the Marine hanging at attention in the shadows. "I was just up at the house."

"Well, come in, sit down, have a drink."

The man seemed greatly amused.

The boy came in, sat down on the broken lawn chair, but refused the proffered bottle.

"You a man or ain't you? Hell, I thought you flyboys were supposed to be able to hold your booze."

That struck home. The boy took the bottle, wiped the top with his hand, and slowly swallowed a mouthful of its harsh warmth. It needled his nose, made his eyes water, and left him breathless, none of which he could hide.

Lucien Quirk's face squeezed into lines for a laugh that stopped as abruptly as it began. The face seemed too old for the muscular chest as the man leaned forward in the cricket-chirping silence. "And what you been up to, Captain?"

"I was up at the pond swimming."

"The old swimming hole, huh. Find any pussy?"

"No." Bobby Dearborn shrugged to relieve the implication that there had been the possibility of such a thing.

"Really, huh? No girls up there want to take their knickers off for a big strong boy like you? A captain in the United States Air Force?"

"I guess not."

"Did you ask?"

"No."

"Well, you gotta ask. They ain't just gonna come to you and give it to you."

"We played king of the raft."

Lucien Quirk ran a hand through his crinkled hair as if trying to decide to laugh or not.

"We blew up a frog with a cherry bomb."

Now the man laughed. "Blew up a frog, huh? You and the Japs. How the hell'd you do that?"

"We put it in an old can and put a rock on top."

"A real bunch of heroes."

The man laughed into the boy's blush, then stopped, as though forgetting why he laughed. He drank from the bottle and fumbled for cigarettes. "Go on, have one."

"I ain't supposed to."

"Says who?"

"My aunt Ernestine."

"She got a nice pussy?"

"I don't know. She's kind of old."

"Yeah . . ."

"And sort of skinny."

"That's all right. The closer the bone, the sweeter the meat. And those old ones know what they're doing . . . except when it comes to cigarettes. Go on, it won't hurt you."

So the boy puffed and blew the offending smoke from his mouth. Lucien Quirk, demonic with glee, held the bottle out to him. "Go on, you gotta be a man."

And he was a man.

And the other man was singsonging:

> "In days of old,
> When knights were bold,
> And women weren't particular,
> They'd lean 'em up against a wall,
> And fuck 'em perpendicular."

"What's perpendicular?"

The man's face swayed through a screen of blue smoke.

"Perpendicular's this country girl I knew in North Carolina by the name of Clara Mae, Clara Mae Wilkins, to be exact, and she never wore any undies and every time I turned around, she had this big sweet ass of her sticking out at me . . ." He stopped and bent forward as if leaning into the memory. "And she'd fuck you till you fainted."

"What happened to her?"

With an effort the boy ignored a tingling in his nose and a knot in his stomach resolving itself in acrid sherry-raspberry belches.

"She went off with another gyrene who could stand up behind her longer than me. Ha, ha, ain't that a son of a bitch."

They sat in sadness. The small noises of summer night deepened the silence, and a moth fluttering against the lantern made shadows move against the walls.

"I gotta go," the boy said finally. But he stayed seated.

"How come?"

"My aunt'll be home soon."

"Where is she?"

"I think she's at her sister's in Lowell, watching television."

Lucien Quirk's tongue flicked out over his lips. "She's quite a lady."

"She's not my real aunt," the boy said back, wine working into truth. "I don't like her."

But the man wasn't listening to the boy. A fantasy rehearsing and transcending the conventions of the flesh occupied his wine-stiffened mind. Something in him beyond sex responded to Janet Vaughn, something he couldn't quite mock or drink away. He laughed anyway, singing at the poor ceiling:

> "You are my sunshine,
> My only sunshine.
> You make me happy
> When skies are gray . . ."

Then he was at the wine again, then holding out the bottle. "Drink up, sonny; it'll make you a man before your mother."

"My mother's dead."

Bobby Dearborn couldn't resist some cheap pride in that; it seemed to make him older, more of a man.

"So's mine," said Lucien Quirk gravely, and they both drank the stunning stuff and shared a brotherhood of motherlessness.

"What's it like to fuck someone?" the boy asked, startling the silence. He had in mind Cynthia Kirkpatrick, naked on a pedestal.

The man scowled, feeling some desecration in the timing of the question. He had been trying to remember his mother. But the wine warmed him and his eyes rolled in a rolling head that stopped to say "It's like . . ." and couldn't think of anything to say. Always the same and always different. And he had too many memories he couldn't remember. "It's like freedom," he said finally, and caught the glint of disappointment in the boy's wide gray eyes. "It's like someone letting you into paradise."

"How do you do it?" the boy prodded, hoping some elaboration on the mechanics might reveal the mystery.

That relieved the man. He had words for that, and Janet Vaughn smiling at him as inspiration flickered and grew with his advice to a young man. But more wine first and another cigarette.

"First you gotta treat them right. You gotta be nice. You can't just grab and fuck 'em like some guys. Women like a little romance. It gets them going, know what I mean?"

The boy nodded, man to man now, and blew dizzying smoke through his nose.

"Right. Show a little respect. Bring 'em flowers. Take 'em out. Show 'em a good time. And talk. You gotta talk to them. You gotta sweet-talk them. Tell 'em they're nice. Tell 'em they got nice eyes. They love that."

A recollection of Cynthia Kirkpatrick's green eyes under foxy eyebrows receded, and the boy put down the cigarette because concentration grew more difficult as inexplicably the bull began to bellow in the barn and as Lucien Quirk, bent from the cot, lipping his words, brought him closer to the primal exercise, removing article by article Janet Vaughn's best clothes on the edge of an idealized bed in an idealized bedroom and stroking the pendulous breasts offered in the poster on the wall preparatory to "spreading their legs."

"Then you do it."

Lucien Quirk shook his head. "First you gotta eat it."

"Eat it?"

"Yeah." The man was enjoying this.

"Her thingee?"

"That's right, her cunt. You get down there and nibble on it a little."

The boy's stomach rolled. "You bite it?"

"Gently, real gently. And stick your tongue in it, too, and give it a lick."

"What does it taste like?"

"It tastes like life itself."

"And they like that?" Bobby Dearborn had to breathe through his mouth.

"They love it. It gets them ready. Now you can slide right in . . ."

"With your cock?" He needed reassuring.

Lucien Quirk barked his wicked laugh. "If you've got one."

The boy nodded. Go on, go on.

The bull's roar boomed.

The man's hands held imaginary hips. His torso moved. "You do it in and out, up and down."

"On top of them?"

"That's right. Or from behind or from the side or hanging out a tree. You just gotta get in there and work it back and forth, up and down . . ."

"Then what happens?"

"Well, pretty soon you get this kind of sweet pain that runs across the back of your ass because her butt's going up and down too and your prick's going in and out of her pussy which is hot and wet and slippery and feels like smooth pink and then you get another sweet pain across your ass just as you start to come . . ."

But the boy was remembering the frog for some reason, the way its torn pink flesh looked when Richie Fox held the match over it, and he had to bolt through the door as saliva filled his mouth just before his stomach gave an awful wrench and spewed out a bilious, cheap wine, purple slurry against the tarpaper of the shack. He felt better for a second. Then it came again, and his mind shrank to this backward flow of matter through his mouth, a bitter retrospect of the chicken and corn and cucumber salad they had had for supper, so that only gradually did the rhythmic whinny of the man's laugh and the bellowing of the bull intrude, followed by a far more alarming sound — the woman's voice calling his name and growing louder and angrier as she came down the path. And the vomit, uprushing again, and the man's mocking hilarity seemed like nothing next to the humiliation that was about to descend.

❧ 6 ❧

"THE HAYING'S DONE. We don't need him anymore."

The woman's voice came across the room from where she stood changing her clothes.

"I need him for the second crop."

Hedley Vaughn lay pale that Sunday morning as the sheet that covered him. One of his bad days. He had waked, feeble from dreams of drowning, in a room that felt bereft of air even though a slight breeze lifted the lace curtains on the open windows. All his life he had risen by five-thirty and been at work by six. By noon he'd have a day's work done and another by the time he turned in at night. Never a sick day in his life before this thing, except for a bout of pneumonia when he was a boy. Now it was going on nine o'clock and he could scarcely breathe enough to keep himself alive. And a woman stood in the room telling him what to do.

"You said there wouldn't be a second crop if the drought lasted."

Hedley Vaughn opened his eyes and squinted at his wife as she unlaced her corset, releasing breasts and belly in amplitudes of white flesh. A shadow of desire, dimmer than dim memory, crossed his heart.

"The storm greened things up."

"I told you what he had the boy doing."

The man crooked his arm over his eyes to shut out the painful light filtering through the curtains. She had told him a dozen times during the past week, if once. Wearily, he spoke. "He'll leave the boy alone. I told him."

"You told him?" Janet Vaughn timed her derision, rustling in the closet for something comfortable and just a little stylish to wear for the day. "A lot of good that'll do."

Anger rose in the man, but he could not sustain it any more than he could the nudge of lust. Damn woman, he thought under his arm, remembering this too was the day her family would come for lunch. A nosy, gawking bunch. And not a lick of work out of the lot of them. The irritation moved him to sit up in his nightshirt and swing his thin legs over the side of the bed.

"Lucien Quirk ain't bad for what he is. I don't know, Jan, what you got against the man. He likes his wine, but I've seen worse. And he is one of your kind."

But his voice sounded estranged in a dizziness that was swirling the light and his wife's anger.

"He's not one of *my kind*, Hedley, and I don't have anything against him, either. I just don't want him around here anymore, that's all. You said it would only be for the haying."

In truth, Janet Vaughn didn't have much against the hired man when she thought about it. She didn't have much she could tell her husband, anyway. Men, she had learned, don't like to hear about other men that way. Put his hand on my backside. Not just a little pat, either, trailing that finger. He never says it, but she knew what he was thinking all the time. That crooked grin and the way he laughed. Hungry enough to eat her. And what she finally couldn't tell her husband, because she could scarcely admit it to herself, was that she had moments of weakness. She was human. Not that she'd ever do anything, not with him, not with anyone, really, even when it got so bad she wanted to scream. She couldn't tell her husband about those dreams Father Fahey said were natural as long as she didn't take pleasure, which she did, resenting the early morning jangle of the alarm waking her to the same every-day sameness. No, she couldn't tell her husband about that or how she didn't want the man around because people talked even when there was nothing to talk about. And to-day was her mother's birthday and she was coming out to the house with Ellen and Ellen's husband, Steven Dunn, and their two kids, and her brother, Joe Jr., and his wife, Liz, and their baby, another Joe, a toddler now, with time flying.

Janet Vaughn pulled on a pair of slacks she'd worn only once, more than a year before. She must have lost weight haying, because they fitted her nicely. She hooked on a bra and buttoned on a navy cotton blouse to match the slacks. Her face in the dresser mirror did appear thinner on second glance. It wasn't just that she'd started to let her hair grow out. She smiled at herself, suddenly happy. Softening, she said: "You did tell him he's not to be here today. Mom's coming out with Ellen and Joe . . ."

"I told him."

The sound of his voice made her turn to look at her hus-band, who sat like death on the edge of the four-poster they'd inherited from his parents and that she had painted cream because the wood was so dark.

"Hedley, are you all right?"

"I'm fine."

But he wasn't. He got up and stood unsteadily in the flan-nel nightshirt that came to his knees, and walked around the bed from post to post to the door that connected to the bathroom through a walk-in linen closet. He wouldn't be helped.

"Do you want me to call Weller?"

"No."

Which relieved her. A Sunday house call cost seven dol-lars. And Hedley insisted they pay. She listened to him in the bathroom in a trance of anxiety, waiting for the crash of his fall. She feared it even as, in a dark and twisted way, she hoped for it as a deliverance for him and for her from his pain. She caught herself thinking of him in the past tense as she gazed at their wedding picture on the dresser she had also enameled a cream color to go with the bed. He stood tall in his tuxedo, head bent over her plumpness, more hair then and a rare smile making him handsome. She had wanted a June wedding, but he had said it was a busy month on the farm. So they married in May and drove to the White Mountains for a week of rainy weather and her husband shaking his head at the poorness of the soil and the food they got in restaurants.

But he's a Protestant and a farmer and too old, her family kept telling her, partly, she knew, because they had picked her to stay home and take care of the old folks. They hadn't known Hedley Vaughn was poor as well and would get poorer. He must have bags of money, they said. All farmers did. They made it hand over fist during the war on the black market. Not Hedley Vaughn. He shipped his milk and eggs and bull calves at government-set prices, because there was a war and because he was an honest man.

They hadn't had much in common. Need, mostly. Life had left both of them on the shelf and there they had tried to make a life. She had imagined her future existence then as a farmer's wife with fine sons and a horn of plenty under the bowers of a rose garden. It was certainly no grand passion they had. It had been more of a willed love, steady and sure if sometimes thin. She had found him generous enough when he knew what she wanted and had the means to buy it for her. He was a considerate, gentle man who had been vigorous if not particularly subtle in the ways of intimacy. Now she loved him even for that.

He appeared in the doorway like his own ghost and came back around the bed, post to post, pathetic in his nightshirt and the room she had feminized. She helped him back under the sheet and sat on the edge of the bed for a while, holding his rough hand limp at the end of a weak pulse, her heart piteous, her voice comforting. But those slacks fitted her again, and she kept alive an ember of happiness for herself as she put the hand back and quietly closed the door and went downstairs to get ready for the family visit.

❧

Janet Vaughn hummed her own tunes as she swept and dusted the house. The old Hoover leaked almost as much dirt as it sucked up and there wasn't much she could do with the kitchen floor, but she savored the anticipation anyway. She savored it despite knowing that the reality never lived up to the expectation. Something always seemed to spoil it. They would get on her about the boy (does the aunt take him to church ever?) or Hedley or selling the farm and buying the little place next to Joe Jr.'s in Dracut, criticizing and tempting her even when they hardly knew they were doing it. Right then it didn't matter. She felt festive, putting out clean towels in the bathroom, where she paused to glance again at herself in the mirror to reaffirm her new thinness, her new face, which smiled back its happiness. She even gave the boy fifty cents for mowing and raking the lawn that stretched from the side of the house to the row of maples that came up along the barnyard. Don't get your new sneakers dirty, she told him, but nicely, giving him a smile with the money. The boy and his aunt Ernestine were taking one of their Sunday trips together. While he waited, she made him a sandwich of the ham she had sliced and placed in layers on a platter she covered and put in the refrigerator. She tried to draw out the boy, but, as always, he kept his distance, saying, she knew, what he thought she wanted to hear. It usually maddened her, but not today. Today she was happy.

The arrival of Ernestine Vaughn to pick up the boy dampened her spirits a little. But, then, her sister-in-law's predictable, constant, and vaporous cheeriness always brought her down a notch or two. The way the woman smiled when you told her her brother was having one of his bad days. The way she rapped on the bedroom door and chirped, "Hi, Hedley," as if she didn't know the man needed to rest. The older woman in her sunny dress and sensible shoes who never looked you quite in the eye spread her cheer uniformly on her brother, the boy, the dog, and Janet Vaughn, leavening it here and there with a murmur of educated pity. Janet Vaughn, who long suspected the cheeriness masked some great despair or hysteria, now thought it masked the nothingness that was there. Ernestine Vaughn, like the boy to whom she was related, was simply one of those people Janet Vaughn could not reach. Today she wasn't going to let it get to her. She was going to be happy. And when they had driven out of the yard, she hummed again at her work, dicing the potatoes she had boiled and left to cool before going to Mass, mixing in chives and mayonnaise and a dash of vinegar before setting them on a bed of lettuce in the willowware bowl that she had found in the attic.

Outside, under a bright sun climbing a faultless sky, Janet Vaughn inspected the lawn the boy had worked on. Brown patches showed from the drought, and she wished now she had watered it. The back of the house needed painting, it was true, but the lilacs she had planted a few years before more or less screened the area from the muck of the barnyard and defined, along with her roses in the ell of the house, the maples, the mulberry tree, and two blue spruces standing sentry near the road, a haven of peace and some beauty. Over the massive, splintery picnic table she shook out a clean tablecloth and placed in its center a glass bowl of water with rose blossoms floating in it, the way she had seen it done in a magazine. The success of it gave her a little flush. She went over her list. Ginger ale for the bottle of Four Roses Steve Dunn would bring. Mom's gift wrapped. Cookies and Kool-Aid for the kids. Ellen was bringing the cake. The heavy metal lawn chairs she had painted green were the one real eyesore. She thought of calling her sister to ask her to bring out her folding chairs. No, it was fine. You could get silly doing these things. Oh, yes, a fresh salad. They always raved about that.

On her way to the garden to pick the lettuce, tomatoes, cucumbers, and scallions she would use in the salad, Janet Vaughn went down the lane to the brooder house to make sure Lucien Quirk had left. That was the one thing that could ruin her happiness today. She braced herself to confront him, to tell him that he had to leave until after dinner time. But Lucien Quirk wasn't there when she peered apprehensively through the burlaped windows, starting for a second at the sight of the uniform, thinking him there, then thinking he had done something to himself, until she saw what it was. She pushed in the door, fascinated by the scene even as she was repelled by it. The disorder, musty odor, and empty bottles appalled her. Looking at the cot, she reminded herself to give him some clean sheets. Pity and a sense of power grew in the center of her revulsion. My God, to have only this. She saw the pinups and remembered her own body in the mirror and what men and women do to each other. She stood for a moment, willingly mesmerized, despite the closeness, the heat, the degradation, and the impossibility of anything like sex with this man, while imagining it with the clarity of voluptuous dreams until the spell snapped and she fled from the place. She bustled along the lower end of the barnyard, going by the hen house and into the garden, where she composed herself by picking ripe tomatoes and cool cucumbers, keeping her happiness intact.

❧

Later she helped her husband dress and walked him to a chair on the lawn to wait for the arrival of her family. They came shortly afterward in two cars, unloading into the dazzling sunlight, greeting her with hugs and exclamations before trooping around the front of the house to the side lawn. There, less demonstratively, they greeted Hedley Vaughn and praised her table, which now sat halfway into the speckled shade of the maple. They unpacked hampers and got things from the house before settling into the lawn chairs, the men more or less together in the sunlight. Ill at ease at first, they groped cautiously for common ground with disjointed small talk as they waited for the drinks being concocted on the table to smooth the way.

"How are things going, Hedley?" someone ventured. They were careful with Hedley Vaughn, because he was an older man wearing a woolen plaid shirt and a rug over his knees on a hot summer day, and sometimes he spoke his mind. "Going good," he said in his company voice. "Got the hay in."

"A good crop?" Ellen Dunn asked, even though she was helping her sister with the drinks and keeping an eye on her children because of the road and really couldn't have cared less about crops, good or bad.

"Not bad, considering the weather." He had in mind the drought.

"Yes, wasn't that an awful storm . . ."

"Yeah, it knocked out power at the plant for more than two hours." Joe Gilooly was relieved to contribute something.

But Hedley Vaughn, Yankee farmer, demurred. "The rain was good," he drawled. "Could have used a lot more."

"Hedley, would you like a rye and ginger?" asked his wife.

"Don't mind if I do."

"Is that Grandpa?" Five-year-old Michael Dunn had his finger in his mouth.

"No, Michael, you know that's Uncle Hedley."

"Unkill Heddy looks like Grandpa."

"And you, Mom," said Janet Vaughn, quickly covering the small embarrassment, "will you take a little with ginger ale?"

"What?"

Rose Gilooly, grandmother, matriarch, old lady, sat in the shade with her hands curled in her wide lap, a thin cardigan over her shoulders, her ailing legs swathed in support hose. She had sharp, judging eyes that shifted in her motionless head and watched people when they spoke. She said little herself, wielding power through silences that elicited confidences and confessions and petitions for counsel as though she were a seer, even though she seldom said anything. It may have been the way she said what she said, mingling blame and significance, as when she told her daughter in an aside that "Hedley doesn't look good," followed by a slight sniff and accusatory arch of eye. In this case it may have been that she resented the man's failing heart. It made her varicose veins and arthritis seem insignificant.

"A little rye and ginger ale?" her daughter repeated.

"I don't know."

Janet Vaughn made her one anyway and one for herself. Steve Dunn took a shot, which he chased with a beer. Joe Gilooly, Jr., took only a beer, and Liz, who had shyly announced her three-month pregnancy, took only ginger ale.

The announcement created a happy little buzz among the women. Liz Gilooly, her freckled face and bland features going milky, supplied the kind of details that seem very important to the beginning and the end of human life. When did she first find out? What did the doctor say? How are her mornings? And Joe Jr.? We planned it, she told them, alluding to the sensitive issue of birth control and drawing a frown from her mother-in-law. Liz Gilooly, quiet and strong in her own right, did not pay court. She didn't bask, either, in the attention. She had been through it before. Little Joe had been easy, a nine-pound boy after an hour in the delivery room. She felt well, she told them. She had plenty of maternity clothes and the bassinet and crib. She hoped for a girl, of course.

Janet Vaughn joined in and tried to keep the envy out of her smiling eyes. Besides envy, a deep, empathetic envy, she felt disqualified to add much, though she had been through it all in her own way. Jessica Lee would have just turned five, and for an eye-misting moment Janet Vaughn could imagine her in little jeans and a jersey with the sunlight in her hair as she played with the other children. She composed herself, pretending busyness with cheese and crackers to go with the drinks.

"Well, cheers," said Hedley Vaughn, who was capable of being gracious when he felt sociable. He nodded at Liz Gilooly. "The best of luck."

"Yes," someone added, "and happy birthday, Mom."

They clinked glasses and the party went up a notch.

The women talked about Mary, who had gone to college and married Vincent Tully of Andover and was said to be having difficulty in her marriage, which, it was thought, explained her absence. The men talked about hunting.

"Seen many pheasants this year?" Steve Dunn, in a baseball cap and short-sleeved shirt, sucked beer from a bottle and let his belly hang over the buckle of his belt. A tall, crewcut man gone to fat, he worked as a quality control inspector at the Raytheon plant in Lowell, which manufactured Sparrow air-to-air missiles. During the hunting season he would drive out to the farm on Saturdays with Joe Gilooly, Jr., and both of them would walk the meadows along the creek with polished shotguns cradled correctly and fecklessly in their arms. They certainly looked the part, in red hunting jackets and plaid, visored caps. The autumn before, Joe Jr. had managed to shoot a squirrel, which he had taken home and finally thrown away when it began to stink up the kitchen. Mostly, it seemed, their harmless fall ritual gave them something to talk to Hedley Vaughn about; he was hardly to be drawn into conversations about whether Steve Dunn ought to buy a new '58 Ford or stick with Plymouths, or how the Red Sox were eleven games out of first place in the American League.

"Seen a few. Dry weather's good for them, I guess." Hedley Vaughn, feeling stronger with the whiskey boosting his heart, turned to the younger man, only the twist of his mouth showing amusement. "Thinking of trying again this year?"

Joe Jr., who was dark and slight and very much under the sway of his pregnant wife, nodded his head as if it were an invitation they might miss. "Oh, yeah, we'll be out."

Hedley Vaughn fiddled with his pipe. "You need a dog," he said. "They'll run before they'll fly and you won't put them up."

"We put up a few last year."

"Ummmm."

It was nearly to the word the same conversation they had every time they talked about hunting pheasants. Steve Dunn, sensing the older man's disparagement, upped the stakes by mentioning how he might buy a .30-'06 and drive up to Maine with some of the guys from the shop to hunt bear and deer. But that fell on silence and made him restless. To occupy their mouths, the younger men finished their beers and belched softly. Then they got up to go for a walk around the farm. It was something they did every time they came out, a ritualistic inspection tour where they poked around the wealth of old tools and equipment in the barn and the sheds, which made them feel superior and poor.

"Take the kids," pleaded Ellen Dunn.

"I wanna see the bull!" cried her son Michael, suddenly remembering.

A disagreement threatened and faded. Little Joe got on Joe Jr.'s shoulders. Steve Dunn took a child in each hand.

"Don't be too long. We'll be eating soon," Janet Vaughn called after the men, who were safe with the children.

"But he doesn't give her anything." Ellen Dunn came in low over her drink with an indictment of Vincent Tully. "He makes more than the rest of us put together; I know because she's told me, and he doesn't give her anything." Her eyes swept the other women, who nodded but wondered at the vehemence. It had something to do with the slighting of Ellen by Vincent Tully, a stockbroker with social ambitions that went beyond attendance at every family get-together of the Dunns, the Giloolys, and the Vaughns.

"It's hard on her," Janet Vaughn added to help her sister, even if she didn't believe it for a moment. Mary Tully drove her own car and had begun shopping in Boston for her clothes. Janet Vaughn was glad merely to be off the family hook, to have the blame shifted so that she didn't have to answer insinuations about herself or Hedley or the farm. She waited for a break in the flow of accusation to say she had to go in for the lunch.

Ellen Dunn ground her cigarette into the grass. "I'll help you."

The relative darkness and coolness of the old kitchen mitigated for a moment its more glaring faults, and Janet Vaughn, as she took the ham from the refrigerator, could almost think of it as quaint. She turned to show the pretty dish to her sister, but Ellen Dunn, lighting another cigarette, started again, coming closer with her anger.

"Mom's worried about you," she said. "She thinks they're taking advantage of you."

Janet Vaughn said nothing at first. Irritation gathered around her as she got used to the dimmer light. This impossible kitchen. She gazed at her sister, who had been one of the three beautiful Gilooly girls, and noticed how she had broadened and coarsened with age and childbearing and how her face, furrowed and puckered around the cigarette, seemed to plead for something.

"I like your dress," she said in a voice that dismissed and forgave at the same time.

"It's an old thing I bought at Bon Marche." Ellen Dunn sounded baffled as she sat down at the table and picked at the potato salad. "You've lost weight," she accused. "I remember those slacks didn't fit you."

Then she started to cry. It wasn't Vincent Tully, even if he could be a stuck-up snob, or Mom's worrying, because she worried anyway. It was her husband, Steve Dunn, star center on the Lowell High basketball team, now a nobody who had turned fat and brutal in marriage. "Now he's talking of moving to Alaska," his wife complained through tears as Janet Vaughn listened and mixed her garden salad with oil and vinegar.

She had heard it all before, if not as bitterly or as melodramatically as at this outpouring. It curiously gratified her to hear about her brother-in-law's nastiness and threats, his nights out, his stinginess. But if she felt happiness at her sister's misery, it was a happiness she was able to return as sympathy. She did this less with words than with presence. As she gathered the food, dishes, silverware, napkins, mustard, pickles, salt, and pepper on two tole trays, she inclined toward her sister, listening and watching. When she had everything ready, she sat down, attending as though she had all the time in the world. It ceased, finally. Janet Vaughn put her arms around Ellen Dunn, kissed, and held her for a moment. When they emerged into the sunlight a few minutes later, their arms laden, they were smiling and talking like old times.

Not even the sight of Gladys Porley's white convertible slowing down to turn into the front yard could penetrate Janet Vaughn's armor of joy. Let her find us here, she thought, resisting an impulse to intercept the woman and her bag of soiled shirts, another sore point among the family. Let her come around the front of the house or through the back door and see us sitting here, having a drink and a picnic and being happy and normal.

Which Gladys Porley did, gingerly stepping across the lawn, her synthetic smile gleaming in front of her. Janet Vaughn made brief introductions, and Gladys Porley, tanned and white in the white sun, smiled more and said pleasant things and could not conceal her essential nosiness even from these abashed people who murmured back at her.

"Well, isn't it pretty back here! And that potato salad, it looks so yummy."

"Thank you."

But Janet Vaughn resisted another impulse to offer the woman a drink. There was an awkward pause.

"Well, I have to go," Gladys Porley said apologetically, as

though declining an invitation. "Charles is playing golf. He'll need his lunch." Then, her smile compressed to poison, she turned to Janet Vaughn and said quietly, but loud enough for the rest to hear, "I left the shirts inside the kitchen door." Loud again, the smile at full volume, "Nice meeting all you folks." And was gone.

She left just as the men, trailing children, came up the lane that led from the main road past the lawn and along the maples to the pastures. The sight of them relieved Janet Vaughn, who did not want to gossip about Gladys Porley and defend the ironing she did for the woman and listen to her mother start in with "if your father knew . . ."

Little Michael Dunn dashed ahead of the rest. "We saw the bull," he said to his mother.

"You did? And what did you think of the bull?"

"It was dirty. I wanna cookie."

"We're going to have lunch right now. Aunt Jannie's made yummy things."

"I wanna cookie!"

And so did Debbie and Little Joe, who joined the chorus of demand.

"Hey, who you got camped down in that shack with the uniform?" Steve Dunn and his belly wanted to know. He turned to his wife. "You oughta see it. Looks like a hobo city down there."

Janet Vaughn opened the cookies to quiet the children.

"It's just someone helping us with the hay."

"It don't look like much help, with all them bottles laying around."

"What is it?" The grandmother perked up.

"Someone from Lowell who's helping us with the haying. He'll be gone soon."

But Janet Vaughn knew that wouldn't settle it.

"Boy, I don't know."

Steve Dunn pulled another beer from the picnic cooler and pried off the top. His comparative respectability made him feel righteous. He stood over his sister-in-law, wanting to know.

· 82 ·

"Who is it?" asked Rose Gilooly.

"Lucien Quirk."

"Lucien Quirk? He's not one of the Highland Quirks?"

"I don't think so. He's from the other side of the river."

"Oh."

Her mother's look and Steve Dunn's bullying belly threatened Janet Vaughn's little glade of joy. She stayed busy at the food and kept up thin smiles for everyone.

"What do you pay him?"

She pretended she hadn't heard.

"What do you pay him?" Steve Dunn persisted.

At that Hedley Vaughn coughed loudly, said "Hey," and motioned for the big man to come over to him. Closer beckoned the finger, a word in the ear. The man bent over and reddened at the words, which came just above a whisper: "Why don't you mind your own God damn business."

That shattered and restored the peace as they sat in glum silence, sawing at the ham and forking the salad from the plates on their laps. The flies buzzing the table seemed louder than usual. The dog came from under the shade of the mulberry tree and sat in front of people, panting for a tidbit. Then a blue jay, bold as his color and silent as an apparition, dropped to the table to steal a scrap of bread. They remarked on the bird. They praised the food. What did you put in the potato salad, Liz Gilooly wanted to know. And Ellen Dunn praised the garden salad, and not just because she knew the Vaughns wouldn't let them leave without giving them bags of the same fresh vegetables. Janet Vaughn fanned the reviving talk with another round of drinks. The crested bird came back. They pointed it out to the children. "He's wearing a hat," Debbie Dunn said, which made them laugh. They began to tell stories. Remember when.

Remember when Joe Jr. came back from the beach and said he'd seen a fish as big as a ship the summer they rented the cottage on Hampton Beach from that miserable woman who came in every day to make sure they hadn't broken anything, and they all laughed at him and kept kidding him until the next day there was a picture in the paper of a whale spouting not far from shore. Remember when Dad played Santa for the PTA and Ellen, who was only five, went along and recognized him. And Dad told her he kept the reindeer on the roof and every time she pestered him to show her, he had to make excuses. And she was so proud. She told everyone her daddy was Santa Claus and when she saw a picture of Santa Claus she'd say, "That's my daddy." And remember when Uncle Jack came back from the war with the Nazi helmet and the funny money he gave to Mary, who went all over the neighborhood looking for a French store where she could spend it on candy.

The sun angled westward, its pickling light shrinking the shade of the maple, wrapping them all in its golden haze. The party lifted on a web of memories spun out by Rose Gilooly, who, pink-nosed with her second drink, dabbed at the tears in her eyes. She even charmed Hedley Vaughn, who discarded his lap rug and leaned forward through his pipe smoke. Janet Vaughn hovered around them all. She kept the children happy and quiet and helped her brother-in-law assuage his injured pride with food. She bustled into the kitchen to make coffee, which she brought out on a tray with cream and sugar and cups. She returned for the cake her sister had baked, and when they saw her coming down the path with it, its single candle lit, they began singing "Happy Birthday."

"Make a wish, Mom," Ellen Dunn said, holding the cake for her mother to blow out the candle.

Rose Gilooly puffed and smiled and dabbed at her eyes and said she already had her wish.

Another car pulled into the yard. It was Ernestine Vaughn, returning with the boy. They came around the front of the house together, a pair, Janet Vaughn noticed, and said hello pleasantly to everyone there. Bobby Dearborn shook hands self-consciously with the men.

"Aren't you getting big," said Rose Gilooly, who had begun to take an interest in the boy. She had spoken obliquely to her daughter about adoption and conversion. He needs a proper upbringing, she had said. "Aren't you lucky to be out here with all the fresh air."

Bobby Dearborn nodded and smiled politely. The Giloolys made him restless. He wanted to gobble the offered piece of cake and leave, but he stayed and answered their questions about the trip he had just made with his aunt to the Higgins Armory in Worcester. He mentioned the different kinds of bolts they had for crossbows, and got into a seemingly technical discussion with Steve Dunn on the difference between the radar-directed Sparrow and the heat-seeking Sidewinder air-to-air missile.

Janet Vaughn poured herself another small rye and ginger ale and finally relaxed into a chair. The party, a real party, buzzed around her. Hedley seemed his old self. Even her mother, beaming back into Ernestine Vaughn's cheery face, seemed happy. And she heard tones in the boy's voice, as he talked air-to-air combat with Steve Dunn, that she had never heard before. Ellen Dunn, her back to the sun, asked them all to say cheese for the poised Brownie. Janet Vaughn smiled as the black box went *click*, trapping the moment. In that instant, reality transcended all her expectations of the afternoon, all the ragged edges of her existence were smoothed over, and she was so happy that she knew it couldn't last.

It didn't. When she looked at the snapshot later — it had been underexposed, making moonlight out of sunshine, darkening them into another age — it had the staining aura of what happened a few moments later. She had been enjoying herself, half-listening to her mother and Ernestine Vaughn, when she heard it or thought she heard it on the edge of the noise a car made in passing. Scarcely breathing, keeping her smile going, she strained to hear. The muffling noise of another car swept by. Nothing. Her pulse jumping, she leaned back to claim her happiness again, disappointed, almost, in not being disappointed. Then the sound came again and froze her face.

You are my sunshine, my only sunshine . . .

Bobby Dearborn was the first to notice Janet Vaughn's silent alarm. It spread like a contagion, and one by one the conversations died. Hushed, everyone turned to the road, where the full-throated song grew in volume. *You'll never know, dear, how much I love you . . .* then stopped as Lucien Quirk materialized, obviously drunk, framed between the spruces, dark against the sun, his shadow reaching. He gimped across the lawn toward them and for a crazy moment Janet Vaughn thought her family idyll could encompass even this (Mom, Joe, Ellen, Steve, Liz, this is . . .), until she saw the long-stemmed roses in paper clutched in his rising hand.

"Hedley . . ." she began.

But Hedley Vaughn did not seem to notice.

Lucien Quirk was upon her, his face slit with a painful grin as he bowed with clownish dignity and laid the roses on her lap. Without waiting for a response, he went on down the lane, whistling the same tune, which hung in the stunned air over them.

"You have an admirer." Ernestine Vaughn broke the spell with the simplicity of truth. Ellen Dunn giggled, and for a moment it seemed that the incident, still fresh as a bad accident, could be defused and dismissed and they could get on with the party. But the party's magic had evaporated. Janet Vaughn caught her mother's glancing eye, and Steve Dunn, making agitated male motions, was saying, "So *that's* the hired man, huh?" and Liz Gilooly, peering down at the untouched roses, said, "But they are beautiful."

They were. Wrapped in green paper and sprigs of greenery, still half buds and deep rich red, they lay firm as flesh on Janet Vaughn's lap. She glanced at them and was torn between an urge to show them she rejected the gesture by throwing the flowers away and worry lest they wilt in the heat.

The sudden booming of the bull distracted them.

"What's that?" Joe Gilooly, Jr., asked.

"The bull," said Hedley Vaughn. He rapped his pipe defensively against the timbers of the picnic table. "He gets to bellowing now and again."

"Boy, it sure sounds creepy."

"I suppose it does. The vet says nothing's wrong with him."

"Who wants another drink?"

Bobby Dearborn watched the woman slide the roses under the flap of the tablecloth and beam a jolly fake smile on everyone. He was surprised by the pity he felt for her.

Another round went around, and the party continued as if nothing extraordinary had happened. Under the gloss of more alcohol, it didn't seem to make much difference that they were merely going through the motions of conviviality. The afternoon died to the monotonous roaring of the bull. Ernestine Vaughn left first. The boy took off his new sneakers and went to get the cows for milking. The families collected their hampers and children and made a trip to the garden for bags and more bags of produce, which Janet Vaughn foisted on them in a sudden panic, nearly embarrassing even them. Take everything, she was saying, take everything, just don't judge.

She knew they would anyway and she knew also that their judgment was not entirely groundless. If the man didn't tempt her, the roses did. That night, when everyone else slept, she went out under a dim moon to retrieve the bouquet. In the kitchen she trimmed the stems to make the roses fit into a china vase. There was no place to put them except the spare bedroom, which opened off the landing next to the boy's room. It was full of odds and ends and hadn't been used much and needed cleaning, but no one would see the roses there and start asking questions. Janet Vaughn sat on the lumpy double bed and looked at the red roses in the white vase on the mantel and began to cry. She cried because they would never understand. No one would. She cried, too, because she felt so pathetic. Other than a few obligatory corsages, they were the first flowers that anyone had ever brought her.

7

THE ROSES lasted more than a week, and for several
days at the height of their bloom gave off a suffocating,
lemon-sweet bouquet in the unvented space of the spare
bedroom. The fragrance permeated the upstairs of the
house until the flowers, ripening like fruit, shed their pet-
als, which littered the narrow mantel and the brick hearth.

Agitated by the smell, which seemed more than a mere
odor, Bobby Dearborn traced its source. The roses looked
perfect against the yellowing wallpaper. He wondered why
the woman, even if she had gotten them from Lucien Quirk,
kept them with the broken bureaus and lumpy bed in the
spare bedroom instead of in the kitchen or living room.
Downstairs, depending on the season and her moods, she
would sometimes arrange pussy willows, loosestrife, or
wild asters in vases and old jars. At night he had heard her
going into the spare bedroom, where she turned on the
wrought iron standing lamp, leaving a crack of light under
the connecting door. During the time of the roses he had
heard her weeping there. Drawn by the sound, half sigh,
half gasp, he had crept silently across the creaking floorboards to squat and peek through the keyhole. In the rank-
ness of the roses and in the silent swelter of the night, he
was afraid she would hear the thunder of his heart, because
by squinting and straining a tearing eye, he could discern

in the poor light her hunching shoulders, her naked back narrowing to an abrupt swell of hip and a deep cleft blurring at the edge of his vision. Flesh or fabric, he saw what men see. His knees hurt and he trembled, his loathing for the woman confused now by the pain of pity and by a nascent lust licking like a flame through his body before resolving itself in a palpable, throbbing ache. Reaching down, he touched his first, tentative thickening.

⒏

Rain became a memory. The August sun sucked at the land, parching it so that the stream shriveled to a brook, leaving its bed of wet mud to dry and crack. There amid festering anthills the boy found death etched with the bones of small animals and fish, and came on the delicate ladder of a snake's skeleton coiled in fossil sleep. Desert seemed possible. The stones he threw, bombs from his imaginary fighter-bomber, landed in explosions of dust. He saw birds panting like dogs in trees where the leaves hung limp and bleaching. During the hot afternoons the thunderheads swelled, mountainous, in the birdless sky, only to misfire and disperse, leaving the air enervating and explosive. And it smarted his eyes now to peer at the land distorted in the shimmering heat.

Hedley Vaughn, brittling in the swelter like other creatures of the drought, watched the sky and checked the calendar and cursed. Were he younger and stronger, he might have *willed* rain, or so he thought. Now the lengthening dry spell seemed some manifestation of his own weakness, as if the aridity of his heart had spread to the land. He didn't believe that, of course, but he felt it, the same way he felt — at some instinctual depth — that the equipment making noise and raising trundles of dust on Mayhew's farm rendered rain meaningless and thereby offended the gods. In practical terms it came down to a hard decision: unless he opened the hayfields for pasturage, the cows would dry up. Each day now their milk production dropped. But without a second crop, they wouldn't have enough hay to last the winter. And even in the drought conditions the second crop nudged upward on the moisture of night air to cover the stubble of the first cutting, making the man wait and hope. But it was hopeless. It didn't rain, and the cows kept breaking out of their dying pasture.

On a day when he had the energy to decide, Hedley Vaughn knocked his pipe against the inside of the sink and announced to his wife that he was going to fence the hayfields and let the cows graze the second crop.

"That means we'll have to buy beet pulp in the spring."

"Maybe."

Janet Vaughn sighed with anger as she sorted the week's eggs according to size and put them in cartons for shipping. Her rage went beyond words. They already owed money to the feed company, to the government, to the hospital, to the doctors, to the bank, to the farm equipment dealer, to Ernestine Vaughn. The debts rose into the thousands of dollars, a wall of obligation that would keep her smothered in that kitchen sorting eggs and ironing a fat man's shirts and arguing with her sick husband about running a farm that kept losing money. More bills. Wiping sweat from her face, she turned to him and saw the late afternoon sun blazing off his glasses, making him monstrous as he breathed smoke. It was hell.

"We'll plant a double crop of turnips for the fall," he said. "The late ones we can trim and store. That'll save hay for the spring."

Hedley Vaughn hadn't expected an argument.

"Who's going to pull them? Bobby will be in school."

Janet Vaughn was not going to break her back in the sleets of November.

"Quirk can do it. He's turned into quite a worker. Sobered up, too." The man hacked and spat into the black sink.

The woman flinched with disgust and her voice trembled. "Where are we going to put him when the weather gets cold?"

"Who?"

"Lucien Quirk."

"The brooder house has a stove."

"It doesn't even have windows."

"Then he can have the spare room upstairs."

Janet Vaughn kept herself under control. "I don't want him in the house, Hedley." She uttered her words quickly and quietly and discovered that the thought of the hired man living in the house with them no longer appalled her. It took a moment for the realization of that to settle in. She erupted then in sudden panic. "Oh, God! God! God!" she cried and moved toward him, her voice hysterical with supplication. "Let's just give up, Hedley. Let's sell this place and move to a regular house. Or we could keep the house and sell the land. You could keep an acre or two for a garden. You could get better. Hedley, you're killing yourself!" She beseeched him with her eyes as well, following his until she could see beyond the glint of glass to his stony gaze.

"You can sell it when I'm dead."

"I don't want that! I don't want you to die!"

But she didn't sound very convincing, at least not to herself. She reached for him to affirm her words with a touch and stopped herself. She tried words again. "If he comes into the house, Hedley, I'm leaving."

Hedley Vaughn merely grunted at her and headed for the back door to get the fencing started. He did not take her seriously. In his world, women did not leave their men. In his world, women loved, honored, and obeyed. He hardly got angry. In the cool of the barn door, he had to stop, however, because he felt squeezed of air. Across the road, through the heated air, he could hear the rumble of machinery and the whack of hammers on Mayhew's farm. He flinched and simply denied the evidence that his world was disappearing from around him even as he watched.

9

LUCIEN QUIRK'S ax sliced into the white wood of the three-inch sapling. After a few strokes the tree quivered, its crown rustling for a moment in the canopy of the hardwood glade, and fell. One-handing the ax, he went along the tree, trimming its branches before cutting and pointing five-foot lengths for fence posts. When he had finished, he gathered the posts and loaded them into the all-purpose farm wagon they had pulled into the woods behind the tractor. Not far away, the boy whacked at a tree. But he was no match for Lucien Quirk nowadays. The man sized up a tree, spat on his hands, and notched with a few deft strokes the side where he wanted the tree to fall. His last swing flashed through the dappled light, cutting into the back of the notch. Without stopping, he trimmed and chopped and loaded the wagon. These days he fell frequently into spells of silence when he had no words for the sake of noise and no dirty ditties for the boy and no glad-mouthing for the old man. It was the same silence he had kept when the transport hove to off Betio, which had lain low and ominous in the distance. He had cleaned his rifle and packed his gear and brushed his teeth and eaten his meals with an obsessive care and consciousness, because these things were all he had left to define a life in forfeit.

Now it was Janet Vaughn who suddenly loomed, distant

and somehow inevitable. She threatened as a kind of final hope, and he was half afraid she wouldn't respond and half afraid she would. Like impending death, she lined the curve of his every thought; she bit into the tree with the strokes of his ax; she came out in his sweat; she drifted blue with his cigarette smoke. He took her rare smiles as gifts from the gods. He adored her hands red from work, the prominence of her front teeth, the comfortable bulk of her body. The simplest things she said fascinated him, and he listened to her voice as though some profound, exquisite personality were unfolding along its husky tones. Lucien Quirk was in love.

Later, the barbed wire unrolled from a spool rigged to the back of the wagon on a length of pipe. Bobby Dearborn drove the tractor slowly while the man dropped the posts off every fifteen feet or so along the unraveling wire. Then they walked it, putting in the posts, nailing the insulators, and stringing the wire. The boy opened the holes for the posts by plunging the weighted, pointed end of the crowbar into the dry ground. Elbows akimbo, legs spread, he drove the bar a foot or more into the ground before levering it back and forth, opening the top of the hole. Lucien Quirk stood by, impatient to sink the pointed end of a post into the hole and drive it firm with the broad side of the sledge, only once in his exertions pausing to make a crack about tight pussy. He propped the embedded post against his hip, and the nail for the cork-sized insulator hammered easily into the green wood. The boy pulled the wire. Tighter, the hired man said, his finger testing the tension as though it were some cord tightening in his heart. He secured it with a wire snap and they walked to the next post.

Bobby Dearborn noticed the change. It wasn't just that Lucien Quirk went into long silences or that his wisecracks came like limp afterthoughts or that he worked like a demon, taking charge and giving orders, as if the farm were his. The man was automatically distracted by the woman. When Janet Vaughn came into sight, Lucien Quirk stopped what he was doing to gaze in her direction, oblivious of the boy tugging at the wire or holding the post. Around her the man soldiered for love, waxing cheerful or concerned, keeping just the right distance, ever alert for her voiced or unvoiced wishes. The boy noticed how, just to be in her presence, the man spent hours of his free time in the garden, picking runner beans or weeding onions. He saw them together snake the black hose down the rows of produce for the snapping nimbus of water that kept the garden verdant in a dying world; or how later, holding a bushel basket, the man disappeared with the woman into the stalky green depths of the corn, where she opened the silken ears on gleaming teeth before snapping them off.

On an afternoon in the midst of the drought, the power failed, knocking out the lights in the house and Janet Vaughn's iron. More than just fuses, said Hedley Vaughn, cursing in the darkness of the cellar. They'd have to call in an electrician. Lucien Quirk, who had wandered into the house with Bobby Dearborn for a drink of water, said he'd take a look at it.

"Could you?" asked Janet Vaughn hopefully. The thought of an electrician's bill rattled her.

Her husband, exhausted by the climb up the stairs, shrugged and sat in the old armchair and opened the newspaper and muttered about everything going to hell.

Lucien Quirk and the boy followed the woman and the halo of her flashlight into the cool cellar of mortared stone that smelled of cobwebs and dank decay. Beyond the old-style washing machine and an ancient, plastered furnace and bins for apples and root vegetables and a wall racked with canned produce, they found the fuse box. The man and woman stood nearly touching as Lucien Quirk played the light over cables leading to the array of fuses glinting back from their sockets, dead eyes in a snarl of wires. He made discouraging noises.

"What's the matter?" asked Janet Vaughn, who feared some irreparable, expensive breakdown.

"It's all rotted," the man said. "You're lucky the place ain't burned down around you." He probed with a finger, and blue sparks hissed.

"Oh, be careful!"

In the penumbral light Bobby Dearborn saw Janet Vaughn grasp the man's arm and let it go immediately, as if shocked by the touch of hard muscle.

"Can you fix it?" she wanted to know.

Lucien Quirk flashed the light along a scabrous wall, found the mains, and opened them. "Can try," he said, probing the frayed cables and loose sockets with impunity now. "I'm going to need a pair of pliers, electrical tape, a screwdriver . . . and some luck. Here, you'd better take the light. And don't forget the luck, huh."

His voice sounded rough and friendly in the darkness, and as Janet Vaughn bustled up the narrow steps she found herself warming to him. Bring me some luck. She felt complimented and slightly mocked. Since when had she brought anyone any luck? Hedley Vaughn dozed in the armchair as she rustled through drawers for the tape and things he wanted. When she found them, she hurried back down the stairs, a little breathless with expectation.

The exertion focused from the man's tensed head and shoulders into his hands as he took apart the fuse sockets, snipped and stripped, twisted and taped gleaming filaments of copper. The boy assisted, holding tools and cutting tape. They worked in a silence broken only by the click of things and the man's voice as he gave the boy orders and muttered about the fuse box. "You need new leads from the mains," he said. "There ought to be more circuits for a place this size . . . See where it's all burned out . . . Someone really screwed this one up."

With his voice, his criticisms, his competence, his orders to the boy, Lucien Quirk enveloped even Janet Vaughn in the aura of his authority. In that cozy darkness, with the light following his expert fingers, she felt secure. They wouldn't burn down. There wouldn't be any huge bill. Her iron and refrigerator would work again. But his display thrilled more than her domestic soul. In the darkness she did not back off when they inadvertently bumped. She found herself thinking of sending the boy away on some pretext so that she might take his place. It was not so much a temptation as a fantasy of temptation. She saw herself in that eerie light alone with the man, half-wanting, half-fearing some overt gesture — a word or a touch — that would be the oil-smooth prelude to frankly graphic scenes that would happen there in the dark cellar as in the safety of her dreams, happening but not happening.

"The light!" his voice rebuked.

"Oh, sorry."

Lucien Quirk finished the wiring, remounted the sockets, and screwed in the fuses. When he closed the mains, a bulb hanging nearby went on, making them blink and revealing an old tub, a low-slung sewer pipe, and the repaired fuse box.

Janet Vaughn beamed at him. "You did it!"

Bobby Dearborn saw the man trying to act casual. But the woman's reaction gratified him so much, he looked foolish and had to turn away. He tried to joke. "Maybe you brought me luck. I don't know how long it'll last."

"But it works! And it looks so much better. Don't you think so, Bobby?"

The boy nodded, bemused himself by the strange, seductive note of approval in the woman's voice. He liked her then.

"Where did you learn all this?" she was saying. "It really looks professional."

Her friendly words, her admiration, knifed to the man's heart. "I've odd-jobbed around," he managed to say in a normal voice. But his eyes, in a quick, furtive glance at the woman, were naked, even to the boy.

Janet Vaughn's guard came up quickly. "Well, I really do appreciate all this. Now I can finish the shirts." Her laugh had an edge of sarcasm. They went back up the cellar steps, once again the boy, the hired man, and the woman of the house.

Even with that revealing glance, Janet Vaughn was not entirely conscious of how utterly she had bedazzled the man. He cringed now in his hobo clothes, hiding his limp, which, though proof of bravery in battle, had become symptomatic to him of some deeper crippling. Out of the cocoon of alcohol and hopelessness, another Lucien Quirk began to emerge. He dug out a toothbrush and a bridge that filled, more or less, the gaps in his smile. On trips to the pond with the boy he took a bar of soap and drew frowns from the matrons of the Village Improvement Association as he stood in the shallows, lathering himself like any good soldier on the move. He didn't go so far as to throw out his faithful pinups, but he took them down and cleaned out the empty bottles and cigarette butts and swept his shack, just in case his fantasies came to life and she stole down to him through the cricket sounds of the night. It was a scene he imagined in vivid, minute detail — her steps, her voice, her hesitations, their embrace — as he lay on his back, waiting and rehearsing the climactic moment with an expert hand.

She invaded his sleep in a recurrent dream, in which they were young and pretty together in an endless weekend of fancy restaurants and plush dance halls where he wore a new suit with padded shoulders and pegged trousers and no longer limped as he fox-trotted her through a silvery gossamer world conjured up from movies of the thirties. Something always went wrong. He lost a shoe. His fly wouldn't zip. He didn't have enough money to pay the check. And she would leave him (they always left him), saying she'd come back, and he would wait and wait until he would wake in cinematic dream time, smack in the middle of the sequence, and smoke a cigarette on his creaking canvas cot and wait for the trembling to stop.

When his disability check arrived, he took the afternoon off and went into Lowell to buy a pair of new chinos, new shoes and socks, and several sporty shirts at the factory outlet on Thorndike Street next to Keith Academy. On the way home he stopped to pick up his dress blues, which he had earlier left at the dry cleaners in Chelmsford. He was back in his shack, with the clothes still unwrapped, when Bobby Dearborn appeared on the step.

"What did you get?" the boy asked.

"I got my blues cleaned, Captain, first time in years. And I got me some new duds too."

"What for?"

"What the hell you mean, what for? You think I'm some kind of bum, huh, that don't need good clothes?"

"I didn't say that."

"You might as well of." But squinting, undressing down to his underwear, Lucien Quirk wasn't really angry, merely more convinced that he was doing the right thing. He carefully removed his uniform from the plastic cover. "I got my blues cleaned while I was at it. Ain't that special, huh?"

"Yeah," said the boy, admiring the dark brilliance of the uniform. "How come you got it cleaned?"

"I was thinking maybe I'd wear it next Fourth of July in the parade. With the medals on it. That'll show her."

"My aunt?"

"That's right. Women like a man in uniform. Makes them take notice." Carefully, so as not to soil them, Lucien Quirk pulled on the stiff trousers, then buttoned up the tunic. He took some time pinning the medals back on. Then he fixed the visored hat in place. "Lance Corporal Lucien Patrick Quirk, reporting, SIR!" he barked, coming to attention, saluting, every inch the Marine again, except for his stocking feet.

"How come you're doing this for my aunt?" the boy asked.

Lucien Quirk took off his uniform with the same care he had put it on and slid the plastic back in place.

"Your aunt is one fine lady," he said finally.

The shack was suddenly quite still and hot, the air stifling.

"But she's married to Uncle Hedley."

"That's right." The man was undoing his other packages. "Look at them shirts. Ain't them beauts?"

But the boy, standing back in the doorway, remained silent and watchful, waiting for an answer.

"That's true," the man said, still opening his packages, repossessing what he had bought. "But when the farmer can't milk his cows, somebody's gotta do it for him."

"But Uncle Hedley has a bad heart," said Bobby Dearborn, not altogether confused by the man's little parable.

"That's right."

"That ain't fair."

The man nodded, as if agreeing. He was hanging up his new chinos and shirts. "That's right, it ain't fair." He took out his cigarettes and offered one to the boy.

Bobby Dearborn shook his head and waited.

The man blew smoke. He looked more sexual than vulnerable in his skivvies and socks. His glance met the boy's and his words came out even and hard. "One thing you ought to know about life, Captain, is that anything's fair when it comes to women."

Bobby Dearborn had nothing with which to counter that. He stood, watching the man get dressed, and tried to dissemble the tremor of challenge and excitement the man's words had aroused in him. He knew something was happening that was real and wrong and natural.

❧ 10 ❧

A THICK, piss-green soup stood knee-deep on the broken floor of the barn cellar where Bobby Dearborn backed in the manure spreader. It was a tricky business. He had to steer in the direction opposite from where he wanted the spreader to go. The high wheels with their heavy treads churned like steamboat paddles in the liquid muck, and with the muffler removed so that the tractor could clear the low-slung entrance, the noise was deafening. He didn't have to back in very far. The dung from the winter before ranged in peaks between the stone foundation and the locust posts supporting the joisted floor above. A single bulb threaded through the planking and lit the cobwebbed darkness, including, at the edge of its glow, an audience of rats that had gathered to watch the boy and Lucien Quirk start on the first pile. Laced with sawdust that was used to bed the cows, the manure had become a heat trap, and steam billowed out from where they dug in their wide forks. The fuming dung clattered on the metal floor of the spreader, which filled quickly. Then the noise hammered as the tractor crawled from beneath the barn into the blinding day.

The stuff flew high and wide from the spinning rotors at the back of the spreader as the boy roared down the field they were getting ready for the turnips. It was a level stretch of some five acres between the garden and the new electric fence behind which the cows grazed the second crop of hay. When the spreader emptied, he headed back to the barn. They sweated again in the acidic, purifying stench, their rubber boots squishing in the muck, rats' eyes gleaming in the darkness. Sometimes the rats squealed as they humped about. Lucien Quirk dug out a nest of pink-bodied young ones. It went into the spreader. The spreader went up and down the field. By late afternoon the field had turned brown with two dozen loads that in the baking sun stank up the valley.

George and Joyce Fullmer, a couple with children who had begun to renovate the old Mayhew house (they had moved out from the city), drove over in their varnished station wagon to complain. Really, they said, the smell had gotten into the house. Janet Vaughn, defensive and obliging, told them the smell wouldn't last long and appeased them with a bag of fresh produce.

The smell didn't last long. The next day Bobby Dearborn began to plow the manure under. He had never plowed before, so he drove the tractor slowly, keeping an eye on the plow blade knifing under the sod, which slid back along the share, a furling wave of polished black earth. The first furrow bisected the field. He came up the other side, matching it, furrow against furrow. His confidence grew. He notched up the gas. The sod hissed along the plow blade. He went up and down, down and up, and the imbricated pattern widened, attracting grackles and starlings that, black and glinting as the soil, were in their element, stalking up-turned grubs.

As he came up the field on a go-around, the boy noticed Lucien Quirk and his uncle bringing out a cow and tying her to the maple near the end of the barn. The cow had come into heat and they were going to breed her. Bobby Dearborn kept plowing. He had seen cows bred before. For all the majesty of the bull, it was a disappointing spectacle, what with the beast's ringed nose snuffling under the cow's raised tail and its scarlet foil unsheathing for its stiff-legged mount and quick, lurching thrust. At one time the boy had thought human sex was as perfunctory, and he couldn't understand what all the fuss was about, except that he also thought it was as infrequent — once a year and then only if you wanted a child. (A school chum who had watched an older cousin and her boyfriend copulate frequently and at length the summer before had set him straight.) So he ignored the scene unfolding under the maple at the end of the barn and concentrated on keeping the right wheel of the tractor against the square cut of the previous furrow, just ahead of the plow point and the turning sod. At the end of the furrow he pulled the cord that raised the point out of the ground, drove across the end of the plowed section, lined up the tractor in the furrow, and lowered the point. Let them breed the old cow. He would rather plow the field and enjoy the heady sensation of transforming reality.

Like executioners, they were leading the bull down to the tied cow. The bull was balking and bawling. The boy came up the field, crossed over, and went down. They were still under the tree with the bull and the cow when he came up again. They were taking a long time, and the boy could sense something going wrong. He saw his uncle gesticulating madly and, as he got closer, could hear his shouts over the roar of the tractor. At the top of the field, he stopped plowing and walked over to them.

Hedley Vaughn held a long wooden pole, the other end of which was snapped onto the ring in the bull's nose. "Get up there, God damn it!" the man cursed. The animal, tugged by the nose, held its mouth open and rumbled in its throat. The cow moved, and Lucien Quirk shoved her back into place. Hedley Vaughn, pale and agitated, tried again, easing the bull's pink snout close to the back end of the cow. The bull wouldn't mount. The man cursed again.

"Bobby, hold her in place," he ordered. Then he gave the ring pole to Lucien Quirk. "Keep him close." Free, the man scooped moisture from under the cow's upraised tail and rubbed it on the bull's nose. They were all in close, tense and sweating, waiting. For a moment it seemed it might happen. The bull's penis unsheathed and the animal gathered as though to mount, when the dog, panting in the shade, got up and barked. The bull roared and with an abrupt, violent twist swung its hindquarters around, knocking Hedley Vaughn to the ground. There was a flurried confusion of hooves and man, followed by an agonized cry from Hedley Vaughn as the bull, prancing about, trampled the man's arms and chest. It would have been worse had not Lucien Quirk yanked the bull toward himself and out into the field. Hedley Vaughn sat up for a moment in the dust. The speckled shade of the maple rose in a swirl as he grabbed at his chest and tried to tell them to breed the cow. Only there wasn't enough air to speak. His face darkened, his mouth opened, and he crumpled onto his side and lay still.

Lucien Quirk handed the pole to the boy. "Take him inside," he ordered. "Then go get your aunt."

It wasn't one of his darker fantasies Lucien Quirk lived as he bent over the stricken man; it was memory. *Corpsman!* he wanted to yell, and involuntarily kept his head low for a moment. It was on reflex that he opened the man's shirt to see how badly he'd been hit. It had gotten so he could tell whether they were going to make it or not. There was a clearly defined cloven hoof mark rising on the man's white skin like the devil's imprint. One of his arms hung limp as though broken. He searched for and found the unconscious man's fluttery pulse. He knelt and put his ear down on his chest and heard his lungs moving, but just. Hedley Vaughn might make it, he thought, if they got him help in time.

Janet Vaughn came down the maple-shaded lane in her shuffling trot, followed by the boy. He watched as she stopped, horrified, several feet from the form lying on the ground. But her voice was calm as she knelt and cradled her husband's head and asked, "What happened?"

"The bull just kind of hipped around and knocked him down," the hired man said. "He got walked on, too. He ain't in very good shape."

The boy drew close, awed by the drama before him. Yet he was detached, aware of the heat and the cow still tied to the tree.

"Hedley," the woman murmured.

"He's out."

"I know."

She took off her husband's glasses so that they wouldn't get broken and stroked the few strands of limp hair from his gray face. She had been through it before, but that didn't help. She still had to resist the luxury of tears and the choking numbness of fear and helplessness. She still had to act.

Lucien Quirk was talking. "We ought to get him to a hospital." The man had stood up and was peering down at her. "Bobby," he said, "why don't you go call an ambulance."

The woman shook her head. For a moment it seemed as though she was going to say something like No, let's let him die. As though that would be the natural, merciful thing to do.

"We'll take him in the car," she said instead, her voice hard, her eyes snapping as she glanced up. Anger had taken over from fear. "It's faster. Last time it took them more than an hour to get here."

Faster. And cheaper. Janet Vaughn was not so panicked that the thought of what this would cost didn't deepen her sense of raw desolation. It was all of a dismal piece — hurrying into the house for purse and keys, then the suffocating air of the sun-baked car as she turned on the ignition, her face in the rearview mirror (looking a fright to be driving into Lowell, she thought, her lengthening hair mussed, and wearing that grain-bag blouse faded to a rag and khaki slacks and old sneakers). The car rocked going down the tractor-rutted lane. Spangles of light played over the windshield in the shade of the maples, disorienting her, making her think it might be a bad dream. But if it was, it wasn't one from which she could escape. Ahead of her, framed in the windshield, she saw the cow still tied to the tree, the dog panting, the boy gaping at her husband lying in the arms of Lucien Quirk. For an instant painful with truth, she wished Hedley Vaughn dead. The wish became a daydream of which she was barely conscious — Lucien Quirk saying, He's gone. You don't need the car. I'm sorry. The boy sad. The dog whimpering. And she could collapse with grief and relief. But he wasn't gone, and she could not sustain even a shadow of that bleak hope as she got out of the car and bent over him again, touching his face, wanting to sob.

Bobby Dearborn and Lucien Quirk gently, but quite unceremoniously, lifted the unconscious man and got him into the back of the car. Propped lengthwise along the seat, half-lying, half-sitting, his head back under the rear window, Hedley Vaughn appeared comic, like a drunk passed out. Janet Vaughn noticed that as she tucked the feet in. It seemed just one more indignity.

She turned to the boy. "Listen, Bobby, I want you to call Saint John's Hospital — the operator will give you the number — and tell them your uncle's had an accident and maybe another attack . . . that he's unconscious and that I'm bringing him in in the car." Putting the situation in words made stark its pathos. Her voice began to break, but she caught herself. "Do it now."

The boy nodded, turned, and ran toward the house.

"I ought to come along," Lucien Quirk said through her window after she had gotten in and started the car.

She paused for a moment. He was right. Something could go wrong. The car could stall. A flat tire. An accident. She nodded a mute yes. Jesus, what am I doing? He got in and she drove ahead into the clearing between the back of the barn and the equipment shed. There wasn't enough clearance for a U turn. She had to stop, back up, go forward, back up, forward again, up the rutted lane, skidding, sliding a little into the verge, then across the yard and onto the road without looking, going fast, too fast, as if chased by death.

Bobby Dearborn came out of the house just as the car left. He had telephoned the hospital. They would be waiting for his uncle, they said. He went down the lane to the scene of the accident. He was waiting for something like sadness to come over him. It seemed only right to feel sad. His uncle had been badly hurt by the bull. He might even die. But that isn't finally what made the boy pause. What moved him was the way the woman had held the stricken man and touched his face. He felt sorry for her sadness.

He untied the cow from the tree and led her into the barn, where he put her in a stanchion. The bull stood in its stall, head down, as if threatening to charge. The boy perched on the top rail of the corral.

"It's the butcher for you, bully," he said aloud to the animal. "Can't even breed an old cow. They're gonna knock you on the head and slit your throat and hang you by your hocks and make hamburgers out of you."

The bull snorted and pawed at its bedding, and the boy decided not to bait it. Not then, anyway. He had work to do. He went down the ramp at the end of the barn and out into the bright day. It surprised him that everything looked perfectly normal under the tree where they had tried to breed the cow. It was as still and as hot as before, with everything in place — the sun, the shade, the lane, the field — as though what had happened hadn't happened, as though reality were mocking itself. He got up on the tractor and resumed plowing. He concentrated on keeping the furrows dead straight, the thick sod turning over, the land burying itself. This, at least, was real.

☙

Janet Vaughn drove with panicked competence and speed through Elmsbury and Chelmsford. In Lowell the traffic thickened. But she knew short cuts. She went right onto

Hale Street, through the tenements, and over the railroad bridge. At the sight of footballers going through drills in shorts on the Keith Academy field, she had to clench back tears again. The football players had been out there going through spring practice that rainy April afternoon Hedley drove her to the hospital. They had an old Pontiac then, and the wipers made rainbows of clarity on the running windshield. He had been caring and gentle with her and the awe on his face when he looked at her made him seem ten years younger. If it's a boy I want him to go to Keith Academy and play football, she had said, only half-joking. If it's a boy I'm going to need him on the farm, he had replied. They had indulged those contentions like luxuries during her pregnancy and on that day, even though, with the pain erratic, she already sensed something was wrong. She had said nothing to him. She was too committed to their happy conspiracy; she wanted to keep believing that they had succeeded.

They drove down Gorham Street, past the project on the left and the courthouse on the right, climbing Church Street to Nesmith. The hospital loomed with the realization of what she had done so that at the last moment, pulling into the emergency entrance, tears welled, and she nearly broke down. But she remained dry-eyed as the professional world took over. Orderlies in white eased her husband from the car onto a stretcher and draped him to the neck with a sheet, transforming him somehow into hospital property. Because the car had to be moved, she gave the keys to Lucien Quirk. Then, hurrying, she followed the stretcher inside. O.R., someone said. Dr. Williams is waiting. Hedley Vaughn's face disappeared under an oxygen mask. A nurse with a clipboard wedged into the elevator with them. She gave Janet Vaughn a quick, appraising glance and began asking questions. Is he allergic to any drugs? Do you know his blood type? How did it happen? Janet Vaughn, who already felt outlandish, tried to explain how he had been trying to breed a cow when the bull knocked him over and walked on him. A young orderly who looked like a college student snickered. The nurse frowned. Anything broken? Janet Vaughn shook her head. She wasn't sure. Our life, she nearly blurted.

They wheeled the stretcher along a corridor and through doors labeled HOSPITAL STAFF ONLY. Janet Vaughn was not allowed through. She stood, relieved of her burden and bewildered. She went lightheaded for a moment and then walked back along the corridor, as though she might find a special room to take her pain and shock. Anxieties ballooned and broke in her like waves of nausea until she found a bench and sat down. She wanted to weep but found she couldn't. She glanced up at a pale statue of the Virgin niched in the wall across from her. Hail Mary, she started to herself, trying to invoke that presence, that other reality to prop against this one. But she couldn't pray, either. The statue remained masonry, a mere token in this temple of man, where the starched white air of science held sway and where the resurrections were only reprieves.

And expensive. A woman from the financial office found her and began another litany of questions. Blue Cross–Blue Shield coverage? Savings? Here before? Oh, *that* Vaughn. Thought the name was familiar.

Then she went to the waiting room. Lucien Quirk brought her a cup of coffee and hovered, a solicitous presence, while she stared off into space or flipped through a tattered March *Look* with Princess Grace and her new baby, Caroline, on the cover. Grace says her baby will have a normal upbringing. The life story of Pope Pius XII. A diamond is forever. Time thinned and stretched and nearly seemed to stop.

"Mrs. Vaughn?"

Startled, she peered up into the rich gray aura of a doctor with silver hair, slate eyes, charcoal suit, impeccable shirt, and straight tie who towered over her even after she had stood up.

"Yes," she managed.

"I'm Dr. Williams. This is my colleague, Dr. DeGraffen. We've been treating your husband."

The voice was a rich, professional purr.

"How is he?" she asked.

"Well . . ." The pause grew ominous. The first doctor glanced at the second and for a moment she thought, He's dead. And it was terrible, more terrible than she could have imagined.

"He's not . . ."

"Oh, no. But he's in very poor condition at the moment." He turned for a confirming nod from Dr. DeGraffen. "His vital signs are beginning to stabilize. Frankly, we didn't expect him to pull through. Your husband is a remarkably strong man."

She had been holding her breath and now let it out. "How badly . . . what happened . . .?

There was another clearing of throats. "Well, first of all the indications point to another major infarction, essentially a repeat of the attack he had last year. That, of course, is the most serious thing . . . Umm, he also sustained several cracked ribs and a fractured ulna — that's a bone in the forearm — on his left side. He also has some bruises and abrasions, but our chief concern is his heart." He went on about a long recovery period, but Janet Vaughn was only half-listening, because she had heard it all before. She was watching his quiet, square hands and how they tented in front of him, fingertips touching, as his voice purred on.

"Can I see him?" she interrupted.

"Of course. A nurse will take you."

Then they were gone and she was walking along corridors with a nurse, through doors, deeper into the place to a white chamber, where he lay, slightly propped, arm in a cast, hostage to oxygen, wired and tubed like something in a monster movie. She had seen him like this before, but it still unnerved her. What had she expected, a miracle? Yes, but without realizing it. His rough hand was limp, and he lay white and withered behind the transparency of the oxygen tent, remote in a world of his own. Hedley, she murmured, my poor Hedley, and pity for him and for herself descended like grace. Still, she didn't cry. She found a chair and sat down, lapsing into the anodyne of mild shock.

A while later she got up and walked, more or less in a daze, back to the waiting room for Lucien Quirk. Together they went out to the parking lot. Lucien Quirk was saying something about driving home except he wasn't allowed to drive in Massachusetts. She shrugged. But then, as she sat in the driver's seat, the car and its farm smell evoked what she had just gone through, and her first sob was an inward gasp of breath. "Why! Why! Why!" she cried and beat her fists against the steering wheel. Her tears erupted luxuriously, wetting her face, making her nose run so that she had to sniffle. She felt Lucien Quirk's hand on her shoulder and did not shake it off.

"He'll be all right," she heard.

She turned her reddened face to him, and her words were broken with sobs. "That's not so. That's the awful thing. He won't be all right. He'll never be all right. They can't do anything for him. And he won't stop . . . Oh, God . . ." She put her face against his shoulder and her cry was a wail of helplessness.

❧ 11 ❧

Lucien Quirk had bits and pieces of several drinkers spread in orderly fashion on the swept floor of the barn in front of the mangers. He had rigged a sawhorse with a vise to hold three-quarter-inch pipe.

"How the hell did you water the stock down this end of the barn in winter?" he asked Bobby Dearborn.

"We ran a hose from a faucet up at the front end."

"That must of been a pain in the ass."

"Yeah," the boy agreed. "A couple of times we had to carry it when the hose froze."

It was hot and not quite airless where they worked at the far end of the barn, fixing the last few of the drinkers that were secured with bolts between every other stanchion. Lucien Quirk had repaired the mangers first, installing new two-by-six uprights and replacing the floorboards where they had rotted through. He worked now stripped to the waist, beads of sweat bunching and running down the chunky muscles that plated his back and chest. Together with the boy, using a hammer and pinchbar, he pulled out the bent nails holding the unconnected main pipe that came overhead along the beams. "Chinese navy," he muttered, as he pried loose the last of the pipe and pulled it down.

Navy. The word sounded a signal for Bobby Dearborn to resume his favorite topic in talking to the hired man: What had it been like fighting in the war? The boy had an endless fund of questions. How big were the Jap guns? How could you tell when they were going to counterattack? He had other, more crucial questions that Lucien Quirk hadn't gotten around to answering. What, the boy wanted to know, was it like to kill someone? What was it like to be really scared? What was courage? The man had been evasive.

"Did you have to spend much time on the troopship on the way out?" the boy asked, seemingly out of nowhere.

"Too damn long," the man said. He had the measuring tape in his hand and was scoring new pipe with a nail where he wanted it cut. "I suppose it wasn't more than a couple of weeks. It felt like years. Being a sitting duck for Jap subs." They secured the pipe in the vise, and the boy, shirtless and sweating like the man, went back and forth with the hack saw. "And then it didn't seem long enough." They kept the cut piece in the vise and threaded both ends of it.

"Why's that?" asked Bobby Dearborn, who guessed the answer but wanted to contribute at least questions.

Lucien Quirk let it hang as he daubed sealing paint on the gleaming threads. One end he twisted into a T-joint before tightening the other into main line, leaving the T-joint poised just above the upright between the two stanchions. "Look at that. Ain't off but a pussy hair." Then, his voice going narrative again, he said, "One reason it didn't seem long enough was that when you weren't in the troopship, you were getting your ass shot off."

Again they measured, cut, and threaded pipe. The man was talking. "I mean the only thing worse than being packed into those tubs like sardines waiting for the Japs to feed you to the sharks was getting off the God damn things." He laughed as if at a private joke. "It wasn't like they were waiting to sell you souvenirs when you went ashore."

The second piece of pipe threaded into the middle of the T-joint and came down the upright to within a couple of feet of the floor. In close, wielding Stillson wrenches, sweating and grunting, the pair twisted on the back of the drinker, then the drinking cup, an iron bowl roughly the size of a large cantaloupe cut in half. They secured this to the upright with carriage bolts. Finally they installed the tongue, a perforated pressure plate that connected to a valve in the back and released water when pushed down by the cow's nose.

"What was it like?" the boy resumed.

"What's that?"

"Going ashore."

"Depended on when you went in. The first guys got the shit chewed out of them. If you went in a couple of days later, they had hot coffee waiting for you."

For a while they worked methodically in silence. The head of the threader clamped flush against the end of sawed pipe. The die bit smoothly into metal, dropping thin bright coils of it onto the floor as the boy worked the ratcheted handle up and down, enjoying the power of shaping steel. They added another length of pipe with a T attached and came down from that to another drinking cup. They took a break.

"What was it really like?" Bobby Dearborn asked, sensing somehow that the man would talk now.

"What's that?"

"The real fighting."

Lucien Quirk sat on the floor and leaned back against the front of the manger. He used a drinking cup for an ashtray.

"It was like this," he said.

"This?"

"That's right, like this, just a lot of hot God damn work." He smirked at the boy's glance of disappointment, then relented. "I mean it was mostly just ass-breaking work ... Slogging through hot jungle with a full pack, carrying one end of a case of mortars with the rain pissing on you and the Japs sniping at you from the trees like monkeys with guns. Then setting up. Some dumb-ass lieutenant, green as scared shit, giving orders. Dig in. Dig in. Try digging in the

· 114 ·

jungle sometime. They don't show that in the movies . . . all the God damn work. Sometimes you got so tired you could go to sleep standing against a tree . . ."

"But the fighting," the boy urged.

Lucien Quirk blew smoke. There were not many words in him for the memories of how bullets thudded into bodies or how human flesh smells sickeningly delicious like any other cooked meat after the flame throwers had done their work. But he tried anyway.

"That ain't in the movies, either. You see, when guys get hit bad they puke and shit themselves and start bawling and crying about not wanting to die. 'Please don't let me die! I don't wanna die!' they'd be screaming, okay. And you know the poor bastard's had it and he knows too, because there'd be nothing left of his guts or because he'd be drowning in his own blood or because he'd have a hole in him too big to plug up and stop the bleeding . . ."

Hunkered on the floor nearby, the boy chewed a piece of clover. Swallows twitted in the full mow above them. The bull grunted in its stall. Otherwise there was the silence of a hot midsummer afternoon.

"You must have been brave" was all the boy could think to say.

"Sheeeit," Lucien Quirk hissed with an oddly dispassionate vehemence. "Brave. Hell, I was scared from the minute I got off the bus at boot camp and saw all that gear . . . the tanks and artillery and machine guns. I knew I was going to get killed. I was scared shitless. And when I got into it I was even more scared."

"Into the fighting?"

"That's right, the fighting. You know what I was scared of?"

The boy shook his head.

Lucien Quirk leaned forward, eyes on the boy's eyes as he snubbed out the cigarette in the drinker.

"I was scared of letting my buddies down. That's the first thing. Then I was scared of being scared. That's what bravery is. That's what it was for me and most of the guys. You get too scared to be yellow. You don't want to go out bawling. You don't want to be that scared. So you had to tell yourself all the time that you were already dead, because you couldn't take it any other way. You'd go crazy. And pretty soon you believed it. You walked around like you were already your own ghost. Only you weren't. You were still alive waiting to get killed. Sometimes you just wanted to get it over with. Pull the pins on a bunch of grenades and go running at a machine gun. I saw guys do it. I did it myself once."

"On Saipan?"

"Tarawa."

"What happened?"

"I lived."

Then Lucien Quirk wasn't paying attention. Something else made him cock his head. A car door slammed out in the yard. "She's back," he said to himself, like a thought escaping. He stood up and pulled on his shirt, ran a hand through his hair, dusted off his trousers. After a moment he turned back to the work.

"All right," he said, "let's get it finished."

They went at it again, sizing, cutting, and threading pipe. They hadn't been working long when the man, ever alert, stopped what he was doing. In the blaze of light at the front of the barn, the figure of the woman appeared, a solid shadow coming toward them uncertainly, her eyes not used to the relative darkness. She wore an old-fashioned suit with a box jacket, which might have made her look uncomfortably formal next to them, except that she carried a jug of Kool-Aid that rattled with ice cubes.

"I brought you a drink," she said with pretended cheer.

The man could not keep his eyes off her. "How's Hedley?" he asked after drinking from the jug and passing it to the boy.

Janet Vaughn nodded as though to give her time to control her voice. Still it trembled. "He's better," she managed.

"Better, huh." He lit a cigarette, flaring the match and blowing emphatic smoke.

"Well, he's out of the oxygen tent." She gave a little, nearly girlish laugh. "He said not to plant the turnips too early."

The man echoed her laugh. "Giving orders, huh. Hell, he'll be all right."

Then the woman, her eyes accustomed to the gloom, drew closer, inspecting. "Oh, you've already fixed some drinkers. Look at all you've done!" She was bending over to peer up inside the mangers while the man, paralyzed for a moment by the swell of her hips, began explaining how it was easy to do when you had the threader and how they had enough pipe to run a faucet into the hen house so they wouldn't have to carry water in there anymore.

Bobby Dearborn watched them, heard the man's voice waxing smooth and courtly. Sweet-talking. As if the woman cared about drinker valves and watering the bull. The boy knew what was going on. He remembered what Lucien Quirk had said about anything being fair where women were concerned. He heard him in the house at night, talking to the woman down in the kitchen until it was late. Hanging around on any excuse. Not that the boy particularly cared. It wasn't fair to his uncle, that was true, but Hedley Vaughn, the time he'd gone to see him in the hospital, hardly looked alive.

It was more disturbing the way Janet Vaughn nowadays went from a nervous laugh to tears, sometimes grabbing and hugging him so that he was like a stick in her embrace, blushing, her breasts too rich and the memory of her nakedness through the keyhole fresh as the smell of the roses the man had brought her. Or like right then, taking him by the hand, kissing his cheek, too friendly.

"Don't you want to go swimming with your friends?" she asked.

"I'm helping Lucien with the drinkers."

"Can't you finish them tomorrow?"

"Hell, yeah," said the man.

"I'll give you a quarter for a cone at Earl's."

"Naw, that's all right."

"You sure?"

He hesitated. He wasn't so sure. Then he thought he might as well. With the woman around, there would be no more man-to-man stuff, no more easy cursing as they worked together, no more war stories. He took the coin, and feeling awkward, oddly compromised, left them to get his swimming trunks and a towel. When he came out of the house they were sitting on lawn chairs together under one of the maples beside the barn. The woman offered to drive him, but he said he'd rather walk. Just before the road began to rise, he turned and looked back. They were still in the chairs under the maple. From that distance and from the way they sat and talked, it struck the boy that they could have been man and wife.

12

Margaret Greenwood's voice came loud and flat through the earpiece of the phone.

"You tell Hedley we're thinking of him. You tell him we'll get in just as soon as we can. We'd have gotten in sooner, only Sy's blood pressure's up again."

"Okay."

"What?"

"I said OKAY." Janet Vaughn's shout rattled the empty house. The woman was hard of hearing. "I'll be sure and tell him."

"What?"

"Okay."

"You tell Hedley . . ."

Janet Vaughn held the receiver away from her, and Meg Greenwood's words ran together in a meaningless buzz. Even then, she could hear the sympathy, a little perfunctory, perhaps, but real enough. Their neighbors, friends, and family, after all, had been through it with them before. The first time they had called in, dropping off a roasting chicken or a cake or a bushel of apples, and Frank Devito had helped in the garden and Harry Manning and the boy had sawed wood for the winter. This time they phoned, mixing apology with curiosity, declaring with their clicks of pity and their get-well cards that she was alone with her troubles. Not exactly alone. She did have the boy and Lucien Quirk, the hired man. And even if the latter was only a wino from Lowell, for friends and neighbors it all weighed in the equation.

"I have to go now, Meg," she yelled into the phone.

"What?"

"I have to go. I have to say GOODBYE."

"Goodbye?"

Janet Vaughn hung up the phone. Not that she had any place she had to go, except, perhaps, to the hospital to visit her husband. And she planned to do that in the evening. It was easier then, with closing time set at eight o'clock. She could leave without apology.

How she dreaded the visits. The drive into Lowell each time revived their nightmarish trips in the ambulance and the car. Each time she wondered what she would find when she got there. The day before she had gone with Ernestine Vaughn and found him in the oxygen tent again, fading, a shadow of the shadow he had become. His sister, she knew, wanted to weep. Janet Vaughn had stood over him feeling only numb, as if all the pity and grief and love she could summon had already been wrung from her.

Even when he was having one of his better days, she found little to talk about. She sat next to the bed in the double room, close to the door and the hall, a stranger visiting a stranger. He was like some old relative (your *husband!*) she had to visit out of duty. Of course when he had the strength, he went on about the farm, asking questions and giving orders, carrying it around with him as though it were part of his sick heart, like a disease he couldn't shake. Pathetic in the johnny tied behind him, he would sit and start: Had the black heifer come around? Tell Quirk to move the herd back to pasture and manure the hayfields. Had they sowed the turnips? Was the bull breeding all right? Thank God for the rain. Then the effort would tell and he would fall back against the pillows on the cranked-up bed.

She found it a relief to take Bobby Dearborn with her, even though she knew it bored him. The old rancor between them had all but vanished, although there was still a wariness in his glance. His "Auntie" came easier now, and she felt something protective in his presence, as though he sensed her vulnerability. She welcomed his company on these visits because he could cheer up Hedley, who reached out a weak hand to grasp the boy and hold him. He became a bond between her and her husband, even, or especially, on those evenings when he didn't go with her. And how's Bobby, Hedley Vaughn would say, and they would both cheer up, as though a fond son had been mentioned.

Sometimes they watched the television the patient in the other bed had brought in. Hedley Vaughn scoffed at it, calling it a newfangled thing, fit for kids and fools. Still, it seduced him, especially Phil Silvers in "Sergeant Bilko," who made him laugh even though it hurt. Mostly they simply sat together in a silence broken by the public address system calling for a doctor or by the nurses visiting the old man in the next bed, who was suffering from complications following a colostomy. Those were the worst times, heavy with foreboding and plain boredom. The year before, at least, there had been hope of recovery and of return to what had been in its own way a normal life. Now the hopelessness hung like a pall, and eight o'clock would come around for Janet Vaughn like a blessing. She would stay a few minutes after the hour, kiss him on the forehead, and flee.

It was strange, because she missed him the moment she got home, missed him in the bed beside her, missed worrying about him. Because she no longer worried about him; it was as if the hospital, the doctors, the nursing staff, even the people who mopped the floors there, did that for her now. The hospital owned him. (And with the way the bills were mounting up, it would soon own everything they had.) She even missed arguing with him about the farm, about selling it. You couldn't do that in the hospital. It might upset him even though, damn it, the farm was killing him. Without him there, she felt defenseless, oddly compromised. A woman gets used to a man, even half a man, around the house.

She could have gone that Sunday to a family gathering at Joe Jr.'s in Dracut, but she had begged off. The last time, at her sister Ellen's, she had felt too much like a fifth wheel, like an old maid aunt, and their kindnesses had cut like cruelties. In one of those awful moments revelatory of family gossip and malice, little Debbie Dunn had approached her and said, "Are you going to sell the farm and be rich when Uncle Hedley dies?" Worse was her mother finally voicing what their eyes said: "You shouldn't be out there alone with that hired man, the one who brings you roses. People will talk."

They were probably right, even if Lucien Quirk had been a perfect gentleman in his own way and a great help, going so far as to talk about putting down a new floor in the kitchen (he knew a place in Lowell where they sold linoleum cheap) and a new sink with a Formica top and chrome fixtures (they're not that expensive). Only now, those things didn't tempt her the way they might have earlier.

Janet Vaughn fidgeted, glanced at herself in the paneled mirror in the living room, the top part of which had been painted with a bucolic farm scene years before by one of Hedley's aunts. Thinner still, she thought, in the black sweater and the kilt of Royal Stuart she had worn to Mass. And with her hair reaching down to cover her neck, she felt attractive and didn't want to change to do the morning dishes or start the dinner or the pile of ironing Gladys Porley had dropped off with a How is Hedley doing? Please tell him we asked for him specially. Could you iron and fold five of these professionally, like they do at Tsongas. Charles is off on a business trip to Chicago. The woman had seemed subdued and decent about it all, leaving the book of Green Stamps without waiting for her usual quotient of gratitude.

Only Janet Vaughn, back and forth in front of the mirror, could scarcely dream of the table lamp with the black and brass base that might rescue her living room so that she could invite Connie Murphy over for coffee. Aside from anything else, it was one of those days when any effort seems futile, when the future — the hopes and fears and expectations — gets canceled, and time shrinks to the stifling present, so that you move from moment to moment in the freedom of a vacuum.

The boy's absence — he had gone with Ernestine on one of their Sunday forays — only added to the emptiness she felt. She had come to depend on him. He was still somewhat remote with her, it was true, but now he let her hug him when she simply had to have someone to cling to, and his glances, shy and penetrating at the same time, had a strange, adolescent empathy she couldn't quite fathom. She shook her hair forward at the mirror. Perhaps her breasts were just a little too prominent for this sweater, for Mass, for Sunday. A pretty widow. She entertained that surprisingly pleasant prospect for a moment before suppressing it. Surely it must be a sin to wish your husband dead. Father Fahey would know. But that wasn't what she wanted. She wanted . . . And that, on a beautiful sunny Sunday in September, was the rub: she didn't know what she wanted. In any event, she remained in her kilt and sweater, black pumps and nylons, to stay pretty, feeling she would need the armor of her attractiveness when she confronted Lucien Quirk, as she would have to, about the locket.

She had returned from the nine o'clock Mass to find the small package gift-wrapped in fine-striped gold and white paper on the mantel in the living room. Bobby! she had thought at first with puzzled delight. A miniature card with the package contained a simple envelope and the words "For Janet" in a rough, unpracticed hand. It wasn't the boy's. It had to be from Lucien Quirk. She couldn't imagine anyone else coming by and leaving her such a gift.

She knew what she had to do. She had to put the card back in the envelope and return the package to him unopened. Thanking him kindly, of course, but remaining firm in saying no when he came in for Sunday dinner. The man was doing so much for them. It was embarrassing every week to hand him his five dollars, more like a rich kid's allowance than a workingman's pay. And that shack.

But Janet Vaughn couldn't resist. Out of some mingling of curiosity and guilt and pity, she was led, against all her best intentions, to undo carefully the paper that covered the white box with ABBOTT'S OF LOWELL embossed on the cover. Inside, a silver, lozenge-shaped locket engraved with a rose nestled in its chain on a pale blue cushion. Its elegance made her go a little faint. And she had never received anything quite like it before. Hedley had bought her a small diamond engagement ring and a gold wedding band, loose now on her thinning fingers, but both were expected, conventional things. She couldn't resist draping it against herself before the mirror, its silver brilliant on the black of her sweater. A lover's gift, it made her, for a giddy moment, feel young and attractive and even sophisticated.

Yes, but it was impossible. It would mean . . . She gave it a last glance, then put it back in the box and carefully rewrapped it to look as though it hadn't been opened, all the while rehearsing her rejection. Thank you very, very much, but you know I can't possibly accept *this* from you. Though dreading having to do it, she relished the prospective drama of it all, because it made her feel like the heroine in a romance, even if the setting was a broken-down farmhouse and the suitor the hired man rather than a young earl in a castle. It wasn't a scenario she could sustain with any conviction. In truth, Janet Vaughn was tempted by the gift, by the man, by her own nagging needs.

Puttering around in the kitchen, she turned on the radio. A voice was screaming:

"I got a girl named Boney Moronie
She's as skinny as a piece of macaroni . . ."

She snapped it off. Such harsh, stupid stuff nowadays. Not like the old music, songs like "I Can Dream, Can't I," by the Andrews Sisters. Janet Vaughn, who had a poor voice for music, sang:

> "Dream on, dream on,
> For dreams are just like wine,
> And I am drunk with mine . . ."

Lapsing into a medley of old songs, singing snatches of them, she tapped her hand to

> "Night and day, you are the one
> Only you beneath the moon and under the sun . . ."

and found herself dreaming of Michael Gavin, the man in her world of what might have been, the man she would never forgive for having caused heartaches that, in the present circumstances, seemed merely indulgent, merely . . .

The sound of scraping feet outside the screen door startled her, making her think of Hedley and how he might have caught her in a daydream. Actually, she was afraid her humming and singing had betrayed the happy mood she had lapsed into. She had barely resumed her stance as the proper housewife by the time Lucien Quirk had made his perfunctory knock on the door and come in, too early for dinner. His face, younger and healthier-looking now with good food and hard work outside, revealed nothing as he uttered a commonplace about the beauty of the day.

"Hi," she said with averted face. Then, sweeping from the room on the momentum of the surprise, even fright, his sudden appearance had given her, she went to retrieve the locket. He was sitting at the kitchen table when she returned with it and placed it in front of him before plumping down in a chair opposite.

"I can't accept your gift," she said abruptly, trying not to sound rehearsed, trying to sound casual and final, but not mean. At the same time, she knew her neck had begun to mottle with color.

The man's face remained impassive as if he were practiced in rejection. He said nothing, but his eyes tracked hers as though searching for some softness.

"It's beautiful," she began to concede, "but it wouldn't be right."

"You opened it?"

"Well . . . yes." Admitting that, she felt at a disadvantage. "I know you mean well . . ."

"I don't mean well. I mean what I feel."

His declaration brought her blush higher. She struggled to maintain a semblance of outward calm while inwardly she was unnerved; her attitude, she felt, seemed conventional and small next to his. And she was flattered.

"I'm a married woman."

It was a last, pitiable defense.

Again he was silent. When finally he said, "I know," she knew he was acknowledging that she had, in the ordinary sense, more to lose than he. This acknowledgment, rather than debasing his gesture in her eyes, gave it a gallant, even noble quality. The depth of his feelings moved and alarmed her, and she couldn't bring herself to say what she should have said at the beginning: I can't accept this gift because I don't feel about you the way you feel about me.

Now she wasn't sure how she felt. She was reduced to shaking her head and repeating, "I can't take it. I just can't accept it." She moved the package across the table toward him and he stopped her, covering her hand with his in a momentary possessive gesture.

"I don't want it back. Give it away. Throw it away." Having worked his hook in, perhaps sensing how deeply, he cut her loose. "You don't owe me anything."

Then he was standing up, the legs of the chair scraping under him, the hired man again, another voice talking. "I was wondering if it would be okay to use the bathtub. It's getting kind of chilly up at the pond and there's no hot water in the dairy. I was thinking of getting cleaned up and taking the afternoon off. Bobby can milk when he gets back. It keeps him in practice."

"Oh, yes, you can."

Janet Vaughn had stood up as well, relieved to be able to be so affirmative, and noticed for the first time the set of folded clean clothes he had brought in with him. Going out, maybe, she thought, wondering where. She led him through the living room to the front stairway and climbed to the landing with him, telling him there were clean towels in the linen closet. She was careful to avoid his eyes. He went on ahead, his limp more pronounced on the stairs, while she stayed on the landing, her heart a heavy pendulum of emotion, her hand trembling on the banister.

In the kitchen she started on their dinner, some pieces of chicken, and tried to ignore the fierce ebb and swell of agitation in her chest. The gold-striped package shimmered in a shaft of sunlight on the table, a magnet pulling at her eyes, tantalizing her until she finally picked it up to put it away in the living room closet. Instead, on an impulse, she opened it for one last peek, and this time tried it on, snapping its tiny circular clasp. She swirled before the mirror, watching her hair skirt up like a fashion model's and the locket moving like something alive just above the swell of her breasts. Then: No, no, no. It was impossible. Communion that morning. Walking in paradise with Jessica Lee. You fool. Hedley nearly dead. Mom practically telling you you couldn't be trusted alone with the man, a wino from Lowell. Grabbing your bum in the hay mow. His finger. Drunk and dumping roses on your lap in front of everyone. And now a trinket. Like taking candy from a baby because you wanted to keep it and wear it around your neck and feel like . . . you silly girl in the mirror.

She had her elbows out and her hands behind her neck, undoing the clasp. It wasn't easy. She placed the locket back in the box and put the box back in the closet and went back to the kitchen. Only now it was the reality of her life she found impossible to sustain — the pile of Charles Porley's shirts, the prospect of driving to Lowell to visit her ghost of a husband, the bills, the goose-pimpled chicken flesh she was breading for frying in this dingy old kitchen, the meat cold and gray as the death we all die.

In a dream, but never more conscious in her life of exactly what she was doing, she washed her hands of the chicken smell and again put the locket around her neck. Going up to the bedroom she shared with her husband, she stood near the linen closet that led to the bathroom and listened to Lucien Quirk splashing water, singing and humming his song: ". . . my sunshine, my only sunshine . . ."

In a state delicious with expectation and fear, she heard him rise in the tub and the released water gurgle down the drain. She pictured him standing there, pictured not so much his nakedness as his vulnerability.

"Lucien," she whispered, calling him directly by his name, something she had scarcely done before. He couldn't have heard her, but his humming stopped as though he had, as though, standing on the threshold, she had no retreat, no turning back to the safe, joyless life she had just fled. "Lucien," she repeated, louder, feeling its glide, *looshun*, on her tongue. The door opened. Expecting him to be naked, she turned away. But he had a towel wrapped around his midsection and was using another to tousle his wet hair.

"Yes?"

He was still the hired man. Then he took in her eyes and the locket.

She had gone as red as his heat-flushed body.

"Do you need clean sheets?" she asked in token pretense. The final move, after all, had to be his.

Lucien Quirk stopped drying his hair and moved into the bedroom, his eyes holding hers.

"Clean sheets?"

Suddenly, as though stricken, she sat on the bed.

"Is everything all right?" he asked, settling next to her,

the towel stretching. "Listen," he began, allowing her a last, slight chance of escape before gently cupping her face in his hands and kissing her softly and then deeply on the lips.

"Oh, God, God," she murmured as his hands flowed, defining her. The towel fell to the floor and her dreams became as real as flesh becomes.

13

THE RED CLOCK, which had a yellowing face and a frayed cord trailing up the wall like a rat's tail, read 8:05, and Janet Vaughn was nagging the boy, who was bent over a bowl of Wheaties. "The bus'll be here soon," she was saying.

" 'most finished," he said, avoiding her glance out of habit. He drained his glass of milk in quick gulps before standing and taking his dishes to the sink.

"And your books?"

"I put them on the chair."

The exchange lacked the animus of school mornings in the past, when he had had to milk the cows and came in with only minutes to scramble into clean clothes and eat his breakfast, the smell of cows on him like a curse, while her anger whined to a rage — hurry, hurry, hurry, and don't eat so fast — and he, getting on the waiting bus with clean suburban kids staring and holding their noses, could have butchered her with a kitchen knife, only the Air Force didn't take murderers.

In the mirror over the sink Bobby Dearborn checked to see if the front fringe of his cropped hair still bristled straight up where he had applied the whiffle stick. It did, but not as stiffly as he wanted it to. His hair tended to lie flat, making him appear, he thought, more like a convict than a fighter pilot. Peering intently at the stubble starting to darken over his lips and down his jaw, he noticed his aunt in the room behind him, framed like an old painting in the dim glass. She slumped in a shapeless dress, hand curled on her lap, listless, her eyes soft with some appeal.

Something had happened. He didn't think that consciously so much as sense it in her giddy, nearly hysterical mood when he came back the day before from the visit to the natural history museum at Harvard. There had been something open, accessible about her, as though he could have asked for anything and gotten it. She had been dreamy one moment and chatty the next, plying him with questions about his excursion with Aunt Ernestine and then not waiting for an answer. She had made a fancy dinner with blueberry pie for dessert and hadn't eaten anything. She had begun to cry in the middle of it, getting up and leaving the kitchen, like a scene in a movie. She's worried about Hedley, Lucien Quirk had said, keeping at the chicken casserole. Now it seemed again as though she had just been crying or was about to. Maybe it was Uncle Hedley again. Bobby Dearborn wanted to ask about him, but he was afraid it would only make her sadder, and he didn't want to do that.

The way the boy watched her in the mirror unsettled Janet Vaughn, who was edgy anyway. She began to move around the room, tidying where there weren't messes and reminding him again that she had put a dime for candy in his lunch bag with the two cheese sandwiches and an apple. He had gotten taller and broader, she noticed. Maybe it was the haircut Ernestine paid for that made his neck look thicker. Like those pictures of Hedley when Hedley was younger, much younger. She winced and continued to fuss, concealing, she hoped, any evidence of what had happened to her the day before. She had expected something so frankly physical to leave visible marks other than the shadows around her eyes from sleeplessness, because her time in bed with Lucien Quirk had been a revelation of the flesh, leaving her both languorous and nervous, fulfilled and yearning, wounded, as though deflowered again. But nothing showed in the mirror or in the boy's eyes, despite his glance. He was his usual self in jeans, zippered jacket, and sneakers, books under one arm. He could have been her son, the way he submitted to her brief hug and kiss, returning the hug with his free hand. An all-American boy. Stay home, protect me, she wanted to cry out, even though she knew what a man's protection entailed. He'd be thirteen soon. That's the age they start. Then the bus honked and he was flying out the door with a "Bye," leaving her in a waft of fresh morning air to face Lucien Quirk, who would soon be coming in for his breakfast.

The air invigorated her and lifted her out of the mood she was in. She took out the ironing board and plugged in the iron and had a cup of coffee before starting to press Charles Porley's shirts. The iron hissed and pointed along the collar, then the yoke, the sleeves, the starched cuffs, the broad back and side panels. The familiar smell of steamed cloth soothed her as the wrinkled shirt turned smooth and crisp under her expert hand. Gladys Porley had ordered several folded for traveling. So she buttoned it and laid it face down to fold it, a two-inch nap along the sides of the bodice that lined up the sleeves she folded at the elbows, a tuck of the tail and a final double fold. Professional. For a few busy moments it seemed that her hardworking, innocent life remained intact. *It* hadn't happened. It could have been a dream.

The sight of Lucien Quirk standing in the doorway of the dairy startled her. He wore a pair of her husband's overalls with the bib pulled high and the trouser legs poked into rubber boots. He whistled as he rinsed the machines, banging metal on metal and pouring milky water down the drain.

She took the bacon out of the refrigerator, peeled off a few slices, and put them into a frying pan over medium heat. She went back to her ironing. It had happened, and the memory of it seeped back, corrosive, palpable as the iron in her hand. His hot skin had smelled of soap and her bra strap snagged and he knelt beside her on the bed to undo it, his thing sticking up like a purple mushroom she wanted to pick and she thought he'd just get on top of her like the others and do it but he was kissing her instead and feeling her all over like a blind man as if he couldn't believe what he had and light as a feather teasing her with his hands and his tongue and just when she thought she couldn't bear it any longer he made her go *oh oh OH* with a long slow stab touching her deeper and wider deeper and wider wider wider until she melted and ran like wax in a flame and the rhythm of it turned to a shudder that kept breaking in her until he lay still and she lay still and thought she'd die or cry and didn't want to think and then didn't have to because he had started firing her again until the white light of the room ran red behind closed lids and she was saying Oh my God oh my God . . .

"Oh my God I am heartily sorry for having offended thee. I detest all my sins because I regret the loss of heaven and the pains of hell . . ." Janet Vaughn murmured the Act of Contrition to herself as she had done all night, punctuating recollections too pleasurable not to be sins. And thinking. To commit adultery once was bad enough, even if God through Father Fahey (the thought of taking to the priest a real sin thrilled and frightened her) would forgive her. It was more difficult to forgive herself for the weakness and willfulness that sent her up the stairs to all but molest the man in his bath. And it wasn't fair to Hedley, even if his condition precluded any confession to him because it might kill him. She sensed and feared most, however, having begun something she could not stop, something beyond the damnation of living in sin, something, a temptation she couldn't quite grasp that was far more profound than the gratification of the flesh. It couldn't happen again.

So again in her dingy kitchen in the middle of ironing Charles Porley's shirts, she contended with the wants of a man. Lucien Quirk had come in wearing her husband's overalls with the cuffs turned up because he'd left the boots outside. And no longer just the hired man. Not that his manner as he washed his hands in the sink and dried them on the towel hanging on the back door indicated any greatly altered status on his part. He kept his distance as he settled at the table with a remark about mastitis in one of the cows. But his eyes looked ready to pounce and his voice nudged, reminding her that they were intimate now. She broke two eggs into the hot grease and poured him a cup of coffee. The normality of it made her tremble. She kept silent and busy, tried to seem natural, angled her body so that she wouldn't appear to be avoiding the gaze she could feel following her.

When she turned to face him with the bacon and eggs, he asked, "How do you feel?"

"Okay."

He nodded and started to eat.

She sat across from him and they gazed directly at each other until she said, "Lucien, I have to talk to you."

"Uh-huh." But the food preoccupied him.

Before this completely unnerved her, she blurted, "It can never happen again. You know that."

He sponged the yellow of a broken yolk with a piece of bread and his lip glistened with fat. Hungry, she thought; how could he be hungry? And the frank puzzlement in his eyes as he wiped his mouth and bent to his coffee vexed her more. He didn't understand.

"I want you to take the locket back." It was a demand and a plea. "I wish . . . I wish . . ." Her eyes went moist and her voice failed her.

"You wish it hadn't happened."

Her head bobbed.

"Well," he started, but stopped to finish his breakfast, chewing his thoughts as the silence conspired around them. Finally, he said, "I can't say I'm sorry for what happened." He reached out a hand and there was nothing sly about him. "But I'm sorry you ain't happy."

Janet Vaughn removed her hand from under his and dried her face with her apron. Composed, outwardly anyway, she sighed and said, "It's just that nothing can come of it."

"Nothing has to come of it."

"Then it ... Lucien, I'm a married woman. I'm a Catholic."

His nod might have been a sneer.

Of course what she said about being married and a Catholic sounded small and paltry next to what had happened. More angry with herself than with him, she lunged with "I'm sorry about yesterday because I don't feel about you what I think you feel about me. I'm not in love with you."

There, it was said. But though she felt better for having taken this stab at the truth, she could feel her resolve giving under the sudden hurt in his gaze.

His tongue busied itself in one side of his mouth and he sucked on a piece of bacon caught between molars, concealing with the nonchalance of a slow nod the sting of her words.

"I don't expect you to," he lied, and offered himself at a lower price. "But we could comfort each other."

"No," she persisted, the word hollow in her heart as the thought of comfort seduced her and the memory of what had happened flashed as their passion had flashed. It would be so easy. They could do it again. Right then. Right there. On the living room floor. On the stairs. Nothing, no one could stop them. There and then. Now. Comfort. She gaped with need but fought it. "No," she repeated with nothing left but negation. "It's wrong. It's a sin."

The man shrugged. "Life is a sin."

She didn't know what it meant, but it sounded like both heresy and the truth. Had he touched her then, taken her hand, she might have yielded.

Instead, Lucien Quirk withdrew. He stood up from the table, poking at a tooth, casual, as though they had been talking about turnips, as though he knew it would happen again and then again and again.

"Speaking of comfort," he said, cocking an eye to include her in his self-mockery, "that shack's going to be getting damn cold at night. I was thinking . . ."

Janet Vaughn rose as well and wished she had remained seated and could appear as offhand about everything as he could. Still, it relieved her to talk about something else. "Oh, yes," she said, her voice and stance proclaiming her again as Mrs. Vaughn, the boss's wife. "You can stay in the spare bedroom. Hedley suggested it earlier." Invoking the authority of her husband seemed strange under the circumstances, but she prattled on nevertheless to the hired man about moving his things into the spare room when she had it cleaned, and cleared the table and raised steam in the sink, propping words and motion between them. Gladys would be in for her ironing. And look at the time. She went on like that until the man retreated to the back door and slogged off in his rubber boots and did not hear the crash of the cup that fell from the woman's trembling hand.

&

Lucien Quirk's dress blues hung clean and pressed with his shirts and chinos in the closet of the spare bedroom. He had pieced together the better of the two broken bureaus and moved the other, with Janet Vaughn's help, up to the attic. She bleached the gray lace curtains, making them plausible again, and the man rewired the wrought iron lamp, for which they found a shade. The room brightened under their touch, despite the stained and faded wallpaper of floral design and the cracked and peeling paint on the trim, the doors, windows, baseboards, and fireplace. The bed, a slatted, sturdy thing painted black, squeaked and had a lumpy mattress. But lumps and all, he found it infinitely more comfortable than the stretched canvas of his cot. And the lumps were not something he or Janet Vaughn noticed during those stolen moments when the old thing whinged and heaved as though party to their lovemaking.

Because it did happen again. His move into the house perhaps made it inevitable. You couldn't consider someone a derelict who slept between clean sheets in your own house. Lucien Quirk had slept there that night and they worked on the room together the next morning with a friendliness that on its surface seemed innocuous enough. She had said she wanted to do it alone, but when he arrived with his things he found excuses enough to linger and lend a hand. Let me help you with that mattress. Let me help you with that bureau. Let me help you. They sweated up the steep, narrow stairway to the attic with the rejected bureau. There in poor light they poked around the boxes and chests, the bits and pieces left by four generations of Vaughns. There was a dress form for a tall, long-waisted woman, a paperback novel in tatters, a parcel of letters, a doll with a carved wooden head, a pair of skates with curved blades, a chamber pot. In an album of old photographs, people in muttonchop whiskers and high-buttoned shoes frowned at them out of the past, as though disapproving. What they found fascinated and depressed Janet Vaughn. All of life's efforts came to this — an attic of leftovers picked over by strangers.

It was a relief to descend to the light and airiness of the spare bedroom. She began to clean out the closet and came across dresses she had worn at her heaviest.

"Good God! Can you imagine me this big!" She held a span of baggy blue cotton in front of herself. "I was huge."

The man lifted his head from the bureau, where he was applying Elmer's Glue-All to a broken drawer runner. He was looking at her face. "You're beautiful in any shape," he said with an unaffected directness that ribboned her heart.

She stifled a sigh and felt the flush warming her neck. She turned away. "God, I never want to be that fat again."

But her words, mostly noise, only emphasized the silence thickening around them. She turned back to glance at where he reclined, still as a statue, on the wide-board floor, golden in that light, watching her. No, she told herself, delving into the depths of the closet, and might have survived the moment had she not come up with a clutch of maternity clothes packed away in the hope of needing them again someday. She let them drop and, with a soft, involuntary moan, turned. He was standing and coming toward her. She waited and told herself it was comfort, only comfort.

But it was more than that.

14

I'M LETTING LUCIEN use the spare room," Janet Vaughn announced to her husband not long after the hired man moved into the house. "It'll be too cold for him down in the brooder house." She said it steadily, right into Hedley Vaughn's trusting face, without fear of betraying herself. She knew the possibility of her committing adultery with Lucien Quirk was not something that would occur to the man. He would nearly have to see it himself to believe it. Infidelity did not often enter his world, and when it did, he refused to acknowledge it except perhaps to tut at some gossip about neighbors or a story in the newspaper. Adultery belonged to an alien class of things, to rock and roll, Hollywood, communism, television, federal troops in Little Rock, organized crime, and city people taking over the land for houses.

Also, he had been too ill for the kind of effort jealousy takes. This time he had been very close to death. Through the long nights and gray days stretching into weeks, time had passed so slowly he had thought it might stop and that would be death. He had suffered pain, the deep, brilliant spasms that left him fumbling for air, and the slow, solid hours of restless discomfort. But he could live with pain and discomfort and the tubes violating his body. What he could scarcely abide was his utter helplessness and the pall of hopelessness that came with it. When will this end, he would ask with his eyes when he could not speak. When will life begin again? It got so he would gladly have agreed to die for a healthy week of walking around the farm, checking, making sure things were ready for the winter. He began to understand why the sick are called patients.

So the fact of Lucien Quirk's moving into the house registered as little more than another necessary detail. Particularly that day when he was feeling measurably better. He sat in the propped bed, his gaunt features tinged with color and his voice with hope as he spoke with enthusiasm about a new treatment the doctors had started. All his healthy life Hedley Vaughn had scoffed at doctors and medicines. It's all up here, he'd say, tapping his head. Or in the blood lines. Now he believed in the miracles of modern medicine because new drugs and the doctors murmuring over his charts and cardiograms like shamans reading bones were his last hope.

"They say it's working out so far. They say if it works, I'll be able to get out of his damn place soon."

His eyes had swept hers then for confirmation.

Janet Vaughn made glad sounds and faces for him. But ambivalence cut her down the middle. Of course she wanted her husband to get better and come home. He was her husband; she loved him, even though that love had shrunk to a kind of tenacious pity mingled with guilt. But she loved him, even though she had to remind herself of the fact. So she sat in the room with the rails on the ceiling and the bedside paraphernalia and gave him what she could of herself. Yes, she nodded, she was sure this new treatment would work, though the last time there were new treatments as well and all of them failed.

A nurse padded by on rubber soles to the patient in the bed near the window whose deodorants and disinfectants didn't quite veil a certain sickly feculence. The nurse's cheery voice rang from behind the drawn curtain. "Time for your shot, Mr. Coughlin."

Hedley Vaughn leaned toward his wife and in a low voice said, "Poor old guy. Had cancer of the gut, and they didn't get it all. Now it's in his lungs and brain. Nice fella, too."

Janet Vaughn already knew about Mr. Coughlin. Her husband had told her before about him, pitying the man's fate, painting a picture of comparative gloom, his way of saying there was hope for him, his way of asking her to hang on. He couldn't know that she had already let go and in her darkest fantasies wished him dead and at best was anxious for the visit to finish so that she could go home. He would never understand — she scarcely did herself — that letting go was her way of hanging on.

❧ 15 ❧

With the advent of late September the skies contracted and deepened and the air had the tang of cider just turned. In the lowlands, where the stream ran cool and full again and where the frost first touched, the bushes flared with color, foretelling the autumnal bloom. The turnips grew a lush carpet of green, and in the garden the drying cornstalks whispered in the tail winds of distant tropical storms. The swallows swarmed and flew south. Each evening now the sun angled down a little more sharply over what had been Mayhew's farm, backlighting with new clarity the frames of split-level bungalows that looked the flimsier for having been tacked with plywood.

Like the season and its spin of heady days, Janet Vaughn's life was constant in its change. Mornings now she shook the ashes from the wood stove and kindled a fire to take the chill off the room. She cleaned the house and cooked their meals and shopped at Koop's or in the dazzle of the supermarket, where she said hello to people she knew and grew weary of telling them that Hedley was doing better but that no (with that sad sigh they expected), she didn't know when he would be coming home. In dreams rich with guilt and in her poor kitchen she sorted eggs and ironed the endless wrinkles from Charles Porley's shirts and heard, sometimes before rising, old Peter the Polack from Golden Vale Dairies reverse the boiler-plated flatbed against the milk house door as he had done for years, to heave aboard the twenty-gallon cans with a great banging of metal on metal.

This was the time of year she canned tomatoes and string beans and, in pickling cukes and onions, suffused the house with the smell of fresh dill and hot vinegar. Together with the man she dug potatoes and pulled carrots for the root bins in the cellar. They chopped cabbage and picked corn, zucchini, purple-black eggplant, the grotesque Hubbard squash. They reaped each other as well, touching and falling like the ripened fruit of the garden, seeded with life in the exhilarating air of those blue and bronze days.

But Janet Vaughn remained troubled. Her lovemaking with Lucien Quirk touched her with a pleasure and guilt that festered, opening in her another, greater yearning she could not grasp or articulate to herself. For though ostensibly gorging now at the feast of life, she felt that something essential was missing. The season may have contributed to the feeling. The lengthening darkness and the sharpening air mingled an atavistic foreboding with a sense of renewed energy and purpose after the sapping heat of summer. But to what purpose? At Mass on Sunday mornings, where she no longer took communion, Janet Vaughn knelt with bowed head and brooded on it.

She grew impulsive. She gave the boy a dollar to buy himself yet another model airplane for simply mowing the lawn and raking leaves. She redeemed her books of Green Stamps for the lamp with the black and brass base to put in her living room; the possession of it gave her an hour of anxious pleasure as she positioned her new article around the old brocade couch in an effort to achieve the best effect. In the end she was disappointed and went out to gather flowers. She brought back fronds of yolk-yellow goldenrod, purple loosestrife, the lace of wild carrots, Turk's-cap lilies from the edge of the lawn, tiny asters of the palest amethyst, her own roses. In the bower of her house she polished and set with candles the heavy dining room table for a dinner of roast pork, gravy, potatoes, string beans, salad, and store-bought chocolate cake, for which, once ready, she found little appetite. At Cherry & Webb she bought on credit a smart fall skirt in gray flannel that clung to her trimming hips and flared in pleats just over her calves, which were shaved and shapely in nylons. She hinted at perfume to Lucien Quirk to go with new lipstick and eye shadow. One evening, alone after a luxurious bath, she put on makeup, scent, new skirt, nylons, sheer blouse, and silver locket. But she had nowhere to take this attractive self. She paced her room, caught in the glass of mirrors like a house-trapped moth fluttering against the solid light of windowpanes.

On an impulse, and out of a mangle of motives, she invited Lucien Quirk to go with her on a visit to her husband. In part, she was being devious. She would show by showing it that she had nothing to hide. Even Hedley Vaughn with his usually keen nose for mendacity would not sniff the lie were it held close enough. It wasn't a rationalization she could abide for long. It only confirmed the wrongness of what she was doing, even if, in bitter privacy, she blamed her husband for what was happening. He had insisted on Lucien Quirk, on hiring him, on keeping him, on bringing him into the house. Well, why not take him to the hospital? She also half-hoped Hedley Vaughn would divine the truth, would shrug his consent, would perhaps forgive her. Finally, she imagined he already knew and had cynically bartered her in a bargain to keep his land and his herd. The farm, after all, was his real passion.

The invitation obviously pleased Lucien Quirk. He finished the chores early to have time to get properly cleaned up for the occasion. He shaved himself ruddy and pulled a brush through his hair and picked lint off his sweater as he checked himself in the mirror. He clattered down the stairs in his new shoes to show himself to her with a big grin and a flourish of tap steps, a little soft shoe and a little soft soap. They might have been going out on a date together. They were so obviously a pair that she panicked at the last moment and asked Bobby Dearborn to go with them. He agreed to, but reluctantly, and she caught a glance from those gray eyes that not long before would have had her boxing his ears. On the silent drive to the hospital she gripped the steering wheel tightly and stared straight ahead, wishing herself as insensate as the fixed trees by the side of the road over whose leaves they swept.

The visit turned out quite differently from anything she expected. Leading the way, scarcely limping, Lucien Quirk strode into her husband's hospital room, his hand out for a vigorous shake as he trumpeted a jovial greeting. "Hey, chief, how're you doing?"

His grinning eyes swung away, came back. Their hands remained clasped.

"I ain't dead yet." Hedley Vaughn met the other's gaze and relaxed.

"Ain't dead for sure. They must be treating you good."

His bonhomie glowed off the polished surfaces in the subdued yellow light of the room.

"Good enough," said the patient. "The food ain't worth feeding to a dog."

"That's right, ha, ha, like the slop they fed us when I had my ass in a sling. Feed it to a dog? Hell, a dog wouldn't eat it!" Then a serious note: "But you are looking better, Hedley" — holding it: "a hell of a lot better" — setting them up: "a lot better, anyway, than the last time I saw you, sitting on the ground like you was trying to milk the bull, ha, ha."

His laughter encompassed the boy and Janet Vaughn, who, still standing in her coat, recoiled at what seemed a mocking and amplified echo of her own betrayal. She hadn't expected this kind of performance. She approached, a reluctant Judas, to peck her husband's cheek. She noticed his farmer's hands, which lay smooth and white on the bedclothes as though embalmed. She shuddered for him.

Yet Hedley Vaughn moved these sepulchral hands to grasp the boy's in another hearty greeting, telling them all to sit down, sit down, as he propped himself up in anticipation of something more than the usual. And she had to admit that the genial mood contrasted with that of her own begrudged attendance, when she spoke without heart about turnips and cucumbers, the cows and the bull — a screen of small facts behind which she huddled with her lie. The two men and even the boy were speaking of the same things, but more naturally. The men in particular had a bond she hadn't suspected. Of course, Hedley was desperate, letting the hired man chummy up to him like that. Common, she almost thought before remembering it was Lucien, her lover, and she blanched at this reflection of her own desperation.

"Bobby here tells me you got the drinkers all working right," the sick man said.

The boy noticed Lucien Quirk stiffening at these words of praise. "Yes, sir," the soldier's voice saluted before it turned on itself and belittled. "It wasn't much. We had most of the bits and pieces kicking around the place except for some pipe. I borrowed the threader from the Dillons."

"Well, I think you did a hell of a job. I couldn't have done it, not in my condition."

The praise embarrassed the hired man, who deflected it with a nod toward the boy. "The captain here did all the rough stuff. He's one hell of a good little worker."

"Eyeah, he's that, all right." Hedley Vaughn turned pleased eyes on the boy. "And he ain't so little, from what I can see."

"That's right."

"Growing like a regular beanstalk."

"He sure is."

A pretty nurse with a pill interrupted this duet of agreement. "Time for your pill, Mr. Vaughn," she chirped from the opposite side of the bed. She poured him water and watched while he swallowed. He might have been a child on his potty or a football team, the way she led the cheers. "Isn't he doing well!"

The visitors were emphatic in their agreement.

"The manure," Hedley Vaughn growled, reclaiming himself from the young woman, who energetically fluffed his pillows.

"We got about half the cellar cleared out," Lucien Quirk reported. "I'll get the rest on the pastures before the snow flies."

"You want to save some for the garden."

The hired man, sitting in the chair next to the bed where Janet Vaughn usually sat, laughed again. "Hell, Hedley, there's plenty left . . . and more where that came from."

The nurse, still smiling, wheeled from the room.

Lucien Quirk clucked out the side of his mouth and jerked his head in a winking motion as he rode the hilarity. "I'd keep an eye on Hedley here, Jan, with all them pretty young things running around the place."

"I ain't too sure I'd be much use to them, condition I'm in," the older man snorted back. But he clearly enjoyed the imputation.

"I'm sure you'd do better than that damn bull of yours."

Janet Vaughn blushed behind a forced smile. The hypocrisy was being spun so thin and so fine, it might not have been hypocrisy at all. As she sat, all nerves, on the hard edge of the chair near the foot of the bed, she couldn't tell whether this man (*your lover!*) was slyly making a fool of her husband in front of her, which would have been unforgivable, or merely, in an attempt to cheer him up, indulging him in the banter of males. Forgive me, Hedley, she prayed, hoping he wouldn't look at her for the truth, because she couldn't lie with her eyes and she knew the truth might kill him. At the same time she resented their rough camaraderie, the bass barking of their laughter. Sex was their ultimate joke, funnier than death. Which she felt rather than thought. They stripped her adultery of its weight and significance. They might have laughed it to a small tawdry thing, the butt of their low jokes. Their bull talk. Perhaps Hedley knew and didn't care. He was leaning forward, head cocked, eyes bright, his old grit showing. She was glad for the presence of the boy. It was as if he understood. His own show of amusement, she could tell, was only politeness.

Then Lucien Quirk, as though sensing her unhappiness, turned to include her in his spell of cheer with a sudden trumpeting about the garden and how the pumpkins were going to be as big as bushel baskets and how that ought to get them a few bucks from Frank Devito. And she was charmed. It was so achingly familiar. It was something lost and forever sought, something big enough to contain all the complications people twist themselves into. It was family. She sat somewhat amazed with that growing realization. He had made them into his family and was playing his parts in it. He was variously her brother and husband. He was Hedley's son and Bobby's father and pal. He was . . . And somehow it didn't matter then if he was nothing more than a consummate charlatan, full of the queasy gratitude the adulterer feels for the cuckold. Because the illusion was better than nothing. He had made a gift of whatever he was. He had touched them all to life. He had seduced everyone now, including the boy, who had forsaken his friends at the pond to dog the man around the farm, starting half his sentences with "Lucien says . . ." And now Hedley, who needed the touch more than anyone. She wanted to reach out and hold all of them. She wanted to weep.

Hedley Vaughn worried aloud about his bull. "We ought to get the vet in again to give him a lookover." He addressed them as one with his eyes, which shifted back and forth with worried, pleading glances. "It could be lonely, you know. Maybe we ought to build a special paddock so it could run with the herd. I read one time where that helps old bulls. And that bull's going on fourteen, come the new year. Hell of an animal all the same. A man from upstate

New York once offered me five thousand for him and that was when five thousand was worth something." He leaned back and closed his eyes and his face appeared sealed, except for the groove of his mouth, which kept moving. "Remember, Jan, how folks used to truck their cows from all over the county to have them serviced before all this foolishness with artificial insemination started? You mark my words, they'll be doing it on people next . . . ain't natural . . ." He dozed against the bank of pillows, his mouth slack around loose dentures, his face delicate in repose, as though age had refined his bones.

Reduced to a vigil, the visitors waited uncomfortably. The woman pulled her chair closer and wanted to take her husband's hand but didn't. The dying man in the next bed groaned in morphined sleep. A nurse whisked by. The intercom called. Time seemed to slow, as though to allow for pain.

Hedley Vaughn woke to the announcement that visiting hours were over. He came to, muttering the loose end of a thought, some fragment of a dream. The embarrassment, which he covered with a cough, colored his abrupt speech. "I'm glad you could make it in, Lucien. I've been wanting to tell you how much Jan and I appreciate what you've been doing. Someday . . ."

Lucien Quirk stood suddenly and blustered disavowal of being owed anything. They shook hands, and the hired man, after some laughing rejoinder about young nurses, retreated with the boy, leaving husband and wife to say goodbye in private.

❧

Later, as Bobby Dearborn lay in bed, he could hear the two adults talking in the kitchen below. The voices, ghostly clear as they carried up the radiator pipe to which he held his ear, did not seem like those of a hired man and the wife of the boss, but of a married couple, more or less equals.

"You were good with Hedley," the woman was saying,

repeating something she had mentioned during the mostly silent ride home.

Lucien Quirk gave what sounded like a dismissive grunt. "He's been through a hell of a lot."

"I mean, you really seemed to get along with him."

Someone struck a match. What the man said was garbled.

"I don't understand." Janet Vaughn sounded exasperated.

"Don't understand what?"

"I don't really understand how you can get along with Hedley . . . I don't see how you can like him."

The man's laugh might have been mocking. "That's simple enough."

"How is it simple enough?"

"Hell, Jan, he took me in when nobody else would . . ."

"He needed you."

"That don't make any difference."

"But I'm his wife!"

Now the boy was out of the bed and kneeling on the floor, his ear near the hole in the floor where the radiator pipe came through.

"I know that," Lucien Quirk was saying.

"So how can you . . .?"

"What?"

"How can you . . ." Her voice dropped to a hot whisper, out of which the boy caught "sleep with me."

There was the sound of a chair sliding, of the man making comforting noises. "He ain't got nothing to do with that."

"He's still my husband."

"I know."

"Then how can you say he doesn't have anything to do with it? He has everything to do with it."

"Hedley ain't got nothing to do with you and me, because I love you."

"Oh, Lucien," Janet Vaughn said after a while of moving

around the kitchen. "I don't know what's going to happen."

Then there was the silence of people sitting in a room together saying nothing. Eventually they turned off the lights and came up the stairs. They took turns using the bathroom. Lucien Quirk went alone into his room next to Bobby Dearborn's. The boy pretended the regular slow breathing of sleep. He listened. A while later he heard or thought he heard or dreamed the floorboards creaking as the man got up and went across the landing to the woman's room.

❧ 16 ❧

"AND HERE'S ONE of Mom smiling."

Ellen Dunn, smiling herself, dealt another snapshot from the pack she shuffled like a cardsharp in the robin's-egg blue of her color-coordinated kitchen.

"Uh-huh," Janet Vaughn murmured, agreeing that it had been something of an accomplishment to make their mother smile. She held, like a weak poker hand, the snaps taken of the lawn party in August. Underexposed, the pictures looked darkened with age, as though what they recorded had happened in some earlier, more innocent time. They recalled for her the attic and the browned portraits of the Vaughn ancestors, clothed in their wing collars and their righteousness. It was just the camera, she told herself. But the haunted sky and the ghostly white tablecloth with the dim figures ranged around it made her wistful. It had all happened before her fall, the new divide in her life. It was all irretrievable.

"That was the day the hired man, remember, brought you the roses. I thought you'd die."

Janet Vaughn nodded and perused her hand. Mom's smile never quite rid her eyes of venom. Hedley smiling. He was such a good man, despite everything. One of herself smiling. Heavier then and happier. But it was, in retrospect, a thin, simpering, dependent happiness; she had made her mother smile.

"Well, Mom had a good time anyway," she said, like a bid or a bet.

"Until the roses arrived," Ellen Dunn came back.

Janet Vaughn sighed inwardly and sipped beer. She had continued to drop by her sister's house from time to time after visiting the hospital, even though it meant talk about Mom's worries and an inquisition of searching glances and unsubtle insinuations about the hired man. She went because the relative normality of her sister's life reassured her and because she was lonely for a closeness that was not infused with sex and guilt. The Dunns lived on Christian Hill in Lowell, a neighborhood of new, modest houses on streets steeply angled over the Merrimack River. There she could relax a little, be an auntie, have a beer, and watch "Gunsmoke" on the Dunns' television. The hulking Marshal Dillon, the anxious Kitty in her saloon, and the philosophical Doc were, she thought, the kind of people who would understand her predicament. She could have driven into Dodge City on a buckboard with Lucien Quirk, and they would have known and would not have judged. In Dodge City she would have been counted among the troubled but the good, which is how she wanted to see herself. The sad fact is that she would have confided in Kitty sooner than in her sister, whom she didn't quite trust.

"Does the hired man still do it?"

"What?"

"Bring you roses?"

Heavy, going on shapeless, Ellen Dunn exuded a hunger for the illicit, for the excitement of sex, which had gone out of her own life. She might not have been so curious had Janet continued to bring her detailed, fascinating complaints about the hired man. When he moved into the house she expected new outrages they could pick apart together. Janet had failed her. Instead of better, juicier gripes, she had practically stopped griping altogether — about anything, about the man, the boy, the farm, her miserable kitchen. And sister Mary or even husband Steve, for all their faults, were paltry stuff for gossip next to the riches she knew her sister was hiding. Their closeness had suffered.

Janet Vaughn blinked in the reflected fluorescence and noticed, as she feigned a laugh, that the table top of patterned Formica needed wiping. "Oh, I put a stop to that long ago." It was a truth of a sort. She elaborated on safer ground. "Besides, I have roses of my own and all kinds of wildflowers. This year they're really gorgeous. Lucien says it was the wet spring and the dry summer. You should come out for some."

And see for yourself.

The other woman was not to be distracted. "How do you stand it?"

"What?"

"Oh, Jan, having this *Lucien* around the house!"

She had mimicked her sister's pronunciation of the name and had pulled her chair closer. Her body hunched and her eyes widened in a silent plea to be told.

Janet Vaughn resisted. "He's there. I have to put up with it. If Lucien left, Bobby would have to do the chores again, and I don't want that. What's the use of complaining?"

"What's he really like?"

"I don't know. He keeps to himself."

It was too obvious a lie for both of them not to feel the shock of the truth it concealed.

Rebuffed, Ellen Dunn stood up to get another bottle of Schlitz out of the refrigerator.

"Beer?"

"I'm fine," Janet Vaughn said cheerfully, but it sounded like another refusal.

"Keeping slim, huh?" Lighting a cigarette, Ellen Dunn went on in a voice edged with sarcasm. "I mean, what's he like around the house? Does he leave messes? Is he a grouch? Does he help at all?" She stopped abruptly, aware perhaps of projecting her own domestic woes. Steve Dunn, still sprawled in front of the television with a beer, was anything but neat and good-natured around the house.

Janet Vaughn shrugged. "He seems tidy enough."

"Steve said his shack . . ."

"That's when he was drinking."

"He's stopped?"

"As far as I can tell."

"Really?" Ellen Dunn swallowed beer and allowed herself a soft belch before leaning closer again and half-whispering, "Aren't you tempted? I mean, if he's sober . . ."

"Sure."

Janet Vaughn admitted to temptation with alacrity, another easy truth. But she couldn't return her sister's glance. She came close to blurting it all out, because it was taking too much to sustain the lies and half truths and evasions and split loyalties that grew out of her infidelity and that spread to entangle everything and everyone she touched. She wanted suddenly to share the guilt and the ecstasy of it, to mention details, to ask advice, to weep with a friend, to have an audience for her lonely passion, for the melodrama her life had become. She tottered for a moment, glancing around, then resisted the impulse. She might have talked, had the kitchen table not needed wiping or had she, at bottom, trusted her sister. But she knew family politics to be as brutal as any other; anything she told her sister would eventually get back to Mom. The grim mouth would judge. They would all turn on her. So she sat peering down at her glass of flat beer and trying to think of something she could say, some confidence or complaint that would signal her essential if qualified allegiance to her sister.

"Actually, he's very handy," she found herself saying.

"Handy?" Ellen Dunn palmed the word and threw it back. "I bet he's handy."

"He wants to help me fix up the kitchen. I'm thinking of putting down a new floor . . . and maybe putting in a new sink."

"What'll Hedley say to that?"

"I don't care what Hedley says. I'm sick of living in that

kitchen with that floor and that sink. If Hedley had his way, we'd still be using the outhouse." She got up for another beer.

"You're really going to do it?"

Janet Vaughn opened the long-necked bottle and poured too decisively. It foamed over, but she didn't care.

"I'm not going to stop living because Hedley's in the hospital."

There, she had intimated everything now. She had also realized for the first time that she would have her new kitchen.

"I thought you had bills?"

"We do . . ." She trailed off, letting beer fuzz the roof of her mouth and trying to think her way around debt to a new floor and a new sink. "We'll just have to have one more."

Ellen Dunn collected the snapshots and put them back in the yellow envelope. "If I were you, I'd just go ahead and do it and not listen to anyone else." She nodded her head meaningfully. "I'd just go ahead and do it."

17

FROM A TIGHTENING KNOT of old wood where she breathed, a gleaming new surface spread to cover the kitchen, the yard, the farm, and the fields. It's much easier to clean, she explained to an angry Hedley. To prove it, she uncoiled the hose across the spreading sheen and turned on the water. See? But it all melted like snow, revealing the old floor, the hired man, the boy, the world she woke to in a sweat of expectation. Because Janet Vaughn was going to have her new floor and her new sink, however distressing her dreams. She would have her new kitchen no matter whether it meant fudging once again the economic reality represented by the ledger of debt she pulled from the old desk in the dining room where they kept the accounts.

On a piece of paper she added up the pluses and minuses. With production, the milk check came to more than five hundred dollars. Devito had given them nearly seventy dollars for the last load of produce. They would get at least a hundred for eggs. And she had some fives and tens squirreled away from produce they had sold that summer. It all seemed substantial enough until weighed against the heft of debt: the Agway grain bill, more than fifteen hundred, on which they wanted at least a hundred and fifty; the land-bank loan, with a quarterly payment due that month; a brusque warning from the Farmall dealer; the semiannual mortgage, due in December (they would have to sell at least a couple of yearlings, with feed low); overdue electricity bill; the vet's bill for the bull; the druggist's calling personally, sugar and acid in his voice; and the hospital charges piling into the thousands, which made it all seem absurd anyway.

She found herself seeking the boy's approval the way she might have sought Hedley's had he been there. "What do you think, Bobby, about doing the kitchen over?" she had asked one evening at supper with a smile and an openness that made him cautious. "Wouldn't a new floor and nice sink make it much better in here?" And it hadn't merely been talk. She had watched him, waiting for some reply, some nod of assent, which he gave, but uncertainly, it not being his place to approve.

"Sure," he had mumbled in his food and glanced around, nodding. He knew something like this was afoot; he had heard them discussing it at night downstairs after he had gone to bed. He sensed, if only dimly, that the talk about improving the kitchen was part of some larger intrigue, some fundamental duplicity in the air around him. He knew his uncle wouldn't approve of any new floor or new sink. In the past, kitchen improvements had been a chronic sore spot. Hedley Vaughn would listen impassively to his wife's pleas as they waxed to outrage. Eyeah, he'd say, we'll get to it, then would change the subject.

Linoleum, Janet Vaughn learned over the phone, cost around three dollars a square yard. So on her hands and knees, pulling and stretching a tailor's tape, she measured the kitchen. Roughly eighteen by fifteen, if you counted the short hall from the back door and the pantry. Two hundred and seventy square feet divided by nine and multiplied by three. Ninety dollars, plus felt and paste. Say a hundred dollars. The kind of sink she wanted plus fittings cost more than a hundred and fifty. But Lucien Quirk said he knew of a place in Pawtucketville where you could get things cheaper.

Clutching her envelope of tens and fives together with the checkbook, she drove with the hired man and the boy into Lowell and crossed the river. She had forgotten how easy it is to buy something, how all you do is give someone money and they give you what you want. Her hands sweated and she bit her lip when the salesman, smooth and snide and reassuring, invited them to buy up the store. They leafed through the heavy tome of linoleum. The boy watched silently as they considered a red and white checkerboard, a flaked, rusty brown, an imitation tile, and a sunflower yellow, before finally picking a simulated old red brick to go with what Janet Vaughn was now calling her "traditional" kitchen.

Choosing a sink was more difficult. The place had an acre of modern kitchens — sinks, fittings, counters, dishwashers, cabinets, lighting, refrigerators, stoves. It wasn't fair. Her head was turned this way and that, and the salesman kept smiling and nudging until she nearly lost her nerve, with the boy watching. At last she settled on a stainless steel double sink with a pull-out sprayer included in the fixtures and a length of three-quarter-inch plywood veneered with brick red Formica for the counter to match the floor. And while they were at it, they might as well paint the walls and the ceiling before laying the new floor and putting in the new sink. And a new light for the ceiling, reminded Lucien Quirk. And some red material for new curtains, which she would get at a fabric shop on the way home. Janet Vaughn was too nervous to take pleasure in the acquisitions. They were buying so much. She handed over the crumpled bills and wrote a check with trembling hand. They couldn't afford it, she kept thinking, as they tied the roll of linoleum wrapped in brown paper to the top of the car and wedged the carton containing the sink into the back seat. It was like stealing, like infidelity.

They stole time, as well. For a week, ignoring all but the essential chores, the three of them patched and painted the ceiling, scraped and painted the wide-board walls an off-white semigloss. It already looked better. After she had made a quick visit to the hospital (telling her husband they were fixing up the kitchen a little), Janet Vaughn worked with Lucien Quirk into the evening until they were exhausted and exhilarated by their progress and the cups of coffee they drank to keep themselves going. Then, creeping up the stairs, they stopped to listen for the boy's regular breathing before culminating the day in the darkness of her bed.

Using a pinchbar, Lucien Quirk and Bobby Dearborn pried loose the old sink and tore out the timbered base on which it rested. The boy played apprentice and watched admiringly as the man constructed a new frame, to which he secured the Formica counter. Laboriously, using a coping saw, the man cut out a section to fit the sink and, with a thick bit in the brace, tapped holes for the fixtures. The sink went in snugly, lipped around by a rubberized gasket. He plumbed the taps and the drain. He turned on the water and made her smile and give them each a big kiss and a hug. He kept going that day far into the night, trimming the counter with a strip of chrome and fashioning doors below from leftover counter material.

The next afternoon the man and the boy pulled up the old floor. They used square-headed spades to scrape up the tar where it stuck to the old boards. Where the nails protruded, they pounded them flat, and where the boards were loose, they nailed them firmly against the joists below. When they had it all ready, Lucien Quirk cut and laid the felt-paper base. Then he cut and pasted the linoleum, easing it into corners and rolling it into a seamless, level expanse.

Janet Vaughn hovered, pleased beyond her dreams and anxious about what people would say when they saw it. The floor went perfectly with the sink counter and with the red and white check curtains she ran up on her sewing machine. Her kitchen gleamed under the halo of fluorescence Lucien Quirk had installed in place of the single hanging bulb. She got the boy to help her carry out the old arm-chair, but she stopped short of throwing it out. The Glen-wood remained. Lucien Quirk blacked its cast iron surfaces and polished its chrome. Still, it didn't belong. The temp-tation to buy a new range gnawed at Janet Vaughn even as her feet squeaked on the new floor and as she gave orders for no boots in the house. But they couldn't afford to buy a new stove and they couldn't afford to heat with just oil. They already owed too much. And there was a more intan-gible account with Lucien Quirk. You don't owe me any-thing, he said when she repeatedly expressed her gratitude. But he drew closer; his gestures became more possessive, his hand coming down on her haunch even with the boy in the next room. And his eyes watched and waited for her to return the declaration of love he had repeated while poised over her, stroking, worshiping, alarming her with his inten-sity. So the old stove remained, sturdy and ugly and old-fashioned, a reminder of Hedley.

The renovations had, for Janet Vaughn, a gratifying ef-fect on Gladys Porley who, mouth agape with wonder, stood holding her bag of dirty shirts in the doorway.

"Well . . ."

"We're getting it ready for Hedley," Janet Vaughn lied, feeling the need suddenly to explain her extravagance even as she saw through the other woman's eyes all the little defects that remained.

"Well, Hedley must be getting better. What a relief that must be for you! It's unforgivable that we haven't been in to see him this time . . . Charles has been so busy, and get-ting the boys ready for school . . . But look at what you've done! A new sink, too! And a new light!"

"Lucien, the hired man, did the hard parts."

"Really?"

"And Bobby helped too."

Janet Vaughn had said too much. To deflect attention from the handiness of the hired man, who had a bed of his own upstairs and moved about the house with the air of a permanent resident, she took the woman into the living room to show her the new lamp.

"Yes, it does go well with the sofa," sang Gladys Porley, who, they both knew, would have died before letting that poor sagging thing into her richly appointed home. But she had kind sentiments. "I'm so glad things are going better for you, Janet," she went on. "You've been through so much." Her mouth grimaced for Lucien Quirk, who had come in and stood, back against the sink in his stocking feet, all but touching his forelock while the woman screeched compliments at him through Janet Vaughn. She had never met a derelict before, not even a reformed one. She stopped abruptly because something, a glance or the man's stocking feet or telepathy, revealed them to her — naked, coiled in an embrace so passionate that she blushed for them and began apologizing for intruding. At the door she recovered enough to turn and blurt something about the shirts. Then she retreated to sit, fascinated and trembling, in the creamy interior of her car.

When Ernestine Vaughn came in for the first time since the renovations, she stepped on the new linoleum as though it were thin ice. Her smile dimmed a shade.

"You've been busy, I see," she declared quietly.

"Yes, Lucien did most of it . . . and it didn't really cost that much," explained Janet Vaughn, because they owed Ernestine money.

"Well, it's very nice," said the older woman, glancing around. "Very nice. But I think Hedley will miss his chair."

18

Bobby Dearborn positioned himself about equidistant from the man and the woman as he leafed through an old *Life* and tried to look serious. They were arguing.

Janet Vaughn was defending herself. "We had to call the service, Hedley. The bull won't breed. You know that."

"You ought to have taken her to the Patersons."

Lazarus-like, dignified in a hospital bathrobe and no longer wearing a cast, Hedley Vaughn occupied the chair next to the bed. He was able to get up now and move around a good bit. He was well enough to be crotchety. Not so long ago he would not have dreamed of taking one of his herd to the Patersons to be bred.

"The Patersons sold their bull. I called."

"What did you breed her to?"

"A Holstein . . . a purebred. We can get the papers."

"It ain't the same. They dilute it, like everything else these days. It'll ruin the herd. We ought to have kept that last bull calf. I could kick myself."

"Well, I don't know what else *we* could have done."

She spread the blame a little. It had been Lucien Quirk, after all, who had taken a managerial tone and told her they ought to call the service. He didn't believe in the dilution of the species. It was true that she agreed with the hired man and had gone out to the barn with him and the boy when the man arrived from the artificial insemination service to breed the cow. The man had brought along a black bag of stoppered test tubes containing, like ice cream flavors, the sperm of a dozen registered bulls — Holstein, Ayrshire, Brown Swiss, Jersey, Guernsey, Angus, Hereford, even Milking Shorthorn. He had put on a long white smock, and the three of them had stood and watched as he reached a rubber-gloved arm into the back end of the cow to clean the dung out of the last few feet of intestine. They had hovered, too engrossed for embarrassment, as though the technician, sudsing off his soiled limb in a bucket of water, might mount the cow himself. It came down to a simple, clinical procedure. He probed the cow's vulva with a long glass tube, slid it in, and blew home the watered semen with an air-filled rubber bulb. The anticlimax left them feeling a little foolish. The man signed a paper, took six dollars, and left with his bagful of bulls. Hedley was right about its not seeming very natural.

"You ought have asked me first."

He had his pipe out and was poking it full of Edgeworth and lighting it, his lips puckering intently around the stem. The bits and pieces of him were coming back. Soon, she knew, he would be in overalls, shambling around the farm, trying to reclaim it, a ghost haunted by a place.

"Well, it was that or let the cow go dry."

Her voice, mechanical and provocative at the same time, struck a false note and made him snort smoke, as though for the first time he sensed the usurpation, the other voice coming through hers. Something else she mentioned in passing tantalized him. If only he could remember.

Bobby Dearborn had gotten to the cover story in the old *Life:* "A Scientific Race Against Time to Launch the First Man-Made Moon." America's first satellite, still earth-bound, reflected crewcut scientists on its convex silvered surface. In another photo its intricate innards were displayed on a table. And a drawing depicted the curve of the Vanguard rocket's projected flight from Cape Canaveral to the edge of space. The boy frowned. Sputnik had just gone into orbit, and he took it personally. The Russians, right then, were high overhead, circling, beeping. He turned to an article about Marilyn Monroe. There was a back view of her in lace-fringed bloomers.

"A new floor in the kitchen, you say?" Hedley Vaughn asked, putting down the bitter pipe. He had remembered.

"We had to. It was all pulling up in front of the sink. The floorboards were rotting."

The boy heard the woman's fib. She had torn up the lino herself. The boards beneath were stained, not rotted, Lucien Quirk had said. But they would rot. He had heard the man and woman convincing themselves, justifying the work with conspiracy in their voices. It was part of the larger sexual collusion they could not conceal from him. He had realized their actual intimacy only dimly at first — in the way the tension between them suddenly became more expectant than defensive, in their coded glances and their sometimes unsubtle contrivances to get him out of the way. And, though he didn't think it fair, he ultimately hadn't judged. It seemed natural that one man would replace another, who, for whatever reason, had left. And he hadn't, in fact, seen it until a few days before, when, peering down at them from the hay mow, he had caught the man, in an act so swift it might not have happened, run his hand down her back and over her bottom. Her protestations had been tactical. Watching them, the boy shuddered. Men touched women like that. Naked. The vision in the keyhole came back. He had undone his jeans to hold himself where his excitement had knotted into blood-gorged flesh.

"Lucien put it down," the woman was saying.

"Is that so?"

"We also put in a new sink and painted the walls."

"And what did all that cost?"

"It was less than three hundred. Sink and everything."

"Ain't the mortgage due in December?"

"We'll have to sell a couple of yearlings. We don't have enough to feed all of them, anyway."

"Who says?"

"You said . . . when you decided to plant the turnips."

She kept her gaze steady and defiant. Her lying had become better with practice.

"I don't remember that."

"You don't remember a lot of things, Hedley."

Janet Vaughn was prepared to get nasty in defense of her kitchen. She noticed the boy's gaze.

"Would you like to go for a Coke, Bobby?"

"Sure."

She fished a dime out of her purse and gave it to him. Then she braced to defend herself. But her husband was leaning back, pale, his eyes closed. After a moment he spoke. "I ought to get back into bed, Jan. Would you help me?"

The cafeteria was empty except for a couple of older nurses in cardigans. Bobby Dearborn sipped a Coke and daydreamed. Cynthia Kirkpatrick had smiled at him in the corridor. It wasn't much of a smile, but at least she hadn't looked away. If he were in her class, he could call her up and ask her about homework assignments. If he were in the Civil Air Patrol, he could wear the uniform with the garrison cap and fly out of Hanscom, looking for missing aircraft. He'd come back to school in his uniform, dead tired because he'd had to parachute with supplies to survivors of an airliner that crashed high in the White Mountains of New Hampshire. He'd become a secret ace and, on the most secret mission in history, the Air Force would send him up in one of the X-designated rocket planes, straight up, higher than any man had ever dared to fly, to shoot down the Russian Sputnik. Cynthia Kirkpatrick would notice him then as she walked in the corridor in her soft sweater and tight skirt and white socks and her penny loafers, hugging her books, with her freckles and chestnut hair and wide lips so fine he thought he might simply inhale them.

As he dawdled back to his aunt and uncle, he saw in the rooms along the way visitors paying homage to the sick with reverent faces, flowers, and other offerings. As though the sick were deities in need of propitiation. He did not understand illness or why old people with their gray, spent lives clung to existence. It would never happen to him. He would never go out like this, mewling in a bed, surrounded by old people. He would go down in flames and glory. He would disappear into mystery. He would get blasted to heaven. If there was one.

When the boy got back to the room, he noticed that his uncle was in bed and the woman had pulled her chair closer and was holding his hand and talking to him in a low, conciliatory voice. Not wanting to intrude, he stood just outside the door, waiting, restless, mystified by the complexities of human love.

❧ 19 ❧

THE WEEK'S COLLECTION of eggs lined the short hallway from the back door to the sink in a row of wire baskets. Janet Vaughn stood at the kitchen table, sorting the eggs according to size. Her hands moved rapidly, from basket to scale to one of three large cartons, as she fingered the soothing shapes in mindless repetition. The color-coded scale registered small, medium, large, extra large, and jumbo. The small and cracked eggs she kept for the house; the jumbo she set aside for Koop's. Some of the eggs were dung-smeared and needed washing, and the odd rotten one that rattled she threw in the stove. When she finished a basket, she stacked it in the woodshed and lifted a full one to the table.

It was a Saturday afternoon. A late October rain stripped the withered leaves from the branches she could see moving in the wind through the beaded windows. The rain alternately pelted and dribbled, was soft and staining, mild as the day was mild in the tag end of Indian summer. Through the window she could look out on the denuded garden and the smear of bright green where the turnip field started. Afternoons now the man and the boy loaded the smaller wagon with turnips to feed to the cows after milking. They had half the field cleared. Soon the hard frosts would come, shriveling even the tough purple tops as the land closed in a frozen fist that would not loosen until late March brought the muds of spring. Mostly her eyes were on the simple aluminum scale and the crates with the honeycombs of cardboard dividers into which she slipped the eggs. Wood chinked as it settled in the stove. She could hear her own breathing, which sounded like sighs. She took comfort in the relentlessness of the rain.

Janet Vaughn had begun to fret with a fear that was also a sublime hope. At times like this, as she stood there sorting eggs with the rain tattering the world, she was absolutely sure. It was nothing as obvious as morning sickness. Her body had not yet responded quite the way it had in the first few weeks of Jessica Lee. Still, she felt or imagined she felt the hormonal tide washing through her abdomen like an inner foaming of breaking bubbles that could make her gasp suddenly and leave her trembling. They had done nothing to prevent it. She rummaged back through the weeks and in the shuffle of days and nights found she couldn't remember when she had had her last period. August perhaps. Her monthly flow, irregular at best, wasn't something she watched very closely. It always came, sooner or later, a true curse. So she wasn't all that certain, after all, and at times the inner foment seemed just another of nature's pranks, like the double yolk sometimes found in a jumbo egg.

But the conviction that she was pregnant, a conviction spun of wisps and wistfulness and real things, grew as the days darkened dramatically with the return of standard time. She lingered in the nursery, where she dusted the bassinet and fluffed the pile of unused diapers, imagining in their softness the smooth skin of a baby. There, with the crib and the sweet dry scent of baby powder, she could conjure up the chubby limbs and tiny hands of another newborn, a being other than the ghost of her Jessica Lee. These imaginings, at times like apparitions, transformed the small room from the sepulcher of her dreams to a shrine of hope. A child now, even as the living tissue of her adultery, would redeem everything, would justify her infidelity and the thousand attendant lies. More than anything, it would simply *be* — her child, her baby, her life.

Then she would remember: *Hedley's coming home.* And the enormity of being pregnant by another man would unhinge her dream and unravel her courage. Then the whip and rattle of the elements intimidated her, and the feel of the eggs no longer soothed. Or, out in the world, talking to her mother on the phone or delivering the jumbos to old man Koop, an erratic, inner tug would make her blanch with fear, as though what she carried was not new life but some secret, killing cancer. She remembered the time that Esther, the oldest Dillon girl, came back from a summer in England and had to be sent away again. The way people went on about it. Gladys Porley's slitting face when she gossiped about it. And Janet Vaughn had made the right noises, throwing her little stone even though she secretly envied the girl — until she came back without her child and had that vacant, wounded look in her eyes. Now it would be her turn. Now Gladys Porley would whisper her name with the neighbors. She could even hear the damning words, the malice tinctured with pity. *Well, what did you expect? I mean, they let him into the house with her all alone except for the boy . . . some kind of derelict . . . from Lowell . . . And her husband in the hospital . . . I mean, really!*

There would be the awkward physicalness of it. To what Mass would she take her newly burgeoning self? People would stare. And with the word getting around, would old man Koop still take her jumbo eggs and stop to complain about the supermarket putting him out of business? Would Gladys Porley take her shirts to Tsongas in Lowell? And Frank Devito, who might be jealous, and Ernestine, whose smile would freeze. Their averted glances haunted her as she picked through a clutch of straw-stuck eggs and reminded herself to tell Bobby to clean the nests. His silences might condemn, too. And Ellen. She wouldn't forgive, because she hadn't been confided in. Not that Ellen would desert her entirely. She would visit — like some brave nun visiting a leper colony — a herald of family outrage. *Mom's heartbroken, you know. The doctor's worried about her. It's her heart. Her liver. Her spleen. She doesn't understand why you did this to her.* And any drip of sympathy or understanding would be rendered at the price of moral slavery. Ellen, she feared, could be as big a bully as her husband, Steve Dunn.

Janet Vaughn fed wood to the fire and went back to weighing eggs and sorting through her dreams and terrors. Hedley was coming home. The day before, his hospital slippers had slapped along the corridor as he walked her to the elevator and rode down with her to the entrance. Two more weeks, three at the most, he had kept saying, his mouth smiling around the stem of his pipe. Couldn't wait. His arm had encircled her shoulder, reclaiming her. So now her hands trembled as they flew from basket to scale to crate. She tried to visualize the scene, the words, the reality of telling her husband she was pregnant. It would be right there, in the kitchen with the new floor. She would sit him down at the table. She would say, Hedley, I have something to tell you. And he would nod and take out his pipe. Hedley, while you were in the hospital . . .

But she could not imagine herself actually saying it to him. She could not imagine him comprehending it, let alone accepting it. And what she could not imagine, she could not abide. So her dream broke then. She denied that anything was happening to her at all and called herself a silly fool of a woman to think she was going to have anyone's baby. It had happened enough times before — the inner tug and the sickish fullness — and she had, except with Jessica Lee, been disappointed. And Jessica Lee . . . The silence of rain was broken by her abrupt whinny, something that was akin to hysterical release, something that left her with the relief and emptiness that comes when a long-suffering loved one finally dies.

Emptiness.

She stacked an empty basket outside in the woodshed and started on a full one. Medium, large, extra large. Brown and white. The odd ones. Like people. Rain quicksilvered the windows. She peered out at the stripped branches and the vague gray sky and saw emptiness. And in that void her truth slowly gathered around her, accumulated with the handled eggs dropping into their slots, resolved before her out of thin air: this life was not enough. It would be the same tomorrow and tomorrow and tomorrow until she got old and sick and blinked off into nothingness. So she palmed the eggs and brooded then, as she had before, on the desolation of her life until the germ of that vital dream sprouted again, and again she hummed to herself, content with merely the hope of a dream. She hummed away the emptiness until finally, still for a moment in a silence defined by the rain and the small sounds of the kitchen, mind and body were one and she knew: life, new life, was inevitable. All the shame in the world could not stop it.

Other doubts and fears gnawed at Janet Vaughn's dream. Even when she could countenance the averted eyes and stiff silences of those she loved, she still had to account to God for what she was doing. That involved suffering more than the finely honed guilt of an American Irish-Catholic upbringing. In the iron logic of her faith and in the deal she had struck with God, Janet Vaughn could not hope for some celestial reunion with her Jessica Lee and at the same time deliberately go about conceiving a child by a man other than her husband. Adultery was a mortal sin. Were she to die then, she believed, her soul would burn in hell for all eternity. Mortal sin made her an outcast from the mythical body of the Church. She could no longer approach the altar rail and take the wafer that opened the gates to that green and white hope of a perfect existence in a time when time was gone. She would not confess her sin and ask God to forgive her. And contrary to the popular notion that Catholics may sin and confess and sin again with impunity, Janet Vaughn understood the more demanding requirements of penance: she would be forgiven her adultery only if she resolved never to commit it again. But that she could not contemplate. Her stolen time with Lucien Quirk still burned with a narcotic, if somewhat diminishing, flame. She might have been able to resist if Hedley had been there or if she had prayed to the Virgin and gone on novenas or simply shared her need with someone else. But there was more than the pleasure of it. Indeed, the pleasure of it signaled its deeper significance. That, embryonic at first, had unfolded with time to a dreadful and thrilling realization as obvious as the flesh of her own body: she wanted a child.

Janet Vaughn wanted a child more than she wanted her own life. Janet Vaughn knew exactly what she was doing and took responsibility for it. She judged herself. She admitted her transgression as deliberate and her passion as purposeful. She was, for a few clear-headed, bracing moments of self-truth, ready to risk the loss of her faith. Jessica Lee was dead and gone. Even if the priest had baptized her, was there really anything beyond the moment you cease and become mere matter? What was that next to the reality of a child, another life? She would risk the essential blasphemy of women who, in having children, provide the only real resurrection of the flesh. A priest more astute than Father Fahey would have accused her of the sin of pride.

But her hand faltered. An egg got away, rolled off the table, and smashed softly on the newspapers she had put down to protect her new floor. As Janet Vaughn gathered the mess of broken shell and ruptured yolk in a peel of newsprint and fed it to the stove, she was touched with terror. God, the divine sorter of men, who separated the clean from the soiled, the cracked from the whole, and the good from the bad, did not have an infallible hand either. In the shattered egg she saw her Jessica Lee, her own life.

A sound at the door made her start. The world, which would judge her more immediately than any God, intruded in the form of Bobby Dearborn. He came in in his tentative way, as though still a stranger in the house, and stood before the sink.

"I was looking for Lucien," he said in his clumsy voice. The sight of the eggs put him on guard. He used to have to help sort them and wash the dirty ones, trapped for hours until he wanted to smash them.

"Lucien," she said, distracted by the flames of the stove and thinking that the boy would not judge harshly. He appeared so much like Hedley now that he might have been her own son if they had had one, although the Gilooly men ran to shortness. She gazed at him until a sudden prickling of fear and realization started: maybe God had sent the boy instead of a baby, and her sin had been to reject him. "Lucien," she repeated, the name dawning on her, bringing her back to the kitchen, the eggs, and the rainy day. "Lucien's gone to Lowell."

"Do you know when he's coming back?"

She shook her head.

"We were going to fix the ignition on the tractor." He could feel acutely the distress of the woman as she began sorting eggs again, her back not quite to him. "I got the starter off and taken apart. I think I've found the trouble." It was an attempt at good news.

She turned from the scale with an expression so strange, she might have been a different person. "Oh, Bobby, will you ever forgive me?"

His puzzlement looked like scorn. "For what?"

She had difficulty putting her sins into words. Holding an egg, she fumbled at it until the truth came. "For being so mean. For not loving you."

He was confused. He had not been asked to forgive anyone before; not an adult, anyway. He shrugged, and she turned back to the eggs, her hands gliding again from basket to scale to crate.

Something remained unresolved in the air as he stood there a while longer, watching her and listening to the gush of water in the downspout outside the window.

"I'll be out in the barn with the tractor . . . for when Lucien gets back."

She nodded her averted head, and he could tell that she was crying again and didn't want him to see. He pretended he didn't notice and kept his voice normal as he repeated about his being out in the barn. He left, lingering a moment in the woodshed outside the door, where the newly sawed firewood, not quite seasoned, gave off a faintly urinous odor. Piss oak, they called it. He had a sense of freedom he wasn't sure he wanted. Strange how easily the glue of the world lets go. At least there had been something binding in the way she used to get mad at him; she paid some kind of attention, even if he had hated it. Now he could come and go as he pleased. He could fix the tractor or play with his friends. Not that Bobby Dearborn explicitly thought all this; it came rather as a sensation mingled with the sad tang of the wood, as a qualm. Maybe, he thought, I should have stayed and helped her with the eggs.

❧

The bus stopped in Chelmsford Centre in front of Page's Drugstore. Lucien Quirk climbed down with the stringed box from McQuaid's of Lowell tucked under his old service trenchcoat, which was more warm than waterproof. He started walking toward Elmsbury, one arm holding the package against him, his free hand cowling a cigarette to keep it dry enough to smoke. When cars approached from behind him, he turned but didn't put out his thumb. The rain blew with the wind, one moment easing, the next moment slanting into trees and houses, dancing and running on the road until it seemed the whole distorted world might liquefy and flow away. Head down, neck wet, mind ticking over, he soldiered on, oblivious of the downpour.

He had begun to think of murdering Hedley Vaughn. It was like an itch he could not scratch. He imagined the act without really wanting to, the scene occurring to him with nearly mechanical dispassion. Janet would be out of the house. The old man, home from the hospital, would be upstairs taking a nap. He would come in quietly with a pillow and gently suffocate him while he slept. No fuss, no mess, no suspicion. Died quietly in his sleep at home after a long illness, the obituary would read. Then, after a decent interval — Lucien Quirk knew and respected the conventions — they would be married. They would live happily ever after.

But he could not sustain the fantasy for long before it snagged on some outcropping of pride. He wasn't a murderer; murderers were bad guys, like bums, and he wasn't a bum. He had killed, but only other soldiers in combat. There was a difference. Besides, she might find out he did it, might *know* and not forgive. He was afraid that, despite everything, she still loved the old man. Each time she returned from the hospital nowadays she announced the imminent return of her husband. He took it as a warning, as a threat. And now too at odd moments she wept to herself. She wouldn't tell him why; she wouldn't let him touch her. Then she'd be all over him, a bundle of need. Christ, he thought, but did women ever know what it was they wanted so badly. So he took one day at a time. Like war. Each day might be your last. One day at a time until . . . until the old man came back and he would find himself out in the cold. Alone.

The rain sheeted. Lucien Quirk trudged on, his head a tangle of love and murder.

&

He hung up his water-heavy trenchcoat in the woodshed and took off his boots. On wet feet he went by the remaining basket of eggs to where she stood, the fixed star of his life. She showed more concern for him, it pleased him to notice, than for the paper-covered floor on which he dribbled or for the package he carried.

"Oh, look at you!" she exclaimed, and from a closet brought out a dry towel. "You'll catch your death. Did you have to walk from Chelmsford?"

The man toweled his head and suddenly felt warm and

exhilarated, more heroic than after any nasty firefight with the Japs. "Partway," he said, and backed against the heat of the stove. "One of the Dillon boys picked me up in their truck. I bought myself a sports coat. I got you a little present, too. It's in the box."

She was already hovering over it, apron up as she wiped her hands, but shy also and afraid that the boy, out in the barn waiting for the man to come back, might come in on them.

"Go ahead, open it."

His drips sizzled on the stove and he watched her intently as she intently removed the string and took the top off the flat box.

"The box from Bon Marche is yours," he said.

"It's a beautiful jacket, Lucien." She held the blue and gray tattersall sports jacket with narrow lapels up to him. "It goes beautifully with your eyes."

He might have melted against the stove.

"I got a tie, too."

"Oh, it's perfect, and a shirt with a button-down collar. You'll look like a college man."

"Look in the bag," he urged. "I got it special for you."

She did so quickly, rifling the bag of a plum-colored sleeveless angora sweater with a plunging neckline. "Oh, Lucien!" she cried and whirled into the living room to look at it against herself in the mirror. "It'll go great with my new skirt."

"That's what I was thinking," he called from the sink, where he wrung out his socks before carrying them, offending things, out the back door.

When he returned, she kissed him full on the mouth. "It's gorgeous," she said, but her eyes were troubled.

"What's the matter?" he asked.

She tried not to sigh.

"Jan, what is it?"

"Everything's beautiful, absolutely beautiful ... But where can I wear something like this? Where can we go?"

"I'll take you out."

Now she laughed. "But where?"

Barefoot, beginning to shiver, Lucien Quirk thought he heard derision. "Maybe we could go to a restaurant for supper. I just got a check, you know."

Quite suddenly it was a serious matter. They might have been high school kids and he was just asking her out on a first date and she had to be a little coy even though she was going to say yes.

"I was thinking about the Spear House," he offered.

"Someone might recognize us."

"What about the Old Oaken Bucket in Westford?"

She made a face. Not good enough. She had gone there with Hedley. Now it seemed to Lucien Quirk that she would object to his desecration of the floor. She was right, of course. Having clothes with no place to wear them is as bad as having somewhere to go with no clothes to wear there.

He said, "There's a place in Lawrence called Bishop's. It's got some kind of Arab food that's supposed to be pretty good . . . if it ain't too far to drive."

It was tough, being a man of the world shivering in your bare feet.

"When?" Her question was an answer.

"Tonight?"

"Okay."

"What about Bobby?"

"Bobby's going to Ernestine's for supper. He'll be out till eleven or later. We don't have to worry about him."

With a little whoop of joy, she kissed the man on the cheek and folded her new sweater and put it away for later. Her hands flew over the eggs as she went back to sorting.

"I'll call the hospital and tell them I'm not coming in. Hedley won't mind if I miss a day. Ernestine's going in this afternoon, anyway. And you should get out of those clothes before you freeze to death."

She tucked away her troubles as if they were so many

eggs; she was happy in a way she hadn't been for years and years. A night out!

Her bedraggled swain, still backed against the stove, his teeth starting to chatter, muttered something about messing up her new floor.

"That's right," she said.

But they were smiling at each other; they were both delighted.

❧

The musk of her perfume and the sweetish tang of his aftershave contended with the homelier odors of the farm that clung to the inside of the car as they drove toward Lowell on their way to Lawrence. It was as though Hedley were in the car with them. Each familiar house and sign and tree caught in the headlights seemed another link in a lengthening chain of betrayal. It was not easy for Janet Vaughn to have fun, much as she wanted to. She had expected so much. She had taken her time making up, using eye shadow, giving a touch of rouge to her cheeks, making her lips and nails a deep scarlet, and sweeping back her hair and pinning to it a hairpiece that matched. Lucien Quirk, in his new shirt and tie, had been quite impressed, glancing sidelong at her. But now she felt like a painted trollop. She could see her mother's eyes narrow and her nose lift. Dressed and smelling like a common whore. Going out with Lucien Quirk, who wasn't even one of the Highland Quirks. While your husband lies sick in a hospital. And their going to a restaurant together, even if it was in Lawrence, constituted a kind of public declaration, an unspoken deepening of commitment, which somehow was all too appropriate, considering the condition she thought she was in. So, steering and clutching and changing gears through Chelmsford Centre, she wrestled with the impulse to turn the car around and drive home and wash off her makeup and go to visit her husband as she had every day since he had gone to the hospital. She might have done just that, only she knew she could not also wash away her adultery or the knot of life opening within her.

Her disquiet sharpened as they entered Lowell. They drove by Palmer News, the Owl Diner, the old armory, her path of sorrows. They went over the Concord River and turned left on Nesmith. The brick pile of the hospital loomed and her hands trembled on the wheel.

Hedley . . . The name choked in her throat. But the old Chevrolet moved them, took them across the Merrimack and right on Route 110, the river road that curved with the flow at the bottom of Christian Hill. They passed the Cathay Gardens, a Chinese restaurant set with Oriental enchantment next to the river. The rain had stopped. Only now did she notice that and the mild, freshening air and, glancing up through the trees, the wind streaming high thin clouds beneath a filling moon.

She went giddy with a sudden sense of liberation and smiled at the figure in the dim light beside her. They were in Dracut, then Methuen. They had left behind her complicated, compromised world. Here, in Lawrence, parking the car, walking along the street toward Bishop's, they were an ordinary couple, unjudged, free. There were Mr. and Mrs. Anderson for the maître d', who had taken her reservation over the phone and who now smiled and armed himself with menus and led them through a crowded, murmuring room spiced with the scents of exotic foods to a high-backed booth against the wall. Janet Vaughn felt the lingering stares. She had drawn the same attention when she was Janet Gilooly on the arm of Michael Gavin. She had gotten them even when she made herself dowdy at the office where she'd worked to keep the males at bay. A small candle flickered on the table. She hunched forward, the clefted swell for her man on the other side.

"This is marvelous," she murmured at him and began to relax.

His hands were busy with his napkin and his eyes kept falling to her décolletage.

"Just like a dream," he said in a dreamy voice.

"A drink before dinner?" The urbane purr of the waiter interrupted their tête-à-tête. Janet Vaughn shrugged her nearly naked shoulders.

"Some wine?" Lucien Quirk offered.

"Sure."

They settled on a bottle of Taylor's, which arrived chilled, its neck scarved in linen. The waiter poured. They touched glasses, and their eyes touched like those of adolescent lovers. The sweet fruity bouquet filled her mouth and nose, and what had merely shone before now dazzled in the uplift of the wine. Butter and sliced pouches of Arabic bread appeared. Together they perused the menu, which to them was a garden of strange dishes.

"The lamb shish kebob looks nice," she said, because at least she had heard of it before and a single skewer didn't cost that much and you never knew what they put in those stuffed grape leaves. Maybe the next time. The waiter, hovering with poised pencil, scribbled their order.

Inadvertently, she caught the lingering eyes of an older, dapper gentleman, a member of a large party at a nearby table. An admirer. She felt the wine burn on her ears and neck. His slight smile and the way he touched the silvered bristle of his mustache seemed pure worldliness to her. It wasn't exactly the world she wanted, but she might bask in the glow of its ambience. It went with the sweet wine and the delicately mint-seasoned green salad. It made her think of the time she went with Michael Gavin to the Parker House and was daunted by the polished wood opulence and the severity of the Negro waiters. She also remembered going to a small Italian place in the North End of Boston, right after the war, where they had checkered tablecloths and harsh red wine from a bottle encased in a wicker basket. But he had been rejecting her then and she had been unable to take the pasta and the rich sauces. She had missed so much! Now she could eat the world. She could murmur sweet nothings to Lucien Quirk's sallies and return his shyly ravenous glances and let the oils of sensuality flow with the wine and the strange, satisfying food. He kept filling her glass. He was saying things — about the boy, the farm, other restaurants he'd been in. It didn't matter. He sat handsome and young-looking in his new jacket from McQuaid's with the thin, navy, collegiate tie, even if his rough farming hands and his common Lowell twang gave him away as he ordered another bottle of wine from the waiter sliding platters of spiced meat and handcut French fries onto the table between them.

The evening rushed, pitched higher to the sipping of the too sweetening wine and the munching of the irresistible fries that somehow went well with the skewered lamb. Now she giggled at whatever trifle he mouthed, leaned back to laugh and show her throat and the riches of her breasts. She wanted hilarity. She wanted them to go with the dapper man to a big house with French doors and creamy ceilings and a phonograph playing Glenn Miller records. And dance as she had danced at the Lowell High Officers' Ball, with all the time in the world. She might flirt with the old boy — whose glances across the shrinking space had grown blatant — and let him see her legs and let herself be the stranger she had become. But in the tizzy of the wine, and with time already congealing around the soft focus of her vision, the gentleman was gathering his family — son and daughter-in-law (she guessed), and grandchildren — was paying the waiter, was giving her a last lingering look that was more sad than flirtatious, was leaving her to spin another dream.

Her dream was reality. She took another big fry and her stomach deflated with a silent belch, followed by a fluttering in her lower abdomen. Her wine-propped smile fell and her face paled. She saw it all mirrored in the sudden concern narrowing Lucien Quirk's eyes as his knife and fork remained poised over his plate, elbows on table, his wrists — he had fine wrists — emerging from new cuffs.

"What's the matter?" he asked.

She waited in a luxury of silence for the flutterings to fade. She put down her cutlery and straightened her back. She had wanted to avoid this. She had wanted one evening of grace before the welter of circumstance overcame her life. She tried to smile and barely kept it from becoming a sob.

"What is it, Jan?" His hand reached across the table for hers.

She allowed him to take it for a moment and then withdrew. "What are we going to do?" she said.

Lucien Quirk had not drunk much wine, but now the need for it rose with a helplessness that turned him rubbery. And the night had been going so well.

"He's coming home, you know."

The man nodded and resumed eating. He could chew and swallow, whatever happened. With bullets stinging the air. You might live. So you had to eat. But he also knew his soldier's philosophy was no good for her. Women needed more than the day-to-day. He chewed and swallowed and eased himself with wine. He braced himself for the beginning of goodbye.

"It isn't just Hedley."

"No?"

"No."

"What do you mean?"

Then somehow he knew. He knew from instinct, from the sound of her voice and the flat certainty of her eyes, what she meant. It was curiously like being told of someone's impending death; the world would change. The pain of an abrupt, wild hope played riot with his heart. Still, he chewed and kept his gaze.

"I think I'm pregnant."

"How do you know?"

"I just know."

He took her hand and held it firmly, the flats of his fingers pressing against her palm. For what seemed a long time he said nothing. Then his words came in a low hot whisper and he bent toward her, pressuring her with his hands and his eyes. "Let's get away from here. Just pack a few things. I've got some money. We can take the car."

It was utterly impossible, of course, and the only thing left to do. She heard herself ask, "Where?"

"San Diego. I've got friends there. I could get a job."

That might have been true, but Janet Vaughn, still too sober for mad dreams, was sipping her wine and thinking how she couldn't leave her new kitchen behind. That was foolishness, but she needed something trivial right then to anchor the immensity of the thing. Her mind kept opening and closing on the fact that if she was pregnant, she had no other choice but to run away with the man.

"You gotta see it. It's beautiful out there. It's warm all year round with these blue skies that go on forever . . ." He was pitching hard and fast, and his eyes, glinting with something of final desperation, held hers. "I mean they've got a park there, Balboa Park, that's as big as all of Boston. Just the park. You gotta see it. They've got these little canyons in it with red and purple flowers growing up the walls and these Spanish kinds of buildings and a zoo and lawns and gardens . . ."

"I can't."

"Sure you can."

"Hedley . . ."

"Hedley ain't gonna care as long as he's got the farm. You know that. He's gonna kill himself on that place whether you're there or not."

She knew he was right despite the hustle in his voice. "Bobby . . ." she started, and the tension lifted to her chest and funneled up behind her eyes and nose at the pathos of it all. Bobby, Ellen, Mom, Mary, Joe Jr., the kids, Jessica Lee, the house, the farm, her kitchen — all the people and places she would have to leave. It was like death, this new life dangled before her by Lucien Quirk. The candle flame blurred through her tears.

"Ernestine will take care of Bobby," he said.

He was stripping her of these people, perhaps of her illusions. Did anyone really need her except him, whose needs, she sensed, might prove bottomless? *Him?* Who was he? Who was she, sitting in a restaurant in Lawrence, the remains of her meal turning greasy as it cooled? Was she Mrs. Hedley Vaughn of Elmsbury, Massachusetts, or Janet Gilooly again, knocked up and living in sin in San Diego, California, with the hired man? The membrane of her life stretched and tore as the impossible became the plausible and the plausible the inevitable.

"When?" she asked, as though sentence had already been passed.

"Tonight." His hand tightened on hers and his eyes bore in. "We can go back and pack a few things. We'll take the car. It won't be stealing. They owe you that much. I've got some money. You've got some money. We can make it there in less than a week."

It was all true. They could go then. She had some money. She could claim the car. Would they even miss her after a couple of weeks? The gossip would die to legend. And who, finally, would care? And San Diego. The flutterings faded and her mood swung around. It might not be all bad. She let herself dream. She imagined blue skies and white buildings and a child in the sun. She could have her Jerusalem now. And they could just do it, pack up and go, just the way they had gone out and bought the sink and the linoleum. They could have a little house near the beach with a new kitchen if it needed one. She laughed, happy with her dream, because that's what it was, a dream, and dreams are safe.

"You'll go?"

"I need to think about it."

She might have said yes, the way he smiled and let go of her hand and went back to his food. "I know," he said, no longer insistent, confident that he had her on the hook of necessity. Time would work for him. "Drink your wine," he urged. "We still have the night."

❦ 20 ❧

Aunt Ernestine had one of her spells. I think I'll drive you home now, Bobby, she had announced not long after he finished his dinner of pork chops and mashed potatoes with the canned green peas he didn't like and the two helpings of brownie and ice cream. I don't feel quite well, she had said, and smiled, as though to belie it. And she had driven him home with her usual authority at the wheel, hardly feigning a hand to the head, her smile intact.

Well, grownups had their world, and damned if he could figure it out. Not that he particularly minded. You could outgrow watching television with your old aunt. You could enjoy being alone in the kitchen at home with the radio on as deeper yearnings stirred in you like a warm wind.

The fat man's voice warbled higher, lingered and rolled:

> "Ah found my threeeil
> On Blueberry Heeil . . .
> When ah found youuuu . . ."

Then Bobby Helms was cooing:

> "You are my special angel,
> Sent from up above . . ."

A tune to moon by, to imagine slow dancing with Cynthia Kirkpatrick, the way they did on "American Bandstand," bodies touching down a long front of bliss.

There was an ad for Chevrolet, America's number one car, followed by some disk jockey patter about a record hop at Keith Academy. Then a bouncer:

"You shake my nerves and you rattle my brain
Too much of love drives a man insane."

Jerry Lee Lewis swept the treble notes, holding them and moving them in a mating trance. The boy's mind thumped and floated with the music. He was jitterbugging with the girl of his dreams. He was holding her hand, walking with her, giving her a kiss, holding her like a lover should. Then he was heroic for her, the *g* forces pressing as his F-100 snapped over into a power dive and the world loomed, rushing up to meet him.

Finally he turned the radio off and rose, restless, trapped in the house and in the house of his body. He drank a glass of milk and went upstairs to look at his model planes. He had an air force now. They climbed and dived and banked on invisible fishing line tacked to the ceiling. There was a gull-winged Corsair, an F-90 Lockheed, a Sabre in position to shoot down a diving MIG 15. His bureau top and the deep windowsill next to his bed looked like the crowded flight deck of a carrier. He picked up the Stuka. Primitive things, he thought. The landing gear didn't retract. Of course, that slowed them up during the dive, made them more accurate with their bombs. A sitting duck for the Mustang, which was superior to anything the Jerries had except for the ME-262, one of the first jets and better than anything anyone had. But he would have climbed to meet it anyway in his P-51 Mustang, with its air-cooled engine and eight fifty-caliber machine guns arrayed along the wings; he would have come at them out of the sun, firing.

He sighed. The fantasies of aerial glory no longer quite sufficed. There was another hidden door to the world, behind which the meaning of the music throbbed. He took off his clothes to get ready for bed, and the pale stretches of his body ached to be touched and to touch in a way that went beyond what he knew of sexual plumbing. In the bathroom mirror he scrutinized the darkening bristle on his upper lip and the angle of his jaw. He had asked Aunt Ernestine if she would get him an electric razor for Christmas. Just for himself. A token of manhood. He got into bed and lay with the lights out, waiting for sleep and for something like revelation.

&

He may have dozed, but mostly he was simply lying in the dark when the lights of the car caught the windows of his room and flickered dimly against the ceiling. Noises filled the ensuing darkness. He heard them in the kitchen below, the low voice of the man wisecracking, the woman's skirling with girlish outbursts of giggling. The boy listened, tense with expectation and trespass. They didn't think he was there; he was supposed to be at Ernestine's until much later. They were coming up the stairs and then into the room next to his. Lucien Quirk was talking about a hotel, the something Coronado, and a place called the Creole Palace, where they would have to go. The light came on, a sharp crack under the door. The boy suppressed an impulse to cough loudly to let them know he was there so that they could continue to hide from him what he already knew. The voices drifted. He caught sentences. "Oh, Lucien, I've had too much to drink." Then the rustle of fabric, the zip and fall of clothes. "Did you see that sweet old man. I think he liked me." Lucien Quirk mumbled something back. The bed whinged.

"I should make sure about Bobby." Janet Vaughn now sounded close enough to be in the same room with him. She checked in a cursory way, standing behind the door and calling his name, but softly. "Bobby? Bobby?" He lay still, holding his breath. Lucien Quirk had come behind her. "He's at Ernestine's," he said. "It's only nine-thirty." Janet Vaughn's giggle turned a husky "Ooooo, look at you."

The boy heard them retreat from the door. He slithered from his bed and edged in breathless silence till his eye smarted in the slot of the keyhole, his blood blazing. Two white forms blurred in and out of his vision. Then he saw them standing naked. Her hand was on him as they kissed, working down. They moved to the bed and the boy could see them better. They were lying side by side, her back to the door, her bottom a white, cleaved globe over which the man's hand played. They shifted about. Her legs had opened like wings as she lay back, but the man's position confused him. His head was between her legs, reminding the boy of pictures he'd seen of lions feeding. He was kissing her there. Eating it, he had called it. The woman's breasts seemed curiously flattened, her eyes closed and her mouth open as she uttered low, unearthly cries. The boy stroked himself, worked his own blister of pleasure as he saw the man kneeling, his passion poised, then lowered to a juncture of fluid thrusting, a pinning, a pursuit even in surrender. The woman moaned as though being subjected to exquisite torture. It grew to a phantasm of flashing limbs and buttocks, of breasts and hair and bodies entwined, her sound rising until she was going *oh, oh, oh, OH!* for an unbearable duration while the boy whipped himself to their time until something melted in the root of his being and a scalding started and moved and came up and off as he felt with amazement and ineffable pleasure the clots of his first spunk slap against the door as the couple on the bed shuddered and quivered into stillness and silence.

ᗏ 21 ᘓ

THE MEMORY of those two figures and how they had coupled remained with the boy like a tangible, poignant presence, and he walked as though under water, through a world gone heavy and buoyant with lust. Surreptitiously he watched them, his eyes averted yet keen, with new knowledge of what people are and do. He saw their glances and listened to their silences and knew. He stripped them of their ordinariness during, for instance, the mundane occasion of a meal, and saw them transfigured again in their embrace. He extrapolated that transformation to the rest of the world and understood that everybody, Smiley Grimes and Harry Manning and Mrs. Terry, his history teacher, everybody had another secret, sexual self. And this other self was so extraordinary, so inflamed with nature, he wondered why anyone put on workaday clothes to shamble about the world at what needed doing.

Even November with its gray fields and dead light took on that painful throbbing glow peculiar to adolescent concupiscence. Now when Bobby Dearborn climbed aboard the school bus to sit in a hard-cushioned seat, he could scarcely look at his schoolmates without envisioning the passionate act from which they had each sprung. These houses in front of which the bus stopped, some prim and middle class, some hardly more than shacks set back amid the gloom of pines, contained behind their mere walls and doors the secret life he had witnessed. So in their modern Colonial, Mr. and Mrs. Teely had undressed and engendered the three Teely girls, who were blond and dimpled and giggled in their innocence. And the whole Langdon clan. That must have been some doing, although the poor mother, worn and raddled, hardly seemed the part now. And in English class, in math, and world history, where they had gotten as far as the Rome of the late Caesars, he watched the budding girls and saw their uplifted breasts and haunches snugged in tapered skirts as delights among which he might someday frisk. Squirming in the oak and iron desk bolted to the floor, he undressed them all and guessed at their spread forms and faces in that humbling and exalted moment of sex. As he sat with a nagging erection, consumed with the urge to reach out and touch, his fingers might have been tumescent.

He could think of nothing else. Sleeving the empurpled ridge of this new sensation, he relived the moment at the keyhole to the limits of specific irritation. Only now it was himself he saw through squinting eyes, sitting with Janet Vaughn on the edge of her bed. She would let him give her a real kiss, mouth to mouth, like the movies. They would talk about doing it (although he could not imagine the words he would use). She would let him feel her breasts as they got undressed. He wasn't sure about putting his mouth down there the way Lucien Quirk had, but he was sure she would understand as she pointed him to the right place, in there, smooth pink, belly on belly, covering her, making her go *oh, oh, OH!* hearing it, feeling it, until his hand-held dream dissolved into the hay or a hanky or the bathroom sink.

At night his dreams were so vivid in their damp and ecstatic culminations that they blurred the distinction between desire and reality. The boy remembered Lucien Quirk's advice to a young man on seducing women. Be nice. Talk to them. Bring them flowers. So he was nice to

Aunt Janet. He helped her around the house and picked up his dirty clothes and smiled at her, but shyly, hiding his blush. The flowers, however, presented something of a logistical problem. The nearest florist was Cal Laughton in North Chelmsford, and roses, he found on calling, tended to be expensive. He had a dollar twenty-five, which he had saved for a model of the B-58 Hustler, a new strategic bomber. It was enough for a Whitman's Sampler at the drugstore in Elmsbury. It took him some time to get up the courage. It was one thing to dream about and plan the seduction of this woman, his uncle's wife, who only months before had been cuffing him around like a puppy; it was another thing to do it.

But he did. On a Thursday he deliberately missed the school bus after school and walked home, stopping for the box of chocolates, which he tucked among his books and his dreams. That night he scarcely slept as on the screen of his feverish imagination he played and replayed the next morning's scene — how he would wait for Lucien Quirk to go out of the house to milk the cows; how he would get up and wash his hands and face; and how, still wearing his pajamas, he would go quietly into her room and wake her if she needed waking. There, he would sit on the side of her bed and present her with the chocolates. Here, Auntie, they're for you. Sweet talk. And here his fantasy faltered. He could imagine no real man talk for his Aunt Janet. The kind he heard in the movies didn't quite fit. *Darling, I love you. Darling, you have beautiful eyes.* It was easier to picture the act itself, her saying yes and letting him lie next to her and then on top of her, doing it, going up and down with that motion that had transfixed him at the keyhole. He spent himself on the sheet and drifted off into a sleep, fitful with dreams explanatory of night noises and of Janet Vaughn taking him down to her recumbent form so that when the hissing and banging of the heating started, he both heard and dreamed of Lucien Quirk thudding down the stairs and making coffee in the kitchen before going out to milk. He woke with a rocketing heart.

❧

"Bobby?"

Janet Vaughn, asleep and not asleep, turned her head to see the boy standing in his pajamas just inside the door leading from the bathroom. He was saying, "Hi, Auntie," in a strange voice, his words chattering, though the chill had gone off the room. She rolled over in the warmth of the bed and sat partly up. She sensed something was amiss but couldn't imagine what.

"Are you all right?"

"Oh, I'm fine," he said, his voice not quite under control. "I brought you some chocolates."

"How sweet of you."

Sleep made her voice huskier than it usually was. She touched her hair. Even if it was only the boy, she thought about her appearance. And he was nearly as big as a man and was bringing her chocolates, which triggered some slight alarm she ignored. It was just Bobby, after all, sitting on the edge of the bed in the old-fashioned striped pajamas Ernestine had bought for him at Bon Marche.

"I got them at the drugstore," he volunteered.

Janet Vaughn felt sufficiently covered in her high-necked flannel nightie to pull herself into a sitting position.

"Go ahead and open it."

Again the boy's voice quavered, and the box was proffered with downcast eyes.

She removed the cellophane, making a sound that reminded her of Christmas, and said something about how thoughtful he was and wondered why. Perhaps it was to signify that he understood. She knew the morning after they had been to Lawrence that the boy had been there the night before and had probably heard them. She liked to think he accepted what was happening without judging.

The rich brown aroma rose from the candies cupped in corrugated paper.

"They had Schrafft's, but I thought you'd like the Whitman's better. You can tell what kind they are." He shivered visibly.

"What's your favorite?" She turned the open box to him and caught him in a stare at the nippled forms of her breasts taut against the flannel.

Her sweets.

He dropped his eyes to the brown shapes. Never had chocolates seemed so irrelevant.

"I like raspberry jelly," he said, for something to say.

"Go ahead and take it."

"They're for you."

"I'll have one later. After breakfast. Here, let me give you a big kiss."

She had meant a motherly smooch. The boy, awkward and off balance, half fell as he kissed back, inexpert but hungry, his teeth touching hers before she could push him back, her face igniting. Now she understood the chocolates.

"I like you," the boy swallowed, the words taking more courage than the deed. The grays of his eyes were dense and naked as they met hers. His pajama front was tented with painful obviousness.

"I like you, too, Bobby, but I have to get up. Lucien will need his breakfast. And you have to get ready for school."

She had pulled back and crossed her arms. She did not get out on the other side of the bed because she did not want to appear to flee him. She knew her smile was awful, but she wanted to pretend nothing had happened. She sat immobile, at once beleaguered and tempted, panicked and languorous, angry and, at some oblique remove, deeply and secretly pleased, which annoyed her.

"I want to do it to you." His words came out stuck together, stark as his crewcut head and his boy's thick lips open in a face pleading with an insistence that seemed undeniable.

"No!" But she didn't move except to bring her hands to her throat. Words would not suffice. She felt herself go moist.

"Just once," he begged out of that curiosity that is need.

"No, Bobby," she managed, woman to man now because his boy's manhood had declared itself through the flimsy fly of his pajamas. She tried not to stare. She was amazed.

"Please!"

"No!"

Her legs swung from under the covers over the edge of the bed, but toward, not away from the boy. The box of chocolates fell and the contents scattered.

The boy tried anyway, bending his knees toward her and holding her with his strong, wiry arms so that she couldn't escape his truncheon of flesh poking at her thighs as her nightgown bunched higher up her legs, revealing the lux-uriant furrow and the frank pout of her nether lips, which, while she went *no, no, no, NO!* and squirmed, he man-aged to brush in his ardor for a silken, paralyzing moment. She was weakening and it might have happened then, only he gasped as though struck and she felt him spill along her leg. She stopped struggling and waited, holding him, as his spasm expended itself.

They were very still for a moment. His breathing was audible. Then he pulled himself upright and was again a boy in his pajamas.

"Get ready for school," she told him, and waited for his gaze to drop and for him to leave the room before letting herself lie under the covers, damp from his discharge and from tears flowing without sobs.

❦ 22 ❧

THE SHOCK OF IT came slowly, as a kind of faith in the incredible. The boy had tried, really, to rape her. The scattered chocolates made it real. She had scurried around the room afterward, picking them up and later burning them in the stove. The scattered sweets of her life. Her eyes were hollow and dry as she ran her iron over the white stretches of Charles Porley's shirts. Her hand shook, and wonder mingled with her anger as the visceral quake deepened, her outrage hissing and steaming where it touched the enticement of the thing. For the boy had made her feel young again despite herself. The memory of it was a breeze touching surfaces beneath the skin. *I want to do it to you.* Then he had gushed all over her like something out of nature, something beyond shame. She was angry with him and angry with herself for wanting to reach out and take him, pluck him like the big green apple he was. But where would that end? The Church was right: out of sin came chaos, the road to ruin, her ruin, his ruin. So the shock widened and the guilt tightened like a looped and twisted rope until she thought she might split and spill the pod of life welling within.

All of which made it difficult to listen to Lucien Quirk, who sat at the table edgy with coffee as the pall of his cigarette smoke rose above him. She had told him about the boy without going into details. She had to tell someone; already she had so much hidden from so many people. And hidden things fester. The man had raged momentarily. I'll whip his little ass, he had thundered. She had said not to say anything. It would blow over. Lucien Quirk had cooled quickly then, his face assuming a sly cast as he included what had happened to her into his arsenal of arguments for their leaving. It'll happen again, he had repeated. Things will only get worse. That and her pregnancy. What will you do when it starts to show, huh? They ain't gonna understand. They'll crucify you. And against all that he propped his vision of San Diego, reciting the litany about palm trees and blue skies, Pacific Beach and Balboa Park. He had the car ready. They could pack secretly over the weekend and leave on Monday. They had to leave now, escape before it was too late, before Hedley came home. He smoked his cigarettes and sipped his coffee and repeated himself.

She didn't say yes and she didn't say no as she moved the prow of the iron over the starched fabric. Escape. She had a sudden suspicion that escape was the pattern of this man's life. She tried again to imagine going away with him, because she had to imagine something before she could do it. But she also had to want something like that before she could imagine it. She slid a wire hanger under the shoulders of the shirt and drew a blank. She could not conjure up the requisite blue skies and warm breezes. She might very well pack a few things and drive away in the car, but she understood there was no escape, no escape from the Mrs. Porleys of the world, who would still bring her their laundry and whom, in the near-mythical city of San Diego, she wouldn't know well enough even to hate. There would be no escape from Mom's judging eye and silences. That judgment would follow her to the moon, to the grave. No escape. She'd still have to dream her dream of Jerusalem with some ramshackle reality where the sunshine and palm trees would be ordinary as dirt. In the end it came down to the little man sitting at the table following her with his eyes like a child. You don't love me enough, the eyes said, knowing, as one always does, the worst. Because she couldn't respond with a straight answer or a straight look, pretending instead to eye the finished shirt critically, then sighing and wondering what the hell she was ever going to do with her life when the sound of a car pulling into the yard made her glance up.

Good Christ!

Through the window, not quite real though reality itself, she saw Father Francis J. Fahey's black Ford pull up beneath the big elm. She saw the priest sit there for a moment before opening the car door and emerging, hatless. In an instant she resumed her role as the respectable if poor Mrs. Hedley Vaughn, sweeping dishes toward the sink and waving at the cigarette smoke and hustling a reluctant Lucien Quirk out the back door. Then, all but breathless, pushing at her hair with one hand, she opened the door to admit this deputy of God.

It began as a ceremony of apology. The priest said he was sorry for just dropping by, for not calling, for not coming by sooner. And Janet Vaughn was too busy apologizing herself to really listen. Bless me, Father, for I do not always keep a tidy house, the dirty dishes in the sink and the pile of Porley shirts being the outward signs of her drudgery and sin. They were both somewhat bemused and jittery as she took his overcoat and he braced himself for yet another cup of coffee that went with this visiting of parishioners.

"Would you like a cup of coffee, Father?"

"Don't go to any bother."

His gaze was circumspect.

"It's no bother at all, Father."

The well-groomed and somewhat fastidious priest, who had been there the summer before, when Hedley Vaughn first went to hospital, didn't mind being led into the neater living room and left while she fled to make the coffee. The casual chaos of ordinary lives never ceased to amaze him.

For Janet Vaughn it was almost a relief simply to have a male in the house who was above sex. He wanted only her soul. Such defiance of nature left her, as it did a lot of women, somewhat in awe. When she had the coffee started, she returned to her guest and sat at a respectable distance, feeling defenseless suddenly without cups and things to rattle about in front of herself.

"Well, I've been meaning to drop by for some time."

Father Fahey, who began in a voice he might have used from the pulpit, nearly put her in a panic. She took it as the start of chastisement or, worse, as a prelude to the inquisition she more or less expected. Why haven't you been to confession? Why don't you take communion? What's this I hear about a hired man working here? But the priest had his own guilt. The face, enlarged by the glabrous pate, reddened as he sensed resistance. She wasn't going to let him off the hook that easily, he thought. He plowed on anyway.

"I've been in to see Hedley a couple of times in the hospital. He's looking much better."

This time Janet Vaughn heard the man's apologetic tone and settled back a little. He hadn't come for her soul, not just yet. "Yes, he was mentioning you the other day." She felt her face smile. "He's always glad to see you."

Which they both knew was a harmless enough lie. Hedley Vaughn believed in the finality of death and had little use for his own tradition and none at all for the Roman variety or its representatives. He barely managed a polite tolerance in the cleric's presence. But the lie, as prelude to any truths they might agree on, eased them both a little. They could get on with the ritual of the pastoral visit and the pain of being comforted.

"He's greatly improved," the priest repeated and took out his pipe to do something with his hands.

"Yes, he'll be home soon."

"That will be a great relief for you, I'm sure." The man's lips sucked and blew in quick puffs around the stem of the pipe. "It can't have been easy for you, these weeks."

She dissolved a little at this pity due her, mingled as it was with the aromatic pipe smoke that reminded her of Hedley. She noticed a bloom of dust on the floor near the window where the gray light touched. "Yes," she murmured and thought how she would have to clean the place for her husband's return even while she planned to pack her bags and run off with the hired man. Her impossible worlds. She could even imagine how the priest would tell others, after the news got out, that she had seemed fine, perfectly fine, only days before. But, then, people can be dying and keep a straight face.

Straight-faced, she excused herself to attend to the coffee. She found homemade cookies the boy hadn't eaten (he would rifle everything she had!) and put them on a plate, mostly for decoration.

Father Fahey protested that it was too much for her to have done, but lowered his spittled pipe anyway to handle cream and sugar. "And the young lad," he baritoned, easier with a cup and saucer to balance (what was the kid's name anyway?). "How is he doing these days?" He had made a few nudges about bringing the boy into the flock, but the husband had a sister, one of the hard kind.

"Oh, fine, Father, fine. He's getting bigger all the time."

"He must be. How old is he now?"

"Nearly thirteen. Thirteen in December."

"He must be a great help to you."

"Oh, yes."

But her cup rattled then. If only she could have dispensed with this pretense of cups and saucers, could have gone on her knees to confess and ask, if not forgiveness, at least understanding from this groomed, black-clad man who had prayed himself above nature. Bless me, Father, for I have sinned. I have betrayed my husband, my family, and my God. But understand that my sin sprang as much from necessity and circumstance as from weakness or willfulness and that I will sin no more. I will not flee with another man and hide my shame. With your help and God's, I will stay and suffer the coming storm and from that suffering gain some measure of salvation. For a moment, Janet Vaughn's eyes swam with the possibility of confession. And she might have started right then, started with a hesitant trickle of words that would become a deluge, had not another car disturbed the gravel of the driveway. It was Gladys Porley, on time to pick up her husband's shirts.

This woman stepped on stage, her social self, patting a wisp back into the marble of her coif and forgiving her washerwoman in a whisper ("I have to go into Lowell, anyway. I can pick them up on the way back"), before advancing, not quite invited, into the living room to ring the rising priest with a smiling enthusiasm quite beyond what was required. Janet Vaughn, in any event, was momentarily reduced to being a spectator as the Porley woman, her hand in the priest's, gushed, ". . . and Charles is a great admirer of yours, Father . . . Charles Porley, Father. You were on the Tercentennial Committee together."

"Of course, of course, and how is Charles doing these days?" The man at least glanced at Janet Vaughn and positioned himself to indicate that his parishioner had not ceased totally to exist in her own house.

". . . and Connie Murphy, Father, is a great friend of ours and a devoted fan of yours, I must say . . ."

Janet Vaughn stood by helplessly in her worn dress, entranced by the woman's crepey, silk-knotted neck. The Porleys and the Murphys drank sherry and played bridge together. And right then, listening to this knowing exchange between the priest and the woman, Janet Vaughn knew she would never surmount that steep wall into the middle class no matter what she did to her kitchen.

"Won't you stay for a cup of coffee?"

"Thanks, anyway, but I really can't." Her head tilted in fake apology to the fake invitation. "I should be running along and letting you and Father Fahey get back to your little visit."

"I was just telling Janet how well Hedley looks." The

priest was signaling his pastoral purposes. Everything aboveboard here.

"I'm so glad. You've been through so much," said Gladys Porley, turning her dazzle on Janet Vaughn, who was warmed and charmed despite herself. Then terrified. If only these genteel people knew. (They would know!) If only they could have seen her and Lucien Quirk at Bishop's together or the boy that morning, coming at her big as a man . . .

Gladys Porley was running along, as she said she must, a word in the kitchen about the shirts while her eyes made a quick inspection with that fascination the better-off sometimes have for the domestic arrangements of the less well-off. And what was the priest doing there? Then she was gone, her coming and going breaking the stiffness between the priest and parishioner, leaving them more susceptible to the rituals of comfort. Her visit had also made things seem trivial, social, and the man had to clear his throat to find the right note on which to resume.

"You've been having a difficult time, haven't you?" he began, picking up on an observation made by the visitor.

"Yes, Father, it hasn't been easy."

She hadn't meant the confessional tone, not quite yet, but the relief of even that small admission was immense. The renewed temptation to go on, to redden his ears with the heavy delicacy of her crisis, was all but irresistible. The blue eyes in the shaved face invited it. His silence tugged. She began to formulate a phrase to start; she voiced a "Father, I . . ." and stopped and peered down at the rug, which was worn and stained with life beyond any real redemption. And in the aftermath of the Porley visit, confession was somehow implausible. They were reduced to suburban truths. And she realized what the priest's answers would be. She didn't trust him to see the complexity of her situation, how others were going to suffer. What did he know of life? A sin is a sin is a sin, he would intone, holding tight his purse of grace. At last she saw, like a new vision of death, death as extinction, that she no longer believed anyway, no longer believed, insofar as she was going to do what she had to do, that forgiveness was impossible. So she sighed and resisted any bloodletting of words then, and the priest coughed again to find his voice.

"Is there anything I can help you with?"

It could have been a plea. Help me help you. But he appeared in some measure relieved. People have such problems. Usually sex or family or both.

"Bobby," she said, throwing him a scrap, "is going through a phase. He's at that age . . ."

She trailed off without elaborating. There were no euphemisms that would suffice. And she had not been circumspect in the occasions of her own sins.

Father Fahey took the morsel gladly and squared himself off with a professional stance.

"Do you want me to speak to George Kendall about him? He might be able to help."

"I don't think so." She didn't want the boy giving the Reverend Mr. Kendall an earful. "It's been a difficult time for him, too, Father."

"Well, Hedley will be home soon."

Father Fahey was rubbing his hands together as though washing them. A man about the house again. That would put things right. The priest frowned slightly, not quite remembering some talk about a hired man helping out with the farm. A few years earlier he might have remembered and would have asked questions. It was his business to pry. Now there were so many new people, with all the developments going in, and they hadn't sent him that second curate he needed. So, remembering a Mrs. Cassidy, who was dying and whom he had to visit, he scarcely noticed the woman holding her breath at some sudden, inner flickering.

It could have been the coffee or the priest indicating that his visit was concluded. But it wasn't either of those; it was the unmistakable sign of new life within her. She kept up a brave front, appearing casual in spite of the tumult of jumbled emotions. Then she was in another kind of panic when the priest rose abruptly, his height and blackness dignifying the room. She waxed voluble, apologizing, clutching at him with words. "More coffee? More cookies?"

"Well, I must let you get back to work," the man said, extricating himself. "If you need anything . . ."

"Thank you, Father," she said, as though hearing her penance. She retrieved his coat from the dining room. Their sense of mutual failure was nearly palpable.

"And tell Hedley I was asking for him if he gets home before I get to the hospital again."

"Yes, Father."

He had his coat on and was in the doorway and just about to leave when he stopped, as though remembering some last detail.

"Would you like a blessing?"

"Oh, yes, Father," she said with sudden gladness and went down on her knees and heard the mumble of Latin above her. She remained kneeling as the door opened, letting in a waft of cold and refreshing air that was the small touch of grace the priest had left with her.

&

Lucien Quirk had let the herd out into the yard so that he could clean the gutters behind them. He was also whitewashing the cow barn, a project he'd started some days before. He did it to impress her, to make her exclaim, to show her how things could be. Anger suffused him as he worked. He kept pacing to the front of the barn and peering through the window to see if the priest's car was still parked in the driveway. The sight of the black Ford, funereal and official, made him hiss through his teeth. Priests. They were good for old women and weak men, with their Virgin Marys and their little bags of tricks. He lifted a hinged plank to hoe the dung from the gutter behind the cows into the cellar below. The priest would get to her, turn her head, make her confess, make her stay. Why else was he there? Sons of bitches could smell trouble a mile away. Like vultures. He went out to one of the bays on the barn floor and brought back a bushel basket of sawdust, which he spread behind the stanchions where the cows stood. It didn't do much good. The animals still lay down in their shit, which dried on their hindquarters like thickening scales of armor. The radio played some song of love. But he didn't hear it as he scraped the accumulation of years of spattered dung and generations of whitewash with a garden edger. The wood was skeletal beneath. Even so, the cows would have it mucked up again in no time.

And the kid going in and trying something with her!

He gouged wood in a sudden fury, getting the stuff in his hair and his nose till he came to the end of the section he was doing. He kicked at the dog, which lay in his way as he went through to the dairy to mix lime and water. The whitewash went on gray and took a while to dry and whiten. He heard a second car drive into the yard and got to the window in time to see Gladys Porley standing at the door. Snobby God damn bitch, he cursed to himself, the way she looked right through you like you weren't there. Nosy cunt, too.

Lucien Quirk, dipping the brush into whitewash and trailing it across the imperfect boards, was staggered by a sudden, profound sense of futility. He had been banished to the barn as though he counted for nothing, as though nothing had happened. They hadn't made love and plans. She wasn't pregnant at all, or if she was pregnant, he would merely get the blame. She would never leave with him for San Diego, because he was only the handyman, milking the cows and feeding the chickens and slapping whitewash on shit-rotted boards for five dollars a week. Because he didn't believe it himself. His whole life had stalled in the act before the act.

He laughed aloud at himself, daubing this stuff on the wall, getting it all over himself. The old deep parch touched off in him and he found himself in the feed room, a walled-off bay with a door, where he groped behind bags for a stash of Pastene. He found it, opened it, and paused. Then he hoisted the bottle. That was better. Then not. It only fueled the chemistry of rage and futility that had him trembling. And jealousy. He imagined her falling for the boy. Women could do that. Fickle as hens. Turn around and they're screwing someone else. It had happened before. He tilted the bottle and let it burn, relief that was not relief. God damn, but he would teach that little bastard a lesson. Hardly thirteen and grabbing at someone who was practically his mother. Christ, what was the world coming to?

He mixed more lime and water and slapped it on, but sloppily now. His rage whitened like the drying wall. He quit working and then started again. He arranged sacks of grain to give himself a place to lie down and saw a rat's tail disappearing through the tinned, ratproof floor. He lay down and got up and lay down again. He brooded. He got up and paced out to the window. Gladys Porley's car was gone, then the priest's. He was at the window when the school bus made a sudden large intrusion of yellow in the pane and left the boy on the side of the road. The man lay down again. He lit a cigarette and nursed the bottle and could not find a rage deep enough to protect him from the blank of despair as the wine eased him, but lower.

❧

Bobby Dearborn and the woman were silent for a time together in the kitchen. Finishing the last of Charles Porley's shirts, she treasured the comforting afterglow of the priest's blessing. From the grace that had touched her she found courage to confront the boy. He had made himself a peanut butter and jelly sandwich and poured a glass of fresh milk from the pitcher in the refrigerator. Except for the silence and the averted eyes, it might have been any other schoolday afternoon. But the silence hung between them with a wary tension that went beyond any impending anger; they were no longer just Aunt Janet and Bobby, but some other, unresolved entity. Her movements as she started on the dishes in the sink were precise and inhibited, as if there were a strange man in her kitchen. And still just Bobby, a gangling seventh-grader with a milky crescent on the fuzz of his upper lip. Their eyes caught and broke as she wiped off the table. He made a second sandwich. She put things away, restoring order, circling. She wanted to reach out and touch him, forgive him. But she was afraid of him and somewhat confused about what she might say.

She had thought a good deal about exactly what she should say to him when he came in from school. Phrases — the threads of the old morality she had been reared with — ran through her head. She would show the boy the way, even though, as she realized, she was hardly in a position to preach the catechetical pieties about the sanctity of marriage and the specialness of love and how all that has to do with sex. Still, she found that she did believe deeply in the old morality. It was what she wanted to impart to the boy. They were her values. And this discrepancy between what she believed and how she acted left her feeling not so much a hypocrite as a sinner. So she circled and fussed until her resolve was reduced to mere anxiety, which she relieved by sitting down and announcing, "Bobby, we have to have a talk."

The boy nodded, silent. His eyes intimidated her with their seeming lack of remorse. He might have been angry. Janet Vaughn was in any event reduced to being the supplicant as she began to speak. Only now her little homily on love and sex came out in wooden bits and pieces, words and phrases about love and respect, about duty and being old enough and finding the right girl.

"You do it with Lucien," Bobby Dearborn said directly when she finished. "I know. I saw you and him through the keyhole."

Good God, he had watched them! The realization jarred her, leaving her weak with sickish lust. They were again a man and a woman, and he was still trying.

"Lucien is very special to me."

"He's just the hired man," the boy said, but not without a twinge of betrayal. Then, recklessly: "He's a wino. I heard you say it."

"A hired man can be special, too, Bobby. There's nothing wrong with being a hired man. And he's changed since he came here. He's not a wino anymore. He's stopped drinking. I helped him with that and he's helped us a lot with all the work . . ."

"I do a lot of work, too."

This display of logic without emotion fazed her, but at least they were talking and she was able to return the intensity of his eyes.

"Lucien is *very special* to me," she said, hoping the emphasis would convey that choice was paramount, too, where sex was concerned.

"But you're married to Uncle Hedley."

"I know."

She let it go at that, because no explanation she could think of then would suffice.

The boy was silent, licking at the whiteness on his lip. Then he asked, "Why can't I be special too?"

She could have laughed or cried at the ignorance and innocence of his appeal.

"You *are* very special to me, Bobby." She spoke without thinking and turned toward him and dared take his hand. "But you're special in a different kind of way."

"A different kind of way?"

"Yes . . ." She fumbled for words.

The boy waited.

Janet Vaughn was left with only the truth, which she voiced and discovered at the same instant. "I think of you as my son."

He put down his sandwich and his brows pulled together in puzzlement. "But I'm not your son," he said. But he seemed doubtful, and he didn't withdraw his hand.

"I know, and I'm not really your mother, but I could be your mother . . . if you let me."

"My mother's dead."

"You can have more than one mother."

She was propositioning him now, pleading for a touch of another kind.

A mother. The notion jumbled further Bobby Dearborn's confused emotions. All day he had brooded on the events of that morning. By turns he had been angry, puzzled, ashamed, and fearful that his trespass had in some way been unforgivable. He had rerun the scene over and over in his mind and tried to figure out what went wrong. Maybe, he thought, chocolates weren't enough. Maybe it took flowers. Maybe it wasn't that easy. And now this woman, Aunt Janet, whom he had loathed to the point of murder and with whom he still wanted to have sex if only to resolve an urge compounded of pride and need and functioning genitals, was asking to be his mother. He swallowed the dry food in his mouth. His confusion verged on disorientation. For a few moments he didn't know what to think. He had never thought of her as his mother; he had never really thought of anyone as his mother. He wasn't quite sure what a mother was. Motherlessness was something he had lived with most of his life. His memories of his own mother were distant and vague — a voice, a warmth, a presence that became an absence to be endured. Out of that deprivation he had salvaged the meager heroism of the loner. Fighter pilots did not need mothers. So his first impulse was rejection. He frowned, but didn't quite know how to tell her that he didn't want or need a mother. And then he wasn't sure. Dimly, through the welter of feelings, the appeal of her overture glimmered, an idea as potent and compelling in its own way as the passion that had moved him that morning — and not altogether unrelated to it. Her hand was warm and her eyes, when he glanced at them, were soft. A mother. He could, after all, have her for a mother and still be a fighter pilot. He could still be a hero. He could be a hero for her.

"I don't know," he said. "Don't I have to be adopted?"

"That's only the legal part. We can do that any time."

They were silent again for a spell. Time itself seemed tremulous as she waited for this miracle to happen. When he turned to her again his eyes had darkened with a faint bloom of violet and his voice was unguarded.

"I could call you Mom?"

"Yes."

"And Uncle Hedley would be Dad?"

She nodded, because she did not trust her voice. But she couldn't help the tears. They came in a quiet flow down her cheeks, and her nose ran so that she had to get up for a Kleenex. She also wanted to stand back and look at him. She didn't quite believe it was happening. But it was. The earth was moving, and the world was becoming something like what she had always hoped for. With a son she had a future beyond her own.

Janet Vaughn had a few moments of bliss then. She told him to do his homework; there would be time enough for him to change his clothes and go out to the barn to help with the chores. She hovered, but not too closely, as she did things about the house. She would have settled now for this — Gladys Porley's ironing done, her new kitchen tidy and gleaming, her boy, her son, bent at his books, reminding her anew that he was a good student and that other worlds would unfold for him who was now hers.

Her reverie didn't last long. It ended abruptly with the sound of Lucien Quirk's boots and the bang of the door as he came in, red-eyed and seething, spattered with whitewash, and trailing the dog behind him. Silent at first, he claimed the sink and then the room, his dirty boots on her floor. The boy peered up from his books; his "Hi, Lucien" was swallowed in the man's glower. Janet Vaughn wiped her hands on her apron and waited.

"Wadijetelldepreest!"

She didn't understand the words muttered at her on the dragon breath of cheap wine.

"I said what did you tell that God damn priest?"

The voice was small, like the man's stature, but its violence filled the room.

Bobby Dearborn stood up.

The man moved on the woman as though to attack.

"Leave her alone," the boy heard himself growl above the inner noise of his racing heart.

"Leave her alone, huh? Listen to hot-pants Romeo here. *You* leave her alone, you little son of a bitch!"

The boy's eyes knifed at the woman. "You told him?"

But she was looking at the man. "Lucien," she warned in a rising tone.

The man ignored her and went at the boy with the quickness of a terrier, catching him with a sucker punch just below the sternum. A dish shattered on the floor. The woman shrieked in alarm and grabbed at him. Another punch missed the boy, who staggered a little and then grappled defensively. Surprise and fear that he might enrage the man further and even a kind of respect kept him from hitting back. Entangled, like a threesome of violent lovers, the dog yipping at their heels, they lurched around the kitchen, just missing the hot stove, knocking into the table, the sink, the accordion of ironed shirts, making sounds that might have been laughing or weeping, so the rap on the door penetrated only to Janet Vaughn, who now was practically riding the man's back as he tried to pummel the boy and saying "I'll go! For Christ's sake, stop it! I'll go! Stop it!" because she knew Gladys Porley was at the door to pick up the shirts but mostly because she was afraid for the boy.

They stopped suddenly, all breathless, and disentangled.

"Are you all right, Bobby?" the woman asked.

The boy nodded, but his eyes remained fixed on the man.

"Then go upstairs." Janet Vaughn was amazed a little at her own coolness.

The boy hesitated a moment before obeying her.

"When?" the man pressed. He had taken her wrist and pinned her with his eyes.

The rap sounded on the door again.

"Coming, Gladys," the woman sang.

"When?" Lucien Quirk repeated.

"Tomorrow," she said, pronouncing sentence on herself. "The day after tomorrow."

She glanced away and tugged at her entrapped hand. He was strong. She knew that she didn't love him and, what was worse, that she never could love him. It was as though the devil had come for his due.

"Why not tomorrow?"

"Because I have to pack and see people."

"You promise?"

"I promise."

So he let go of her arm and went out the back way with the dog. Janet Vaughn picked up the shirts and opened the side door. The Porley woman swept into the very presence of scandal, and Janet Vaughn was frankly telling a lie, a tale about the dog going mad and wrecking the kitchen; and the absurdity of the lie was somehow understood to be in direct proportion to the enormity of the truth it hid, leaving the other woman speechless as she fished for dollar bills in her purse, trying to imagine what was happening and what would happen next.

Bobby Dearborn sat on the bed in the gelid air of his room and waited for the shaking to stop. He might have wept in his fear and anger and sheer confusion were he not the dry-eyed sort, Captain Robert S. Dearborn of the United States Air Force. Only now his model aircraft poised around the room with their decal insignia seemed pathetic to him, the poor emblems of a dream that no longer sufficed for the human complexities engulfing him. An older, simpler fantasy had revived. He would run away. He would go to Canada. He would go to the north woods and live like a trapper, hunting and fishing for his food. He'd wear buckskin like Davy Crockett and build a log cabin deep in the woods where no one ever went.

He had tried to run away before, right after he had arrived at the farm. The kindly old cop in the cruiser had picked him up before he got to Chelmsford Centre. She had raged at him for a week. This time it would be different. He had some money saved. He would fill the rucksack Aunt Ernestine had given him with food. He'd roll up some blankets and strap them to the top. He would go at night. He would wait outside the railyard in Lowell and catch a freight for Montreal. He shivered and paced as the dream emerged as specific possibilities, as details of the real. He would, for instance, take a frying pan and a pot for making coffee. He would take the double-barreled shotgun, breaking it down into barrel, stock, and hand grip. Then he stopped.

Mrs. Porley had long since left in her car. The silence in the kitchen below was broken by a regular, disturbing sound. With his ear to the radiator he could tell that it was Janet Vaughn crying. Well, she had told Lucien about that morning. He still felt the anger of embarrassment. But he had to struggle to keep his anger and his dream of escape; the sound of her sobs touched him where he was raw, in his sex and, deeper, in his heart. He was again confused, his simple answer in disarray, and he found himself going down the stairs to the kitchen.

Janet Vaughn was at the table, huddled as though to keep her misery private.

"Auntie . . ."

She raised a tear-swollen face. For an instant, with her jaw clenched and her eyes sore, it seemed she had reverted to what she had been and might lash out at him. He feared that then more than before, because he no longer had hate to prop against her. But Janet Vaughn had found a tissue and was composing her face.

"I'm sorry, Bobby," she said.

"For what?"

"For telling Lucien."

Her apology made him uncomfortable. "That's all right," he mumbled, blushing at the sense of easy grandeur that forgiving gave him. And he was awkward, being near someone he might call his mother.

He drew closer. "Are you okay?" he asked.

· 213 ·

She smiled, superior and easy with him, reaching out a hand to take his. It all might have been a private joke between them. "Are *you* okay?" she echoed. "He didn't hurt you?"

Bobby Dearborn shook his head, withdrew his hand, and sat down next to her. "Why did he get so mad?"

"Men are like that."

He nodded his agreement, as though he knew.

"I'm sorry about this morning," he managed to say after an effort.

She touched his face before turning away to hide her eyes. "Those things happen," she said.

They were both thinking the same thing when he voiced it: "What are you going to do when Uncle Hedley comes home?"

He hadn't meant to upset her again, but it was as if he had put a slow knife into her, the way she shuddered, the pain flowing into her face as she put a fist to her mouth to keep back the tears. "I don't know," she said. "I just don't know."

And in her distress he saw, like a revelation, how small were his own troubles.

She was cheerful a moment later, asking him whether he would like some coffee. "There's some left in the percolator."

"Sure."

"And some cookies?"

"Okay."

So they sat for a while, friendly, not altogether at ease, not quite what they had been, not yet mother and son, just two people at a kitchen table having coffee.

❧

Later, when the cows began to bellow their hunger in the cold twilight of the barnyard, the boy went out to let them in and to start the milking. The radio pulsed with the machines, and the cats gathered for their lap of milk. Out on

the wide floor running down the center of the barn, he
lifted and secured the wooden hatches in front of the cows'
mangers. The breath of the animals steamed the air. On the
other side, the bull, thinner now, snorted and pawed at his
bedding of straw. All around above them hay filled the barn
like the coat of a huge shaggy beast turned inside out. The
boy went warily, afraid he might come on Lucien Quirk
and have to defend himself with words or fists. That punch
in the kitchen resonated. He wanted both to avoid the man
and to find him. He wanted to explain. Didn't he say everything was fair as far as women were concerned? Hadn't he
told him how to do it? Still, guilt of another kind had
started.

He climbed the nailed ladder to the loft, which was lit
by a single naked bulb that, high on a beam, gave off just
enough light to work by. It took a lot of effort getting the
hay down. The packed, knotted stuff came loose in wisps
and small clumps that had to be worked like veins in a
mine. He piled it on the edge of the mow, then pushed it
over, hearing it thump on the floor below.

When he had enough hay down, he went to change the
milkers and filter the milk. He dawdled at the radio over a
song, "Love Is Strange," by Mickey and Sylvia, before remembering he had to feed the cows grain before giving
them hay. The tune rang in his head, a siren song redolent
of lush places and sweltering nights. The wide door of the
feed room scraped along the floor as he pulled it open. He
fumbled for the light and stopped with sudden fright as it
went on. Lucien Quirk sprawled on a bed of sacked dairy
feed, pug face to the ceiling, passed out. The empties were
on the floor.

"Lucien," the boy whispered loudly, wanting to wake the
man and also leave him sleeping. Something like compas-
sion stirred in him. "Lucien," he repeated, "Lucien, are you
all right?"

A dead eye slit glazed for a moment and closed.

The boy filled the feed cart and wheeled it along in front

of the frantic cows, scooping grain in rough proportion to the milk each was giving. When he returned, the man was as he had left him, slack-faced in the sleep of a drunk.

Bobby Dearborn went to change the milking machines, all the while thinking of the man in the feed room as some strange, secret treasure. He went back again. But he couldn't rouse the man to get him up and come into the house, where it was warm. Finally, because there was nothing left to do, the boy shook out some empty cotton print bags and covered him. He whispered good night, turned off the light, and closed the door.

❧ 23 ❧

THE ACTUALITY of running away with Lucien Quirk registered only gradually with Janet Vaughn. It accumulated with all the small things she touched and held to pack or leave behind. In the attic the Vaughn ghosts might have been whispering about her as she retrieved the three-piece set of imitation leather luggage, a wedding present she had used on her honeymoon with Hedley. They had gone nowhere else with the luggage except for a weekend to the Eastern States Exposition to see the prize cattle. Now she would use it to run away with the hired man to San Diego, California, another world. The peculiar airlessness of tragedy made her gag as she maneuvered the suitcases down the steep attic steps and opened the largest one on her bed. How much of my life can I pack into this space, she asked herself. She boggled at her actual movements, sighed heavily, but could not weep as she made the small choices that were necessary for the final choice. Things were mute in their accusation. She couldn't leave the mother-of-pearl brush and mirror set or the inlaid rosewood box where she kept her few bangles and beads, including the silver locket. Or the matching lamps with the figurine bases and the decent silver in the living room closet or the set of embroidered Irish linen that was too good to use. And that willowware bowl out of which she had dished so much potato salad. And the set of maroon towels she had bought to go with the curtains she made for the bathroom. Her new kitchen. She knew it wasn't just the things themselves, not entirely, anyway; it was the things as the tangible webbing of her life in that place.

This sentimentality about things also kept her from seeing beyond them to the real horrors of what she contemplated. The intensity of her love for Hedley and Bobby, for her mother and sisters and brother and their families, for Ernestine and even for Gladys Porley, took her unawares, opened up in her like a wound she was afraid to look at. She would make of them ghosts that would haunt her, even as she could still feel the glower of her dad behind his newspaper as he withdrew his love. And the silence of those Vaughn ancestors in the attic with their fixed, severe faces would be Ernestine's silence as that smile finally faded to an unspoken What did you expect? And the old racial judgment stung again, because she would be, finally, the Irish maid, Gladys Porley's washerwoman and favorite charity, skipping town with odds and ends and the wino handyman. In the nursery she kept immaculate she pondered what she might loot from among the baby things. She could have wept again for that little ghost then, for her investment in what had been lost and in what she was to lose. She sighed so deeply it hurt. The very air seemed solid.

Still, her hands moved, picked up these things, and packed them into suitcases and the cardboard boxes to fit into the trunk of the car. She pushed deep into the closet for the maternity dresses and found most of them too heavy — she had worn them in winter and very early spring. It would be warm in Southern California all year round. And dry, like a desert. It did not seem natural. She worried that there would be no peepers in the spring or crickets in late summer. She wondered if there were real trees, like elms and maples, and lush days in June when the rain could sing. She already missed those Octobers shot with flame and knew she would never wake up again on a January morning after a blizzard to find the world blue and white and silent. She discovered suddenly that she was a New Englander, that she was rooted here, that she could kiss the boards under her feet, could treasure the monstrous old stove, could treasure what she thought she despised rather than give them up for the blankness of the unknown. It was, finally, like death; in the yard below the car waited like a hearse.

Yet she continued, however mechanically, to embalm bits of her life to take with her. She packed the silver and left the linen; she found a maternity shift that might do even in the heat. She acted in dumb terror because she had given her word that she would go and because, ultimately, she was pregnant by this man. She was trapped in this version of reality because she had rehearsed a thousand times, awake and asleep, the shame that would envelop her as her condition grew obvious. For all her courage, she was afraid of that and of Lucien Quirk. He was capable, she thought now, of murder. As he lurked and hovered, hanging around on flimsy excuses, she saw something desperate in the shift of his eyes, which were edged about with the fire of cheap wine — the pit she was to save him from. She didn't hate Lucien Quirk for this; it was simply that she didn't love him, couldn't love him, and that was worse. In some ways this failure of love was the worst failure. Love might have redeemed her, she thought, might have made her thickening middle appear as more than some crude indulgence of instinct, the literal weight of her sin. She trembled to find her faith intact after all. God was letting her have her deepest wish — her child, her Jerusalem, her San Diego, her hell.

❦ 24 ❧

THE CAR'S READY. It's got a small oil leak in the block, but it should get us there okay."

Lucien Quirk had sobered up, though some false bravado left over from the wine starched his queasiness as he sat at the table, ostensibly making plans but actually, she guessed, testing her resolve.

Too numbed to think, Janet Vaughn responded with minimal nods. The road map of the United States that he had unfolded on the table terrified her.

"I think we ought to go south first, right down to Georgia and then across." His hand, pointing, came down the coastal plain and swept west through Alabama, Mississippi, Louisiana, Texas, New Mexico, Arizona, and she was in the fourth grade again with Sister Clemency, learning how to spell the names of the state capitals and how there were belts for cotton, corn, and cattle. Now it was an alien vastness with unimaginable distances from her own little state tucked neatly in the upper right-hand corner of the map.

"I'll help you drive once we get out of state," Lucien Quirk was saying, prodding her for some kind of affirmation, though he knew she had a suitcase already packed and hidden away in the closet upstairs. "We'll stop at the Grand Canyon. You'll get a kick out of that." He took her hand, and his voice softened. "It'll be okay, Jan, I promise. We'll see the country. We'll have fun." He committed his eyes, but she looked away and withdrew her hand. All she found in her heart for this man now was some rancid residue of affection. She glanced again at the map and this time found it too constricting: there was no place she could flee this fleeing.

"I know it ain't easy," he was saying from behind her, "but we ain't got a choice. You know that."

The map, with its veining roads and rivers, its small towns spotting like a rash, misted over. She nearly cried, "No!" then, nearly told him she couldn't go and that she would stay and suffer and make others suffer rather than leave. She stood but did not turn. He was close behind her, hands on her hips, then moving up, over her breasts. "Jan," he began thickly. She could feel him against her bottom. She remembered with regret other days in the same place, bending, tugging at her clothes to let him, quick and wanton, standing up, like an animal in rut. Now the chemistry had changed. Now his readiness did nothing except remind her that she was his.

"No," she said and pushed his hands away. "I don't feel well. And I still have a lot to do."

She didn't actually have much to do. She was mostly packed and free. It had been her dream to be free, free of all this work. Now she found herself clinging to the work. She vacuumed the floors and rugs, oiled and polished the furniture, came down both stairs a step at a time with a damp rag and got on her hands and knees in the bathroom to leave it shining. She went out into the frosty day to clean the storm windows that had been fastened to the kitchen casements. Up on a stepladder she applied the pink paste that dried to a dust and wiped away, leaving her ghost against a mineral sky. Shading her eyes, she could peer in at what would be hers no more.

Later she took out the ledger and paid what bills she could. In a note to Ernestine Vaughn, she explained which bills had been paid, which checks were due, and how Hedley had to sign them for her. That morning in the Lowell Five Cents Savings in Elmsbury Centre, she had cashed a check for two hundred and fifty dollars for herself. They couldn't really afford it, not the way the hospital bills were piling up. And it seemed such an extravagant amount; it seemed like stealing. At the same time it was a paltry sum to show for ten years of marriage and work, the work of marriage. It was as though she had put a very cheap price on herself. Of course, they would be taking the car. She would be taking herself as well, stealing herself from her husband and from this place, this life.

Penning in her readable script goodbye notes to her family, Janet Vaughn wet the writing tablet with tears. Each note came out differently, yet phrases repeated themselves: Please believe that I love you very much . . . I will miss you as long as I live . . . You won't be able to understand why I'm doing this, but . . . Please believe that I didn't have any choice . . . I did not want you to suffer on my account . . . I love you . . . I love you . . . I love you . . . She could write nothing to her husband, though. The words she left for the others would not come for him. Her treachery and love ran too deep. They canceled each other on the plain white of the paper, and she crumpled one false start after another and threw them in the basket. For the boy, her son, who hovered now, watching and suspecting what was happening, she bought a ham, a brick of processed cheese, and several boxes of chocolate chip cookies. She planned to leave these treats for him on the table, along with the notes to her family and Ernestine. "Oh, Christ," she cried aloud, "it is like death!"

On her last visit to her husband in the hospital, she remained virtually speechless as they sat in chairs next to the bed.

"It's okay, Jan," said Hedley Vaughn, sensing the depth of her dismay, confusing it with the collapse that sometimes comes with relief. "I'll be home soon now," he repeated to reassure her. "Three, maybe four days now, the doc says, if the tests are good. He says the old ticker's working like a regular clock." He laughed then, his old dry chortle. "He says just to make sure that damn bull doesn't walk on me again." He talked on, garrulous for a while about sleeping pills he needed, about the farm, about the old man in the next bed who had been taken away, presumably to die. She put her arms around him and held him. It was her way of being held. Her tears wet his cheek. His hand, soft from the hospital, rubbed hers.

"It's okay now," he soothed; "it's all over. Everything's going to be okay."

The kindness in his voice only magnified the enormity of what she was about to do. Her leaving would dumfound him, possibly kill him. She had thought of hints she might strew around: What would you do, Hedley, if anything happened to me? Forgive me for everything, Hedley. Remember that I will always love you. Or even a straightforward, quiet confession, right there in the hospital: Hedley, I'm pregnant. I'm leaving you to go to California with Lucien Quirk, because I don't want to have a child here that will be a living insult to you the rest of your life.

But she barely spoke. Words went chalky in her mouth. She remained past closing time, staying with him until a nurse came in and told her she had to leave. Even then, after putting on her coat, she lingered. Finally, abruptly, she fled down the corridor, her shoes rapping on the polished floor as she went by the hushed rooms and took the stairs, moving.

❧ 25 ❧

THE DREAM revolved like a torture wheel. A soft green spot on the brown map of California grew until a thread of blue became a tree-lined river with fields beyond where they were all going — Hedley, the boy, Lucien, the cows, the house, and the barn, pulled by one of those powerful new tractors and a logical force that explained as well why she was blooming with child, which mollified her mother, indeed, made her happy enough to smile, Janet Vaughn's happiness sharpening until it touched terror and the dream collapsed like a pricked balloon so that she dreamed she was awake and facing (with the intensity of a dream) the stark dilemma of her life until she could bear it no more and the brown map swam under her again as she sought the soft green spot and the thread of blue.

The morning was eerily like any other when she woke. The room was cold, with the heating just starting to bang the pipes. Things had to be done. Lucien Quirk had gotten up and made coffee before going out to milk the cows. He had also lit the stove so the kitchen was warm when she came down from dressing in the chill upstairs. She started breakfast. The scarred black frying pan that she had for so long wanted to throw out and replace with one of those shiny aluminum things had the weight of a precious object in her hand. Bacon would never smell the same in California. Did they even have it there? She called the boy. She made oatmeal and toast and orange juice from a frozen can. She put two eggs sunny side up when she heard his footsteps on the stairs and had to hold her breath for knowing how she would never hear that sound again.

❧

Bobby Dearborn came into the kitchen apprehensively. He had sensed for some time what was happening. It was the foreboding in the air, the hush of covert busyness, the half-packed, poorly concealed boxes in Janet Vaughn's room. Still, he didn't quite believe it. He took her guilty glances and evasiveness as signs that she hadn't forgiven him. A couple of times, half joking, testing her mood, he had called her Mom. She had paled and averted her face. And he had heard them in the kitchen at night, Lucien Quirk talking with new authority in his voice about going south and then west. He could hear the woman's silences as the man said enough for both of them. And there had been something too easy for the boy about the reconciliation with the man after the row in the kitchen. They hadn't even talked about it. The day after the fight he had helped the man, who was all sobered up, change the oil and put a new fan belt in the Chevy. He had been tense with embarrassment, afraid they still weren't friends. The man had been first vague with preoccupation, then blustery in his cheerfulness, clapping him on the back as though nothing had happened, as though it didn't matter that something had. Finally, the boy knew they were leaving, knew it instinctively, the way a dog knows when its master is about to leave.

Now, at breakfast, with the woman hollow-eyed from sleeplessness, departure was in the air, palpable as a coffin. They avoided each other's glances as he pecked at his food. The minutes hummed on the clock. There had been so many ruptures in his life already, one more didn't seem significant. He could not abide the sad scenes in movies — the death watches — because they took so long, because the tension became unbearable. Get it over with, get it done, he wanted to yell. Life resumes on the other side of disasters.

But he turned suddenly to gaze at her, making her start. "You're leaving with Lucien, aren't you?" he accused.

Janet Vaughn didn't deny it. She tried to avoid his eyes, but couldn't.

"Aren't you?" he repeated, a boy now, panic in the whine of his voice.

She nodded.

"When?" he insisted. "Today?"

She nodded again and found her voice. "We're driving to California." Voicing it to him made it real, inevitable, intolerable.

He stared right at her and his voice was pure and piercing. "I thought you were going to be my mother."

Janet Vaughn flushed, then sighed. "I am . . ."

His expression changed to a quizzical frown. "Then why are you going away?"

"I have to." She said it and didn't believe it. She wiped her hands and sat at the table with him as something more of an answer hovered.

He didn't press; he sat and waited, watching her as the clock moved and the logs settled in the stove.

"Because . . ." She struggled but couldn't tell him. "Your uncle Hedley . . ."

"You don't have to tell him," he said, willing to share her betrayal that much.

She resisted touching him. She sighed and closed her eyes and took a deep breath. "Bobby, you don't understand. It's not just that . . ."

"What is it?"

Janet Vaughn shook her head and covered her face. When she looked up at him he saw that the mystery was enormous, bigger than life, then life itself as she shocked him, whispering, "I'm pregnant." Beyond anger or pity, he was awestruck by the ever-unfolding complexity of life, by the logic of its deepening. And what he felt as he regarded this woman in her modern-looking slacks was not jealousy in the ordinary sense, but the residue of jealousy, which is irrelevance, a sense of no longer counting. He was an orphan again, a ward of the state.

"You won't be coming back," he said evenly, cutting to the heart of the matter.

Hunched forward as though with stomach pain, she was averting her face and shaking her head as her hand groped blindly for his. He held it and was moved by her plight and by his own part in it. Another kind of manhood was dawning in him.

Then it was time to go. It was after eight. The school bus would be there shortly. Then it was there, its honk like a knell. The boy wanted to be gone. Rangy and clumsy in the jeans and cowboy shirt Ernestine had bought him, he rose and embraced Janet Vaughn for a trembling moment. "Don't go," he blurted and was going himself, grabbing his books and jacket, pushing through the flung door, running for the impatient bus.

※

Her face was still a mess when Lucien Quirk came in.

"Well, I gave the stock enough to hold them for tonight," he announced, a bounce in his words as he ignored her tears. "We'd better get on the road. I figure we can make New Jersey by nightfall." He was gentle with her for a moment — an arm around the shoulder, an understanding smile. But not too gentle; he kept some soldierly steel in his voice. "All right, let's get moving. It's always great to get moving." Despite his limp he bounded up the stairs, and she followed him with halting steps, as though she had taken on his wounds. From her room she heard him splashing in the tub and humming his tune. It brought back the summer and everything they had done and that she wished now could be undone. Because sex leads to possession and she was possessed now, looking at herself in the mirror or making her deserted marriage bed (for the last time) or carrying what she had packed down the stairs, one moment manic, full of hectic energy, the next utterly enervated, hearing voices — Hedley's, the boy's, her mother nattering in a corner, her sister Ellen saying, Jan, Jan, Jan, right in her ear.

Spry in a clean shirt and chino trousers, Lucien Quirk descended the stairs with duffel in hand. His freshly shaven face glowed ruddy, and some straightening of the back made him seem less short. His voice commanded her. The boxes would go in the back seat, her flat luggage in the trunk. Quite suddenly he was no longer the hired man she had reclaimed from booze and to whom she paid five dollars a week. He was . . . In fact, she didn't know quite what he was. She knew only she no longer held sway, that it no longer seemed her own house. She saw a stranger with a duffel bag and a cardboard box of things that had taken him a few minutes to pack. Deft and quick, this man was uprooting her from what she had and what she was. He was in the kitchen and in the yard, backing up the car and opening the door, coming and going, getting more alien with every word and gesture. He even seemed a little common, with his cheap shirt and cigarettes, like a million other ordinary men. Hedley, at least, was never ordinary. And in what was left of her mind she could imagine too clearly now how poor and pitifully drab this new life was going to be. And still she brought out the letters for her family and the food for the boy; she neatened things up and held the door open and assented with her actions to what was happening. She was dressed lightly in slacks and a thin sweater for traveling, and the cold air knifed at her. She simply felt she had no choice. She would do it if it killed her, because she had said she would do it, because she was pregnant, because, in a state bordering on shock now, she could no longer imagine not doing it, because misery has its own disabling weight, and that finally made her helpless, a victim.

How smoothly and quickly it went! The car was packed; the food and letters were arranged on the clean table in the neat house. Everything was ready. Nothing was ready. She said goodbye with a glance and was at the side door and going out when the phone rang.

"Don't answer it."

The man's voice ordered, and his hand on her arm propelled her out the door, which locked with a click behind her. The ringing persisted, followed her out into the cold beside the car, where she finally broke from his grip with annoyance and stood listening, knowing only her mom would let a phone ring forever. It tugged at her like a lifeline and she followed it, breaking from the man in a shuffling, woman's run around the back to the unlocked door, breathless and crying as she lifted the solid black instrument to her head.

"Janet!"

"Hi, Mom."

Janet Vaughn was silently and copiously weeping, sniffling and blowing her nose and saying she had a cold. Her mother's accusatory voice drilled in her ear. "You know Mary wants us all for Thanksgiving."

"Uh-huh."

"She wants you to make the pies."

"Uh-huh." Janet Vaughn did make a good crust.

"Will Hedley be able to come? You say he'll be home from the hospital soon."

Janet Vaughn found a tissue and blew her nose. She ignored Lucien Quirk, who had come in and was pacing and scowling and holding up his wrist with its cheap new watch. Her voice steadied. "We'll have to ask the doctor."

"Well, Mary wants to make sure Hedley comes if he's able. She wants you to bring Bobby along, too."

"Bobby might stay with Ernestine. She'll be all alone."

"Well, I don't see why Ernestine can't come," Rose Gilooly said with some testiness. "I'll talk to Mary about it."

"I'm sure Ernestine would love to."

"Mary may not want her."

"That's okay too, Mom." Janet Vaughn, self-possessed now, stared right back at Lucien Quirk, who was tightening his jaw with impatience. "I have to go now, Mom; I'll call you later."

She hung up the phone but did not move.

"Come on, we've gotta get going."

Janet Vaughn remained motionless and silent for several moments.

"Well?"

"I can't go with you."

The man snorted at her. "Yeah, sure. Let's talk about it in the car."

Janet Vaughn stayed next to the phone, which was on the desk in the hallway to the dining room.

"I can't go," she repeated.

Lucien Quirk approached with fisted hands. "What the hell do you mean, you can't go?"

"I have to make pies for Thanksgiving at Mary's. That's my other sister I told you about. She's the one that lives in Tewksbury in a real nice house. We're all going. You can probably come, too, if you want to."

She knew she sounded insane, but she didn't mind. It was something of a refuge. She spoke with such maddening calmness and certainty that Lucien Quirk, unnerved, was both gnashing his teeth and laughing until his face resolved itself into an intimidating incredulity and his voice hammered the other reality at her.

"What the hell are you talking about? We're going to be in San Diego for Thanksgiving. Now let's get in the God damn car before I do something I don't want to do."

She walked around him into the kitchen, taking possession of it again. "I have to make the pies for Thanksgiving," she repeated, a statement that was beside the point and exactly the point. She began to collect the letters she had spread out.

"All right, let's go."

"I'm not going."

"I said let's go."

"No."

He hit her wrist and grabbed it, spinning her around so violently that she almost fell. He jerked her erect and pulled her close to his contorted mouth.

"Listen, God damn it, you're going out that door with me and we're driving to San Diego and I don't want to hear any more shit about pies and Thanksgiving."

"No, I'm not."

"Yes, you are, lady."

"No, I'm not."

He pulled at her. She dug her heels into her new floor. They shouted and screamed back and forth, struggling, knocking over a chair, before they stopped and stared at each other, breathless, his hand still around her wrist like a manacle. His face flamed.

"What the hell's gotten into you? Everything's ready, for Christ's sake. You can't back out now!"

"I'm not going." She pulled at her trapped hand. "I'm not going anywhere with you."

He released her and in the same motion slapped her hard. But she stood, facing him down, her eyes leveled into his. Movie talk became real.

"You can hit me, Lucien, if you want to. You can break my bones. You can kill me. I'm not going with you."

He hit her again, but it was a pulled punch that became a caress as his hand stayed on her cheek. After a moment she covered his hand with hers in a gesture of comfort for his having lost what she knew he wanted so badly.

"You're going to get a big belly, Jan. You know what that'll mean if you stay here. People can count."

He was pleading now, seduced by the sympathy in her eyes. Losing.

The woman picked up the chair and sat on it at the table. For his sake she tried to keep the joy of her relief from showing.

"I don't care what they say, Lucien. I can't go. I can't leave this place."

"You can try."

"No, I can't."

"Remember the night we went to Lawrence to that place. Remember the fun we had, huh? Remember how you felt free."

He lit a cigarette and smoke fanged through his nostrils. Otherwise he might have been a little boy begging his mother for something.

"That was for a night. This is for a lifetime."

He settled next to her at the table and took her hand, gently this time. His fingers trembled on hers.

"Just try getting in the car. We'll drive for a while. Just try it. If you don't like it, I'll bring you back."

She shook her head.

He became agitated again. He got up and paced to the sink and back.

"It's because of me, ain't it?"

"No."

"You ain't let me touch you since that priest was here."

He stood working his jaw, the pain and threat growing again in his voice.

"Father Fahey doesn't have anything to do with it."

He sat down again and started stroking her arm and talking to the side of her face.

"They're going to crucify you when they find out you got my kid. They ain't gonna let you forget it."

"I don't care. I can't leave."

"It is me, ain't it?"

"No, Lucien. If things were different . . ."

"Things are different. What's your mother and your sisters and that priest and Hedley gonna say when you're out to here?" He gestured in front of himself.

Janet Vaughn bowed her head and repeated, as in a litany, "I cannot go, I cannot go, I cannot go . . ."

The man was up, fuming, circling. "What's gonna happen to me when he comes home?"

"What do you mean?"

"When Hedley gets here."

"I don't know."

"It's out in the God damn chicken coop for me, ain't it?"

"You have your room upstairs."

"I mean with you, with you and me."

"I don't know," she said before her silence grew dangerous.

"It ain't going to be the same, is it?"

"How can it be!" she cried. "Hedley's coming home."

His intake of breath was audible. His hands worked. "Hedley! God damn Hedley!"

"Lucien, please try to understand."

"Come with me."

"You know I can't."

He had gone down beside her on one knee in supplication and had taken her forearm in his hands. "We can start a new life."

"No," she said, but mechanically, as though the pleading and refusal had become a ritual.

"I'll get a good job. I'll take care of you."

"I can't."

"Yes, you can, you just don't want to."

His voice had hardened and the grip on her arm tightened.

"Lucien, I can't. I would if I could. I just can't."

But she didn't look at him when she said that.

He begged. She said no. They stopped for a tense, trembling silence. Then a strangled sound broke from him and the grip on her arm became a powerful tug as she was pulled off the chair and down onto the kitchen floor, where he mauled her, ripped at her clothes, exposed and splayed her on the cold lineoleum. She didn't resist, but yielded like something dead so that there was only the suck and thud of mere meat, an irrevocable violation that culminated in a desolation of upside-down chair legs, table legs, the ceiling, the weak sun in her eyes. The weight finally lifted. He stood over her, finished, buckling himself, his face written with cold rage at this final rejection, his words pointing at her heart.

"When that son of a bitch comes home, lady, I'm going to kill him."

He left, slamming out the back door.

She lay as though stunned. Then, slowly and carefully, she picked herself up as if she were one of the pieces of her broken life.

❧ 26 ❧

W HERE'S MY CHAIR?"

Hedley Vaughn stood stooped next to the kitchen table while his wife helped him out of the ancient overcoat he had worn home from the hospital. It was plain to Bobby Dearborn that all the changes disconcerted the man. The quiet smile of expectation that had flickered around his eyes and mouth on the way home in Ernestine Vaughn's car had thinned to a tense neutrality.

"We put it in the attic," said Janet Vaughn, hanging his coat near the door. "It needs fixing."

"I want it back."

His nostrils tilted and flared as though sensing the deeper usurpation.

"Then I'll get it fixed and bring it back." His voice quavered as she smiled at the boy and the other woman, bringing them to share the blame.

Bobby Dearborn waited apprehensively. His uncle, though weak, exerted a presence that once again dominated the house. It hardly seemed credible now that what had happened had happened. And was still happening, because Janet Vaughn, on the offensive, flaunting her new kitchen, was still pregnant and would become more so. And when those two realities collided, as inevitably they must, the world, the boy thought, would not be able to bear it.

That collision appeared imminent. Every glance, gesture, and word seemed to tell the tale. The very shininess of the new floor, waxed for the man's homecoming, glittered with the trespasses of Janet Vaughn, Lucien Quirk, and himself, because he counted himself among the sinners. He had tried. He would share the blame when the flammable truth spilled all around them.

"But don't you think it's a whole lot better?" Janet Vaughn asked.

The man grunted. "It must have cost an arm and a leg."

"Oh, it didn't, Hedley. We did it ourselves."

"I think it's a great improvement," said Ernestine Vaughn, smiling as she sided with her sister-in-law.

"And I'll cover your chair and bring it down and everything will be okay." Janet Vaughn took her husband by the elbow and pointed him. "Let's go into the living room."

Things seemed safe again as the man, again the patient, obeyed, trooping in with the others. Still wearing his good suit, he acted for the moment like a guest in his own house. He sat stiffly on the sofa while the light, filtering through lace curtains, touched his face with waxy ghostliness. Below in the cellar the furnace roared, making the radiators hiss and hit false notes; even in the coldest weather the Vaughn house did not have the heat on at full blast in the middle of the afternoon. It was all very awkward, with coffee and cake, Ernestine smiling, and the boy staying in the background.

"Where the hell's Lucien?" the man asked, as though that might be what was amiss.

Janet Vaughn glanced at the boy. "Have you seen him, Bobby?"

"He's out in the barn, I guess. Or maybe gone to town."

Bobby Dearborn couldn't just come out and say that the hired man was in the feed room passed out with cheap wine and had been that way for several days — since the day he and Janet Vaughn were supposed to run away. He couldn't tell his uncle that it was just as well, too, because there was no telling what the hired man might do or say if he were to sober up. So the boy dissembled, not exactly lying, but not telling the truth either. He glanced back at the woman and felt the mesh of mendacity tighten around him.

Then there was silence as they fumbled for something to talk about. There was only so much you could say about the weather. The boy gulped his cup of coffee. Ernestine smiled into a vacuum. Hedley Vaughn shifted about, agitated, as though afflicted by the thick unease in the air. Being passive and waited on was exactly what he hadn't wanted. The house, all clean and smelling of polish and fresh paint, reminded him of the hospital.

"I need a pair of scissors," he said out of the blue. When his wife fetched him a pair, he slid the blade under the plastic name bracelet on his wrist and snipped it.

"I've been waiting to do that ever since I went into that damn place," he announced.

He relaxed then, smiled, and said the cake was good. With the coffee helping him, he rose and went to stand in the short hallway that led to the kitchen.

"I suppose it needed doing," he conceded, turning back to the others. "Did a good job, too. Only I want that chair back . . . next to the stove, where it's warm."

When Ernestine Vaughn left a few minutes after that, the boy thought it would finally happen. He thought his uncle had been waiting out of courtesy for his sister to leave. His heart jumped when the man said, "Well, I think it's time for a little talk." It was strange too, because his uncle Hedley was smiling as much as he ever smiled.

Bobby Dearborn glanced quickly at his aunt, but could read nothing from her face. She had moved to sit beside her husband. The boy sat in an adjacent armchair and braced himself. His uncle's words came, so different from what he expected that for a moment he was disoriented.

"I hear, Bobby, from your aunt Janet that you're going to be our son."

Dry-mouthed, the boy managed a "Yes, sir."

His uncle was leaning toward him, strangely human. "And that's what you want?"

"Yeah." He made up a smile out of relief.

"Well, I'm damn glad. It's the best thing that's happened for a while." His benign gaze took in Janet Vaughn, whose face squirmed with emotion. For a moment, the man's hand on the boy's shoulder, the woman touching both of them, they were a little family, happy with a happiness that would only deepen the shattering that was to come.

&

Later, after he had rested for a while, Hedley Vaughn donned a warm shirt and washed overalls, woolen socks, and rubber boots. In the woodshed he put on a lined denim barn coat that came below his waist. Shaky still and pale, but his old self in these familiar clothes, he went out to reclaim his farm.

And out in the barn, amid the rich stink of manure, the tarragon scent of hay, the visible, biblical breath of the animals, the straight old wood, the burlap and hayseed and sawdust roughness, amid the smells and textures of a lifetime, Hedley Vaughn finally felt at home. Had he been of religious bent, he might have likened this sense of reclamation to a kind of resurrection. But he was not schooled in exaltation or in exultation, for that matter. His soul was as simple and sturdy as the pegged beams and nailed boards framing the life around him. He was not particularly conscious of what it all signified, because, in the end, he did not stand outside the existence of the hay-filled loft, the breathing herd, and the pale light admitted by the cobwebbed windows. These things were what should be.

Indeed, he rather quickly turned to business. Stick in hand and followed by the dog, he went down the back of the herd like a general inspecting a regiment. It all seemed shipshape enough. The broken drinkers had in fact been fixed. A new pipe led to the hen house. There were signs of competent carpentry. The whitewash pleased him, though he never saw much use in it himself. Out on the barn floor in front of the cows, he peered in at the bull. The animal was looking poor and mean, its pink snout frothing around the brass ring. Armed with a stick, the man formerly would have thought nothing of opening the heavy gate to the pen and going in. Now he stood outside and frowned. Should have kept that last bull calf, he said to himself as he poked around. He looked in on the hens. He checked the bay to see if they had enough sawdust. He tapped with his stick the poised barrel of crude molasses. He went into the feed room.

For a moment he did not comprehend. The form lay on the bags as though on a bed and appeared unconscious, then awake, then hostile, the eyes angry and red. Back on the bottle, the older man saw with a disappointment that wasn't altruistic. "Lucien, how are you doing?" he said.

"I'm doing fine. How are you doing?"

The man gave no indication of moving, but lay there, in a barn coat, propped partway up, with a bottle handy.

"Well, they let me out of that damn hospital."

Hedley Vaughn stood over the other man in the manner of an attending physician. When the other merely stared, he added, "Jan gave you a bed in the house, didn't she?"

"You could say that."

"It's warmer in there."

"I like it here fine."

The farmer cleared his throat. The man's unfriendliness disconcerted him. "Barn looks good," he complimented.

Lucien Quirk grunted.

"You sure you don't want to come in out of the cold?"

"I'm sure."

"Suit yourself."

The farmer turned from some muttered rejoinder and closed the door after him, puzzled and annoyed as he went out through the cow barn and across the half-frozen muck of the barnyard. Not everything was that shipshape. He felt some uneasy connection between things — the bull, the hired man drunk, his chair gone. He shrugged it off and inspected the young stock huddled under the hen house. He walked around the equipment sheds and out into the turnip field, where a few leftover purple tops still showed green against the dun land. It was a bright, brown November day with a fresh northeasterly breeze chasing the intermittent clouds and the polished leaves underfoot. As he poked through the thatch of dead vegetation in the garden, he fretted himself with plans. He would plant turnips again and buy more chicks for the hen house come spring, and keep the next bull calf and . . .

Across the road on Mayhew's stripped and violated farm, the plywood-clad forms of the new houses sounded with interior work and looked flimsier than ever to the man. He stood for a long spell, his back to the strengthening wind. Those houses won't last long, he thought with grim satisfaction. Someday they'd fall down and blow away, and the land, which would always be there, no matter what they did to it, would heal itself, would revert to forest or farm, to what it was meant to be. In these matters time was on his side, even if his own stock of it was running out.

"What the hell's happened to Lucien Quirk?" he asked his wife when he got back to the house.

"I think he's been drinking again," Janet Vaughn replied, not quite lying and not really telling the truth. The truth had grown too monstrous to tell.

"Well, he sure is cranky as hell."

Janet Vaughn said nothing.

"Is he able to work?"

"Most of the time. He does the morning chores. Bobby does the night chores when Lucien's not able."

The man glanced around him. He was lost in this gleaming kitchen without his chair. He sat at the table. "When did it start?"

"A week or so back, I guess."

Hedley Vaughn rubbed his gray face and made a noise.

If he sensed anything concealed from him, he didn't show it. He sat for a moment and the expression on his face softened to something like receptiveness, as though understanding some of what she had gone through. "It ain't been easy, has it, Jan."

Janet Vaughn's knees went weak and her eyes freshened. But she didn't sit down and she didn't weep, because she was afraid that if she did, she would tell him everything. The urge to do that festered within her, grew like a malignancy that might finally consume her. She wanted to spew it all out — the affair, the pregnancy, their plans to run away, the boy's advances — everything. Because she had never had anything really to hide from her husband. Because she would have to tell him soon anyway. Because she wanted his forgiveness or at least his understanding. At the same time, she had a thousand rationalizations for not telling him anything. He needed time to settle in. It would only spread the misery. It might kill him. And it was all quite incredible, so he might not believe and understand the facts and circumstances of what had happened; he would hear only the wickedness. And she feared the judgment of his eyes.

"I'm all right," she said. "The worst is over."

❧ 27 ❧

In fact, the worst, as she had feared, was only just beginning. She had to help her husband up the stairs, one step at a time. There were mornings when she had to help him out of bed and into the bathroom. She had to make sure he took the right pills at the right time from the array of bottles on the bureau. As soon as she could, she bought some red fabric and ran up a slipcover for his old chair on her sewing machine so that he could have a warm place to sit and read the paper or doze and fidget, because he couldn't do much else. He had spells that frightened her, and sometimes he slept in the chair with his mouth open and was so still that she thought him gone. And always the weight of the impending, inevitable revelation of her condition lay heavily on her heart.

Hedley Vaughn was not the only semi-invalid she had to take care of. Lucien Quirk in his drinking bouts exhibited a variety of drunkenness — the fastidious tippler, clean-shaven and with a wheeze to his breath as he went about some morning chore; the jolly type, but never quite jolly, with his face inflamed and his mouth ribald and eyes with hooks grappling at her; then mean and foul-mouthed, staggering about, interfering with the evening chores; at least once or twice helpless at night in the feed room so that she had to go out with the boy to bring him in. He came, half dragged and half carried, his head lolling as he muttered curses and threats. In the woodshed they took off his boots before wrestling him up the stairs and rolling him into bed.

Drunk or sober, Lucien Quirk hovered around her. He had a knack for ubiquity, for being in the very place — the kitchen, the yard, the hen house — just as she arrived there. Cornering her, he would alternate between cajolery, begging her to leave with him, and when he was drunk, threats, often involving her husband. She did not quite believe that he would do anything to Hedley Vaughn. That was, after all, the stuff of Ellery Queen novels and the movies she had seen as a teen-ager. But then she would start to think how desperate the man was and how, at a certain point of intoxication, he had a quiet, murderous intensity about him, particularly in the way he glanced at her husband. He wouldn't do anything cold bloodedly, she thought, but might purposefully drink himself out of control, drive himself to the occasion. So she remained watchful, keeping an eye on Lucien Quirk the way she might watch a cat around baby chicks.

Bobby Dearborn saw what was happening. Much of the man's harassment of the woman was obvious to him. He could guess what the urgent whisperings were about when he came on the hired man and the woman alone in the house or out in the barn. He felt the man's hoverings and saw the awful need in his eyes. And one night, as he hunched over the kitchen table doing his homework, she came over and sat next to him. "Prepositional phrases," she said with fake cheer, peering down at his English book. "They can be used for adjectives and adverbs." Then she sighed and said what she wanted to say: "I think I am going to go crazy."

He pushed the book aside. "You mean Lucien?"

She nodded and moved closer to hold him by the arm, but really to be held. "Is he out there now?"

"He's in the feed room."

"Drunk again?"

"I think so. He was asleep."

"I suppose we have to go get him."

The boy made a shrugging motion. "I put the old horse blanket on him. He's okay for now."

"Oh, Christ, I wish he would just go away. I wish he would leave me alone." But she didn't cry. Her exasperation had gone beyond tears.

Her helplessness made him feel only more helpless. In some ways he was still torn between the two of them. He brooded about it. He sided with the woman now and at times thought of the hired man as the villain. But it wasn't that simple. Lucien Quirk was a Marine. He'd been in combat and won the Bronze Star. And when he wasn't drunk and bothering Janet Vaughn, they were still friends. And the boy was still just a little afraid of him.

"Do you want me to anything?" he asked, falsely adult, as though there were something he could do.

Her face was against his shoulder; she was taking deep breaths at the flutterings within gone awry. "Just be here," she said. "Just be here."

It nearly came to a head the Saturday before Thanksgiving, not long after Hedley Vaughn came home. They were sitting down to soup and sandwiches when Lucien Quirk came into the house in a jocular mood and began kidding the older man. "Bet you miss those pretty nurses, huh, Hedley," he joked, and winked at the boy. There were little false smiles all around. Then: "See you got your old chair back, huh? Can't sit in that the rest of your life, Hedley, ha, ha. Stick around and we'll have you pitching hay in no time. Ain't that right, Jan?" He sat down with them and began to cut closer. Bobby Dearborn noticed that his aunt had stopped eating. He saw her blanch when Lucien Quirk, the words rolling out of him, stopped and asked abruptly, "Have you told Hedley yet?"

"Told him what?" she asked, her voice calm, showing character.

"Oh, come on. You said you were going to have to tell him some time."

For the boy it was like watching torture. He glared at the man.

The woman had risen and gone to the sink on the pretext of looking for something. She had to struggle now to keep her voice normal. She knew that her husband behind her had paused to listen.

"I don't know what you mean, Lucien." She said his name sweetly, trying to disarm him.

"Sure you do."

"What is it, Jan?" asked Hedley Vaughn, who, oblivious for the most part to the war of nerves between his wife and the hired man, now watched both of them.

"I don't know."

She kept her back to them. This was, in some ways, what she feared most — having it thrown in her husband's face (and right in front of the boy) as though it were some dirty joke, something small and common and obscene.

Lucien Quirk, who had been drinking before he came in, kept her on tenterhooks, teasing her to tears before, sputtering into his soup, he spit it out. "I'm talking about the cow we had done the artificial way."

Janet Vaughn wiped her eyes and came back to the table. Her soup had cooled. The grease slick on it made her feel sickish. "I already told Hedley about that," she said, giving herself away a little.

The man went mock-jocular again, his mean streak showing. "Well, that's good, because a fellow in Hedley's position ought to know who's breeding his cows. It ain't that old bull, I can tell you that."

"That's right, and it ain't the same," Hedley Vaughn began. "They dilute it and you give it time and that'll weaken the herd . . ."

Janet Vaughn spooned her soup around. She was relieved to hear her husband lapse into his diatribe against artificial insemination. No one else was listening. Lucien Quirk was watching her and the boy was watching him, glowering, as though he might go right across the table and hit the man.

Lucien Quirk wasn't asleep or even particularly drunk — just on his way — later that afternoon when Bobby Dearborn, doing the chores, came across him. The hired man reclined in his usual place on the grain bags, old blanket over his legs, bottle open on the floor, old milk can lid for an ashtray. "Well, if it ain't the Air Force come to feed the cows," he chirped when Bobby Dearborn pushed the door open to get at the grain.

The boy ignored him. He had been seething quietly all afternoon with fantasies of revenge, denunciation, with simple rage. He wanted to go out and slay the fire-breathing dragon in his lair. But his very anger kept him in check. He was afraid not merely of the man but of himself as well. He had begun the milking and thrown down hay and put off as long as he could the confrontation. Now he stood there, too wound up to speak.

"What's the matter, Captain? Cat got your tongue, huh?"

In response the boy yanked hard at the bag of dairy feed piled high over Lucien Quirk's head. It came loose, thudding to the floor, knocking over the wine and dislodging the bag underneath, which slid down with force against the man's back.

"Hey, what the hell!" The man was scrambling from underneath the hundred-pound bag of grain and grabbing at the cheap bottle of wine spilling like blood on the floor. He turned on the boy. He was short in his stocking feet, but his ill-shaven face, usually pallid, flared with sudden anger.

"You wanna start something . . ."

"I ain't afraid of you," said the boy just at the moment when he was most afraid.

The man gestured with a fist. "Who the fuck you think you are?"

The boy stood his ground. They were face to face. "Why don't you leave her alone," he said, finding courage in anger.

"Why don't you kiss my ass."

"You're supposed to be a Marine."

"That's right, sonny boy. I'm a Marine and I earned it."

"Marines don't bully women around."

The man drew closer, jutted out his jaw. He stank. "Listen, pal, what I do with women ain't any of your fucking business."

Now the boy met the man's eyes straight on and endured the unbearable tension of that closeness. Without thinking, he said, "Aunt Janet's my business."

"Oh, yeah? How the hell you figure that?"

The man was already relenting, feeling at himself for a cigarette.

"She's going to be my mother."

Lucien Quirk laughed, not altogether derisively. It became a shivering cough. He moved back and sat down on the edge of the grain bags, fumbling at a match for his cigarette.

"You ain't the only one," he said after a while.

"I know that." Bobby Dearborn remained standing. He still had anger to play out.

"She's going to have my kid," the man said, as though he didn't quite believe it.

"So why don't you treat her better?" the boy persisted with unanswerable logic. "It ain't easy for her, you know."

"The old man'll find out sooner or later."

"That ain't an excuse for doing what you did."

The man seemed on the verge of flaring again, but instead he subsided more, slumping in his pathetic blanket, mouth to the bottle, then the cigarette.

"She should of come with me," he said, as much to himself as the boy. "I mean, what the hell's she got here. A barn full of stinking cows . . . Christ, the old geezer's already half dead . . ."

The boy couldn't answer that. His anger was dissipating to pity for the man; his victory was hollow. He didn't push his point; exhortation was beyond him. He sensed too the helplessness of the man, how he had come out of a hole and was falling back down it.

"You wanna drink?"

"Naw, I've got to get the cows fed."

He opened the bag and spilled it into the cart. He scooped grain at the swinging heads. He changed the milkers. Everything was the same and everything was different. When he went back the man was still there, hunched forward with the blanket around his shoulders and the bottle between his feet.

Bobby Dearborn was embarrassed at not having anything to say. The man was staring straight ahead. It was cold, and the acrid smell of the spilled wine tainted the sweetness of the grain.

"Do you want me to leave the light on?" the boy asked.

The man didn't move or glance up. "It don't make any difference," he said.

❧ 28 ❧

DESPITE EVERYTHING, Lucien Quirk could still be a gentleman where Janet Vaughn was concerned. He could revert to the man who, not that long before, had been her lover. What he simply could not do was comprehend the depth of her refusal. He was puzzled that it now offended her to have him come into the bathroom while she was in the tub (even though he whispered, knowing that Hedley Vaughn was asleep in the next room). She understood that it hurt him when she shrank from a casual caress or wouldn't go up into the hay loft with him. She knew his response to these rebuffs was the cheap sherry he kept in the feed room, which he drank to salve his pain until, half drunk, he groped at her again, fumbling for what she could no longer give him.

Deprived even of hopelessness by her pregnancy, Lucien Quirk lived the cruel quandary of the fallen-again boozer: because things were intolerably bad, he drank, knowing that would only make them worse. He would get too angry, too down, to resist the easy escape, the self-exile of lying in the hellish chill and half-light of the feed room, smoking cigarettes and firing himself with cheap wine as the rats scuttled and squealed in the floor beneath him.

He got up in the mornings shaky, his memory of the day before blotted and smudged. He jagged himself sober with black coffee so he could milk and feed the cows and clean the steaming gutter behind them. He could go in then and clean himself up and be decent when he sat down with the man and his wife, Janet Vaughn, whose very presence in the room made him shaky again. He would try to be casual as he waited for some small sign, some acknowledgment that he was more to her than the hired man, that what had happened between them would or at least could happen again. He met a wall. Her eyes, her voice, her movements, even the way she sat at the table, kept him at a distance. Even her seemingly friendly familiarity with him, the way she enunciated "Lucien," had something posed and synthetic about it, as though she were trying to prove that everything was and had been aboveboard. Her sham pleasantness would disarm and disorient him because it evoked those other mornings in the kitchen when they were easy together, so easy that he could reach and take her with a touch or a glance. Now she cringed at his approach and after breakfast escaped to the cold living room to wait for him to leave.

Beaten, he would retreat to the barn to find something to do. But in winter there isn't much to do on a farm, and he would dawdle at some project he had no heart for. Thirst lined the emptiness within him. He would start down the road. At least walking to Elmsbury Centre for a couple of bottles of wine had some purpose to it. It was a task with a beginning, a middle, and an end, even if that end was the feed room, where he tried to numb himself against heartache and where, tormented by memories of their lovemaking, which returned to him inflamed by loss, he would pull at himself, mingling those memories with explicit dreams of reconciliation till he oozed on himself, emptied, disgusted, and as miserable as ever.

He did have one rather shoddy hope left. He hoped that when Janet Vaughn's belly got too big to hide, shame and fear would drive her to leave with him. Where else could she go, he asked himself over and over again. Who else would take care of her? And, under the circumstances, he didn't mind being a last resort. Lucien Quirk was accustomed to last resorts. It gratified him to see the alarm he had caused when he threatened to tell Hedley Vaughn everything that time at lunch. She had nearly panicked. She had acknowledged him then, all right. But he knew he couldn't do that too often. It might drive her to tell the old man everything herself. That fear made his hope turn feeble, because he could imagine her sticking it out. It was not the worst thing in the world to have a bastard, even the hired man's bastard. Things like that happened all the time. People learned to live with their mistakes, especially when the mistakes were children. But he had scared her that time, he would tell himself, and run it through again, wearing his one thin hope to nothing.

Hopeless then, he shivered on the hardening sacks of dairy feed and egg-laying mash and listened to the private lives of rats and worked his anger in the stiff air. That's my kid, too, he cried to his inner court of outrage. He had rights. He was owed because of all the things he had done for her — the chores, the kitchen, the turnips, the wood cut, the things fixed. Without him they would be cold and hungry. And those things he gave her. That locket. That sweater. Taking her out and making her feel like a lady. Hedley Vaughn never did that for her. There were a lot of things Hedley Vaughn hadn't done for her . . . or to her. Couldn't. And she'd liked those things well enough at the time, her eyes going big and her hands handy, grabbing at his life. Now she wouldn't look at him. It was all Hedley now. Practically feeding the old guy and tucking him into his chair. Are you all right, Hedley? What do you want, Hedley? Is there anything we can get you, Hedley? Hedley. Hedley. Hedley. God damn Hedley.

There was finally some relief in rage, in the dark fantasy of murder. Scenes of Hedley Vaughn's sudden death flashed like film clips through Lucien Quirk's mind. The bull goring him against the wall. An ax cleaving his skull. A quick burst of automatic fire making him bounce that funny way. Or, more probably, a pillow held firmly over his face until the muffled struggles ceased.

With each replay, the scene with the pillow grew more explicit and detailed. It went from fantasy to possibility. Lucien Quirk did not work up any elaborate plans, but he knew that the man rested after lunch and that he would have his chance if the woman were ever to drive off to the store for a few minutes. So he was alert in the early afternoon, lurking and listening for the sound of the car starting. In cold blood he would finish the job the bull started.

But it was a forlorn prospect for Lucien Quirk. Even his anger had something blighted and half-formed about it. One of nature's spendthrifts, he couldn't begrudge them the work, the time, the little money, or even the love he had spent. And though he might provoke himself to dream of murdering Hedley Vaughn, he really had little more against the man than his continued existence. Beyond everything, impervious to booze and any rage he might engender, Lucien Quirk feared that even if Hedley Vaughn were gone and even if he were to sober up and be his best self, it would not be the same again. The magic bond that had brought them together had snapped. Child or no child, she didn't love him and never would. So he cursed and drank and peered up at the cobwebs gathering in his dimming vision like the darkness of that sleep which is beyond sleep.

❧ 29 ❧

J<small>ANET</small> V<small>AUGHN</small> began spotting on Thanksgiving Day, when the family gathered in the Colonial-style house of her sister and brother-in-law Mary and Vincent Tully. Bobby Dearborn had come along, but Ernestine Vaughn had begged off, saying she needed to visit an elderly aunt surviving in a New Hampshire nursing home. Lucien Quirk had not been invited, and in any event he was not to be found when they left the farm that morning. Janet Vaughn sighed and checked herself again. She had almost expected the flecks of blood she found on the crotch of her panties. The symptoms, which she knew too well, had begun a few days before with a persistent ache in her lower back and a bloated, crampy feeling in her gut. Now the signs of blood made it more or less definite that she would miscarry. For a moment, sitting there amid the tiled curves and gleams of the Tullys' opulent pink and black bathroom, she resisted any relief or sorrow. The spotting would stop, would not become a flow, she told herself without quite believing it. She so wanted to be a natural mother like her own mother, like her two sisters. She sighed but resisted weeping. Her dream, however nightmarish, was ending as the others had ended — in a tiled place, a bathroom, a doctor's examination room, a hospital. She wadded herself a sanitary napkin of toilet paper and flushed the john. She rinsed her hands and peered at herself in the mirror. Older-looking, she thought, noticing a few threads of steel in her hair and a crease starting on her cheek that makeup no longer quite covered.

"Are you all right, Jan?" Ellen Dunn paused in her peeling of potatoes. "You look peaky." Her glance, concerned, inquisitive, even a little hostile, intimated that she sensed the magnitude and perhaps even the substance of what was happening. It had happened before.

"I'm fine," Janet Vaughn lied, her smile ghastly as she sat with them at the kitchen table, a grand affair of wood, metal, and Formica. Her sister's hard sympathy made her vulnerable. "It's just my curse," she said to the others, betraying more than simple annoyance at the monthly ordeal. She began peeling the small white onions, which made her sniffle anyway so that she had to stop and blow her nose in a paper towel.

"Jan, you're sure you're all right?"

Now it was her sister Mary, elegant behind an apron on which she wiped floured hands.

"It's the onions," Janet Vaughn insisted.

It was the onions and the blood and the Tullys' gorgeous modern kitchen, with its cabinets and counters and the picture window opening on the fenced backyard where Bobby Dearborn and Joe Jr. and Steve Dunn and the little kids played a ragtag game of touch football.

"Why don't you go in with the others for a while and have a drink?" Mary Tully, who loved her older sister, if now at some small social remove, was both solicitous and firm. She could sense a crisis beyond the menstrual breaking in the other woman and she didn't want it to ruin the day. Her touch was a comfort and a command.

Janet Vaughn kept up a brave front for another few seconds. Then her face collapsed and her body sagged as she crumpled into a real weep, holding her head and sobbing vehemently in an outburst that, like a summer storm, was too intense to last long. It stopped as suddenly as it started.

The others drew around her in a close circle, protective and curious at the same time. Liz Gilooly, swollen now with child, took the knife from her. "I can do these, Jan," she soothed. "Mary's right, you know; we can do all of this. Go in with the others and have a drink. Keep Mom happy."

"It was the onions," Janet Vaughn tried to joke as she composed herself.

She did not want to be excluded from this group and its talk of children and things, but she fled upstairs to the bathroom to check again and to fix her blotched and ruined face. A numb acceptance of her loss and her defeat was settling on her now. She would never be a mother. And if not that, what else could she be? Keep Mom happy. That would be her role. An auntie, handy if the baby sitter doesn't show up. Practically a spinster. She rinsed and powdered and composed the shell of her face. She went down the stairs practicing her holiday smile though inwardly she was a jellyfish of emotion,.

The long living room was ranged with reproduction Victoriana, velour wingbacks, an Empire couch, spool-work end tables, marble-topped whatevers, all sunk in a thick wall-to-wall nap. A painting of idealized New England farm life hung over the fireplace, where a real fire crackled and spat. Elbow on mantel, Vincent Tully stood in festive brown jacket and sporty tie, practicing his squirehood while talking stocks and bonds to Rose Gilooly and Hedley Vaughn. This pair sat on the sofa, one shawled and the other lap-rugged, indisputably the old folks.

"Well, here's one of the ladies!" the host proclaimed. "What will you have to drink, Jan?"

Vincent Tully was a big florid man, black-haired and blue-eyed, oblivious and charming, something of a relief for Janet Vaughn, who trembled with a kind of emotional nausea. Breaking down in front of the others like that. And on the verge of it again. God help me, she prayed.

"Anything," she managed in a normal voice and took a wingback and pretended interest in the fire.

"How's yours?" the stockbroker was asking Mrs. Gilooly, who nodded noncommittally, which meant yes. Hedley Vaughn couldn't drink because of his medication.

"Not even a small one?" Vincent Tully tempted.

"Well, maybe a small one."

The younger man chinked ice into glasses, poured Canadian Club and ginger ale, was full of himself and generous. He included Janet Vaughn in the sweep of his eyes.

"I was just telling your mother she ought to get out of those old fart bonds and into the stock market. The return's much better and right now the market can't go anywhere but up."

"My brother Edward lost everything in the crash," Rose Gilooly said sourly, taking her drink and sipping it. "If he'd stayed in government bonds like he was told to he would have been a millionaire. He died in the poorhouse."

Vincent Tully, master of the fire, poked at a log. "That was then, Mom. Times have changed. They've got borrowing margins now, regulations, bank insurance . . . It can't happen again."

Hedley Vaughn made a doubting noise. "Heard that one before."

The other man backtracked easily, with a laugh and a crack about death and taxes, before launching into a recital of technicalities to keep himself from being bored, one suspected, as much as to entertain his guests.

Janet Vaughn looked around her and immediately began thinking of covering an old wingback they had in the attic. Of course she could never hope to have anything like this showroom of furniture and furnishings. She would never have a ruddy-faced husband poking at the fire or freedom from drudgery or the poise that comes from having all the bills paid. Or a baby . . . her heart quaked and she pulled back from the thought, steadying herself like an adolescent drunk keeping his eyes open to avoid being sick. The implications began to reverberate. She had lost more than the possibility of new life. The depth of her deception opened before her. She would have humiliated, even killed, her husband with a child not his own. And Lucien Quirk. She blamed herself there as well. She had made and unmade the man, so that now, reduced to the wretch he was, he lay shivering somewhere on the farm in a drunken stupor. And Jessica Lee. She had condemned her to limbo, because however much she confessed and took communion and prayed, she would not be able, she knew, to revive the hope and the dream and therefore the possibility of that perfect green and white existence in the hereafter with her lost child. All of her moral debts suddenly seemed due. She was glad Vincent Tully had made the drink strong.

She felt a need to confess or at least tell someone her news, someone like Ellen or even Hedley. Someday perhaps. There was no one else there, except Bobby Dearborn, of course, who knew. She gladdened at the thought of him. Leaning back in her chair, she could see him through one of the floor-length windows out in the yard playing with the others. He was bigger than Joe Jr. now and a little awkward in the way he ran and caught the ball. The sight of him reassured her. Now, she thought, he really is my son.

Her depression began to lift. The sight of the boy, the fire, the whiskey, the balm of Vincent Tully's unctuous voice, began to soothe her. The relief was simply too much. She stopped resisting the thick, unsubtle luxury around her. It was true that she would never have all this, but she had it now and for now it was enough.

The others began to drift in. Liz Gilooly, serene in her pregnancy, drank ginger ale and was solicitous. Those outside came in, and the children were suddenly all over everything, faces flushed and noses running from the cold. Vincent Tully piled logs on the fire and used a heavy hand with the drinks. His wife fretted about the cooking meal and the children messing up the furniture.

Bobby Dearborn wasn't there, and Janet Vaughn started to worry about him. "Where's Bobby?" she asked, afraid suddenly that she had lost him, as well. He's still outside, someone answered. So she put on her coat and went through the kitchen into the yard in search of him. The brown, blustery day daunted her, made her feel exposed and weak. The boy's absence panicked her. The world seemed utterly empty. Then she saw him coming down the lawn-lined street and through the gate at the front of the house.

"Aren't you coming in?" she called, sounding more accusatory than she meant to. She knew he was uncomfortable with her family.

"I just went for a walk," he answered when he got to her.

"What did you see?"

"Just houses."

They were near the kitchen door but didn't go in. Without agreeing to do so, they walked through the backyard and into the more formal part of the garden at the other side of the house. The Tullys had made an attempt at privacy there with a hedge of yew behind which were a flagged path, a bird bath, and an old-fashioned stone bench. Janet Vaughn was too preoccupied for her usual envy. She sat abruptly on the bench and motioned for the boy to sit next to her.

"It's all over," she said enigmatically.

He didn't understand.

"Everything's going to be fine," she went on, looking the other way, controlling herself.

"Are you okay?" he asked.

She nodded and held her midsection. "I've lost it," she was able to say, but conveyed more with the hands on her stomach.

The boy was embarrassed. "Do you need a doctor?"

"I'll be all right."

Bobby Dearborn couldn't imagine what was happening right then, and he was too shy to ask. This seemed more intimate than sex. He took her arm. "Shouldn't you lie down?" he thought to say.

His concern and touch nearly undid her. "Oh, Bobby!" she cried. "You really will be my son, won't you?"

He could only say yes and nod his head to show he meant it. Her paleness and the way she seemed older made her more like what he thought a mother ought to be. They sat silently for a while, no longer needing words. "We ought to go inside," he said finally when she shivered in the chill. Which they did, side by side, as though they had been mother and son all their lives.

The Lowell-Lawrence football game came, play by play, from the radio in the background. Vincent Tully glowed with his drink-making. Attended by Joe Gilooly, Jr., Steve Dunn sulked amid the Tullys' finery and played the prole with a shot of whiskey straight and beer from a bottle. It was getting boozy.

Janet Vaughn, her color returning, found herself helping to keep Debbie and Michael from wrecking things. She made them take off their shoes and sat them on the arms of the wingback. They thought it great fun.

The little boy rolled big eyes at her. "Have you seen the bull?" he asked with awe in his voice.

Janet Vaughn jollied him with mock horror. "Oh, yes, isn't he big!"

"What's the bull's name, Auntie Jan?"

"Lancaster."

"That's a funny name for a bull. Why is he called that?"

"Because he's a purebred. His mommy and daddy and their mommies and daddies all had names like that."

Debbie giggled and her brother frowned. "He has big horns, doesn't he?" he said.

"That's right, he's got big horns."

"And if he got out he could kill you, couldn't he?"

"That's right, he could. That's why we keep him penned up all the time."

"Mommy says you have the bull there so the cows can have babies," little Debbie said. She wore a pink frock and had a red ribbon in her blond hair.

"Debbie, go away. Bulls aren't for girls."

"Well, Mommy told me. The cows need the bull to help them make babies."

"But he can still kill you with his horns, can't he?" the boy said, appealing to Auntie Jan.

"Oh, of course he can!" Janet Vaughn exclaimed her reassurance as Debbie, giggling now, whispered hot in her ear something about the bull, and the little boy, disgruntled and defeated, wandered off to beg his mother for another cookie.

After several attempts, Mary Tully got the tipsy crowd into the long dining room and settled down. On a formal table (with matching chairs and sideboard), the feast was spread with thicknesses of linen and silverware and settings of matched china with a pattern of pale blue fleur-de-lis. The smaller children had a table of their own near the door leading to the kitchen.

Michael and Debbie squabbled until their father, flustered by drink and the relentless display of the Tullys, came down on them with an ugly growl, leaving them tearful and everyone else subdued.

But only momentarily. Vincent Tully rose from behind the roasted bird to say the Catholic blessing. Then his wife, in a performance they had no doubt worked out ahead of time, rose from the other end of the table to toast her mother and wish for the speedy recovery of Hedley. Glasses clinked. The white wine flowed and the plates were piled with carved light and dark meat and spiced stuffing and mashed potatoes running with thick giblet gravy. There was orange winter squash and quick frozen peas unnaturally green and the small white onions tamed in cream sauce as well as rolls and butter, an aspic salad, hearts of lettuce, and more wine. The talk was desultory at first. Pass the salt. More wine? Are the kids okay? Another helping of turkey? Light or dark? Who won the game? Isn't the stuffing delicious? And quickly, to the clink and scrape of plates, satiation set in as people, with appreciative groans, refused second and third helpings and then helped themselves to more.

Janet Vaughn joined in. She didn't eat as much as the

others, because she had, or thought she should have, a queasy stomach. She nursed a tremulous, fragile happiness. She was surprised at how her world had begun to brighten. Released from the impending terrors of her pregnancy, she felt born again in an appreciation of the world she had and might have lost. She began making resolutions. She said an Act of Contrition and planned to confess that Saturday and take communion on Sunday, a prospect that filled her with joy. Then she would tell Lucien Quirk what had happened and try to help him, but as a sister. That might be, she knew, the most difficult thing she faced. Still, she was able now to imagine a different future. She thought about enlisting Ernestine Vaughn's help in getting Hedley to sell enough road frontage to pay their debts. Maybe he could be talked into giving up the milking herd and keeping only dry stock. If he got well enough, she thought, she might take a job as a secretary. That would make life much better. She peered around the table and realized how much she loved this family, for all their flaws and petty jealousies and rivalries. She wanted to raise her glass and tell them just that and how in the future she would be more kind and caring. And Bobby. He was sitting next to her, more now than a sympathetic presence. She couldn't resist putting an arm around his shoulder and giving him a squeeze. She raised her glass. She gave thanks.

❧ 30 ❧

I<small>T WAS</small> early afternoon, a week or so after Thanksgiving, when Lucien Quirk went down the line of cows, opening the tops of the long, wood-lined iron stanchions to let each horned head swing free as the cows lined up in orderly fashion to go through the big doorway into the barnyard. The man hadn't had a drink in nearly three days. He was just about out of money and had a bad head cold. Mostly, though, he was trying to keep sober because of a marked change in Janet Vaughn's attitude toward him. She had been ill herself, staying in bed nearly all of one weekend, and then had appeared more subdued and noticeably friendlier. There was even something apologetic in her eyes and voice when she spoke to him.

He lifted the hinged planks and went along the gutter with a shovel, pushing the dung into the cellar. Maybe, he kept thinking, she was changing her mind, was getting ready to leave with him because her pregnancy was starting to show. He had noticed her wearing a lot of loose dresses and skirts lately. Her new attitude, in any event, had jolted him into sobriety. He again took more care with his appearance and at the same time practiced a deliberate circumspection in her presence, leaving it to her to make the move. He'd been too hard on her before. He shouldn't have hit her. She wasn't the kind that liked to get hit. So one moment he was absolutely sure she would be coming to him to make plans. What else would explain her seeming change of heart? He couldn't believe his luck, and the next moment the old doubts would begin to gnaw and his blood and guts would grumble for the quench of wine. And sometimes he thought she just felt sorry for him because of his cold, which made his eyes smart and his nose run. That was something, but not nearly enough.

He was sweeping the place, getting it thoroughly clean before putting down the sawdust, when he glanced out the window and noticed the car gone. Hedley Vaughn was alone, in all likelihood dozing in bed. The sudden flush of opportunity struck him with an anxious joy. It was exactly what he had been waiting for. He was free to act now. He stood for a moment as excitement tightened him and as the old sensation of combat, fresh and unpleasant and fascinating as ever, came over him. The adrenaline surged, but his tension was quiet and he stopped thinking or seeing, except for what he was doing — moving swiftly and silently to the woodshed, where he shucked his boots and coat. He entered the house noiselessly, patted the dog next to the stove, and checked the clock to see how much time he had before the school bus dropped the boy off. He had an hour. He needed only five minutes. He went through each room downstairs to make sure she wasn't there. His limp gone, he went up the stairs as though part of the silence. He looked in each room before gliding through the bathroom and into the master bedroom, where Hedley Vaughn lay supine, eyes closed and mouth open in a twitchy doze. There was a pillow lying beside his head.

Lucien Quirk had pictured himself as simply doing it — taking the pillow and holding it down against the man's face while he knelt on his shoulders, pinning him to the bed until he died either of a heart attack or suffocation. Now he was in that picture, moving around to the other side of the bed to pick up the pillow. The quiet intensity of it grew, and he was moving as well through memories, moving up an exposed beach to where the dense vegetation rattled and spat death all around him. Noiselessly he took the pillow and then paused at what sounded like the car returning. Holding the pillow, he went quickly into his own room, where, from the window, he could check the yard. No car. He returned through the bathroom to place himself on Hedley Vaughn's side of the bed. Excited, he still remained calm and deadly as he calculated how he would have to plant a foot to hoist himself atop the dozing form before bringing down the pillow on the drawn lips, the thin, prominent nose, and the eyes sunken under a broad brow.

Lucien Quirk, the lovesick, heartbroken, five-dollars-a-week, on-again, off-again wino hired man, could do it. He could kneel on the man and blot out his face with the pillow and push down until the body went quiet under him. He could do it despite the daily proximity, even his friendliness with Hedley Vaughn, who had taken him in when no one else would. He could do it, risking the possibility that Janet Vaughn might somehow *know* that her husband hadn't died in his sleep, that he had murdered him, and would never let him near her again. He could do it even if it meant reducing himself to a criminal and therefore a bum, because his desperation during those long hours of misery in the feed room had reached a point where just about anything was justifiable.

But the soldier, Lance Corporal Lucien Quirk, USMC, Good Conduct medal, Purple Heart, Bronze Star, could not do it. He could not do then what he had done best in his life, which was to kill, because murdering a sick old man in his sleep was not combat. Snuffing out a life like that would besmirch the courage that had made him a good soldier, even if that courage was only a fear of fear. It would cancel a sense of self for which he had paid an enormous price on and beyond the battlefield. It would dishonor the uniform, the medals, and whatever red, white, and blue entity these things stood for. It would mean the end of honor, and honor, a worn, irreducible knot of pride, was really all that this soldier had left.

So the moment passed, and Lucien Quirk put the pillow back and left the room and the house as silently as he had come into them.

❦ 31 ❧

On an overcast December day smelling of snow, Ernestine Vaughn sat at the kitchen table in her long gray coat and sipped a cup of tea Janet Vaughn had poured for her.

"How is Hedley feeling?" she asked of her brother, whom she had come to take to the hospital for an afternoon of tests.

Janet Vaughn finished putting wood in the stove and rinsed her hands in the sink.

"I think the cold weather bothers him more than it used to," she said. "I'm wondering if we shouldn't get an electric blanket."

"Well," the other came back, cupping her hands around the teacup, "the cold bothers me more than it used to. I guess the blood thins when you get older."

Janet Vaughn made an agreeing noise and busied herself at the sink, mostly because she had never really learned to relax around her sister-in-law. The friendliness, the generosity, the very normality, of the older woman disconcerted her. There she was, offering to have Christmas dinner in her apartment for the four of them "because I know you haven't been feeling very well" and "because it's been years since I've had an honest-to-God tree in the place." She even offered to invite Lucien Quirk, "though I understand that might be a problem." Janet Vaughn could not tell what, if anything, Ernestine knew of her affair with Lucien Quirk. If she did know anything, she certainly kept it to herself. Indeed, the woman's consistent appropriateness could be maddening. If only she had stooped to judgment or frowned some disapproval, she would have been easier to take. One might at least react. But Ernestine Vaughn did not judge or frown or make claims. She was taking half a day off from a job she enjoyed to drive her brother to the hospital, where she would have to wait around for the better part of an afternoon.

"Oh, I can shop to kill time," she said, diluting her goodness, making it easier to swallow. "Actually, I could look for an electric blanket for you and Hedley," she continued, as though thinking aloud. "I might find one on sale. And I was going to look for an electric razor for Bobby. He mentioned wanting one some time ago."

"I'm sure he'd like that," said Janet Vaughn, who felt envious. She wanted the boy to ask her for such things.

"I thought we might both give it to him . . . for Christmas."

"That would be nice."

But Janet Vaughn was irked by her own smallness as their talk drifted again. She went to check on her husband and came back to wipe dishes and put them away. Then, seemingly out of the blue, Ernestine Vaughn said, "I understand from Bobby that you and Hedley plan to adopt him."

The younger woman wiped and rewiped her new counter top. She had meant to discuss their plans with Ernestine, but she hadn't found the right opportunity. It had been left among several other important things she was going to have to tell people. And she was afraid that Ernestine Vaughn, out of possessiveness, might oppose it. She had her arguments marshaled in advance. We're the ones who have taken care of him, she was going to say; it's what he wants; it doesn't mean he'll have to be a Catholic; you can still be his aunt Ernestine.

"We've thought about it," she responded, testing the water.

"Well, I think it's a wonderful idea."

Janet Vaughn could not hide her surprise or pleasure. She wiped her hands on her apron and sat down at the table. "I'm so glad you feel that way," she said.

"My goodness, how else would I feel? I think it should have happened long ago. You didn't think I'd object, did you?"

There was something contagious about this woman's openness. Pouring herself a cup of tepid tea, Janet Vaughn said, "Well, you did find him, Ernestine, and you always have been very special to each other."

"Oh, I know, but you and Hedley took him in. You're the ones who've taken care of him. And I know it hasn't always been easy, especially for you. He's a Vaughn, and I know what they can be like. You've been a good mother to him."

The tribute flustered Janet Vaughn with a new appreciation of herself. It was true. For all her spites and rages and disappointments, she had tried to be a good mother. She had tried to love him.

"That's the kindest thing anyone's ever said about me," she murmured and on an impulse kissed the thin cheek of her sister-in-law.

There was a moment of rare empathy. Then Ernestine Vaughn's smile dimmed a little. "Well," she sighed, "I suspect Bobby will outgrow his aunt Ernestine, at least for a while. Boys are like that."

Janet Vaughn touched the other woman again. "Oh, you'll always be his favorite auntie. You've done as much for him as anyone. I think he loves you better than anyone."

Hearing her husband come down the stairs, one step at a time, she got up. It was not one of his good days. She went to the desk to get some papers he needed and was touched to see his sister rise to greet him and help him on with his overcoat. They were more than brother and sister, she realized as she saw them out the door; they were older folks; they were from an earlier, tougher generation, from a time when family took care of its own and people endured pain quietly.

Still, it was a relief to have Hedley out of the house; he required so much attention. And there had been times during the past few weeks when Janet Vaughn did not think she would survive. The miscarriage had been severe, a bloodletting that left her faint and bedridden for several days. She knew she should have gone to see Dr. Weller, but she knew, too, that he would have surmised what had happened. And she had been through miscarriages before. She still had pills left over from the last time. She took those as prescribed and felt better. In the end she accepted the miscarriage as God's will, as fate, as something she could not do anything about. She would never have children of her own. At least now she had the boy. Theirs was a bond that grew stronger every day. And now Ernestine knew about the adoption. That was another weight off her mind.

Like confession. She had gone shortly after the signs of the miscarriage started and had burned the good priest's ears with more details than he wanted to hear. She had sensed that Father Fahey, in not chiding her or preaching at her as he dispensed penance, had recognized in her sins a dimension of human tragedy beyond his categories of right and wrong. She believed in the sin herself. She believed she had fallen from grace and was now in some measure restored. But she had not returned to quite the same grace or the same faith she had known earlier. She no longer sought refuge in a green and white paradise with her lost child. She still took communion and prayed for forgiveness and salvation, but she wasn't sure anymore what salvation meant.

She finished tidying up the kitchen and went upstairs to lie down until the boy came home. The house had a dank chill about it, and she left her clothes on when she got under the covers. There, warming, she began to hope that her life could heal. She had confessed. Ernestine knew about the adoption. Next, she would tell Lucien Quirk she was no longer pregnant. She had meant to as soon as the miscarriage happened, but fear and pity made her procrastinate. She wasn't sure what he would do. She half hoped he would leave, but she also felt responsible for him. She wished she could help him. Perhaps Hedley would sell some road frontage and sell the herd for beef cattle. There were jobs at Raytheon for secretaries . . . Bobby could have time to study . . .

Arranging her life, she dozed off, sleep coming in a thin gauze of inner light where half-conscious thought and dream fretted back and forth — the boy, the hired man, the farm, Hedley, the life she had carried and not quite relinquished. She both heard and dreamed the sound of someone coming up the stairs, which creaked, and she woke to find without surprise Lucien Quirk at the foot of the bed, watching her.

&

His suppressed vehemence charged the room like some poison explosive gas a spark could ignite. He wasn't drunk, but it seemed from the deflected intensity of his gaze that he wasn't quite sober either.

"I'm thinking of leaving." He spoke quickly, breaking his words, as though he had rehearsed them.

The woman nodded at that and kept her expression serious and noncommittal.

"I'm heading for California."

"Yes," she said.

Silence hung like the chill in the air. She heard him sigh, a venting of pressure. "You don't really give a damn anyway, do you?"

She caught the contortions of his face, a seething blunted by some mad distractedness. It occurred to her to be frightened, but it wasn't something she felt.

"You don't give a damn what I do," he went on. "Go to California. Stay here. Drop dead. You don't care."

"I do care."

"I don't believe you, Jan. I don't believe anything you say. You lied to me. You promised . . ."

"Lucien, please . . ."

"You did, you promised you'd go with me and then you wouldn't. You got what you wanted, got your stud service, just like I was some kind of God damn bull . . ." He tried to laugh, but the sound strangled in his throat.

"That's not true," she insisted quietly.

"Then come with me."

"I can't."

He moved threateningly to the side of the bed. "What?"

"I said I can't."

Janet Vaughn pulled herself into a sitting position. The possibility of violence made her feel sick. The light thinned, then thickened, went gray and blue. She shivered and crossed her arms to hold herself.

"Sure you can. You don't want to. You never did. You played me for a sucker. Ain't that right, a sucker?"

She shook her head.

He sat on the bed. The fractured blue of his eyes didn't quite focus as he stared at her. He was berating her again as she sat there, trapped, knowing she must suffer it.

"I told you once I was scared. But I ain't scared anymore, lady. I don't care what happens to me, to you, to anybody."

He waited to see what effect his veiled threat was having. Fear at least was some kind of response. She might have offered him that, but she remained calmly, maddeningly unafraid. His hand reached out and took her by the wrist, but easily, as his voice modulated to an urgent plea. "Come with me, Jan. Come right now, while we've still got time. There ain't nothing for you around here. You can't call this living with him living. Christ, you're more his nurse than his wife."

"He's my husband."

"He ain't hardly alive."

"Lucien, I cannot go with you!"

"Why the hell not?"

Now his eyes focused, braced and ready for the truth the way he had been ready for bullets, as though he were finally and truly beyond fear.

She said it pointblank, into his eyes, between his eyes. "I can't go with you because I don't love you."

He absorbed it with a blink, hit but not mortally. He kept moving, looking for cover. "You loved me enough to get into bed with me."

"That's all over."

"You loved me enough to be having a kid with me."

She glanced away. He pressed her.

"What's going to happen when he finds out you're pregnant? Huh? You can't hide that much longer." His grip on her tightened and his eyes bore in. "What's your family going to say? They're going to know. They can count. And how are you going to walk around this town and look people in the face, huh? How's your kid, our kid, going to grow up? What are they going to call it, huh? The Vaughn bastard?"

"No."

He snickered his bitter triumph. "What do you mean, no? What the hell else are they going to call it?"

"Lucien, I'm not pregnant anymore."

"What do you mean?"

"I lost the baby."

Voicing it to him somehow magnified the loss, made it real, so that tears welled hot, then cold on her cheeks.

"I don't believe you."

But he did. He had drawn back, and the odd sound of his voice touched and alarmed her. He could still be scared.

"It's true."

"When did it happen?"

He clung to his skepticism as to a thin hope.

"It started around Thanksgiving. It came a few days later when I got sick . . ."

Not roughly, but with a sudden strength she couldn't really resist, he pulled down the covers and pushed up her dress. She moved then to help him, to show him the belt she still wore, the Kotex pad, the small but still evident stain of blood.

"I'm sorry, Lucien. It just happened. I didn't want it to. I should have told you. I was too . . ."

He had fallen on his knees beside the bed and buried his face in the flesh of her stomach. He shook as though with sobs, a spasm that came and went quickly. But for a long time, it seemed, they remained like that. When he finally stood up, he appeared quite composed.

"We could try again, you know. We could leave for California and try again."

Janet Vaughn pulled the covers over herself and straightened her hair. She no longer felt cold. She could sense the finality of things.

"I care for you very much, Lucien, but I can't go with you."

He said nothing more. He was nodding, as though finally understanding. He knelt down once more and put his arms around her and kissed her on the side of her face. Then he left. She heard him go down the stairs and out the door.

❧

Lucien Quirk hitched the tractor to the small wagon and drove it down to the sheds behind the barn, where a large mound of sawdust from the sawmill had been dumped. He shoveled on a load of this stuff, which smelled to him poignantly of nothing. It went under the cows and sopped up their piss and dung. It was useful, cheap, neutral stuff. Expendable, like him. A front-line leatherneck. Go up there, Quirk, and take out that machine gun, the lieutenant ordered. And you obeyed even though a couple of grunts had already tried and were pinned down or blasted away somewhere between you and where the Japs were dug in, spitting fire. Now you were the hired man. Five dollars a week and nothing. He drove the load of sawdust up to the barn and left the tractor turning over as he unbolted the great door at the front and pushed it back on its rail. He backed the rig deep into the barn, back to the empty bay beside the one next to the bull's stall. He worked automatically, digging at the stuff, shoveling it out into the empty bay. Fighting had been automatic, too. You couldn't think about it when you were doing it because you'd freeze. You'd go crazy. It didn't make any sense to go into a crouching run from one tree to the next, the brush snapping all around you with Jap bullets. Like a wind as you got closer, close enough to use grenades, then your bayonet, sticking them. His world went abstract. Dead Japs. Dead Marines. C rations. Sawdust. Another load. The December sky, gray and bleak as death, sucked at him, emptied him, so that he might have been invisible, a mere shade, grayer than the grayness that he envisioned death to be. Corpse-gray.

It occurred to him then in a decisive yet vague way that he had to leave. There was nothing left for him there anymore. No hope, no dream. He felt like sawdust. Mere stuffing. He backed the second load into the barn and left it there. He closed the big door and went into the house and up to his room. He began loading his things into the duffel. It was what he did every time he left a place. All the while now, however, he kept trying and failing to imagine where he would go. He was like a prisoner trying to scramble out of a doorless cell. Yet he felt more confused than trapped. He could not stay there and still he could not leave, because there was nowhere to go. It was as though he could no longer imagine his own life. The world closed in on him until, with a small astonishment that even had some of the pleasure of discovery about it, he realized that he was dead. Not physically, perhaps, but that was a mere technicality. That was something he could fix, being handy.

So he acted again, unthinking and automatic in his movements. A Marine with a Marine's sense of decorum, he shaved quickly in the bathroom, being careful not to nick himself. He looked at himself for a last time. He looked through himself, a dead man. He had no fear. The trousers of his uniform were tight, but it was a discomfort he could ignore. He buttoned on the tunic and checked the medals. The shoes weren't exactly regulation, but they would pass muster this time. He brushed his hair and put on the visored hat. Then he stuffed the rest of his things into the duffel bag and carried it with him out to the barn.

In the feed room he swigged from the bottle more out of habit than for any infusion of courage. He had gone beyond that. You don't need courage when you're not scared. He allowed himself a last cigarette, smoking it about halfway down before stamping it out on the floor. Then, careful to keep his uniform clean, he made two trips up the nailed ladder to the loft. On the first trip he carried up his duffel and set it on one of the high beams. He came back down to find something to stand on. A bushel box looked like the thing. Jack of all trades, he mused to himself. Master of none. Except killing the enemy. It had taken too much of him. It didn't leave enough of him for living. But he was handy, knew his knots, for instance. He played the guide rope through his hands until it stretched between him and the hay tongs, hanging over him like a giant spider. He wished now he'd turned on the single bulb that lit the mow. But he had just enough light from the high window to work by. He sighed but didn't waver as he gauged the length of rope he would need and fashioned a sturdy slip knot. He set the box on edge, then stood on it, using the rope in his hand to steady himself. The length was just about right. He didn't hesitate. His momentum was like a willed spell. He had now, if anything, a kind of anticipation of liberation. He got off the box and took off his hat and shoes. Then, making sure the box was in place, he reached up and grasped the rope, hoisted himself up, and slipped the noose over his head. He kicked the box away and fell. For an instant he thought he had botched the job because his toes touched the hay beneath him. But not enough. The hay wouldn't support him. The noose tightened sharply around his neck, shocking him alive as though to give him time for death, which is the final terror of living, which subsided for him in a slow choke of agony and relief as the last thing he saw was the window in the apex of the barn, its light dimming as peace descended for Lucien Quirk.

৵

"I can't find Lucien."

"I think he's gone."

"Gone?" the boy said.

"He's left. He took his bag and his things."

The woman sat, pale and subdued, in the living room with the green afghan from the nursery over her knees. "I'm sorry, Bobby," she said and gestured for him to come closer. "We'll miss him." She took the boy's hand. "And you'll have to do the chores in the morning. At least for a while."

"That's okay," he said.

The hired man's leaving didn't disturb him overmuch. It reverberated with earlier losses. People come and go. You don't always get to say goodbye.

"Uncle Hedley . . . Dad . . . has gone for some tests. Ernestine should be bringing him home soon." She let his hand go. "Could you feed the hens for me and pick up the eggs? There's cookies in the jar near the breadbox."

The boy ate cookies and drank milk. He changed his clothes and started early on the chores. First, though, he checked the feed room to see if the hired man was there. He found an open bottle of sherry standing on the floor as though just left there. "Lucien," he called out, sure now that the man had not gone. He poured egg-laying mash into two pails and lugged them down to the hen house. The tractor and wagonload of sawdust partly blocked the floor in front of the cows, but he was able to work around them. He kept expecting to see Lucien Quirk step from behind a door or a beam. Where could he have gone, he wondered. The hens gave off a loud whirring noise and came clucking as he emptied the mash into the hoppers. He watered them.

He lifted the hatch covers on the nests and took out the eggs to put into the wire basket. The brooding hens pecked at his rifling hand, but he pushed them aside. He began to miss the man. Life would be poorer without Lucien Quirk, even if he were only to lie half drunk in the feed room. He skipped quickly down to the brooder house, thinking he might be there, but it was empty save for the pathetic sticks of furniture.

The boy dawdled around the radio for a while before cleaning the gutter behind the cows. He saw Ernestine Vaughn's black Chevrolet leave the yard as Hedley Vaughn walked into the house. Behind him Elvis wailed about a party in the county jail. Finally he started the milking, rinsing the machines and going into the house for a pail of warm water. His aunt and uncle, his mom and dad, were in the kitchen. He could tell from their silence that they had been disagreeing about something. He ran hot water into the pail and listened as the man and woman went into the living room, where they continued arguing. We can't keep the cows, the woman was saying. Bobby can't do all the work. He has to have time for an education. Lucien Quirk is gone. He took his things and left.

The boy went out and checked the feed room again. "Where is he, Digger?" he asked the dog. The animal sniffed around the bags and whined. With the warm water the boy washed the udder of a cow and slipped on the four rubber cups. Milk surged. He put the second machine on. So the man had gone. It was another lesson in life — men can't share a woman. She had chosen. She hadn't gone with him, so he had left. He went back to the feed room and picked the string on a bag of Blue Seal Dairy 16 and dumped it into the heavy feed cart, which he rolled down in front of the cows, scooping the grain at them. It meant doing the milking in the morning again, cleaning the barn, getting the smell of cows in his hair. The bull bellowed. The boy threw him a half-scoop of grain. Its horns crashed against the timbers. Bobby Dearborn no longer baited the beast. It had grown too wild and nasty. He went back to change the machines.

He was about halfway through the milking when he went up the ladder into the loft to throw down hay for the cows. In the light of the single, flyspecked bulb, he pulled and tugged at the packed stuff and rolled it over the edge to the floor below. Dimly he could hear the regular suck of the machines and the noise of the radio. He was working out a long knot of hay when he saw something that made the hairs on the back of his neck bristle. Something lay on the transverse beam just beyond the next mow. It was Lucien Quirk's duffel. "Lucien," he called, "are you there?" He began to climb higher into the loft, glad, knowing the man was still there, probably drunk. "Lucien," he called again. Then he saw him in the crepuscular light, his head bent forward, in uniform, standing oddly at attention. The boy clambered higher. "Hey, Lucien . . ." He stopped, neck hairs bristling again as he saw the tongs and the short stretch of taut rope and knew without knowing exactly what had happened, because no one, not even a Marine, could stand that straight and high and still on the piled hay of a loft. "Christ," he murmured, then "Lucien! Lucien! Lucien!" But the silence was that of the dead, and the boy could smell the excrement where the man had soiled himself. Fear and mystery held him transfixed. In the dimness he tried to look into the man's eyes as though they might tell him something, as though death were a myth you grew up with like Santa Claus, as though, if only he were to get a knife and cut him down and get him some sherry, he might be all right. But the eyes saw nothing and the boy yelled "Lucien!" again to hear his own voice, to affirm that he himself still lived. He backed slowly through the hay, keeping an eye on the corpse, waiting for the man to crack a joke, to say it was a game, and knowing he wouldn't. The magnitude of it burst in him with a strange elation as his feet touched the floor and he went racing along the breezeway to the house.

"Bobby, your boots," the woman started.

"It's Lucien," he said breathlessly. "I found him in the loft."

Janet Vaughn rose quickly, sensing the worst from the boy's manner. "He's there?"

"I think . . ." Bobby Dearborn gulped, but held steady. "I think he hanged himself," he blurted, getting the word right, "from the tongs with the guide rope."

"What do you mean?" But she knew what he meant.

"He's in his uniform, just hanging there."

"Ain't surprising," Hedley Vaughn said with dryness. But he too had risen.

Janet Vaughn did not quite believe the boy and at the same time knew he told things straight. She got out the big flashlight from under the sink and started out to the barn. The boy followed, as did the man, but only after stopping long enough to put on rubber boots and a warm barn coat. The woman told the boy to wait below while she climbed the ladder to the loft. Morbid expectation and fear had turned her blood to oil. She went clawing up the ladder and then up the hay. She turned the flashlight on and in its powerful, narrow beam saw him in bits and pieces — the bent head, the buttons on the tunic, the gleam of the medals, the stocking feet that might have been standing on the hay.

"Lucien," she called quietly, approaching, hoping, as the boy had, to hear him whoop the end of some elaborate practical joke, something he'd rigged to get her attention. "Lucien," she repeated, her voice moist and nasal with tears. "Oh, Jesus, Lucien." She saw the box he had kicked from under him and smelled the stench of his death. Pity and desolation and guilt clenched her heart so that for a moment, unsteady in the hay, she nearly fell. "Lucien," she repeated in a chant, "Lucien, Lucien, Lucien . . ." She moved close to him and kissed his face and touched his hair and his tunic. "Oh, I am sorry!" she cried. "I am sorry! Please forgive me . . . Oh, please, please forgive me." Then, beyond any articulation, she knelt before him and wept hot bitter tears.

A while later she heard her husband calling from below. She roused herself and turned off the flashlight, which had fallen in the hay. She kept her eyes down, not wanting to see again what she blamed herself for. She plowed back through the loft and came hand over hand down the ladder.

"What is it?" Hedley Vaughn asked.

The boy, who had begun to pull some of the hay along the barn floor to feed to the cows, stopped to listen, but at a distance, feeling this was something between the adults.

"Bobby's right," the woman said, invoking the boy, as though he might share the blame. "He's hung himself." Her voice broke and she babbled into her hands. "He's dead, he's dead, Hedley, he killed himself."

The man put his arm around her, comforting. "Here, here," he crooned, "it's all right."

"He didn't have to do that," she sniffled, glad for her husband's touch and yet wary of her own on him, as though her touch had the power of death. "We could have taken care of him."

"Eyeah, we could have."

"He could have had a home here."

The man cleared his throat and spat, as though clearing his mind and heart of the matter.

"That's what the booze does to you when you let it. Damn good worker, too, when he wasn't on the stuff. Damn . . . I suppose we've got to call the police and have them come out and take a look."

Janet Vaughn pulled away from her husband. In his voice, in the callous dismissal of his words, she heard the lie she had perpetuated for so long. It was a deception she could no longer tolerate. With the courage of her grief, she told him.

"It wasn't the booze, Hedley," she said in a flat, controlled voice. "It was me."

The man acted as though he hadn't heard her and glanced around as though to get on with what needed doing, as though he had guessed something had happened between his wife and the hired man and didn't want to hear about it.

"The police . . ." he started.

"It wasn't drink, Hedley; it was me," she insisted, looking at him directly, wanting him to know the truth from her eyes. "He wanted me to go away with him."

"You say . . .?"

"He wanted me to leave with him, Hedley. He wanted me to go away . . ."

"Go where?"

"California."

"He was just a drunk."

"No, Hedley, he wasn't just a drunk. It wasn't just cheap wine that made him go up and . . ." She faltered, seeing again the head, the uniform, the man in the pathetic stillness of death. "It was me. Don't you understand . . . while you were in the hospital." She all but said it.

Hedley Vaughn perched himself carefully on the edge of the feed cart. With tremulous hands he took out his pipe and tobacco, as though with these things he might defend himself.

"It was like that, huh?" he said.

She nodded, fearful and at the same time relieved, feeling an enormous weight begin to shift off her. She had finally told him.

"And he wanted you to go to California with him?" That somehow intrigued the man as he studiously poked tobacco into his pipe, avoiding her gaze.

"Yes, Hedley."

"You didn't want to go?"

"Never."

He glanced up quickly and away, his gray eyes hard behind his spectacles. "But you and *him* were carrying on?"

His incredulity daunted her. "You weren't here, Hedley. It happened. I didn't want it to and then I did. It was wrong. It came natural, like a bad storm."

She wanted to reach over and touch him, to comfort him.

She wanted as well a sign that he might understand and forgive her.

He struck a match, and blue smoke plumed from his pipe, hiding his eyes. "You and him together, huh?"

"Yes, Hedley."

He murmured something inarticulate then and sat for a spell, smoking, his head averted. He sighed when he turned, not quite to her. "Well, I reckon things like that happen to folks . . ."

He stood up. He wanted to leave it at that, because he did not quite comprehend what his wife had told him. He knew what *it* was, but he could not encompass its significance, except perhaps as part of the larger, painful confusion surrounding his heart attack and hospitalization. This talk of herself and the hired man, of California and running away and God knew what else, he toted with his other losses — of work, of simple power to do and decide things, of the weeks lying helpless in that bed, a dislocated time, more distant now than old memories. He did not understand her vehemence or even why she was telling him. Perhaps what she told him was shocking, but no more shocking than the oxygen mask or the endless needles or the faces frowning over his cardiogram or the way his world had shrunk to a room and the dimming light of the window, to the bed, to his tubed and taped hands, to his breathing, rhythmic with a pain that was all he had left of life. So she had carried on with the hired man, and the hired man had hanged himself. What was he to do? He did not have the strength for outrage. Even then a suffocating pressure had started in his chest, and he mostly needed to get out of the cold and back next to the warm stove with a rug over his lap where he could doze and hope to wake up feeling stronger. He was reduced to survival.

"Hedley . . ."

". . . and I guess we'd better call the police to come and see to it."

He made as though to start away, and Janet Vaughn,

shivering because she hadn't worn a coat, was afraid it would end like this, with no condemnation and no forgiveness, so that what had happened would stand between them forever.

"You don't understand, Hedley!" she cried. "It was me. I wanted to have a baby and I got pregnant and then I lost it just like I lost the others."

The man brought a hand to his chest and stood as though wounded. What she said cut to the disappointment they shared, the failure of their life together. "Lost it?" he said through a haze of pain.

"Yes, just after Thanksgiving. That's why I was so sick. He thought when it began to show that I would go away with him. But I wasn't going to go. I couldn't. I was going to stay here and tell you about it. Then I lost it and I was glad because I didn't want to hurt you. I told him today I had lost it and I think he just gave up hope and . . ."

She rattled it off at him, emptying herself.

He nodded and pulled on his bitter pipe. He understood more than he wanted to.

"It happened, Hedley. It wasn't just a fling. It wasn't just something evil."

"And you wanted a baby?"

"I've always wanted a baby."

"That's true, ain't it. And you lost it?"

"Yes."

"Like the others?"

"Like the others."

They were silent then against the sounds of chore time, of restless animals, the milking machines, the radio playing.

"We've lost lots of things, ain't we, Jan," he said at length in a voice of shared and utter sadness.

Now she let herself go a little with a stifled sob, lifting a fist to her mouth. "I love you, Hedley. I always have, even when . . ."

The man glanced up at these words to see that his wife

was shivering and desolated and in need of comfort. He was too much of a Calvinist to presume to forgive. Her trespass was a trespass and would remain, like a knot in the grain of things. Yet he was not without the capacity to feel her misery and sense his own complicity in what had happened to her.

"Are you all right now, Jan?" he asked gently.

Her *yes* was barely audible.

He seemed about to add something when a sharp inner crick made him open his mouth and bring his hand to his heart.

"Hedley . . .?"

"Just a little jab," he managed, and was weak again, in need of her help.

She dared embrace him then, holding him, being held, both of them clumsy as they conjured up the beginning of reconciliation from the moment.

Finally she pulled back and kissed him on the face and wiped at her own tears. "Let's go in where it's warm," she said.

Hedley Vaughn, pale with pain, was nodding and patting the pockets of his jacket.

"My pipe," he said, and stooped to retrieve it from the hay near where he was standing. Only it wasn't where he thought it was, and he had trouble finding it because the pain and the pills and all these other things confused him and made him feel like a damn fool, on his hands and knees groping for what he couldn't see in the shag of timothy. And by the time he did find it, a thin stream of smoke was rising dead straight out of the pile. A nearly soundless *puff* was followed by a crinkling lick of flame. The man and woman remained stupefied for a fatal moment, in thrall, as though this not quite believable commotion of smoke and hide-and-seek flare had been sparked by and was emblematic of all that had gone wrong and all that they had suffered. Janet Vaughn stood as transfixed as her husband, afraid that divine judgment quite literally was at hand. She had sinned. A man hung dead in the loft as a result. It was all consequential.

The fire was also quite real, crackling in the pile, shocking them to a kind of controlled panic as the man began to stomp on the thing with his rubber boots and the woman yelled at the boy to bring a pail of water.

"What?" said Bobby Dearborn, then saw the fire and went charging into the dairy to fill a pail, which he brought, slopping, back to where the man might have been possessed, the way he tramped on the thing snarling in the hay, spreading it more than putting it out. It hissed at the flung water and sent back a billow of steam, but lived, insidious, devilish, deeper and wider than seemed reasonable. The boy ran for another bucket and the woman searched frantically for the length of hose they'd had there to water the stock before Lucien Quirk fixed all the drinkers. It still appeared manageable as they doused it with buckets of water. It flared and died, smoked and fumed, seemingly on the point of extinction. Then from the middle of the pile a solid core of flame erupted that the boy's offering of water diverted only for a moment. The dog barked and whined and slunk behind the man.

The fire was escaping, running along a ridge of hay dust on the floor, sputtering like a fuse. A ball of lit hay fell into the feed cart. With awful beauty a fringe of fire climbed a cobweb, fell, and climbed again. The man and the woman and the boy blinked and covered their mouths in the ashen air as they contended with a blaze. Janet Vaughn finally found the hose, attached it to the valve in the cow barn, turned on the water, and waited and waited while the thing hiccuped and belched, then stiffened and poured. But too late. The stream of water the woman aimed first here and then there seemed merely another effect, incidental to the main event. Twisting up into smoke thick with volatile flecks, flashing scarlet and orange blades of fire chewed along the hay the boy had earlier begun to pull in front of the cows. Sparks flew. Tendrils of smoke appeared higher, disappeared, appeared again. The loft immediately over the cow barn caught.

Things otherwise remained normal. The lights stayed on. The milkers chugged away down the line. A voice on the radio advertised a men's store in Lowell. And Hedley Vaughn, in serene shock, had pulled back from the blaze and was watching it with the disinterest of a spectator.

"Hedley, go outside!" Janet Vaughn yelled at her husband.

He seemed not to hear her. He remained there, his glasses red with reflected flames, watching the growing conflagration.

"Hedley!"

He didn't move.

"Hedley, go outside!"

She turned, looking for the boy, but kept working the hose, as though the fire were something that needed tending.

Bobby Dearborn was moving along in front of the cows, dropping the hatch covers on the mangers.

"Bobby!"

He finished what he was doing and came running.

"Take your uncle outside and run in and call the fire department."

The boy stared at her as though he might disobey.

"What are you going to do?" he asked, his voice loud against the rising din.

"I'm going to get the cows out," she shouted back. "Call the fire department and then stay with your uncle!"

The boy took his uncle by the arm and led him through the door that opened in the middle of the sliding wall at the front of the barn. The dog followed them.

"You stay here, okay?" he told the man. "Take care of Digger."

Hedley Vaughn nodded vaguely.

Bobby Dearborn turned and ran toward the house, caught in the drama of what was happening — Lucien Quirk's suicide, the fire, the destruction, and the urgency

— yet removed from it, keeping a cool head, thinking that this is what war must be like.

After the boy left, the woman dropped the useless hose and began letting the cows out. The fire, no longer dancing and mocking, was going about the steady, serious business of burning the place down. It now involved much of the barn floor and the lower mows on either side, which, filled with dry hay, went up like torches, crackling fiercely. High in the loft the pair of owls that nested there swooped in confused circles around the body of Lucien Quirk, unable to escape through the two open windows that had become, like the vents in the cupola, chimneys for the thickening smoke piling up from below. A cat sat on a beam toward the back and let out a long melancholy yowl. Rats and mice scurried everywhere.

The cows bunched and bawled and milled about in the narrow confines of the cow barn, reluctant to leave even as smoke leaking through the manger covers tinged the air. Janet Vaughn yelled and swung a broom at them. What cows did go out into the darkness of the barnyard tried to get back in. She wouldn't have got them out without the boy. He came back into the barn and stood near the door, keeping out the cows that were trying to get back in.

"Did you call the fire department?" the woman shouted, as much to relieve her anxiety as to be heard above the noise of the herd.

"They're on their way."

"Where's Hedley?"

"He's out front in the driveway. He's okay."

She drove a cow down to the door, and they both pushed it through.

"I think the barn's lost," she said, wiping her smudged face. "I hope they get here in time to save the house."

"The man said they'd be right here."

She clung to him for a moment, then turned and went back for another animal.

Just outside the barn where Hedley Vaughn stood it was quiet and dark. It might have been any other night in December, were it not for the snapping rush of the fire's noise coming dully through the closed door and swirling in his head. For a while the farmer waited under the starless night while this momentous thing happening to him nagged through a murk of confusion. Some enormous deed needed doing. He stood patiently nevertheless and stamped his feet to stay warm. Gradually, as his heart settled and as oxygen reached his brain, the noise inside his head shifted and became the noise behind the door. Memory returned in sequence — the hired man hanging himself, Janet telling him about herself and the hired man, the barn on fire. That last fact registered again with a mental jolt, and another, even sharper anxiety nearly unhinged him once more. What was it? To confirm things for himself, he opened the door and peered in through a sudden waft of smoke. The floor was a meadow of flame that rose, unbroken, up the sides, hollowing back the hay on both sides and lapping under the boards of the high central mow. The man did not gape with anything like horror or fascination. He was too old, too sick, too much of a Yankee for that. He recoiled instead from the fire's gaudiness, its cheap trick of transforming things, his things, into light, heat, and smoke. His things. He watched as the fire engulfed the engine and tires of the tractor. A moment later the fuel tank blew with a greasy *whoosh!* spewing gouts of flaming gasoline into the sawdust. He started when several rats, one of them singed and smoking, ran over his feet. An owl on fire crashed to the floor near the door and tried to hobble toward it. The man remembered his bull.

Had it been necessary, Hedley Vaughn would have gone through that hell to save his prize bull. But it wasn't necessary; he could still get to it through the back way. Holding his chest, he went at a short-stepped trot along the side of the barn, followed by the dog. The back door, which he found easily enough in the dark, was fastened from the inside with a small hook and eye. He pulled at it with both hands, back and forth, until it opened suddenly, releasing several more panicked rodents and a complaining cat. He hesitated a moment to catch his breath, then started up the steep ramp. The dog did not follow.

It wasn't just stubborn pride that sent Hedley Vaughn heaving onto the barn floor, where the fire, a creeping wall of incandescence obscured by recoiling smoke, had jumped the burning tractor to start on the empty stall next to the bull's pen. What impelled him to do this foolish thing was an ideal. What that bull represented finally was the closest thing to perfection the man had experienced in life. It was a perfection he had wrought himself, insofar as he was the first to see it in the beautiful head and long back of the bull calf. Later he had seen it reflected in the eyes of other farmers when they brought their cows to be serviced. He had known that perfection most palpably — he had lived it — in the herd of blue ribbon milkers he, a poor farmer with little more than a hundred acres and some of that woodland and swamp, had bred like magic from this one animal. It didn't matter that the bull had been failing. That was the nature of old males. What remained was the memory of perfection. What remained was the ideal.

He had thought of no special strategy for saving the animal. Despite the urgency, the heat, and the billows of smoke, he planned to do more or less what he had always done — prod or coax the bull into its stall with a bit of hay or a scoop of grain, secure it, attach the ring pole to its nose, and lead it out. But he didn't have any grain or hay or the time to wait for it to come on its own. He tried anyway. He found the ring pole and tapped it on the floor near the stanchion. "Here. Here," he called. The bull, its head lowered in a back corner, butting the wall, did not move. Hedley Vaughn hesitated. He could hear his wife and the boy in the cow barn getting the herd out. That was good, he thought, his head going dizzy with the fire and smoke and a tumble of thoughts about a new barn and buying Canadian hay and yes, the bull, his prize bull. The man opened the gate to the pen and went in.

Prodded from the back, the animal at first wouldn't move. Then, as though trying to cooperate, it lumbered to the front of the pen and put its head into the stanchion. But before Hedley Vaughn could get the stanchion shut, the bull pulled loose. Swinging its head, it came for the man, who jabbed back with the pole and backed up, cursing, getting out and closing the gate just in time. His heart fluttered painfully and he coughed, his world closing down to a miasma of heat and moving, unsteady light. He opened the gate again and went after the bull, which wouldn't go into the stanchion, which lowered its horns and came at the man. They sparred against the curtain of fire. Hedley Vaughn managed to grab the nose ring, but he couldn't get the pole attached. He went faint as the fire moved in a spin of red. The bull knocked the pole from his hand and drove him from the pen. This time the man didn't get the gate shut in time and the bull came through it, straight at him, bouncing him back against the manger covers before dropping its head in a deft flicking motion that caught the man in midsection, turned him, and tossed him like a rag doll through the opening to the ramp. The man banged his head when he hit, but didn't lose consciousness until, sliding and tumbling, he reached the door leading outside. There, the dog whined and licked his face. The bull, frenzied by the fire, rammed into walls and beams until, by chance, he went through the gate back into his pen.

Begrimed, their eyes irritated to tears by smoke, Janet Vaughn and the boy emerged from the dairy into the yard like divers coming up for air. A blowtorch of flame issued now from the window high in the front of the barn and lit the yard below with a flickering, curiously festive light. It might have been an old-time Fourth of July bonfire, the way cars began to pull over and the way the curious gathered in little knots to gaze and say the things people say at a fire. Among them Charles Porley could be heard, asking in his deep bass voice if there was anything he could do to help, if the fire department had been called, if there was anyone in the barn.

The sight of the flames made Janet Vaughn gasp. In the tumult of getting the cows out, she hadn't thought much about what was happening. Now she knew that the barn and therefore the farm really were lost and that their lives would change completely, for better or worse. Even as she watched, the fire erupted through the roof near the cupola and roared at the night sky, illuminating in its garish light the verdigris bull on the weathervane. Lucien! she remembered. At least he was safe in death; the flames could do no worse than what the rope and life had done to him. But it made her fear for the safety of the others.

"Bobby!" she called, making sure he was still there. And he was, tall and somehow much older-looking in the firelight reflected on his face. She clung to him again and peered around the yard at the people dazzled by the fire. Charles Porley was saying something to her, but she wasn't listening because the familiar form she sought unconsciously and then consciously was not there.

"Bobby, where's Hedley?"

The boy peered around. "He was here a minute ago."

"Did he go into the house?"

"I don't know. He could have after I came out."

"Have you seen Hedley?" she asked Charles Porley.

"He wasn't here when I arrived," the neighbor said. "Has the fire department been called?"

Janet Vaughn was nodding at this large man looming before her as she went into a panic again, but slowly, as though it were a thing releasing methodically within her, stabbing at her as she ran toward the house, calling her husband's name. She knew he wasn't there, but she raced from room to room with fear for him tearing at her heart and then with fear for herself, because she knew, flinging into the yard again, that he was in the barn and that she would have to go in after him.

In the yard she cried his name again.

"I don't think he's here," said Charles Porley in a voice sounding of doom.

Janet Vaughn peered up at the intensity of the fire and blanched. The approaching but still distant fire engines added their wail to the hysteria of the flames. Too late to help. She started for the dairy, followed by the boy.

"Please don't go in there," he said.

"Bobby, I can't leave him in there."

"Then I'm coming with you."

They were in the dairy. She picked her flashlight off the floor. "No, you're not. You have to stay here and tell the fire department what's happening."

She gave him a last quick hug, and when he protested again that he would come too, she looked directly at him and said, in a strange, compelling voice, "Bobby, obey your mother." Then she turned and went through the door into the cow barn.

In an agony of indecision and for a few precious minutes, measured out in heartbeats and audible respiration, the boy stood outside the door. Obey your mother. He heard the fire engines arrive and went out to watch the helmeted forms unreel hoses and attach them to the hydrant across the road. Then, thinking like his uncle, he remembered the back way and took off at a sprint along the side of the barn.

Some of the mangers near the front of the barn were in flames, and the smoke in the cow barn had thickened as Janet Vaughn made her way through it. But the lights were still on and the radio played. She went down the line of stanchions, calling her husband's name. Near the center of the barn she pushed up a manger hatch and dropped it immediately as a blast of hot smoke hit her face. She caught a sickening whiff of her own singed hair. She nearly tripped on a kicked-over milking machine that still chugged, sucking at the smoky air. Her eyes tearing with irritation, she pushed up another manger cover and held it open with her shoulder as she straddled the boards in front of it.

The smoke, though rising rapidly now with the upward suck of the fire through the roof, was thick enough to make her gag. She peered through its bright swirl and tried to get her bearings. Just then the lights and radio behind her went off. Numb with fright and choking on the smoke, she recognized through the din of the blaze the rhythmic rapping of the bull's horns against the wall of its pen. She turned on the flashlight and aimed it across the barn floor in the direction of the noise and saw something that made her heart thump painfully: the gate to the bull's stall was open. Hedley had been there. He might still be there.

She was terrified then. She did not want to leave the manger and go out onto the barn floor, with the fire creeping closer and the smoke thick enough to kill. And the bull. She wanted to turn back, to flee to safety, to Bobby, to her family. She wanted to live. But she couldn't leave her husband if he was in there somewhere.

"Hedley!" she screamed, and found herself going across the floor to the heavy timbers of the bull's pen. All but holding her breath, she stood there with her flashlight's beam probing through the bright smoke. She could discern the bulk of the animal clearly enough where it stood, a great wedge shape in the far corner, its head down against the wall. The heat from the nearby flames scorched her face. She gagged once again and nearly fainted and remembered a fire drill lecture in school about putting her face near the floor to breathe, which she did, coming up for air enough to look again through her smarting eyes. Her heart hammered as she saw a dim form, something oblong, that lay in the corner opposite the bull. It could have been a bunch of hay or some bedding. She thought it was her husband.

She hesitated. She put her nose close to the floor and tried to breathe. She sobbed and called out his name. And then, because she was sure he was in there and because she could not leave him there even if he was dead or dying, because she already blamed herself for the death of another man and because courage is cumulative, she went through the gate into the pen in a quick, huddled movement. She found not her husband but only the animal's salt block mounted on a plank and partly covered with dunged straw. Sidelong, she saw the massive dark shape of the bull move. She turned to flee. She glimpsed in the light of the approaching fire the gleam of the brass ring as the beast came for her. She tripped as she tried to get out of its way, and the bull's horn caught her right shoulder and cracked it against the wall in a flash of breathtaking, amazing pain, making her drop the flashlight and leaving her arm hanging useless. "Hedley!" she screamed as a clump of hay fell flaming to the floor from the mow above, lighting up the gate that she stumbled toward, only to be hit and lifted from behind and thrown against the heavy timbers. She tried to rise. She was crying and retching in mortal terror as more of the barn floor flared with crackling fire, and she saw as well as felt this huge, horned thing snorting after her as she tried to drag herself over the timbers with her good arm. Its swinging horns snagged her dress and pulled her down. She crawled away on one hand and it was at her, prodding and hurting her shoulders and sides. She found the dropped ring pole, rose up, and fought back. She screamed at it and tried to get to the gate. Then it had her. It caught and spun her around and she stared with horrified disbelief at its fire-lit eyes and stubby horns as they lowered to pin her, this time squarely against the closely spaced timbers, its movements deadly and precise as its great, concentrated weight gored her, exploding her breath and snapping her ribs as she clung to consciousness because she knew consciousness was life even as her mouth filled with blood and she knew she would perish, her last cry mute as more hay fell blazing with a light that for her grew brighter and brighter and she heard faintly but distinctly someone calling her "Mom! Mom! Mom!"

❧

"Mom! Mom! Mom!" Bobby Dearborn was yelling, in a panic of fear that she was trapped in this fury of flames. "He's out here! He's safe!" He tried several times to go in, brave without knowing it, but the fire was more than solid. The sleeve of his barn coat caught and he had to shuck it, retreating. "MOM!" he shouted. "MOM!" But all he could hear was the manic roar of the fire and the barn booming as it started to come apart like a ship sinking.

❧ 32 ❧

THE TWO DAYS immediately following the fire had for Bobby Dearborn a suspended, time-out-of-time aura. He stayed with his aunt Ernestine. He slept and ate a lot. He had to keep reminding himself that it had happened. When the phone rang, he thought it would be Aunt Janet, his mom, calling from wherever she was. He kept expecting her to ring the doorbell. The times they returned to the locked house to feed the dog and pick up some of his things, he had gone from room to room, feeling her particular presence in everything, knowing she wouldn't be there and yet hoping, through some suspension of the rules, that she would be still alive, would come down the stairs and ask him to go out and feed the hens. He half-expected to find her in the hospital room with his uncle when they went to visit. She wasn't, of course, except in the disoriented mind of Hedley Vaughn, who kept asking for her, keeping her alive and giving the boy a bleak, disturbed hope that she was somewhere and would return.

Ernestine Vaughn bought him a new charcoal-gray suit, a white button-down shirt, and a plaid tie. Dressed in these clothes, a stranger to himself, he accompanied his aunt to the wakes. They went first to Lucien Quirk's at a funeral home in the French-Canadian part of Lowell. Next to the casket, which was draped in an American flag, a Marine in uniform stood at attention. But only a few people showed up during the hour that they sat in the formally nice room and kept a vigil with the soldier. A dark-complexioned older woman in black came in, knelt, and prayed. She clutched rosary beads and spoke to them in apologetic French. "Cousine," she explained, "pauvre Lucien," then left.

Shortly afterward Bobby Dearborn and his aunt also left and drove back to Elmsbury and the Prentice Funeral Home. It was a big Victorian pile trimmed with gingerbread, sided with aluminum, and hooded with awnings that, in the spotlights, gave it the incongruous air of a seaside resort. The extended Gilooly family were already there, clumped defensively by themselves, the men grim-faced in their suits and the women in dark dresses, their makeup ruined with weeping. Rose Gilooly took the boy and held him close until, embarrassed by the grisly feel of corset and the smell of her old lady's talcum, he struggled free. The coffin, a heavy piece of polished maple furniture of ominous dimensions, stood on a trestle banked by sprays and wreaths of flowers, the sweetish odor of which Bobby Dearborn would forever associate with death.

He had difficulty connecting all this with Janet Vaughn, because he couldn't bring himself to imagine that she was in that ornate box surrounded by flowers. The grief of the Giloolys touched him, however, and made him fear the worst. He kept peering around at them and at all the people who had known her — old Koop the grocer, Meg Greenwood cupping her ear, the elderly Jewetts, Harry Manning awkward in a suit, people from Lowell he didn't know, the new couple from across the road, an utterly distraught Gladys Porley with husband in tow — and thought at any moment that she would appear among them. The priest led them in prayers. More people arrived; others left.

The boy and his aunt stayed through it all and were the last to leave. Together, without the others to distract them, they knelt at the priedieu before the coffin and said the Our

Father out loud. Ernestine Vaughn cried a little and then smiled through her tears. "I'm hungry," she said. "Let's go home and make something to eat."

The next morning they drove to the funeral home and from there went in the cushioned, purring smoothness of the limousine to the church. The coffin was ahead of them in a big Cadillac hearse, as though this is what death meant — ease at last. They entered the already filled church and took seats in the first pew at the right. Bobby Dearborn found the Catholic ceremony impressive, compared with the hymn-singing and prayer-reading in the Congregational church. The gorgeously robed priest, flanked by acolytes, each bearing a rifle-size candle on his hip, prayed in a strange language. In dignified procession they came through the altar gates to asperge the coffin. *Kyrie eléison*, Father Fahey sang in good voice. *Christi eléison*, the choir answered from behind them. The boy resisted a surge of feeling then. The weight of the voices bespoke death, but still he did not quite comprehend that what remained of her was in this trunk of polished wood and brass fittings resting on the catafalque in the aisle. He turned around and peered at the familiar faces as though she might be among them, might smile at him.

An early snow had begun to fall. At first it melted, merely dampening the gray, mid-December world. Then it began to stick and accumulate, so the air and the ground drifted together in a healing whiteness. People came out of the church with heads lowered, blinking against the big flakes, licking them off their lips. The procession of heavy cars moved with muffled slowness through the dense swirl with windshield wipers arcing. They went through Elmsbury Centre, bedecked for Christmas, and up Middlesex Road, slowing before the farm, the ruin of the barn half lost in the obscuring snow. One by one the vehicles, the flower car, hearse, and limousines, then the rest, nosed into the old cemetery, where deeply rooted ancient trees stood, emblematic of something like resurrection.

Now, sensing the finality of things, the boy panicked a little. But the priest, still praying from a book and shaking holy water, and a green rug of imitation grass covering the grave and a mound of earth, and the people, heads bent against the snow, continued the comfort and necessary deception that ritual brings. Bobby Dearborn wiped the snow from his eyes. The coffin was on the ground next to the green rug, on which the whitening snow fell. But near where he stood a section of the rug had been inadvertently rolled up, and he saw with a shock the frankly sliced raw earth of the grave and some of the gravel waiting to be shoveled back in. Now he knew she was in that fancy box. He knew that after all the prayers and words and rides in limousines, they were going to lower her into the earth and cover her up. Something close to his heart dissolved and rose, hot and moist, behind his nose and eyes. He held on to Aunt Ernestine's hand while the world distorted through a lens of tears as he wept, because she was gone, gone forever, and he loved her.